HEATHENS

This war just took a turn for the worst
and navigating my way to freedom
might just cost me my life.

Sheridan Anne
HEATHENS: Depraved Sinners #2

Copyright © 2021 Sheridan Anne
All rights reserved
First Published in 2021

This book is a work of fiction. Names, characters, places, and incidents are products of the author's imagination. Any resemblance to actual events or persons, living or dead, is entirely coincidental.

Cover Design: Artscandare
Editing: Fox Proof Edits
Formatting: Sheridan Anne

In case those batteries ran out after PSYCHOS, this is your warning to go get some more! Also, add wine to your shopping list because you're gonna need it!

Please enjoy this image of me booting your ass off that cliff!

CHAPTER ONE

The smell of gasoline lingers in the air, wafting from the wreckage beside me as I stare up into the barrel of Roman's gun. His eyes darken just as a gunshot rings through the night. My body flinches as a raw, terror-filled scream tears from deep in my chest, certain I'm dead. But as Roman topples toward me and barely catches himself against the wrecked car, my eyes widen in horror.

A gasp lingers on my lips as I take a mental note of my body. There's no searing pain, no blood, no life slipping from between my fingers. That bullet was supposed to be mine, yet somehow, I'm still breathing.

The headlights from the wrecked car spread a soft glow through the property as Roman's pained curse fills the air. He clutches his side as disbelief filters through his obsidian eyes. I watch him in horror, and as he moves his hand away from his waist, there's just enough light for me to see the bright red blood seeping through the front of his shirt, staining his fingers.

"No," I breathe as he hovers over me, the gun still in his hand as his hard gaze drops, taking in the stain quickly spreading from his waist.

Rage pulses through his stare and it doesn't take a genius to know that this isn't somewhere I want to be. All hell is about to break loose, and I'm stuck on the ground with a shard of glass protruding from my stomach. Nowhere to run. Nowhere to hide.

I swallow hard as his eyes shoot back up to mine. "Don't fucking move."

Roman spins, immediately clocking the gunman across the expansive property. The man is not alone. Two others stand on either side of him, all three of their guns raised high. It's hard to see from here, but there's something eerily familiar about these men.

"Who are they?" I gasp, a soft whimper tearing from my throat the moment the words pass my lips. My hand clutches the shard of glass as my heels dig into the cool grass, desperately trying to propel myself away from Roman and what's bound to be a fatal shootout.

No one shoots at one of the DeAngelis brothers and expects to get away with their life. If you're stupid enough to take a shot, then you better make it count. Unfortunately for these fuckers, they just sealed their fate, but I can't find it within myself to hate them because their recklessness just bought me precious seconds. Without them, I'd already be dead.

Barely a moment has passed when the three strange men begin

spreading out, knowing that one missed shot at Roman puts their lives in immediate danger. There's no doubt about it, they will die tonight, the only question is, will I die along with them?

Roman clocks their every step, somehow managing to keep a skilled eye on all three of them as they move in different directions.

Anger washes over his face and he clenches his jaw, clearly not in the mood to be dealing with this shit while he has his heart set on killing me for the crime he believes I've committed against Marcus. He's unforgiving, brutal, and lethal. A man like Roman doesn't hang around to ask questions. He acts first, thinks later, and this may be my only shot at keeping myself alive.

Roman groans and crouches down, hiding behind the wrecked car as he looks back at me, irritation strong in his fiery eyes. His jaw is clenched and his breathing labored. It's clear that the bullet wound through his waist is causing him pain, but it's not enough to slow him down. He's a machine, a soldier, just as his father raised him to be.

He reaches for me, and I flinch as he wraps his strong hand around the glass protruding from my stomach. My eyes widen, realizing what he's about to do. "No, no, no, no, no," I rush out, the fear overwhelming my already aching body.

Too fucking late.

He grips the glass and yanks it out of my waist as a searing pain tears through my stomach. "FUCK," I cry, tears brimming in my eyes. The glass is tossed aside, shattering on the wide driveway, but Roman doesn't give me a moment to recover. He grabs my arm and gives a hard tug, pulling me closer to the wrecked car and keeping me hidden from the three men who want him dead.

"Don't fucking move," he demands again, the smell of gasoline getting stronger in the air.

I search his deadly eyes, still trying to pull myself away from the man who wants to end my life. "What does it matter?" I spit, tugging my arm free and holding onto the groan as each little movement reminds me that I was just in a car wreck. "You want me dead anyway. I might as well take my chances with these guys."

Roman leans in and grips my chin between his strong fingers, making it impossible to pull away. "You're not going anywhere," he growls, relentless with his tight grip. "You shot my brother and shit like that will not go unpunished. Make no mistake, Shayne, you will die by my hand, but not like this. I want to feel your screams shattering my eardrums as your life slowly slips away."

"I didn't do it," I cry for what feels like the millionth time. "That hooded bitch shot him. She told me to run, she wanted me gone and I told her no. I wanted to stay with him. I would never hurt him like that. Why can't you believe me?"

Roman scoffs and looks back toward the three men slowly moving in, finally releasing my chin. "My castle is a fucking fortress, Shayne. No one gets in or out without me knowing. I knew you were fucking stupid, but I didn't take you for a liar."

Fury pulses through my veins, the very thought of being labeled a liar grating on my every nerve. I'm a lot of things, but not that. "I'm not lying," I spit through a clenched jaw, pushing up off the cool grass to protect myself better when I should be trying to get away.

"After everything you've put me through, do you honestly think I'd do something like this? You're wasting your time coming after me when you should be trying to find her. You've had me locked up, for fuck's sake. If I did this, then where the hell did this car come from? Where would I have gotten the gun? Your stupidity is allowing her to get away."

Roman laughs, watching me like some kind of pathetic injured animal hobbling along, one who he plans to shoot just to put it out of its misery. He stands, keeping his disgusted leer on me as he checks over his gun. We hear the discreet sounds of the three gunmen creeping in closer and Roman slowly turns, more than ready to destroy them, his bullet wound barely even a thought on his mind.

He glances back at me, the silent warning sharp in his eyes, and just like that, he's gone, slipping into the darkness like a deadly shadow intent on raising the fucking dead … or at least, adding a few men to their exclusive club by giving them a non-refundable eternal membership.

Silence fills the property as my head spins, the blood loss starting to fuck with my vision … or maybe that was from hitting my head during the crash. I'm almost certain I've torn open old stitches, but what does that matter when I'm about to get sliced and diced? I might as well help the process along.

The silence gets louder, and with each passing second, the nerves turn into dead weights in the pit of my stomach, the lingering smell of gasoline making it that much worse. With a whispered groan, I roll myself to my knees and creep out from behind the wreckage, desperate to see what's going on. Roman never told me who these guys were, but if I had to take a guess, I'd say these are his father's men. Nobody else would be foolish enough to come here and take a shot at Roman like this. Though, I'm quickly starting to realize that the men in this fucked-up world don't often come equipped with brains.

Everyone thinks they're better than the next, stronger, wiser, fiercer. They're all fools, assuming they have Giovanni's protection, though nothing compares to Roman, Marcus, and Levi. Being one of Giovanni's men is the same as painting a target right in the center of your forehead and parading around in front of a bunch of psychopaths, daring them to take a shot.

I catch sight of Roman slipping in behind the shadow of the bushes, his body barely visible in the darkness. His back is to me, but I don't doubt that he's somehow still watching, still waiting for me to make a stupid move just to give him another excuse to end my life.

He takes another step and disappears out of sight, leaving me to watch after him, my heart thundering erratically. My stomach twists with nerves as my body grows heavier by the second. Tonight has been a fucking mess, but I'm not about to call it quits yet.

The hooded woman set off a series of events that not even she would have been able to foresee. Despite her bullshit escape plan, I think she was actually trying to protect me, or at least trying to get me away from the brothers, but maybe she just wants me out of her way. She reminded me a lot of Ariana, wanting to take claim over the three men in this world who could never be claimed.

God, I hate that bitch. If there was some way I could sink my claws in and destroy Ariana without destroying myself in the process, I'd do it. She's a leech with a hard-on for Roman, and because of that, she feels entitled to fuck with me.

This hooded bitch shot Marcus and took him away from me right when I thought he and I were starting to build some kind of … fuck, I don't know what it's called. It sure as hell isn't a relationship, and I'd be fucked if I were to label it as a friendship. We were building something, that's for sure. Changes were happening and the dynamic between us was shifting. He didn't trust me, and I sure as hell didn't trust him, but we were heading in that direction. It could have been great between us, but now he's lying on his bed, bleeding out with his brother's hands buried deep inside his chest. No matter what happens here tonight, there's no way I'll ever be able to see him again.

Levi and Roman will do everything in their power to save him, but they're also going to do everything in their power to end me, and from what I've come to learn of the DeAngelis brothers—they won't stop until they get exactly what they want.

Fuck. That bitch better hope she never crosses me again because I will make her life a living hell, though hopefully the boys finally see that I'm telling the truth. Then I won't have to worry about making her life a living hell; they'll do it for me and turn it into an Academy Award-winning performance.

Minutes pass before I hear the telltale sounds of a fight, and my eyes flash across the wide yard, desperately seeking them out. Grunts and groans echo through the darkness and my nerves skyrocket, hating the idea of not knowing where each of the men are.

A gunshot rings out, making me jump, and just as I catch sight of three more men slipping onto the property, a shadow looms over me. My eyes widen and I suck in a deep breath, ready to scream, but his big hand clamps over my mouth, muffling the sound.

Ignoring the stabbing pain in my stomach, I kick out, desperate to get free as he tears my dirty knees up off the ground. My fingers dig into his skin and I feel my nails tearing thick ribbons into his flesh. "Ahhh, fuck," the man spits, throwing me down as he shakes out his bloodied hand.

Digging my heels into the ground, I scramble back, barely feeling the tears as they flow freely down my face and splash against my collarbone. He laughs, watching my pathetic attempt at escape as he walks forward, stalking me like a wild animal. We move almost as one toward the front of the wrecked car, and as the glow from the headlights finally hits him, I recognize him as one of the men who snuck into my room and dragged me right out of bed.

Anger pulses through me and I grab a fistful of dirt and throw it up into his eyes. He curses and the small distraction gives me just a moment to clamber to my shaky feet. Without looking back, I launch myself forward, not giving a shit which direction I'm heading, just desperate to get away.

Pressing a hand over my bleeding stomach, I try to keep myself alive. The man roars in frustration and bolts after me like lightning until a bullet whizzes past my face.

The roaring stops as the man's heavy body falls to the ground, but I barely get a chance to look back before Roman's familiar tone is tearing through the property. "GET THE FUCK OUT OF HERE. RUN."

My eyes widen in horror, my gaze darting around to see that there's more than just a handful of Giovanni's men. There's a fucking swarm of them and they all have him in their sights.

As a general rule, Roman never tells me to run. His reckless confidence outweighs the possibility that things might not go his way. Even when backed into a corner, running is not an option. For him to tell me to run now could only mean one thing—Roman DeAngelis has finally met his match.

Not one to wait around and try my luck, I take off like a fucking bat. My feet pound against the hard ground, each step sending me soaring toward the thick forest surrounding the massive castle. A distant thought that my father is out here somewhere filters through my mind, but he's the least of my problems.

Low hanging branches and bushes snag on my skin, cutting shallow tears into my flesh as I whip past them, the overwhelming fear too great to even register the pain. My ankle twists under me but I keep going, unsure how many more of Giovanni's men are hiding in the woods.

BANG!

A loud explosion tears through the property, the sound deafening as the force of the explosion launches me into the air. I scream and I'm thrown headfirst into the thick trees as the blasting heat hits my back. Fire burns through the property and as I crash to the ground, my heart races.

I crawl to my knees, looking back toward the open field of the property.

The car. I've been smelling gasoline in the air since the crash, but an explosion never entered my mind. Is that why Roman told me to run?

My eyes are wide, searching from left to right, terrified as the fire lights up the forest around me. I push back, scrambling to my feet, ignoring the aches and pains overwhelming my body. I have to get out of here. I have to find freedom.

The darkness is horrifying, and with each step, it feels almost as though it's swallowing me whole, but I won't let it. I will survive the night, and when the sun shines again, this bitch is going to rise like a fucking angel. Though, there may not be anything left for me to go back to. There's no way Marcus will survive, and I'm positive that Roman will be dead within the hour. Once Giovanni's henchmen are through with Roman, they'll go after Levi next.

A piercing whistle cuts through the air, and I stumble as the familiar sound of paws hitting the hard earth picks up behind me. Fear pounds through my chest, certain that Roman has sent his wolves to tear my throat into ribbons of flesh, but when the wolf moves in beside me and matches my pace, the fear fades into a distant hum. I don't see the wolf in the darkness, but I know he's here, either watching over me or making sure I don't do anything that's going to get me killed before Roman has a chance to do it himself.

The wolf acts as my protector, pushing out in front and leading me through the trees as the sound of Giovanni's war echoes through the property behind me.

My pace slows as my head grows dizzy. I won't be able to run for much longer, and as if sensing my unease, the wolf pauses and glances back at me, his dark eyes glistening against the subtle moonlight.

He stares at me for a lingering moment and I can't help but think that this wouldn't be happening if he were running with any of the brothers. Fuck, I bet the wolf even thinks I'm pathetic.

Mustering up all the energy I have left, I push myself forward and follow wolfy through the thickening trees until I fall forward, landing on my hands and knees, clutching the wound at my stomach. "I can't," I whimper, tears streaking down my face as the wolf steps into my side and nudges my ribs, pushing me to keep going. "It's too much … I can't."

A low growl vibrates through the big bastard and he bares his teeth at me, a silent message telling me to get my ass moving or he'll drag me there one limb at a time. Letting out a broken cry and sensing that he won't give me a choice, I crawl along the forest floor, putting one knee in front of the other while whimpering as the small stones and twigs tear at my skin.

The wolf leads me right into a dark, lonely cave and relief pulses through my veins like a shot of whiskey to an alcoholic in withdrawal. The cold cave is creepy and probably full of secrets I don't ever want to know, but for now, it's my only salvation.

My groans echo through the cave as my back slams against the natural stone wall. I clutch onto my body, holding myself tight and putting pressure on my wound as my head tilts back, closing my eyes and sending a silent prayer up to the god that I don't even know exists. In times like this, I have to hope there is something bigger out there, some kind of guardian angel watching over me when I can't do it for myself. I'm not ready to die yet.

The blood continues to pour as my energy quickly drains, and when shivers begin taking over my body, the big wolf moves into my side, pressing his weight against me and resting his head in my lap, lending me his warmth. Knotting my fingers into his fur, I hold him close, knowing that sooner or later, someone will come for me, and when they do, I'm going to be ready.

I've come too far to just give it all up now, and despite how much I need to run from the DeAngelis brothers, I need them more now than ever because, without them, I don't stand a chance at destroying their father.

CHAPTER TWO

he wolf's soft growl vibrating through his chest is my first sign that something isn't right.

My tired eyes snap open to find a dark shadow hovering over me as his strong hand curls around my ankle. I get the smallest glimpse of Roman, his face masked by darkness with nothing but rage pulsing through his dark eyes. In a split second, he turns his back to me, his long hair pulled up into a messy nest as the late moonlight shines through the opening of the cave.

A loud gasp pulls from deep within me, my eyes widening in disbelief. It's not possible. The odds were stacked against him. There were too many of them. He should be dead.

Blood splatters cover his skin, his once white shirt completely stained deep red, but it's impossible to tell what percentage of that blood is his. He was shot only a few hours ago. He should be passed out on the ground, withering in pain, not traipsing through the woods searching out his next slaughter.

His nails bite into my flesh and a strangled scream gets stuck in my throat as he tugs on my ankle, pulling me after him. My back slams to the ground with a heavy thud and I cry out, my body too tired and exhausted to fight him off.

"NOOOO," I whimper, frantically trying to pull myself free, knowing that after the bullshit he's just endured at his father's hands, there won't be any more games. He means business, and this time, he won't be fucking around. Chasing me through the castle and listening to the fear in my voice as I cried, whimpered, and screamed was just his warmup. Shooting out the tires of my getaway car, that was the pre-game, but now, he's ready for the main event, and I know he won't stop until my heart is nothing but a scarred, steaming mess at his feet.

Roman drags me through the entrance of the cave, my back scraping against the hard, uneven rock as the big wolf falls in beside Roman without another glance my way. He knows his master and he will be loyal until his dying days.

Vertigo hits me, the sudden movements proving too much for my exhausted body. "Stop," I cry, pulling against my ankle, using my other foot to slam into his wrist and hoping that in some twisted turn of fate that I can get myself free, but even if I did, where would I go? Roman DeAngelis is a fucking beast. He would track me down in seconds, his big-ass wolf sniffing me out like a juicy steak with his name on it. "Let me go."

Each word painstakingly torn from my throat is like a whimper of defeat. I can cry and fight until my world turns black, but we both know there's only one end game here. All along, all the pain, fear, and terror, it was all just leading to this, but I'm not surprised. Despite their wild promises not to hurt me, I always knew my time in this world was limited.

Twigs, stones, and low branches scrape over my skin as my head continues to spin, bouncing against every rock in its path. I try to grip my stomach, the blood still seeping out of me in painful waves, but I can't do this much longer. The darkness is coming and I'm terrified of what's going to happen when the sun decides to shine again.

"Please," I sob, tears streaking down my bloodstained face as my heel presses against his hand, desperately trying to push it off my sprained ankle. "I didn't do it. It wasn't me."

I repeat those words over and over again, hoping just once he might stop to hear me, but it's fruitless. He's not a man to change his mind. He sees things right to the end, no matter how fucked up they might be. He's a fucking psycho through and through. A goddamn heathen with a hard-on for death.

Fucking hell. Why did I have to be kidnapped by a bunch of fucked-up brothers with daddy issues?

"Roman," I cry, demanding his attention but getting nothing but his back. "ROMAN. FUCKING HEAR ME. I DIDN'T DO THIS. LET ME GO."

A frustrated growl tears through his chest and in the same moment, he releases my ankle, dropping my body weight to the hard ground with a loud thump. He spins on me, his tall, wide frame looming over me like a wicked stalker closing in on his latest obsession. The wolf stops, turning to watch my inevitable fall from grace, not even a hint of remorse in his jet-black eyes.

My heels dig into the ground, catching against a fallen branch and I use it to push myself back, my hands trembling the closer he gets. "I hear you," he tells me, his deep tone low and filled with a deadly venom, a sound that sends chills sweeping down my spine. His head tilts to the side, that angry scar daring me to try and run. "The only problem is you were the only one there. The gun was in your hands. The guilt and blame rests on your shoulders, and now my brother is dead."

My eyes widen, his words piercing right through to my broken soul. "No," I demand, pushing against my heels again, putting more space between us as my words struggle to fly free over the lump lodged in my throat. "No. I refuse to believe that. You're lying. He's not dead. He can't be. I'd know."

"So, tell me," he says, stepping with me and crouching down, dropping his hand back to my ankle and dragging me back toward him. "What do you suppose I do to the girl who took my brother's life?"

My chest aches, my heart thundering as the true weight of the situation falls over my shoulders.

Marcus is dead.

Gone. Taken from me by that fucking psycho hooded bitch and I'll never get the chance to make it right, never get the chance to watch the blood drain from her body as I take her pathetic life. Marcus was the sweetness in a sour world, the sun in this looming darkness. He was fucked in the head, a complete nutcase with a hard-on for chains, drugs, and a tight pussy. And while he put me through hell, he also opened my eyes to a lifestyle I didn't know I wanted. He could have meant something to me, could have been more had I let him, and now he's gone.

Levi and Roman are going to … fuck, I can't even think about it.

I'm not just the girl they think shot him, I'm the girl they believe killed their brother. This is so much more than just a simple bullet through the head, this is grounds for hell. The devils inside them are coming to play and they're not going to leave until they're satisfied.

Sobs tear from my chest as Roman's eyes darken and narrow to irritated slits. He leans toward me, his fingers pressing against the gaping wound in my stomach. "Say your prayers, Empress," he spits, his tone mocking and full of wicked secrets as I scream, the pain too great to bear. His lips twist into a psychotic smirk and darkness falls around me.

Hot, searing pain cuts through me as a pair of hands are lodged deep inside my stomach. My eyes spring open and a loud, terrified gasp pulls from between my lips. Blinding white lights blur my vision as my chest lifts up off the hard bench, desperate to ease the torrential burn. Strong hands slam against my shoulders, forcing me back down with an impenetrable force, and as the hands dig deeper, feeling around inside my body, I scream with everything that I've got.

Stars dance in my vision. I never knew pain like this was even possible.

My heart pounds heavily in my chest and I hear it in my ears, rapidly beating at an inhumane pace, telling me it's only moments from giving out. I try to breathe through it, clenching my eyes, but it's too much. I can't handle it.

"STOP," I wail, my hands clutching onto something velvety, yet corded and strong. "MAKE IT STOP."

Something sharp digs into me, tearing right into my flesh. I fight against the pressure on my shoulders, frantically trying to get away from whatever the hell is causing this agony. This is it. This must be what death feels like. This has to be my version of hell.

A wicked laugh cuts through my misery and my eyes spring open again, fighting against the blinding white light. I blink a few times, forcing myself to focus on the man standing over me. Roman hovers at my head, his dark, lethal eyes locked on my face, watching the pain in my features. "Stop," I yelp, sobbing relentlessly as I plead for this agony to end. I don't know what the fuck he's doing to me, but I know he holds the reins. He holds the power. He always has.

"No can do, Empress," he says, his tongue rolling over his bottom lip as though he's never been so turned on in his life. "You've been a very naughty girl."

"Keep her still," comes a gruff voice from my side.

My wide, terrified gaze snaps down to Levi who stands beside the table, a needle and thread held skillfully between his bloodied fingers.

He hums to himself, enjoying his moment, blissfully unaware of the havoc raining down over me, as though he doesn't currently have his other hand shoved deep inside my body.

His obsidian eyes glance over the tip of the sharp needle and a sick grin cuts across his full lips as he dives back down, digging the needle straight into my flesh. Another hot, searing pain tears at me and I scream as my hands snap up. My nails dig deep into Levi's waist, clawing at his skin like a hot knife through butter. "STOP," I shriek, more than aware of the fact they bypassed the whole numbing part of this bullshit home surgery.

As if only just realizing that my stomach is connected to the rest of my body, Levi's brows furrow and he turns to meet my haunted stare. His eyes are sickening, filled with pain and fury. He looks nothing like the Levi who fucked me on the roof, nothing like the calm and content man who I watched play his drums. This man right here is the lethal DeAngelis brother who I've always heard so much about in the news. He's the relentless, psychotic man who will callously murder on a whim, he's the man who would take every last scream out of a victim before brutally taking their life with a fucking smile on his face.

How could I have allowed myself to see anything other than that in these wicked men?

His hand moves inside me and I watch in horror as the corners of his lips lift into a twisted smirk while blindly digging the needle back into my body. My nails cut deeper as his blood pools beneath my fingers, but I doubt he even notices. "Why would I stop?" he questions, his tone void of all emotion. "I'm having so much fun."

Nausea swirls deep in my gut and I see dark spots dancing across my vision, warning me that I only have a few moments before unconsciousness claims me again. My gaze shoots back up to Roman who's holding me down, his strength like nothing I've ever experienced before, but just as his dark eyes fall back to mine, I feel Levi's fingers moving around inside me just moments before he digs even deeper with the needle, piercing right through my injured flesh.

A haunting scream tears from my throat and I turn my face, clenching my eyes as the smell of blood overwhelms me. He doesn't stop, doesn't relent, doesn't even give me a chance to breathe as the tears stream down my dirty face.

Roman presses down harder, his strong arm jammed up beside my face. I don't even think, just open my mouth and bite down as hard into his warm flesh, desperate to relieve the pain any way that I can.

Roman doesn't move, doesn't flinch or even take note of the pain as my teeth dig into his arm, and when Levi removes the needle from my stomach and I release my grip on his arm, he takes my chin in his hand, forcing it up until my eyes are focused only on his. "There she is," he tells me, heat and desire pooling through his lethal, obsidian stare. "The real Shayne has come to play."

CHAPTER THREE

Sharp, pained breaths rip through my raw throat as I come to, waking in a too bright room with my arms and legs strapped to the small surgical table. My gaze shoots around the room to find both Levi and Roman hovering close by, not letting me out of their sight for even a moment.

Throbbing pain circulates my body but the shock of being alive manages to somehow mask it, if only a little, but it doesn't make sense. They want me dead more than anything, so why the hell did they save me? Do they believe me? Did they find the girl and realize I was telling the truth? That they fucked up more than they will ever know?

No. It couldn't be that. Surely if they knew the hooded bitch existed, they'd be groveling, or at the very least allowing me some kind of pain relief while I heal. I wouldn't be strapped down in this surgical bed, unable to move, unable to run, and I sure as fuck wouldn't have felt Levi's hands moving inside me as he stitched me up. Their games are only just beginning.

Levi sits to my right, his back pressed up against the wall and I can't help but feel that something isn't right. He almost appears regretful … broken, torn down in a world that he rules. His brother died so I get it, he has every right to feel like a fucking shell, but that doesn't give him the right to tear into my body with his bare fucking hands. Though what does it matter? I won't be walking out of here.

I cut my gaze across to Roman before Levi catches me staring. Roman sits perched on a table similar to the one I've been strapped to, his back pressed against the wall. His shirt is gone, and he grips a pair of tweezers in his hand, a grim expression etched into his face.

My eyes widen as the tweezers dig deep into his waist, feeling around for the bullet that was lodged in there so many hours ago. A soft gasp escapes my lips and his dark eyes immediately snap up to mine. He narrows them as a darkness settles over his features, that twisted, wicked man returning.

He stands, dropping the tweezers onto the table as I feel Levi's hard gaze resting upon his brother, probably taking pointers on Roman's technique. I bet these assholes even sit down with each other after their brutal slaughters to go over everything that happened, giving pointers and criticism, working out how to be even more fucked up on their next little outing. It's probably one of their most treasured bonding moments, something their father can really be proud of.

Roman strides right into me until I can feel my fingers brushing against his warm skin, the dried, splattered blood of his enemies rubbing up against my arm. The need to pull away rocks through me, but with my arms strapped down and my body in the worst kind of agony, there's not a damn thing I can do about it.

His skin is soft, but I can feel the strong cords of muscle lingering beneath the surface, muscles that remind me what a man like this can do. I've had more than my fair share of dealings with Roman DeAngelis, and I know his capabilities well.

Roman props his hand on the table beside me, the inside of his wrist pressed against my ribs. He does the same with his other hand and slowly leans into me, his face hovering mere inches away from mine.

I swallow hard, fearing what this heathen has in store for me. His lips twist into a wicked smirk and I can all but feel Levi's stare resting upon his older brother. "Game time," Roman murmurs, those two words holding more weight than any single word should have the power to.

Tears well in my eyes but I fight them back, refusing to let them fall as I shake my head. "No," I tell him, my voice breaking out of fear. "I've already told you; I didn't do this. Please, just give me a chance and I'll tell you exactly what happened."

Roman laughs. "A chance? Empress, you've had more chances than anyone who's ever been under my protection. Your time for chances is gone. It's a shame though, Marcus was the one who would have enjoyed this the most, and now he's gone and he'll never get to experience the sweet sound of your screams echoing down the long hallways as your life drains away."

"You're sick," I spit, my jaw clenched as anger washes through me, my chest constricting at the harsh reminder of Marcus' death.

His dark eyes shimmer with laughter and he moves in just a little closer, his voice dropping to a near whisper as I hold back tears of grief. "Exciting, isn't it?"

I don't respond. What's the point? He has his mind set, and seeing as though Levi isn't saying a word, I can assume that he's more than happy to go along with Roman's bullshit. "I have to be honest," Roman continues. "You've surprised me. I didn't think you'd last longer here than just a few measly days, but here we are with all this history. It's a waste. You could have gone far in this world. I know Marcus had high hopes for you. Hell, that fucker would have signed a marriage certificate just to call you his."

An ache settles into my chest, my heart breaking for the millionth time, unable to believe Marcus is really gone. It was only a few short hours ago that he was buried deep inside me, making me feel truly alive. He fell asleep holding me in his arms, something I never thought possible when it came to a man like Marcus DeAngelis.

Seeing the pain in my eyes, Roman laughs and pushes up, giving me just a little more space, but he doesn't dare step away from the side of the surgical table. "Why?" I croak out over the sharp lump in my throat. "Why bother saving me? You pulled that glass out of my stomach, you told me to run when your father's men were closing in. You made sure I was far enough from the car before it exploded. Why would you do that if you were still going to kill me? Why bring me here and put me back together? You should have just let that guy snap my neck. What's the point in saving me?"

Roman's face softens and for just a moment, I can picture the sweetest words coming out of his mouth, telling me that he couldn't bear the thought of losing me too, that seeing me broken and destroyed would have killed whatever good parts were left inside of his black soul, that he couldn't take away the woman his younger brother fought so hard to protect. But when he leans back down to me and his voice drops to a hushed whisper, a chill sweeps through my body. "The point," he mutters, that deep tone slicing straight through me like a blade, "is that I can't enjoy killing you if you're already dead."

Burning rage pulses through me like a swarm of angry bees, and as Roman pulls back just an inch, I can't let the opportunity slip through my fingers. My wrist flexes as much as the hard straps will allow and with a vengeful force, I slam my fingers deep inside the bullet wound at his waist. Digging my nails into his flesh, I let him feel my wrath the same way I'd felt Levi's hands deep inside me, but when the fucker doesn't even flinch, helplessness washes over me. "I hate you," I seethe, wishing things could have been different, that I could still be struggling back in my shitty apartment, never having met the DeAngelis brothers.

His lethal stare bores into mine, the venom seeping out of him in waves. "You're a liar, Shayne Mariano," he mutters in a chilling tone, briefly dropping his gaze to his waist, taking in the way my shaking hand falls back to my side, his blood coating my fingers.

I shake my head, the tears now freely falling down my cheeks. "I didn't lie."

"You lied about shooting Marc," he says, continuing as though I didn't say a word. "And you're lying now."

My jaw clenches as a wild storm brews beneath the surface. "I'm not a fucking liar."

His finger brushes over my collarbone, sailing down between my breasts, making sure to bypass every harsh bruise coating my skin before finally coming to a stop over my stitched stomach. His obsidian eyes come back to mine as I sense Levi getting up and slowly moving across the room toward us. "You don't hate me," he says, capturing my whole attention as my heart thunders wildly in my chest. "You couldn't hate me even if you tried. You want me, you want to know what it'd be like to feel my hands all over your body, to feel my lips moving with yours, to be the one woman who could tame the wild beast inside me. Even after everything I've put you through, you would still kneel before me. You don't hate me, Empress, not even a little, and that cold, hard fact does nothing except make you hate yourself."

"You're wrong," I spit.

He tsks me, the irritating sound instantly playing on my nerves. "That's just the thing," he mutters as I feel Levi stepping in beside me. "I'm never wrong, and deep down, you know it. Being with me and my brothers, locked up in our little haunted house, has been the fucking highlight of your miserable life. You've been fucked harder than you've ever been before, experienced more thrilling emotions than you've ever felt, and fuck, Empress, you've even managed to grow a fucking backbone, but it's not enough to save you."

Levi meets Roman's hard stare over the top of me before dropping his cold gaze to mine. His fingers play at the side of my strap and as it breaks free, I suck in a deep breath, only now just realizing how restrictive the straps had been. "I'm giving you one last shot," Levi tells me, reaching down further and adjusting the surgical bed until I'm sitting. "Tell me exactly what went down with Marcus last night, and if you're honest, we might even kill you quickly. Lie to us again, and you will experience the full wrath of the DeAngelis brothers. The choice is yours."

I stare into his eyes, hating this version of him. He's not the man I've been getting to know, not the man who held my knee under his father's dining table, the man who would watch over me everywhere I went, the man who scooped me into his arms after finding me in the woods, broken and beaten after being tortured in a bathtub. He would whisper sweet words of encouragement, willing me to be okay, willing me to pull through, but this man who stands beside me is void of all emotion. It's like someone flipped a switch and the humanity drained out of him, leaving nothing but the chilling man from every child's worst nightmare.

My fingers curl around his wrist. "I didn't do this," I plead to him, letting him see the true pain and torment hidden deep within my eyes. "I would never hurt Marcus like that. I swear, I've been telling you the truth."

He shakes his head. "It's not possible. No one can enter our home without us knowing about it. You're lying to us, Shayne, and now's the time to come clean."

"Don't do this to me, Levi," I beg him, squeezing his wrist, willing him to come back to me, to find that goodness that I know is buried deep inside him. I quickly glance toward Roman before looking back at Levi. "A woman slipped into my bedroom in the middle of the night. I wasn't sleeping well. Marcus gave me ecstasy and I'd never had it before. I was coming down after the high and I saw a shadow. At first, I thought I was going crazy but then she stepped into my room. She was in a black hooded cloak that went right down to her feet. Her face was covered but I could see that she had dirty blonde hair."

"Convenient," Roman scoffs. "I'm sick of your bullshit story. Last chance. Who were you working with? Someone had to have given you that gun. Was it Ariana? Did she get to you during my father's dinner?"

"What?" I breathe. "No. Are you that fucking messed up that you just assume every last person is out to get you? Ariana wanted nothing during that business dinner except to get her rocks off. She's a dirty whore, but she's not fucking stupid. She was pissed when I turned her down, but she sure as fuck wasn't plotting some fucked-up revenge against you assholes. Besides," I add, my frustrations getting the best of me, "if I were going to be stupid enough to try and kill Marcus, I would have slit his throat while he slept and then ran for my fucking life. Only an idiot would have shot a gun in your stupid castle. That bitch set me up. She told me to leave. She didn't want me here, but I told her no. I didn't want to leave, and after everything that went down with your father and the fucking Miller brothers, I knew I was safer here, but she wasn't having it."

"Come on, Shayne," Roman laughs. "You can do better than that. At least try to make it believable. You expect us to believe that some hooded bitch just came strolling into our home in the middle of the night, not alerting us or even the wolves that she was there. Somehow pulled up a getaway car to the front fucking doors and got a code to get through the entrance. Right."

"I swear, I'm telling the truth," I seethe, trying to pull my back up off the table but the pain that shoots through my stomach keeps me grounded. "She snuck into my room and when I tried to wake Marcus, she pulled the gun and told me not to. She said she wanted me out of here, that she didn't want me to go through the same bullshit you'd done to her. She said you three were hers, so maybe you should be asking yourself how many crazy bitches you've been fucking with. This shit ain't on me, this is all you."

Levi growls and takes my chin, forcing my gaze to snap back to his. "You better be fucking careful with what you're insinuating here because it sounds a lot like you're blaming my brother's death on us."

"Maybe I am," I spit, that same vengeful wrath bubbling deep inside me. "I don't know who this bitch is but she sure as fuck seemed to know you."

Levi's hand drops to my throat, his eyes narrowing with hostility. "What did Ariana offer you to kill us?"

Fucking hell.

My nails dig into his strong arm, desperately trying to pull it away, my breath coming in sharp, shallow pants. "I told you, she had nothing to do with this, though I wouldn't fucking blame her if she tried."

"Well, luckily for your fuck up, she'll never get a chance," Roman growls.

Levi releases me and I let out an amused laugh. "You think I'm supposed to give a shit what you do to that bitch? I owe her nothing, but you're only hurting yourself. After all, you're the one who's been hanging off her every word since high school. Tell me, I'm curious how she reels in the famous Roman DeAngelis. Does she leash you like a dog? Spank your ass when you've been a bad boy?"

Roman's hand whips toward me so fast that I don't see the gun until it's pressed right against my temple, the metal cold against my clammy skin. "No," Levi rushes out, throwing his hand up and knocking the gun away from my head. "Not until we have answers."

Roman's heated gaze doesn't leave mine and in a flash, he brings the gun back and shoots.

BANG!

My whole body flinches, pain rocking through me from the movement as the bullet sails straight past my head, lodging deep into the wall behind me. "THE FUCK IS WRONG WITH YOU?" I scream, shoving my hands against his chest to force him back, but my body is too weak to move him even an inch. "I TOLD YOU I DIDN'T FUCKING DO IT. The hooded bitch did. I refused to run and she said she would make me. She shot him. Not me. I tried to stop her. I screamed for her not to do it. He saw her. Marcus saw her, I know he did."

"WELL MARCUS IS FUCKING DEAD," Roman roars, his voice ringing in my ears louder than the gunshot.

Tears track down my face and I look back at Levi, the desperation pulsing through me like never before. "I … I didn't … Why can't you just believe me? I wouldn't hurt Marcus like that. I didn't do it. It wasn't me."

Levi watches me for a silent minute as the tears fall and splash against my chest. "Sorry, little one," he says, his eyes darkening like haunted shadows during the coldest night, not a hint of regret swarming in those obsidian pits of torture. "Not good enough."

And just like that, Levi nods toward Roman who turns and walks out of the small room, taking the tweezers with him as he goes. I look up at Levi as the door slams shut behind Roman, leaving us alone in dead silence. I know that this is going to be hell.

He steps in closer and my heart races with fear, terrified of what he has in store for me. He reaches down and pulls the strap back over my body, tightening it with a hard tug until the breath is forced out of my lungs. "Hold still, little one," he tells me, skimming his gaze over my body. "This is only going to hurt a little."

CHAPTER FOUR

Shivers take over my body as I hear the haunting noises of Levi's drums coming from deep within the castle. It's been over twenty-four hours since he walked out of here, leaving me a bloody mess. He was cold and calculated, using everything he knew about me, using my own fears and nightmares against me.

The way he tied me down, the way he took that knife and trailed it over my skin. I've never screamed like that. Not when they first kidnapped me, not when they chased me through the maze, not even when faced with death.

Levi is brutal. He's relentless and lacks any kind of decent human traits. He didn't hurt me the same way Lucas Miller had, he didn't leave me gasping for breath or bleeding out on the table, yet somehow his fucked-up mind games were so much worse than anything I've ever endured.

Levi DeAngelis is a psycho. He gets off on my pain, loves the way I flinch when he comes near me, yet every time he met my eyes, there was something there, something deep inside him telling him he should stop. But the years of relentless torture from his father, drilling into his sons that giving up is weak, that was the voice that kept him going until he saw it right through to the end.

To stop is to show weakness and Levi DeAngelis is anything but weak.

So why the fuck am I lying here in a pool of my own blood, desperately wishing that I could forgive him? Deep down, he's a broken soul who needs a ray of sunshine to break through the darkness. His drums offer him a release from his binds, but the moment he puts those sticks back down, his binds tighten and he's stuck in that relentless cycle.

Why do I do this to myself? Until I start seeing them as the bad guys, I'll never be free of this.

Roman though, he can go and fuck a donkey for all I care. He's callous and cruel. When Levi was left to torture me, I could see a shimmer of hesitation in his eyes, but not Roman. He was ready to go for the kill, to end it all with the flick of his wrist, but he won't, not until he gets the answers he thinks he's looking for.

The brothers have been back a few times, switching out turns, both of them determined to break me, both relentless in their tactics, their manipulative little mind games, and sickening skills. I've never wished for death like I do at their hands. Fuck, I thought being taken by Lucas Miller was the worst thing that could ever happen to me.

How could I have ever known the three men who swore to protect me would be the very men to bring me down?

I stare up at the ceiling, my body shaking, but it's almost impossible to tell why. Maybe I'm cold, maybe it's out of pure fear, or maybe I just need to close my eyes and sleep off the mental and physical exhaustion. All I want is to get out of here and never look back, but that'll never happen. Since the moment the bullet plunged into Marcus' chest, my fate was sealed. I should embrace it. Hell, Roman and Levi would probably like that. It'd make their torture sessions that much easier on them. After all, no one likes to go to work, only to be stuck with someone screaming at them the whole time.

Fuck that and fuck them. Hell, even if I did somehow get out of here, where would I go? My apartment would already be housing some other poor fucker, and I can guarantee after a million missed shifts, I no longer have a job. I bet my turd-tastic landlord enjoyed cleaning out my bedside table and discovering what a little whore I am for those things. May you rest in peace, Tarzan. It was fun while it lasted, but don't be fooled, the moment I can, I'll be replacing that little bastard with Tarzan 2.0.

My bladder screams for release and my stomach growls for a good meal, though I sure as fuck won't be relying on the DeAngelis brothers for that. I bet they're hoping that I'll just piss myself so they can come in here and humiliate me a little bit more. Though, watching grown adults pissing themselves isn't exactly something new to them. In their line of work, they literally see it all.

My gaze shifts around the room, desperately trying to keep my mind off … everything. My body aches, my bladder hates me, and my heart is overwhelmed with grief that Marcus didn't make it, but it's not something I can allow myself to dwell on right now. I have to focus on myself, focus on surviving.

I haven't taken much notice of the room that I'm in. There's been a lot going on, and every time I think that I'm going to have a moment to myself to finally breathe, one of the brothers walks back in to fuck with my head. It takes me only a minute to realize that I've been in this room before. One of those first few days after the brothers had taken me. I sat in here, laid back on this very surgical bed and spread my legs for a doctor doing a thorough physical examination. He inserted a birth control rod into my arm … or at least I think it's a birth control rod. One can never be too sure when it comes to the DeAngelis brothers. There's also a tracking device inserted in there somewhere, though my guess is that the two are somehow connected.

The doctor had died only moments after our appointment, and that's partially because of my big mouth. He tried to help me. He warned me about what happened to Felicity and that one move cost him his life. The brothers have sworn to me that the guy really did deserve it, that he wasn't a good man and that his babies were better off without him, but what do they know? It's not like they have a good father figure to compare him to.

I've made it a personal mission not to think about the appointment I shared with the doctor. Actually, a lot of the bullshit I've experienced in this castle has been pushed to the back of my mind. None of it has really been good apart from a few occasions involving roofs, chains, and narcotics shoved up my ass. But here I find myself thinking back to that moment with the doctor. He gave me the full rundown of the contraceptive he was putting into my arm, and at the end, he was kind enough to leave me a bag full of first aid supplies in case I found myself in a shitty situation, and hell, if this ain't a shitty situation then I don't know what is.

If I could somehow get over there, reach up to the high cupboard he left the bag in, then I'd be able to clean myself up. Hopefully there are some strong painkillers in there to ease the ache that's completely overtaken my body. I'd give anything for a morphine smoothie, just to be able to lay back on this fucked-up little surgical table for ten minutes without feeling the gut-wrenching pain that's overloaded my body for the past twenty-four hours.

My eyes rest on the high cupboard, devastation heavy in my chest. Getting from here to there is so much harder than it ought to be. My body has reached exhaustion, and here I am, willing it to keep going, to keep fighting, to find relief knowing that if I were to get caught, I'd pay for it with my life.

The straps have been left loose, but they're still too tight to easily slip out of. If I had the energy, I could wriggle free, but at what cost? The stitches deep inside my stomach are bound to tear and the rest of the cuts and bruises covering my body are going to scream until I stop moving. Not to mention, the only way out of this is by sliding to the bottom of the table and dropping to the ground. After getting thrown around in the car wreck and having Roman drag me through the woods, my body isn't going to forgive me for allowing further torture.

But what choice do I have? Staying here and suffering like one of their many victims isn't something I am capable of doing. Sure, I may run at every chance I get, but running means I'm also fighting. Hell, they didn't want to keep me around because of my 'yes boss' attitude. They like my fiery personality, they like when I fight them at every turn, and they sure as fuck love it when I tell them no … especially Marcus.

Closing my eyes, I take a deep breath and think of small thoughts. I suck in my barely-there stomach and after mentally preparing myself, I start wriggling, cursing myself as the pain comes back in full force. Every little movement has the stitches pulling inside me, tearing and popping as tears immediately fill my eyes, but I don't dare stop. I push myself harder, knowing that if I were to stop now, I'd never see it through to the end. It's like giving yourself a Brazilian wax, you just have to go for it. Otherwise, you're spread-eagle on your bathroom floor, one foot propped on the bathtub, the other on the toilet with wax stuck to your coochie, tears in your eyes, and regret heavy in your heart.

"Just tear it off like a Band-Aid," I mutter to myself, trying to find the will to carry on.

Inching my way down the table, my hips and shoulders get stuck on the straps and I'm forced to twist to free them. "Ahh, fuck," I whimper, the movement sending searing pain shooting through my stomach but I push through, having gone way too far to even consider giving up now.

My ass is freed and as my head slips under the first strap, I exhale a breath of relief. I'm nearly there. So fucking close. I can taste freedom.

Hell, I don't even know what my version of freedom is right now, but anything other than being strapped to this table is a huge win.

I get through the bottom strap and just as expected, I fall straight off the end of the surgical bed, dropping like a heavy sack of shit without a shred of energy to keep myself balanced. Breathy whimpers, gasps and pants fill the room and I do what I can to hold them back.

Pushing through the agony, I flip to my knees and ignore the blood pooling on the ground beneath me. My knees slip in the blood as the deep cuts on my back scream for relief. I'm almost positive that wriggling down the table would have opened the cuts again, but that's the least of my problems. If I somehow survive this, then I can focus on getting myself the help I desperately need.

Reaching the side of the room, my fingers lock onto the small desk the doctor had been sitting at during our appointment. With every last ounce of strength I possess, I pull myself up as pained groans and grunts fill the room. I bite down on the inside of my cheek, trying to keep myself as quiet as possible, knowing even the slightest noise would alert the boys, even despite Levi pounding into his drums upstairs. Hell, I wouldn't be surprised if the brothers had set up some kind of surveillance in here, making sure their little play toy stays exactly where they left her.

My feet shake as I get them under me, and I fear even the smallest movement would have me toppling over, so I keep one hand gripped firmly to the desk as my gaze lifts high above me to the cupboard containing all the goods.

Letting out a shaky breath, I reach up on my tippy toes, whimpering as the ache burns through my stomach. I'm so close. I will not give up now.

My head spins but I push myself further, fighting for everything I am until my fingers are finally gripping onto the bottom of the cupboard. Tears rest in my eyes, blurring my vision as I struggle to get my fingers under the door. Clenching my jaw, I push through the pain, forcing myself up higher until the door finally comes open. Without wasting another second, I grip onto the bag and yank it out, letting it tumble to my feet. The exhaustion hits me and I collapse into a bloodied heap along with it.

My back slams against the lower cupboards as the tears fall from my eyes, crashing against my chest and mixing with the dried blood. I take three slow breaths, desperate to relieve the ache and give myself just a moment of peace before forcing myself through hell all over again.

The seconds tick by painfully slow, and before I know it, I'm gripping onto the small white bag and fumbling with the zipper. The contents spill out onto my lap, just as my guts will be doing if I don't hurry up and get my shit together.

Painkillers fall from my lap onto the stained tiles and I scoop them up like a junkie desperate for her next hit. My fingers shake as I try to get the little container open and instantly hate myself when they spill out onto the ground. Grabbing three, I pop them into my mouth and cringe as I swallow them dry.

My breathing becomes labored as my movement drains all my energy, but I'll push myself until I physically can't go on. Collecting every bandage in sight, I get to work, starting with my stomach. I bite down on my lip as I press the bandage to my skin, applying pressure to try and ease the bleeding. Blood instantly seeps through the bandage and I double up, needing to save some for the cuts on my legs, arms, and back.

Breathe in. Breathe out. Apply pressure. Groan.

Tears stream down my face and I'm forced to bite the back of my arm to muffle my scream as the agony becomes too much.

I repeat the process until there are no bandages left before finding alcohol wipes to quickly clean the dried blood staining my skin. It's been a few hours since the boys' last visit and I know my time is limited. If I can at least get out of this room and hide out somewhere long enough to regain some of my energy, I might just have a fighting chance.

Picking up the last alcohol wipe, I hear a soft clatter as something falls to the tiles beneath. Glancing down, I find a small sterile blade that must have been hidden beneath the mess of bandages, wipes, and supplies. My gaze locks on it for a long moment, staring at it as though it's daring me to pick it up.

I swallow hard and let out another heavy breath, hating the thoughts twisting through my tortured mind.

I can't. That's insane. But what choice do I have?

My hands shake as they hover over the small blade, and mustering up every last ounce of drive, I grip it between my fingers and bring it to my mouth. I tear open the thin sterile packaging with my teeth, and before I allow myself to back out of this fucked-up little plan, I dig the blade deep into my arm.

Biting down on my tongue, I will myself not to scream as my hands continue to shake. Blood pools under my bite as the blade tears through the flesh of my arm, slicing painfully through the muscle. Tears stream down my face and I breathe heavily, sharp pants ripping from deep in my throat.

Images of Lucas Miller holding me down begin to surface through my head, his knife digging deep into my skin as my world came crashing down around me, but I push through it, determined to see this through despite the terror pulsing through my veins.

Blood trails down my arm, pooling beneath me, and just when I think I can't handle it, I feel the small contraceptive device hidden deep within the muscle. Relief swirls through my chest and I drop the blade, frantically searching the small bag for a pair of tweezers.

"Fuck," I whimper, coming up empty before glancing back down at the mess I've just made of my arm. I shake my head, knowing what I have to do, but not having the stomach to do it. I stabbed Marcus in the fucking hand, survived Lucas' bullshit, and found the courage to shoot my own goddamn father in the knees. If I can do that, then I can do this too.

Fuck. Fuck. Fuck. Fuck.

Letting out a shaky breath, I promise myself that if I somehow make it through this, I'll splurge on a new McClitoris 3000 and ... I go for it.

Sucking in a loud hiss, my fingers dig into the bloody flesh, feeling around until they finally curl around the little contraceptive rod. Nausea pulses through me as my body grows weaker by the second, and just when I think I can't go on, I grip onto the small device and yank it out of my arm with a low, pained groan.

The small rod clatters to the ground as my hand slaps over my arm, desperately trying to control the bleeding. "Holy fucking shit," I breathe, swallowing the blood in my mouth while trying to calm my racing heart. I stare down at it, catching my breath, and as the blood seeps away, I see a small green flashing light staring back at me. Putting myself through that kind of hell was all worth it.

The need to crush the little tracking device floods through me but I leave it alone, kicking it under the table. I can't risk crushing it and setting off some kind of silent alarm on the boys' phones. It's not worth it. For now, I need to get the fuck out of this room.

I drag myself across the small room, leaving a trail of blood in my wake. My hand grips the door handle and I pull it down, letting the door swing open and I fall forward, landing flat on my stomach. I groan low, but I'm one step closer to freedom with the door open. I can't stop to cry about it now.

Getting my hands and knees under myself, I crawl through the doorway, inching myself through the downstairs area until I come out into the massive ballroom that I once thought was the most impressive room in the castle.

Shuffling across to the side of the room, I pull myself up against one of the many expensive statues lining the room. I bite down on my lip to keep me from groaning in pain, and when I finally get to my feet, I forge ahead, determined more than ever to get the fuck out of here.

Clutching onto the white walls, I leave my mark with every small step I take, holding in each grunt of pain. Finally breaking out of the ballroom, I see the long hallway ahead, the very hallway that leads right to the front door. "Come on," I mutter to myself, willing myself to keep going.

My knees fight me with every step, desperately needing to give out. Hell, if that happens, I'll be worming my way to the door and down the fucking steps. All I know is that I cannot stop.

To hell with Roman and Levi. Adios, motherfuckers. I'm getting out of here today. Levi can take his hot as fuck roof sex and his ginormous cock and shove it up his goddamn ass. And as I ride off into the sunset, I hope he's watching me from the window as I flip him off and bolt out of their reach like my ass is on fire.

The mental image puts an oomph in my step and I stumble down the hallway, my gaze locked on the front door.

"Only a little bit further," I mutter to myself. "Come on."

I'm going to do it. I'm going to get out of here, and when I do, the world is mine for the taking. I won't be sitting back and hiding for the rest of my life. I'm going to lie in wait, and when the time is right, I'll fuck them up like never before. They're fools to think their father is their biggest threat because they'll never see me coming.

Taking my final step, I reach the front door, relief pounding heavily through my veins. Whatever pills I took before are making me feel like I can do the impossible, and while the pain is still in the forefront of my head, my ability to push through has risen.

My bloody fingers curl around the door handle as I taste the sweet smell of freedom on my lips, but when I yank down on it, it jars, locking me in. I try again and again and the panic surges through me. "No," I breathe, my gaze shifting over the massive door. "NO!"

Hot tears spring in my eyes as my chest heaves with heavy pants. I forgot about the keypad, Giovanni's electrical lock keeping the brothers trapped like prisoners in their own home, keeping them trapped in here with me.

FUCK!

I sink to my knees, the devastation hitting me like a fucking freight train as thick sobs get caught in my throat. My head falls forward, slamming against the heavy door. "Fuck. Fuck, fuck, fuck."

A chill sails down my spine as two large shadows fall over me. "Well, well," I hear Roman's gruff tone piercing through the silence. "It seems that someone hasn't learned her lesson."

I spin around, pressing my aching back up against the door just in time to see Levi bending low, his arms curling around my waist like two impenetrable forces. "NOOOOOO," I scream, trying to get away, but it's too late. He hauls me over his big shoulder and locks me down with his arms over the back of my legs.

"Don't worry, little one," Levi chimes, excitement brewing in his deep tone. "I promise, we're going to have so much fun."

CHAPTER FIVE

LEVI

The rhythmic beep of Marcus' heart monitor flows through the room, the single noise the only thing managing to keep me calm. My fingers itch for my drumsticks, but not even they can ease the rage burning through my veins.

How the fuck could she do this to him? Was this all part of her sick game? Get close enough to strike? Get us when we're down? It's fucking dirty, but we shouldn't have been so surprised. In this world, the only people I can rely on are my brothers.

Fuck, Marcus never saw her coming, but I'll be fucking damned if I let her play that same shit on me. It'll never fucking happen. Hell, if she doesn't learn her lesson after attempting to kill my brother, then I'll make fucking sure that she knows to never step out against us again.

Shayne Fucking Mariano. I'm not going to lie, that little bitch has balls of fucking steel. If I wasn't so damn furious with her, I would have bent her over that fucking surgical table and fucked that tight ass until she came.

Damn her. This bullshit hold that she has over me is going to hell, right along with that tight little cunt of hers. Hell, she'll be right in her element there. I bet she'd even get on her hands and knees for the devil and let him have his wicked way with her. But joke's on him because a girl like Shayne Mariano is going to sink her precious little claws in and rule over his goddamn kingdom until she's burned it all to ashes around him.

She's a fucking spitfire.

A soft groan flows through the room and both mine and Roman's heads snap up to our brother. Marcus is a fucking fighter and I'll be damned if he allowed a fucking bullet to take him down like that. Fuck, I would have killed him myself, and damn it, I'd have enjoyed it too.

My gaze shoots to Roman who sits across the room in complete silence. He's been like that ever since Shayne first ran. She got further under his skin than he would ever admit, and he's fucking pissed that he allowed it to happen. Roman has always been the protector, the one who does the shit he doesn't think Marcus and I are strong enough to handle. He's our big fucking brother, but he has the heaviest heart I've ever seen. He shoulders all the bullshit, which is exactly why he was the one to go after her. He didn't think I could handle it, didn't think I should have to. Hell, he already knows what it's like to lose the woman he was in love with and he didn't want to see that happen to me, but fuck, I'm far from in love with that little double-crosser.

Our father's been using our little playground for his own games lately, and though his men took our home by storm to find one of their missing prisoners, our father will hold us personally responsible if Marcus were to die. Roman keeps his stare on Marcus, knowing all hell will rain down over us the moment our brother takes his last breath. Though our father would need time to replenish his security after sending a wave of jackasses here. Anyone would think that asshole would have learned his lesson by now, but the fucker ain't that bright.

My father will get what's coming for him, and when he does … fuck, it's going to be a beautiful thing, something that we will celebrate for years to come.

Marcus' eyes slowly open and the relief that pounds through my veins is like nothing I've ever experienced before. I sit up straighter as Roman does the same, leaning forward to get closer to our most fucked-in-the-head, beloved brother.

"Marc?" Roman mutters, his face ashen, the terror in his eyes shining through like two beacons of light in the darkest storm, finally allowing himself to be vulnerable to his emotions.

Marcus' hand falls to his chest, and as the pain registers, his face twists into a cruel cringe. "What the fuck?" he mutters, letting out a deep breath and attempting to sit up, groans and grunts coming out with his every move.

"Don't be a fucking hero," I rush out, watching as he settles back onto his bed, not fucking happy about it either. "You're gonna tear your stitches."

Marc shoots a pissed-off glare at me, but fuck, it's the best thing I've ever seen. "Levi's right," Roman says. "You need to stay put for a few days, let your wounds heal. The bullet nearly nicked your heart. We nearly lost you, man."

Marc grunts, scrunching his face as his hand rubs over his chest, not capable of letting it be. He glances down, taking in the thick bandage across his chest before glancing up at the drip connected to his wrist. He mutters to himself and relentlessly tears the drip right out before throwing it away. "Where the fuck is she?" he says, getting straight to business.

"Don't you worry about her, she's not going anywhere," Roman says. "We're not going to kill her just yet. We thought you'd like to do the honor. But I swear, man, if you take too long to make it happen, I can't guarantee that I won't beat you to it."

A strange pull tears at my chest at how effortlessly he talks about taking Shayne's life, but I keep my mouth shut. Roman wouldn't like to hear me having second thoughts. After all, DeAngelis men don't change their minds. We make a conclusion and we stick to it, and Shayne knows what's up. She knew the consequences of what would happen if she pulled that trigger, and she did it anyway. Fuck my heart and the guilt darkening it, we need to see this through.

"Get fucked," Marc mutters, rolling his eyes as he turns his attention back to me. "Who the fuck is she? It was too dark. I didn't get a good look under her hood."

My back straightens and I shoot my gaze across to Roman as my heart drums a little faster in my chest. "What the fuck are you talking about?" I question as Roman's face turns a sickly shade of white. "What hood? Shayne was the one who shot you."

"Shayne?" Marc says, his jaw clenching as Roman slowly stands. "Shayne was trying to stop her. The bitch in the fucking black hood came in and shot me. If it weren't for Shayne, she would have got a clear shot between my fucking eyes. Tell me you didn't let that bitch get away?"

I shake my head, my hands clenching at my sides, the need to beat a rhythm on my drums pulsing heavily through my veins as the dread overtakes me, the images of the past twenty-four hours flashing through my head like a fucking movie playing in HD. "We … we thought Shayne shot you," I say, looking back at Roman, my eyes wide and terrified for what we've done.

Marcus throws the blankets back, rage pouring out of him as Roman stands in dead silence, the horror crashing down over his shoulders just as it's doing to me. Marcus slides out of bed with a pained grunt, most likely tearing each of the stitches inside his chest. He steps up to me, meeting me eye to eye. "TELL ME YOU DIDN'T?" he roars, seeing the horrifying truth shining through my eyes as he wobbles on his feet, the blood quickly draining from his cheeks. He grabs the front of my shirt, trying to pull me in, but he's just too weak. "WHAT THE FUCK DID YOU DO TO HER?"

FUCK! What the hell have we done?

The guilt weighs down on me and I drop to my knees, my stomach twisting with disgust. The things I did to her, the torment and horror

… FUCK. She's never going to forgive me. All along, she was trying to tell us, she screamed until she was blue in the face and I just kept hurting her, I just kept going, calling her a fucking liar and demanding the truth.

Shayne … my precious fucking Shayne. What have I done? What kind of monster am I?

Marcus turns and looks back at Roman, barely steady on his feet. "YOU," he spits, striding across the room like he didn't just have life-saving surgery. "IF YOU HURT ONE FUCKING HAIR ON HER BODY, I'M GOING TO SPILL YOUR GODDAMN USELESS BLOOD."

Roman looks back at Marcus, slowly shaking his head with dead eyes, his heart lying out on his shoulder, begging Marcus to take it and crush it between his capable hands. Marcus rears back and with one sickening blow, cracks his fist across Roman's face, sending him sprawling back against the wall, and I don't doubt that had he had the energy, he would have gutted him right there without a goddamn hint of remorse.

Without another word, Marcus turns and meets my hard stare. "If she doesn't make it, I'm holding both of you fuckers personally responsible. What we have planned for our father will look like child's play compared to what I will do to you."

I nod, swallowing hard over the lump in my throat. "If she dies, I'll fucking beg you to."

Marcus storms out of the room, determined to find his girl and make things right, but Roman calls out after him. "Wait," he says, his voice full of regret, self-loathing, and devastation. "There's something you need to know."

Marcus stops in his tracks, turning back to stare down Roman in a way I've never seen. "What?" he growls, the feral pitch in his tone enough to send even my blood cold.

Roman sighs, his gaze dropping to the ground. "We …" he cringes, his gaze slowly rising to meet our brother's as he clutches the side of the bed to keep himself upright. "We told her you were dead."

Marcus just stares, not moving a fucking muscle as he tries to keep himself from putting a bullet straight through our heads. Each of us has fucked up in the past, we've all had moments that we've tried to forget, but nothing quite like this. "From now on," Marcus says, his tone dropping to a lethal whisper, the threat coming through loud and clear. "She is your goddamn queen, your fucking *Empress.*"

Roman nods and just like that, Marcus turns and stalks out the door, the anger wafting off him in waves, a clear message that once he's through with Shayne, he's coming for us and we better be fucking ready.

My stare lingers on my older brother, the man who I've looked up to all my life, my one role model, friend, and confidant. I gape at him in horror. "What the fuck have we done?"

CHAPTER SIX

The door busts in with a loud BANG, slamming against the inside wall of my surgical prison cell. My eyes snap open, terror pulsing through my veins as my heart leaps into action, beating wildly like a fucking thunderstorm rolling in over the ocean. "NO," I sob, tears already springing to my eyes at the sheer thought of Roman and Levi coming back for more. "Please, no."

I've had enough. I can't do it anymore. Short of putting a bullet through my head, there's nothing else they can do to me.

They broke me.

I'm done.

No more running. No more fighting. I have nothing left to give. Perhaps they will see the difference and go easy on me. Perhaps they may take pity and finally put me out of my misery. Who am I kidding? This is the DeAngelis brothers. They don't take pity and they sure as fuck don't allow mercy killings. They'll push me past my final limit until I'm a pathetic heap of nothing, forgotten and abused, and only then will they end my miserable life.

They won't change their mind. They're too blind to see the truth, too stubborn in their ways to even listen to reason. I've done everything I can, and now I have to suffer someone else's consequences at the hands of the men who I thought could have meant so much more.

"I'm gonna fucking kill them," the voice murmurs as I hear footsteps on the tiled floor, storming toward me. I instinctively pull away. "Shhhhh, baby," he continues, the familiar tone breaking through my fear. "I'm here now. They're not going to hurt you anymore. I swear, you're safe with me." Hands land on my legs and quickly move up my body as I desperately try to blink back the tears that blur my vision.

I flinch at the familiar touch, immediately kicking them away. "DON'T FUCKING TOUCH ME," I scream, the sheer terror raw in my voice, a clear indication of what they've turned me into.

I was a fool to allow myself to get so close to these men. I knew what they were capable of. I should have kept my distance.

"It's me," the voice says, frantically gripping onto the straps that hold me down, desperate to free me. "It's Marcus. You don't need to be afraid. Roman and Levi are through hurting you, they know you didn't do it, and fuck, they'll do whatever it takes to make it up to you. I swear to you, Shayne. You're fucking safe here. It's over."

My head snaps toward him, my eyes wide as I stare in disbelief.

No. This is a trick. Marcus is dead. They told me he was dead, but here he stands right before me.

Marcus stares back at me, his beautiful face a mask of pure horror, taking in exactly what his brothers have done to me. His chest is bare, and I gape as blood trails out from beneath the thick bandaging across his chest. His skin is pale and it's clear he shouldn't be out of bed, but I don't have it in me to berate him on his stupidity as I can barely believe he's here, standing before me like a fucking avenging angel here to save my fucking life.

"Marc ..." I breathe, my eyes trailing over every damn inch of him as they slowly fill with tears of ... fuck, I don't know. Relief? Joy? Happiness? Disbelief? "I ... I thought you were dead. They told me you were dead."

"I know, baby," he says, finally getting the straps free and tearing them away from my body before reaching for me. His arms curl around me like I'm the most precious fucking thing he's ever seen as he holds me tight, not giving a shit about my injuries, just needing to have me close, and fuck, I think I need it too.

He pulls back slightly, taking in my haunted eyes. "Do you really think I can be taken down by a fucking bullet?" he smirks, trying to appear cocky but his exhaustion and pain rule over everything else. "I'm Marcus DeAngelis. I'm a fucking god."

"I ..." a loud sob cuts off my words and he pulls me back in, his hand falling to the back of my head and slowly trailing over my matted hair, doing his best to soothe me as I cry into him. The overwhelming grief and relief rattling me like never before.

"You're safe," he whispers, the pain in his tone all too real. "I'm going to take care of you."

I press my hands against his strong stomach, his skin clammy to the touch as I push him back a step, just needing to take him in. "How … I …" I cut myself off and take a few slow breaths, trying to grip reality. "They thought it was me," I tell him. "I tried to explain. I screamed, but they wouldn't listen. They just kept … it hurt so bad and they wouldn't stop. I … I just …"

"I know, and trust me, they're going to be punished for what they did to you," he says, taking my face in his hands and staring deep into my eyes, silently promising me the world. "I won't let them get away with this, Shayne. I'm going to see to it that they make it up to you twofold."

I shake my head. "I don't ever want to see them again," I tell him, hot tears stunning my eyes at the very thought of having them in my life. "Please, don't make me."

Regret flashes through his dark eyes, and without saying a word, I know that's not going to happen. "I'm sorry, babe. That's not an option, not around here. You don't need to fear them, not anymore."

"They tortured me, Marcus. Not fearing them is easier said than done," I whimper as his gaze drops over my exposed stomach, taking in the horrendous injuries from the car wreck. "You didn't see what they did to me. You're not the one with the images in your head, the memory of Levi's hands inside of you while Roman held you down. You don't know what it was like running for your fucking life with your brother bounding after you, so don't insult me by telling me that I don't have to fear them anymore."

Marcus lets out a heavy breath, meeting my eyes. "Don't assume because of my name that I've never run for my life. I've been in this exact situation, Shayne. I know these scars just as well as I know my own." He pauses for a beat, adjusting his weight to lean against the surgical bed as his voice slowly gets weaker, the pain shining through brighter. "I know my brothers. I know their techniques because they're the same as mine, and trust me when I say, they went easy on you."

My brows furrow as I move across the bed, discreetly giving him more space to rest. "Why would they do that?" I question. "I thought they wanted me dead."

He shakes his head. "They did want you dead, but they assumed you shot me, and while we may be a little fucked in the head, we are loyal to our brothers. They were waiting to see if I would live because had you been the one to shoot me, they knew I would have wanted to kill you myself."

My eyes widen, the words on his lips terrifying me to my core. "And if you had died?"

"Hierarchy," he says. "Roman is the eldest, so he would have taken the kill."

"That is so fucked up," I say as he slowly lowers himself to the bed beside me and takes my hand in his. "I won't forgive them."

He shrugs his shoulders. "That's your prerogative," he says. "It is what it is, there's no changing that, but I know my brothers, and they will fight to earn your forgiveness for the rest of their lives if that's what it takes. They are forever in your debt … unless you wanna make things interesting and get even."

"Get even?" I grunt. "How the fuck am I supposed to do that?"

"I could hold them down while you go at them with a machete, though that's no fun since Roman would just lay there and take it."

I gape at him in horror. "Absolutely not. Fucking up your brothers with a machete is off the table, despite how good it sounds right now. I know you get off on that kind of shit, but unlike you, I have morals. Besides, if they're going to get fucked up, it's going to be my brand of fucked up."

A soft knock sounds at the door and I glance up to find Levi hovering in the doorway, Roman slightly behind him with the two massive wolves peeking in through the gaps. "Who's getting fucked up?" Levi questions nervously, his voice wavering and unsure, a quality I've never heard coming from this beast of a man.

Marcus stands, a curse on his lips as pain cuts through his chest. "You know fucking well who's getting fucked up," he says, thick irritation in his tone.

Levi nods, his eyes casting down to the ground, accepting what will be without question. He looks up through his thick row of lashes, his usually bronze, warm skin looking a sickly shade of white. "May I come in?" he questions, the hesitation in his tone putting me off. "Your wounds need to be looked at, and your stitches …"

"You're fucking kidding yourself if you think I'm about to let you anywhere near me," I spit, the hatred in my eyes piercing right through him as I will myself not to cry, the very sight of him throwing me back over the past forty-eight hours to each of the times his hands came down over my body.

"Please," Roman mutters, stepping in closer to Levi, the regret heavy in his obsidian eyes, looking absolutely sick with himself. "Your wounds need to be cleaned and bandaged properly. Otherwise, you're going to get an infection and the healing process will take longer. Please, just let us fix you up and then I swear, we'll never touch you again, not unless you ask otherwise."

My gaze flicks to Marcus who looks about ready to pass out. "Can't you do it?" I ask, trusting him with everything I am despite the fact that, no matter which way I look at it, he still has DeAngelis blood pulsing through his veins.

"Come on, babe," Marcus says, his breathing becoming shallow and labored. "I know you're not blind. I'm barely going to last another minute before it's lights out. I know it's hard, but you can trust them. They won't hurt you."

I shake my head. "Then I'll wait until you regain your energy. I don't want them touching me."

"Shayne," Levi mutters, slowly creeping through the door. "Look at you. You tore your internal stitches when you tried to break out of here and you've bled through every single bandage on your body. You can't risk waiting. We need to get you set up on fluids and morphine sooner rather than later. Your body can't take this for much longer. Please, just let us do this for you."

"YOU DID THIS TO ME," I yell, the tears stinging my eyes as I try to sit up. "You're standing here demanding that I trust you unconditionally, trust you with my body when you've done nothing but destroy it. You hurt me, Levi. You were supposed to be the good one.

You destroyed me. How am I supposed to trust you when you couldn't do the same for me?"

"I'm sorry," he says with devastation written across his face, the two very words the brothers once promised me they'd never say. "If I could take it all back, I swear to you, I would."

"I told you," I say, my voice breaking. "I told you so many times, but you wouldn't listen. Every single time. You refused to believe that you two could have missed something, that the poor kidnapped chick could have been telling the truth. Instead, you chose to doubt me despite every single sign telling you that you were wrong. You chose to believe that I would try to hurt Marcus, that I'm somehow out to get you, and now your mistake has cost you more than you could ever know."

"What's that supposed to mean?" Roman questions, his eyes narrowed, cautiously watching me as Levi falls to his knees at the end of my bed, his forehead dropping to the hard mattress.

I clench my jaw, the anger swirling deep in my gut as I take in the two men who look like complete strangers, not the men I've come to know. "It means that while I wasn't out to get you before, you can guarantee that after what you've done to me, I sure as hell am now. You need to watch your backs. I will make this right, and when I do, you two are going to stand there and take it like fucking soldiers."

Roman's eyes drop away just as Marcus' body goes limp beside me. I suck in a gasp and turn his way. "Marcus?" I demand, shaking his arm, panic tearing through me like a bullet out of its chamber. "Marcus? Fuck. Wake up."

"He just passed out," Roman mutters. "He's fine, he'll come to soon, but you might not if you don't allow us to patch you up."

I shake my head, clutching the edge of the surgical bed to try and sit up. "If you guys are so good at what you do, then you shouldn't have an issue talking me through it. You assholes will never lay a hand on me again, not even if it means saving my life. Is that clear?"

Levi's shoulders sag even more as Roman looks back at me, regret heavy in his gaze. "You have internal stitches that need to be fixed, Shayne. Don't be a righteous fool because you want to prove a point. Know your limits. I know you want to stick it to us but doing this is only hurting yourself more."

"Get fucked, Roman," I snap, seething at him with every ounce of energy left in my body, hating that after everything I've done to keep myself alive, he still doubts just how far I'll go. "I said I can do it."

Roman glances back at Marcus, tossing up his options and I don't doubt he's considering knocking me out and doing it himself, but he wouldn't dare, not now and especially not when Marcus would tear him a new asshole afterward. He's in enough hot water as it is, and judging by the way Levi rests on his knees, Roman's got absolutely no one to back him up.

Roman sighs and walks across the room before hashing in a code to a locked cabinet and pulling out enough first aid supplies to fill a hospital. He looks back at Levi, catching his eye before indicating to their passed-out brother. "Move him. She's gonna need all the space she can get."

Levi nods and gets up, his head still hanging low as he moves in beside the surgical bed and reaches for his brother. I instinctively flinch and he pauses, meeting my stare with a broken one of his own. "I'm sorry," he murmurs, holding my gaze for a moment too long. I'm forced to look away, and as if assuming his half-assed apology was supposed to fix everything, he sighs and pulls Marcus into his strong arms, his devastation showing bright and clear.

I watch as Levi strides out of the small room with Marcus, walking out of here with my only security blanket and carrying him as effortlessly as though he was holding a newborn baby. With Marcus out of my way, I slowly shuffle back to the center of the bed and keep my eye on Roman as he gathers everything I'll need to put myself back together.

He places everything on the edge of the bed, being careful not to brush his skin over mine. "Are you sure?" he questions, glancing up to meet my terrified stare.

"Of course I'm not sure," I throw back at him. "I'd give anything to not be in this position, but it sure as fuck beats allowing you to put your hands on me."

Roman doesn't respond, just drops his gaze back to the first aid supplies and starts preparing what I need. A moment of silence passes between us, and as Roman holds up a small needle and starts measuring something out, Levi strides back into the room, thankfully leaving the door wide open. Though it's not like I'd be able to get away from them, not even if I tried.

Levi sits across the room, his heavy stare locking onto my body and trailing over every single scratch, bruise, and cut, even the ones he didn't have a damn thing to do with. "What?" I snap, glaring across the room and hating how much those stunning dark eyes still seem to call to me.

He softly shakes his head as though he can't seem to find the right words, confusion marring his perfect face. "I just …" he cuts himself off as he presses his hand to his chest. "Something … it hurts right in here. I've never felt … I don't know what this is."

I let out a heavy sigh and turn my attention toward the first aid supplies in Roman's hands. "It's grief. Heartache. Regret. Sorrow. Despair. Whatever the fuck you want to call it. It's what happens when you screw up and your whole fucking world comes crumbling down around you. Though I don't expect someone like you to understand what that's like. You've never known what it means to care for anything that doesn't share the same DNA."

"I don't like it."

My venomous glare pierces into his dark gaze. "You don't like the feeling? Or you don't like the fact that deep down inside, you're still a weak human who has absolutely no control over his emotions? You're nothing better than the rest of us."

His eyes harden, and for a minute, I must have forgotten who the fuck I was talking to, but he doesn't respond, simply drops his gaze back to the wounds covering my body.

"Here," Roman says, placing the small syringe needle down beside my hand, being cautious not to allow his fingers to brush up against mine. "This is an anesthetic to numb the area. You need to inject this all around the wound, inserting only a little bit as you go."

I swallow hard and pick up the small anesthetic needle, having seen this plenty of times from working at the bar when things get a little too rowdy and the paramedics need to be called. I hate getting needles just as much as the next guy, but doing it to myself is going to test me. Though it couldn't possibly be worse than digging out the tracking device in my arm. The only difference is hopefully this time, I'm not going to feel it.

Letting out a shaky breath, I hold the needle over my skin and stare, knowing that until the anesthetic actually starts to work, it's going to sting like a bitch. Then sucking in a terrified hiss, I push the tip of the needle into my aching skin.

"Ah, fuck," I grumble, my lips twisting into a cringe.

"A little bit further," Roman instructs, leaving all the bullshit behind just to make sure I don't injure myself further. "Then inject the anesthetic."

I do as he says and after a slight pause, I move to the next section and repeat the process over and over until there's no anesthetic left in the syringe. "How long is this supposed to take?"

"A few minutes and then you'll be able to start stitching yourself up," he mutters, getting the suture kit prepared and pushing a few pills toward my hand, again being careful not to touch me. "Take these. They'll help with the pain until I can find you something stronger."

I meet his eyes for a moment before hesitantly taking the pills, and before bringing them to my mouth, Levi stands, his dark eyes flashing with unease. "Let me get you a bottle of water first," he says, his gaze dropping to the ground, not waiting for a response before he strides out of the room.

Not a word passes between me and Roman while we wait for Levi's return, and they're the most brutal silent moments of my life. Curses, screams, and anger sit on the tip of my tongue, begging to fly free, but I swallow each one of them, now not being the time for us to get into it.

Levi returns a moment later and hands me the bottle. Instinctively, I reach for it, my blood turning cold as his fingers brush against mine. I pull away as quickly as humanly possible, taking the water with me and hating the pain that rests in his features, but not feeling sorry for him one bit.

The bottle of water is still sealed and a breath of relief pulses through me before I put the pills into my mouth and open the water. They go down with ease and the cold water hitting the bottom of my empty stomach only goes to remind me just how fucking hungry I am.

"Alright, you should be good to start," Roman says, drawing every ounce of my attention as he places the suture kit down beside me. He pushes the limits as his fingers come a shitload closer than they had before and my body tenses, waiting for him to retract. Hell, he's probably jealous that his youngest brother somehow managed to get away with touching me without me bitching him out, but unlike Levi, Roman is the one I have vivid memories of, chasing me through the castle, the car wrecking from his bullet, and his gun aiming right between my eyes. Roman and I will never be cool, no matter how hard he tries. Some things a girl just can't come back from.

Trying to keep my mind away from the tragic memories swarming through my mind, I take the needle in my hands, check the wound is properly numbed, and meet Roman's heavy stare. The sooner I get this over and done with, the sooner I'll be back beside Marcus, his warm arms wrapped tightly around my waist. "What do I do?"

CHAPTER SEVEN

Steam fills the bathroom as I step out of the shower and pull my towel around me, cautiously patting my healing wounds. It's been two days since Marcus woke up and two days since I've been treated like the goddamn queen of this castle, and I fucking hate it.

Don't get me wrong, a bunch of sexy-as-sin mafia men treating me like the sun shines out of my ass is what my wildest dreams are made of, but knowing why they're doing it makes me sick. There's nothing genuine about it, just two brutal men regretting their decision to think of me as a piece of meat on a butcher's table. I'm sure once their guilt wears away, so will their need to treat me like royalty.

After drying myself off and cracking the door, the steam fades away and I can clearly see the stranger staring back at me through the mirror. This isn't the girl I grew up with, the girl who was shit-scared of her father and who put herself through hell just to survive. This isn't the girl who found the courage to leave when she was barely eighteen, who somehow pushed through four years of bullshit to finally come out the other end a stronger woman. This girl staring back at me is a stranger. I barely know myself anymore.

My body is covered in more cuts and bruises than I've ever had in my life. More than I ever received from my father during my whole eighteen years of hell with him. There are deep bags beneath my eyes, my cheeks have started to hollow out, and I can see all too much of my collarbone through my skin.

I need to get back to normalcy. I need to find freedom, happiness, and health, and this is not a place for healing, especially with three broody assholes who can turn on you in the blink of an eye. Not to mention their father who likes to drop countless guards on the property to attack at the first sign of movement.

Fucking Giovanni. I hate that guy. He's a piece of shit, though the hell he put me through is nothing quite like the hell he's rained down over his sons for an entire lifetime.

Shit, there I go feeling sorry for those bastards again. I have to stop thinking of them as broken souls or as victims in their enormous castle. They're monsters; even Marcus is the direct result of what their father created. They're not to be toyed with, not to be trusted, and sure as fuck not to be loved.

After towel drying my hair and watching as it falls in damp waves down my back, I toss my towel into the hamper and grab my gorgeous champagne silk dressing gown off the side of the massive bathtub. Threading my arms through the holes, I let out a satisfied sigh. I've never had a dressing gown before, especially not one quite so luxurious. It's the softest thing I've ever worn and I'm not going to lie, with my body still so sore, it's the only piece of clothing I've been able to wear over the past two days, but I absolutely hate it. I only have this extraordinary gift because of what the guys did to me.

Bullshit gifts have been appearing everywhere. An expensive perfume in the living room, a diamond bracelet on my bedside table, the matching necklace gift wrapped in the dining hall. It's getting insane, but I'm not stupid. I like shiny things, and the longer I keep my mouth shut about it, the longer the gifts will keep coming. There have been at least six gifts so far and they're always something small, professionally wrapped with a little note attached. None of the notes ever say who it's from but my guess is Levi. Roman is too stubborn for that shit.

Taking the two long straps dangling by my side, I tie a loose knot at my waist, careful not to pull tight over any of my injuries. My gaze scans down my reflection in the mirror and feeling more feminine than I have in weeks, I turn and leave my private bathroom.

It's getting late in the evening and my lights are dimmed so I don't notice Roman hovering in the corner until it's too late. My heart leaps into action, beating right out of my fucking chest as my whole body flinches and comes to an immediate standstill.

The small flinch has the soft silk slipping from my shoulder and opening wide, exposing the curve of my breast and leaving me anxiously grabbing the material before it falls even lower and my whole tit falls out. Only nothing else matters as I take in Roman, covered in darkness. He takes a hesitant step toward me and I gasp as the blade held firmly between his skilled hand catches in the soft moonlight streaming through my window.

"What are you doing?" I rush out, backing up a step and grasping tighter onto my gown, my throat still hoarse and sore from the endless screaming I've done over the past few days.

Roman holds his hand up, spreading his fingers in a show of innocence, gripping the handle of the knife to his palm with only the strength in his thumb. "I'm not going to hurt you."

I don't stop backing up until my spine is pressed firmly against my bedroom wall, and only then does Roman stop, allowing me some space. My eyes flick toward the door, closer to Roman by miles. If I have to run, I'll never make it.

"Don't," he mutters, reading my mind so effortlessly, though he's been in situations like this more times than I can count, he would know every single type of reaction there could possibly be and he would know how to outsmart every single one of them. "I told you, I'm not going to hurt you."

I scoff. "Forgive me if I have a little trouble trusting your word. After all, these scars on my back didn't get there by themselves."

His eyes drop, and for a fleeting second, I see a wave of regret rushing through his system, completely overpowering him. Though it's gone almost quicker than it came, his ability to mask his emotions is like no other. "I understand," he says, his tone formal and straight to the point, not something I'm used to when speaking to these guys.

They usually prefer a little mind game in their babbling bullshit. After all, what fun is a normal conversation if they aren't making a girl shit her pants before they've even gotten to the 'how are you?' portion of their discussion? "I'm not here to beg for forgiveness. I know that's not something that will come easily. You're going to have to learn to trust me again, trust that I have good intentions when it comes to you, and I get that I could be trying to earn that trust for the rest of my life."

"Don't hold your breath," I tell him, my body slowly starting to relax, though I sure as fuck keep my distance. "Though, on second thought, maybe you should."

Roman just stares at me, not appreciating my comment in the slightest. Though, he'd be a fool if he thought he could hide in the darkest corner of my bedroom with a knife after everything he's put me through and not get even a little bit of bullshit attitude. That's not how the world works, and it sure as hell is not how I work. He's stalked me through this castle too many times not to know that.

"Why are you here, Roman?" I sigh when he doesn't make an effort to hurry this shit show along.

He gently tosses the knife into the air but keeps his dark gaze on me as it flips in front of his face. The blade comes down and he catches it in his hand, the sharp edge digging into his palm. He doesn't flinch despite the sting I know he must be feeling. Instead, he simply holds out his hand, offering me the handle.

All I can do is stare at it, knowing how much power that blade holds, but I'm not stupid and I'm definitely not in the mood for his games. "Take it," he urges after I make it more than clear that I have no intention of following his lead, especially when there's a knife involved. He knows how I feel about knives since Lucas Miller decided to use me for surgical practice.

I cross my arms over my chest and fix him with a stare that could rival one of his own. "Why the hell should I?"

"Because," he says, stepping closer until his face is mere inches from mine, kicking my heart up a few gears. "This is the only opportunity I'm going to give you to settle the score. Take it or leave it."

I gape at him, far too consumed by his words to even acknowledge how fucking close he is. "What the hell is that supposed to mean?" I question, though I'm pretty fucking sure I already know.

"Stop acting so ignorant. You know what I'm offering," he tells me, his tall frame looming over me, though with the blade on offer, I suddenly don't feel so intimidated. "I took pleasure in hurting you and I would have ended your life had you pushed me far enough. It would have been simple. A quick slice across your throat and it all would have been over. I'm offering you the chance to even the score. Take the knife, Shayne."

My gaze meets his and I hold it for a moment before finally reaching out and taking the knife in my hand. The handle is sleek, cold, and dark, just like every aspect of Roman's soul. My finger presses to the very tip and I apply a little pressure, watching how the tip digs into my skin but doesn't quite pierce it.

The sheer layer of blood rests along the curved blade from Roman's palm, a stark reminder of just how sharp this thing really is. I release my finger from the tip and let the blade dangle in my hand, watching as that single drop of blood runs down and falls from the tip. It hits the expensive silk of my dressing gown and only once it's completely absorbed do I glance back up and meet Roman's heated stare.

"Let me get this straight," I start, pushing away from the wall and watching as he moves with me, backing up a step, probably for the first time in his life. "You got off on hurting me. You chased me through the castle, probably hard as a fucking rock as I screamed, telling you over and over again that I didn't do it. You shot out the tire of the car and caused a wreck that could have easily ended my life and then stalked me while I scrambled away with a piece of glass protruding from my stomach. You dragged me through the woods. You left scars all over my body. You held me down while your brother performed surgery on me. I was awake, Roman. I felt his hands moving inside my body, and now, after everything, you come into my room with a knife, and assume that if I get the chance to tear your flesh into ribbons that it's suddenly going to make everything okay?"

Without another word, I slam the knife into his chest, the blade resting along the length of his wide pecs still glimmering in the glow of the moonlight. Though the blade doesn't pierce his skin, I still get the sweetest satisfaction over the way his body tensed.

I step around him and walk to the door, holding it open and silently waiting for him to get the hint and walk out of here. Only the fucker doesn't move.

"I know you and your brothers don't know much about being normal fucking people, but let me give you a clue," I growl. "When a woman stands at her door with a fucking scowl stretched across her face, that's your cue to get the fuck out."

He shakes his head and tosses the knife to my bed, turning to stare me down. "I see it in your eyes, Shayne. You want this. You want to hurt me just as I've hurt you. You want to hear my pain, feel my skin grow clammy beneath your touch. You want me to fear my life slipping away just like you did."

My eyes narrow as anger pulses through my veins, and without thinking, I walk back toward him, feeling the power getting me high at having a man like Roman DeAngelis at my mercy. "Don't doubt me for one second," I seethe. "I want those things more than you could know. I dream about how it would feel to put you down just like you wanted to do to me, but I see right through you, Roman DeAngelis, and you're nothing more than a lost little boy desperate for someone to come along and save him. But get it through your thick fucking skull, that won't be me. Doing this, taking that knife and letting it slice through your skin isn't doing me any favors. It doesn't even the score. All it's good for is to make you feel better about the hell you put me through because of your lack of judgment and inability to trust anyone who isn't yourself. I refuse to give you anything that will make you feel any less of a monster and I refuse to act out in a way that would make me any more of one. The weight of what you did is going to rest on your shoulders, it's going to consume you until the day you die and that will be the sweetest revenge I'll ever get."

Roman stares at me, his heated eyes locked on mine in a silent battle between wills, but there's no way I'm budging on this. He won't be let off the hook by a little slicing and dicing, and I sure as hell won't be giving up a part of my own soul just to make him feel better about what he did. I know my limits, and from here on out, Roman DeAngelis will not be breaking them.

I hold my ground, refusing to be the weaker person, and after a slight pause, Roman turns and stalks to the door, leaving the knife in the center of my bed like a challenge, daring me to stab him right in the back. He steps into the doorway and pauses, glancing back at me. "I know you'll never forgive me, but one of these days you're going to have to learn how to be okay with me, because no matter what, you're not going anywhere. You're stuck here, just like we are."

"What you're failing to see, Roman, is that you're the one who's going to have to learn how to live with me. From here on out, I'm the queen of this goddamn castle, and you're the piece of shit who tried to cut her down," I tell him. "And for the record, it's a two-way street. I have to learn how to trust you in order to survive in this world, but you need to do the same for me. You want me to trust you blindly, but you didn't trust me when it mattered most. I told you I didn't do it, but you refused to listen. You didn't even hear me when I screamed, so until you come to the party and meet me halfway, you and I have absolutely nothing to talk about. From here on out, you're dead to me."

And with that, he walks out of my room, leaving me standing just a little bit taller, while also hating that he's right. Our situation doesn't change the fact that all four of us are prisoners in this castle, and long, endless days are going to be torture if they're filled with hatred, anger, and pain. It would be a shitload easier on everyone if we could all learn how to live as one, something I thought we'd mastered before all this shit went down. But in trying to make things easier for myself, I'll be making life easier for them too, and right now, that's the last thing I want. So from here on out, torture is my best friend. A life of hell is going to be worth it if it means they're going right down with me. Besides, I have Marcus with his wicked tongue, skillful fingers, and devilish need to make me his dirty little whore. For now, he's all this girl needs.

CHAPTER EIGHT

A soft creak filters through my room as the door slowly swings open. My gaze falls toward the door, my heart leaping right out of my chest as though history is about to repeat itself. Since Roman walked out of here a few hours ago, my head has been even more of a mess than it usually is. Having another stranger sneaking into my room in the middle of the night just ain't gonna cut it.

Without skipping a beat, I lean across my bed, holding back a pained cry as I stretch out and turn on the lamp that rests peacefully on my side table, which is exactly what I should have done the night McHooded Bitch snuck into my room. Consider me officially educated on the consequences of not knowing who and what is around you.

Flashbacks of the hooded woman circle my mind as a dark shadow moves into my room, but as the light from my lamp floods the room,

I find one of the massive wolves making his way toward my bed. He plonks his furry ass down and looks up at me, his dark eyes almost as scary as his masters'.

"What do you want?" I murmur, keeping my voice low to not alert the boys that I'm awake. Otherwise, they'll be down here with some bullshit excuse like they were just checking on my injuries, not stalking me to make sure I wasn't attempting my fifty-third escape.

The wolf moves his head toward the door while keeping his eyes firmly locked on mine and I can't help but feel as though he's trying to tell me something. "I don't speak mutt," I tell him, almost certain that this is the wolf Roman ordered to follow me into the woods. It's pretty dark though, so I can't be too certain. This big-ass creature led me to safety and kept me warm in that cave, but the second Roman showed up, the little double-crosser turned on me, and I realize now he was just trying to keep me alive so that Roman could have his fun. And here I thought all animals were supposed to have some kind of innocence about them, but it turns out, this wolf is just as corrupted as his owners. The only difference is the wolf can't be blamed for his actions.

The wolf seems to glare at me, not thrilled with my lack of obedience, though how can I give in to his demands when I have absolutely no idea what the fucker wants? It's like trying to work out what the DeAngelis brothers' ulterior motive is with me—it's useless. I'm pretty fucking certain they don't even know themselves.

I glare straight back at the big ball of fluff, almost daring it to make a move. If the fucker wants to be a stubborn asshole, then I'm more than happy to sit here all night. "I'm waiting," I tell him. "Explain your bitch ass."

A soft growl rumbles through his chest and I blanch, my eyes widening in horror, wondering if the fucker somehow knows that I'm being a spiteful bitch. He doesn't move, doesn't blink, and doesn't make another damn sound until I finally give in and make my move.

I throw my blanket back and painstakingly lift myself into a sitting position, hating the way my muscles scream for revenge deep inside my stomach. Twisting around, my feet drop to the soft carpet and my toes instantly squish into the welcome softness beneath them.

As I raise myself up off the bed and grab my silk dressing gown, the wolf stands and makes his way to the door, glancing back at me to make sure I understand to follow him. Letting out a sigh, I pull my gown around me and follow the big wolf.

He struts with his head held high, way too proud of himself for so easily being able to manipulate me into doing his bidding. We step out into the long hallway and he goes slow, somehow knowing that I'm still not at full speed yet.

"So ..." I say, glancing down and meeting his jet-black stare. "Have you got a Mrs. Wolf? Pups? Maybe a side piece? I know that's frowned upon, but I know how you dirty-minded little freaks like to get down, mounting every she-wolf you come across. I bet Marcus taught you everything he knows."

The wolf huffs and turns back to look down the hallway, having absolutely no desire to spill all the juicy details, but if I had to take a guess, I'd say this guy here is a lady-killer.

The furball leads me right down the hallway and finally comes to a stop outside Marcus' bedroom door. He looks up at me with a smug expression before prancing into Marcus' room and collecting a treat right out of the fucker's hand.

I prop myself against the doorframe, looking in at Marcus as he sits up in his bed, his wide, tattooed chest on display with his wound exposed to the world. My lips press into a tight line, and as the wolf turns and bolts back out the door, his mission complete, I'm left staring in wonder at the man I still can't believe is right in front of me.

"You know, there are more practical ways of getting a girl's attention than sending a messenger dog to come and get her."

Marcus scoffs. "If he knew you referred to him as a messenger dog, he would have torn your throat right out."

"Oh really?" I grin, crossing my arms over my chest, the amusement building like rapid fire in my chest. "He didn't seem to mind when I called him the wolf version of a kinky whore."

Marcus raises a brow, arching it high as his lips pull into a devilish smirk. "Come here."

I grin right back at him. "Now why the hell would I want to do something like that?"

"Don't tempt me, Shayne," he says, his eyes darkening with hunger. "You know damn well that I'll get out of this fucking bed and drag your ass over here. Do as you're told."

"Ahhhh, so that's how it's going to be, huh?" I question, my eyes shimmering with silent laughter. "You know, with that big gaping hole in the middle of your chest, I bet now is probably the only time I could outrun you."

Marcus narrows his eyes on me and in an instant, he throws his blankets back. "Don't count on it."

My eyes widen like saucers. "What the fuck do you think you're doing?" I shriek, running toward him and pushing my hands down over his shoulders to keep his stupid ass in bed, not giving a shit if the sound of my cries wakes up the other two devils who reside in this castle. "Are you stupid? You were shot two days ago. You need to stay in bed."

Marcus laughs and snaps his arm around my waist with a speed I wasn't prepared for, lowering me down over him, his hard cock pressed firmly against my pussy.

He doesn't say a damn word, just looks at me with those deadly eyes, a silent message passing between us—his plan worked flawlessly. "You're an asshole," I mutter, unable to be mad at him.

He grinds up against me and I laugh as his eyes sparkle. "Would you have preferred that I came to you?"

I let out a groan. He knows damn well that I would have bitched his ass out if he'd risked getting out of bed to come and fool around in my room. Though I'm sure he would have found a way to earn my forgiveness. Unlike his dickhead brothers. "Alright, fine," I mutter, my hands dropping to the tight muscle of his abdomen. "You win, but did you really have to send the wolf? He looks at me like a chew toy."

Marcus raises a brow, curiosity deep in his eyes. "Would you have preferred that I sent one of my brothers to go and get you?" he questions. "The wolves will warm up to you in time. They're not the nicest motherfuckers to get along with."

I roll my eyes. "You know damn well that I wouldn't have preferred your brothers. What I would have preferred was letting me spend the night in bed, not having to worry about anything sneaking into my room."

Marcus scoffs and grinds his thick cock against my pussy again. "And miss out on all of this?" he teases, reaching up and gently pulling the silk tie at my waist until it falls free. His fingers slip inside my gown, traveling up over my shoulder and pushing the material aside, letting the gown fall to my waist, exposing my naked body below.

My skin instantly reacts. My nipples pebble as a shiver travels down my spine, my body longing for his touch. "You're fucked in the head if you think I'm about to fuck you," I tell him, doing my best to focus on anything but his calloused fingers trailing over my skin. "You have a bullet hole in your chest. Not to mention, a bullet hole that should be bandaged right now. If you laid still enough, I bet I could see right through it. The last thing you need is me bouncing around on top of you."

"On the contrary," he says, his eyes darkening with the most wicked type of hunger. "That's exactly what I need."

Heat floods me as I watch the way his devilish gaze travels over my body. His fingers roam over the curve of my breast and drop down past my waist, his soft touch skimming over my skin and tickling me in all the right places. Then with a sharp jolt, he pulls me forward and I catch myself against his chest, being careful not to press down over his bullet wound as the position has my clit rubbing up against his veiny cock, teasing and enticing me just like he intended.

"You've got me right where you want me," Marcus whispers, his lips gently grazing over the sensitive skin of my neck, making me tilt to the side, desperately needing more. "When else will you ever get complete control like this? I'm flat on my back with nowhere to go. I'm at your mercy, Shayne. Take what I know you need from me. Take control, baby, just like I know you want to."

Well fuck.

Marcus moves his hips beneath me and while I know deep down that I should be pulling away, that I should be distancing myself from him, there's no way in hell that I have that kind of self-control. He may think he's at my mercy, but he's never been so wrong. Marcus DeAngelis is a fucking weapon, and any woman would be afraid of the things a man like this could do.

Marcus reaches up, his thick fingers curling around my jaw, and brings my face to meet his. Before I can even let out a needy sigh, he's pulling me in, pressing his warm lips against mine and dominating me despite his declaration of handing over control.

He kisses me deeply and I return it twofold, letting him know just how down I really am. His hand drops from my jaw, traveling down to the base of my throat, and as he gives a gentle squeeze, I rock my hips back and forth, letting him feel just how wet I am for him.

Marcus groans and the sound is like a shot of adrenaline rushing through my veins, completely taking control and making me feel alive for the first time in days, but it's got nothing on the way my clit feels grinding against his velvety cock.

Fuck my wounds. Fuck his bullet hole. There's no better healing than this.

Raising my hips just slightly, I reach down between us and curl my fingers around his cock, giving it a firm squeeze before pumping my fist up and down, letting my thumb curve over his tip to feel that small bead of moisture.

"Fuck, Shayne," he mutters, his tone deep and filled with desperation. "Take me. All of me."

And without another word, I guide his thick, long cock to my entrance and slowly sink down over him as he stretches my walls and fills me to the damn brim. I suck in a gasp, my eyes rolling in my head as his other hand takes my hip. "Shit, Marc," I groan, not daring to move as my body adjusts to his size, wanting to soak up every little bit of pleasure on offer.

"I know," he mutters, his lips gently brushing over mine as his cock twitches, making us both groan as I clench around him. "I need you to fucking move. Your tight little cunt is gonna be the death of me."

Raising myself up from his chest, I prop my hands against his stomach. As my tongue rolls over my bottom lip, he becomes mesmerized. "I thought the ball was in my court?" I remind him, slowly shaking my head. "The control is mine. I'll move when I'm ready."

His fingers dig into my hip as a soft growl rumbles through his chest. His eyes flash with a devilish darkness that completely consumes me, and as a grin slices across my face, I can't help but rock my hips back to feel the way his thick cock slowly moves inside me.

Not being able to grip onto the tight skin of his stomach, my hand falls to his on my hip. My fingers weave between his and as my hips move forward, taking him again, I squeeze his hand hard, throwing my head back in pure ecstasy. "Fuckkkk," I moan, rolling my neck as my other hand falls to my chest, slowly roaming over the soft curve of my breasts and leaving a trail of goosebumps in its wake.

"Shit, babe. Keep touching yourself," he tells me, his eyes fluttering with the overwhelming pleasure as I keep moving over him, clenching my walls and squeezing him tight. "Just like that."

I don't dare stop, slowly picking up my pace as I feel Marcus' long cock slowly moving in and out of my pussy, my arousal spreading between us. His fiery gaze remains locked on my body, watching the way it moves, watching the way my fingers tease my nipples and the way they skirt over my sensitive skin. Only when they drop lower and take full advantage of my aching clit, his eyes flame with need. "Fuck, Shayne, I've got to taste you."

Without skipping a beat, I lock my eyes onto his and bring my fingers up before trailing them over my lips. My arousal spreads, glistening in the soft light coming from the hallway, and I watch the way desire rocks through him.

Gripping onto the headboard, I slowly begin to lean toward him, not stopping my torturous slow movements up and down his cock, groaning and moaning as he massages deep inside me, his cock hitting me right where I need him.

My face hovers just in front of his, and I pause for just a moment, watching as he raises his chin, all too ready to accept my offering, but he should know that it's never that easy when it comes to handing over control. "It's all mine," I tell him just as my lips raise into a grin, and before he gets the chance to take what's not his, my tongue shoots out and rolls over my bottom lip, tasting myself.

Marcus flinches, his hand at my throat gently tightening before he pulls me lower and kisses me so fucking deeply, taking what's left of my arousal. His tongue sweeps into my mouth, fighting for dominance, and only when I'm panting for oxygen does he release me. "Just because I'm giving you control, doesn't mean that I have to play by your rules," he tells me, his eyes lighting up like a damn firework as a smug expression crosses his face.

Fire burns through me, and as I pull back from him, I can't help but kick this game up a notch. Keeping my grip on the headboard, I use it to stabilize myself. I need to prove to Marcus that no matter what, when the control is mine, everyone plays by my rules.

I fuck him hard, raising slightly on my knees so that I can bounce on top of him. I come up just high enough that I can feel his tip at my entrance before slamming back down with a desperate groan. I take him again and he watches the way my tits bounce with my movements. "Fucking hell," he hisses between a clenched jaw, his fingers digging into my skin. "Again."

I give him what he needs, my head tipping back with ecstasy, and despite my better judgment, he pulls himself up, leaning his back against the headboard before curling his arm around my waist and pulling me in tight against his body. "Fuck me harder," he demands. "Squeeze that tight little cunt. I want you to fucking own me."

Holy fuck. This man.

I take him harder and faster, my skin quickly growing clammy with a sheer layer of sweat, and as I clench my eyes, his lips press to my throat, sucking and nipping at my sensitive skin. His hand trails down my body, grabbing a handful of ass before slipping further and feeling the way my pussy takes his cock. His fingers trail over my arousal and he spreads it up to my ass, making me realize that when it comes to Marcus DeAngelis, I will never truly have control. Then without warning, he presses his fingers into me.

I let out a soft gasp as my eyes roll in my head. "More," I groan, pushing back against him, and damn it, he doesn't disappoint, giving me exactly what I need.

"Fuck, Marc," I cry, feeling that familiar tightening deep inside me as my ass clenches around his fingers. "I'm going to come."

"Hold onto it, baby," he tells me, his other hand tightening on my hip. "I'm gonna come with you."

My head falls forward and I bite down on his shoulder, desperate for my release, and when I drop down over him and clench around him, it's all I need to throw me over the edge. My orgasm tears through me and I let out a soft cry, my fingers digging into the headboard as my world shatters, my pussy convulsing around Marcus' thick cock.

"Oh, fuck, fuck, fuck," I cry, throwing my head back as the pure ecstasy pulses through my veins, completely taking over.

Marcus sucks in a hiss as his warm seed pours into me, and I've never felt so fucking high. "Shit, Shayne," Marcus murmurs as I ride it out on his cock, slowing my pace until my hips are gently rocking back and forth.

I take a moment to catch my breath as I meet his heavy stare. "I, umm …" I start, my lips twisting up into an embarrassed smirk. "I didn't mean to go so hard. I hope I didn't hurt you."

"Hurt me? Babe, you brought me back to fucking life."

A soft laugh pulls from my chest as my hand falls from the headboard and drops around his strong neck. His fingers brush over my skin, gently trailing over my more serious injuries. "Are you good?" he questions, not taking his eyes away from mine.

I nod, the elation drumming through my body and making me feel more at ease than I have in days. "I'm good," I tell him, hating just how good this feels as getting too close to Marcus DeAngelis is probably going to cost me my life. Hell, his brothers have more than proven that to me.

He lets out a breath and as a seriousness comes over him, dread fills my stomach. "We have to talk about wh—"

"Don't," I say, cutting him off. "Don't ruin this by asking me about your brothers."

"I'm sorry, babe. I've got to know what your plan is. They're my brothers, the two men who have always had my back. I fucking hate them for what they did to you, so I get it. But if you're planning on slitting their throats in their sleep, then you've gotta let me know so I don't fucking kill them first. I'd never take that away from you."

I gape at him, wondering if I heard him correctly, but seeing the horror on my face, he pulls back, his brows furrowed in confusion. "What's the matter?" he questions, his thumb softly trailing back and forth over my skin. "Is slitting their throats too easy? Do you need me to train you up on something a little more … gory? OH!" he adds, his eyes widening with excitement. "What about castration? You're in a good position for that one, especially Levi. He'll whip it out for you any day. The fucker would never see it coming."

"Whaaaaat … the fuck is wrong with you? I'm not castrating your brothers."

His face falls. "Oh, not even a little? You could just take the tip, or maybe just a ball? That way they could probably still fuck. It might hurt a bit, but they're fucking animals. They'll push through the pain."

"You're insane," I tell him, pausing to watch him, unsure if he's actually joking. "I, ummm … I don't know if you're being serious right now."

Marcus shrugs his shoulders. "Dead fucking serious, babe," he says, his expression sobering. "They put their hands on you when they knew what you meant to me, and if taking their life is what you need to be able to sleep at night, then it is what it is. It'll suck, and sure, I'll probably fucking resent you for it, but I'll find a way to live with it."

I shake my head as my heart pounds wildly in my chest, desperately needing to ask him what he means by *'they knew what you meant to me'* but having much larger fish to fry. I'll have to circle back to that one later. "I'm not taking your brothers away from you. I don't … I can't even stomach the idea of taking their lives. They thought I shot you, and I know that's no excuse and I have absolutely no idea why I'm defending them right now, but I understand why they hurt me. I'm just so damn pissed they didn't have it in their hearts to trust me when I said I didn't do it. They were scared, they didn't know if you were going to make it and in their eyes, I was the one who had taken you away. At that moment, they needed someone to blame, and unfortunately, it had to be me."

Marcus shakes his head. "No, that's not okay. It's unacceptable."

"I agree," I tell him, needing him to stay calm. "I'll find a way to make them pay for what they did without hurting them … or maybe I could hurt them just a little, but I won't be taking their lives. That's too easy. I want them to live with regret, live with the knowledge of what they did to me."

Marcus laughs, his lips twisting into a sinister smirk. "That's not how we've been trained to deal with shit," he explains. "When someone fucks up, their life is taken. That's part of the reason Levi has been so wrecked. He's not ready to die and he thinks death is coming his way. Roman though, he's been living on borrowed time for years. He's already accepted his fate."

"I'm not killing them!" I rush out, the thought of Roman already being prepared for death not sitting well in my stomach.

"I get that," Marcus says. "But you need to understand what's going through their heads. They're fucking devastated over this."

My gaze drops and I fall from his lap, scooching into the space beside him and refusing to meet his obsidian eyes. "That's on them," I murmur. "I hope they're fifty shades of fucked up over it. They decided not to trust me and I shouldn't have to bear the guilt for that. If they're worried I'm going to try and kill them in the middle of the night, then that's on them. After everything we've been through, they should know me better by now, and that goes for you too."

"Okay," he says, his big hand dropping to my thigh. "I get it. You want them to suffer in silence, but where does that leave me?"

Glancing up, I meet his heavy stare, unsure of what he could mean. Though when it comes to the DeAngelis brothers, I rarely know what the fuck is going on. "What do you mean?"

"My brothers," he clarifies. "You have your way that you'd like to deal with them, but that leaves me awfully unsatisfied."

Pushing up to my knees, a wide grin tears across my face. "Marcus DeAngelis, you wouldn't be asking me permission to fuck with your own brothers, would you?"

He laughs and catches me around the waist before yanking me hard against his chest, remembering who the fuck he is. "I suppose I'm not."

And just like that, his lips come down over mine and I climb right back over his lap, more than ready to start all over again.

CHAPTER NINE

My stomach aches as Marcus sleeps soundly, more than content having me in his arms. On the other hand, I've barely slept in days, not even with the safety of Marcus by my side. Though, who could blame me? This castle isn't exactly a place that screams safe haven, and the last time I fell asleep with Marcus didn't exactly turn out so well. This castle is my hell. I've been tortured and held prisoner here by the very men who sleep just down the hallway. I'd be insane to trust that I'm safe here.

Marcus rolls and his arm flops right over my stomach, and I suck in a sharp, pained gasp as silent tears fill my blue eyes. "Holy mother of sweet baby Jesus," I hiss through a clenched jaw, grabbing his heavy arm and trying to push it off me. "Get the fuck off me, you big pile of steaming swamp turd."

Marcus groans and grunts in his sleep, probably pissed that I had the audacity to disturb his slumber. "Mmmmm, what's wrong?" he murmurs, tightening his grip around me and pulling me closer which, in a perfect world, I would have loved.

"MY STITCHES, ASSHOLE. GET OFF ME!"

"OH, FUCK!" Marcus scrambles back, his eyes springing open as he flies back on the bed. He grabs the thick blanket and pulls it down to inspect my stomach, gently running his fingers over it in the darkness to check that every stitch is still in place. "Did I hurt you?"

"No," I tell him, though we both know I'm lying. I scoot to the edge of the bed and glance back at him as his face falls. "I just need to walk it off. I've been cramping for a little while."

He rolls his eyes and goes to get up. "Come on, I'll show you where the good shit is," he says, reading my mind, knowing damn well that I was about to go and search every cabinet downstairs until I found the pain meds that would surely help me pass out.

My eyes widen in horror as he tries to climb out of bed after me. "No," I say, leaning back and pushing him down into his mattress. "Don't be an idiot. I'll just be a minute and then I'll come straight back here. You can't be up and walking around for another few days."

"Oh, please," he scoffs, getting comfortable again while failing to hide the pain written all over his face. "I'm a fucking beast. I could walk laps around you."

"Right," I laugh, watching the way his head falls onto his pillow and a deep sleep consumes him. I shake my head, unable to look away from the sight. He looks so peaceful and innocent when he sleeps. The hard lines of his face soften and the darkness seems to fade away. He looks so pure like this, though I bet his dreams are anything but.

A fierce jealousy cuts through me as I grab my silk dressing gown and tip-toe out of his room, not wanting to wake him again. I've never been able to sleep like that, not even when I was alone in my apartment and my biggest problem was keeping hidden from my father. Life has never been kind to me. Each night was always a struggle. I'd have to have my TV on with the sound almost on silent, just enough to block out the noise of the busy city outside my window. The lights had to be off, but I couldn't stand complete darkness. Then once I had everything the way I liked it, I would stare at the ceiling for hours, my mind spinning with the thought of someone breaking through my door … someone just like the DeAngelis brothers.

Who would have known …

There's enough light so I don't have to bother finding a light switch as I step out into the long hallway. I can see almost perfectly, though creeping around in the dark when Roman and Levi are close by probably isn't the best idea either. I can only imagine what would happen to me if they thought I was someone else.

Reaching the stairs, I pause to take a breath. Thirty steps in total. I can do it. At least, I hope I can do it. Walking in a straight line isn't so bad. I don't have to focus so much and there's definitely not as much jostling around, but stairs? Holy fuck. Who would have known walking down a set of stairs would cause me so much panic?

I grip onto the railing with everything I've got and go to take my first step down. Pain immediately shoots through my stomach as my muscles clench, and I silently curse myself for not asking for pain meds sooner.

I take another step and then another before my breathing turns into loud hisses of pain. Hell, it'd be a shitload quicker if I just threw myself down the stairs head first. At least that way, I wouldn't be able to stop myself until I hit the bottom.

I struggle through one more step before a gruff scoff sounds from directly behind me. I barely get a gasp out before Levi is scooping me into his arms and flying down the rest of the stairs, Roman hot on his heels. "Put me down," I screech, my voice echoing through each of the empty rooms.

Levi hits the bottom step and places me back on my feet, holding me steady until he's sure that I have my balance. I push his hands off and take a hurried step away from him, rejoicing in the flash of pain that crosses his face. "Sorry," he mutters as Roman joins him. "You were hurting. It was just easier."

I narrow my gaze on him, hating the way they stand together like an impenetrable force, both more than ready to take me down at a moment's notice, but as I look them over, I realize they're both fully dressed. "Where the hell are you going?" I question, trying to hide the pain that tears through my stomach as I take in their black attire, clothes they commonly wear when they're about to fuck someone up.

"Business," Roman mutters, not willing to give much more than that, though he's already said enough. I know exactly what kind of business they plan to do tonight. "Why are you out of bed? You should be resting. Walking around is only going to tear your stitches."

"Not that it's any of your business, but I was trying to get something to ease the pain," I tell him, only moments from questioning him about their little business outing when he cuts me off.

"Pain?" Levi questions, his eyes wide as his back straightens. "Why's there pain? It should be starting to ease by now. At least, eased enough for you to be able to sleep through it."

I scoff, crossing my arms over my chest. Clearly this guy hasn't experienced an evening of fucking while your guts are torn to shreds quite like I have … though it's hard to gauge the kinds of things these guys have done in their lifetimes. "Well if I didn't spend my night fucking Marcus into a coma, then I probably wouldn't have quite so much pain. But you know what? If I also didn't have a bunch of psychotic assholes kidnap and torture me, then I wouldn't have any pain at all. But shit happens, right?"

"Come on, babe," Levi says, creeping toward me and making me pull back before he finally gets the hint and stops. "When is this going to stop? I told you, we're not going to hurt you anymore. Never again. I want to make this right, but you're not even giving me a chance to earn your forgiveness."

My brow arches and I look directly into his gorgeous dark eyes. "Hurts, doesn't it?" And just like that, he understands my game plan, they both do. Though after barging into my room with a knife only a few short hours ago, Roman should be well acquainted with my devilish little plan.

Levi takes a hesitant step back, his heart clear on his sleeve as he lets out a heavy breath. "At least … allow me to get the painkillers for you. They're up high in a cupboard and you won't be able to reach, not without hurting yourself in the process."

I hold his stare for a moment longer before finally nodding. "Fine," I mutter, dropping my gaze and glancing away. Levi doesn't waste a moment, rushing off toward the massive kitchen and leaving me with his brother.

I turn to follow Levi, not wanting to be left alone with Roman, though I don't see why I'd favor Levi. They're both just as guilty.

"Stop," Roman says, his dominant, alpha personality somehow recovering after his pathetic display in my bedroom. I ignore him as best I can and keep myself moving, not even remotely prepared to give in to his will. He groans and follows me. "Shayne. Stop," he demands, more forceful, the tone of his voice sending shivers down my spine.

I can't help but spin around, fixing him with a hard glare. "Where the fuck do you get off ordering me around? I want my fucking pain pills so I can get back to bed and pretend none of this happened."

He steps closer to me, his eyes just as hard as always. "When the fuck are you going to stop messing around and face us like the fucking badass I know you are?"

"Why would I want to do that?" I shoot back at him. "I want nothing to do with you. I'm not some love-sick puppy who's going to hang off you three assholes. *I'm your prisoner.* Perhaps you've forgotten that. But what you won't forget is that I'm not here to make you feel better about hurting me. If you want to earn my forgiveness, then do that, prove to me that I should trust you, but what you're not going to do is step up to me like this and try to force it down my throat. That's not how it works."

"Fuck, Shayne. Do you really think I know how this works? I've never had to earn someone's forgiveness in my life because everyone I've ever hurt is fucking dead, and for good reason," he growls. "To me and my brothers, it's either black or white, there is no in-between. And you? Fuck. You're right in the middle of that, somewhere none of us have ever ventured before. So, forgive me for not having the slightest fucking idea how to deal with you. You're a mystery to me, a fucking supernova explosion."

I stare up at him, my chest heaving with heavy breaths as he watches me right back. His eyes are wild with unease and his hands ball into tight fists at his side. Neither of us say a damn word, and as the tension grows between us, my heart only races faster.

I swallow hard, preparing myself to tell him just how much I despise him when he steps into me, his strong hand curling behind my neck as he pulls me in, my body pressed right up against his. A gasp leaves my lips, and before I get a chance to push him away, Roman's soft lips are coming down on mine.

He kisses me deeply, full of power and regret, and damn it, so much fucking passion. My hand presses into his wide chest, trying to push him away, but as his lips move over mine and his tongue pushes into my mouth, I sink into him, my eyes closing with overwhelming need.

A soft moan pulls from deep within my chest as I become putty in his hands, soaking up every last ounce of him as I kiss him back. His hand remains at the back of my neck, holding me there as his fingers trail into my hair. His other hand grips my waist and slowly curves around my hips, exploring my body like he's never had the chance to do before, and in this moment, I'm all his. That is, until I remember what the fuck these hands have done to me.

Panic surges through me. What the fuck am I doing?

I tear my lips away as I use every last ounce of strength within me to push him back. My hand cracks across his face with a loud *SLAP* as we both stare at one another, completely dumbfounded. "What the hell do you think you're doing?" I shriek, my chest heaving with erratic gasps as my palm stings from the hit.

Roman just stands there motionless, his eyes wide and full of confusion, and it's as though he doesn't even know himself. "I, umm ..."

Levi comes striding back into view, stealing my gaze away from Roman as a wave of guilt washes through me, though it shouldn't. Whatever Levi and I had before is gone now, and it's not like Marcus and I are exclusive, so technically I'm free to kiss whoever the hell I want, but it shouldn't matter because I'll never allow Roman to do that again.

"Here," Levi says, dropping the pills into my hand and passing me a glass of water as he glances between me and Roman, his brows pulling together. "Take these. They're strong so they should work quickly."

I nod and immediately pop them into my mouth, looking anywhere but at the two men hovering around me. Pressing the cool glass to my lips, I take a small drink and swallow the pills, hating that I can still taste Roman there. It's intoxicating. Scratch that. *He's intoxicating.* He always has been right from the start, but he's not mine and I don't ever want him to be.

I feel Levi's stare digging into me as I lower the glass from my lips, his eyes narrow on mine. "What's going on in here?" he questions, his tone dropping low.

"Nothing," Roman snaps, turning his back and striding to the door. "Hurry up. I want to get this over and done with before we miss our chance. Father has only given us a week of freedom and we're quickly running out of time."

Levi watches me a second longer before taking off after his brother, and as they disappear down the hall, I watch after them, unable to comprehend what the hell just went down, or why I can't help calling after them. "Wait," I rush out, my feet involuntarily following them down the long hallway toward the front door. "Where are you going?"

Roman pauses, his back stiffening as Levi stops and turns back to me. "It's just business," he says. "Go and lay down on the couch. Marcus will help you back upstairs when he wakes."

I shake my head and walk toward him. "What kind of business?" I question. "Bullshit errands for your father, or is this personal?" I pause and watch as both Levi and Roman's gazes harden, silently answering my question. Tonight has everything to do with their plan of overthrowing their father, and damn it, I want in.

Roman steps in beside his brother. "You don't want any part of this, Empress," he says, his stare digging into mine as if he'd been reading my thoughts.

"You wouldn't know a damn thing about what I want, Roman," I say as I slowly walk toward them. "But you can be damn sure that if your plan to overthrow your father is still in the works, then I'm going to be right there to watch that fucker burn. I'm not some pathetic bitch who's going to sit back and watch from the sidelines. I've already lost too much not to reap the rewards. So, if you're building an empire, then consider me officially head of the game."

And just like that, I stride past them toward the door, only stopping when they don't follow. "Hurry up, boys. The clock is ticking."

Levi glances at his eldest brother and a silent message passes between them before they both sigh and nod, giving in to my every will and demand, just as they should. "If you get in my fucking way," Roman growls, stepping into me, fury raging behind his eyes at not only being bested but because he showed his true cards by kissing me. "Then it's your head on the chopping block."

"Wow. Death threats, huh?" I laugh, raising a brow, knowing that even if he wanted to, he would never hurt me again. "If forgiveness is your endgame, then I should warn you, you're already heading in the wrong direction. But don't be fooled, if I get in your way tonight, then your only acceptable response is to move the fuck aside."

Then just like that, Levi strides past me, walking toward the internal garage door and holding it wide for me. "After you," he tells me, watching as I walk past before I hear his softly muttered words flowing behind me. "This should be interesting."

CHAPTER TEN

Roman brings the black Escalade to a stop outside a gorgeous mansion, a few hours' drive from the city. It's huge, but has nothing on the boys' castle or even their father's family home. It's clear this is a product of old money though, just like everything else in this fucked-up mafia world I've been dragged into.

The driveway is long and windy but as Roman kills the headlights and creeps closer to the front door, I see the home in all its glory, not even the dark night can hide its beauty. "What's up?" Levi questions, glancing at me from the front passenger seat. "You look weird."

"It's just … this home," I say, taking in the intricate lines of the two-story sandstone building with its tall columns and circle balconies overlooking the wide expanse of property around it. "I've never seen anything like it. The skill it must have taken to build this, even just the imagination to put together the design. It's like a scene right out of a movie."

Roman scoffs. "Yeah well, in a perfect world, it would have been mine."

My brows furrow, glancing toward him in the driver's seat as he cuts the engine. "What's that supposed to mean?"

"This is my uncle's property, gifted to him after my father locked us away and made him his second in command. That position was supposed to be mine when I came of age, and along with it, this property."

I stare at him in shock as he looks out the front windshield, pretending he doesn't see me gaping in his rearview mirror. "That's … kind of depressing," I mutter, glancing across at Levi. "Were you and Marcus supposed to inherit cool properties too?"

"Yep," he says, his dark eyes hardening. "Currently occupied by our younger cousins, living our lives while we're locked away out of fear."

"No shit," I breathe. "So what are we doing here? You're not about to kill your uncle, are you?"

Roman laughs. "No, he'll be saved for last, right alongside our father. He's been out on business for the past week, leaving us this perfect opportunity to right some wrongs made by his son, Antonio. He's a swine, not worthy of wearing the DeAngelis name."

A chill sweeps down my spine and something tells me that tonight is going to be a mess, but the excitement brewing in both their eyes shows me just how badly they've longed for this moment. "Does Marcus know you're doing this without him?"

Levi grins as he grips his door handle and pushes it wide. He glances back at me. "Don't you worry about Marcus," he says. "Tonight you should be worried about not getting in the way. Antonio won't hesitate to use you as a human shield, especially once he realizes our intentions. He's the type to go down fighting. He'll be sure to let off a few rounds first and, considering that he knows you mean something to us, you're likely to be his target."

Well, fuck.

"Coming?" Roman mutters stepping out of the Escalade and looking back at me. "Though, I understand if you'd prefer to hide out in the car. Things could get a little … messy."

The unspoken insult rests on his lips as I sharpen my glare and flip him off, reaching for the door handle. I help myself out, avoiding Levi's outstretched hand purely out of spite, and I don't miss the way his eyes darken as I stride past him like he's not even there.

Making my way around the Escalade, I stand front and center, knowing damn well I shouldn't be here and that one missed step or fall could put us all in a shitty situation, but despite the way I hate the boys, I know they'd protect me with their lives, even if it meant sacrificing their own.

Levi and Roman stand on either side of me, all three of us peering up at the massive house that should have been Roman's. "So, how are we supposed to do this?"

Roman's brows furrow and he looks at me as though I've never organized a break-in before, but like … he'd be right. I sure as fuck haven't. "We walk straight through the door."

"Huh. That simple?"

"What were you expecting?"

I shrug my shoulders as we start moving toward the gorgeously carved stairs that lead to the impressive entrance. "I don't know. In the movies, they climb trees and break in through the second-story windows."

Levi grunts, struggling to hide the smirk crossing over his delicious lips. "We're not fucking cat burglars."

"Oh yeah?" I argue. "Tell me that out of all the houses you've broken into, you've never once stolen anything."

A guilty expression crosses his face and he quickly wipes it away, but he's far too late and the image is already etched into my brain. "That's what I thought," I murmur under my breath, my voice lowering as we near the front door, only there's no need for my silence as Roman steps right up to the door and busts it down with a heavy kick.

The door splinters as it flies right off the fucking hinges and I gape in horror. "You would have woken everyone up," I seethe, my gaze shooting around the foyer as though I'm about to have assholes jumping out at me left, right, and center.

"That's exactly the point," Roman mutters, casually walking through the destroyed entrance, his boots crushing the splintered wood below.

Hesitantly, I follow him in, being careful not to tread on any of the wood, seeing as though I was in too much of a rush to find clothes and a pair of shoes, leaving me in nothing but my silk dressing gown that Levi hasn't been able to stop staring at. Though it's no secret that the boys would have left without me had I even attempted to leave their sides to dash upstairs to find a change of clothes.

Levi follows behind me, pressing his hand to my back to help me over the destroyed door, and while his touch makes me flinch, I kinda need it there.

Getting past the entrance, Roman leads me through the property as though he specifically knows every little twist and turn, every tiny little walkway and stone that makes the beautiful home. "You designed this, didn't you?" I mutter, refusing to look up to see the smug expression across his face.

"Sure fucking did. Built it with my own goddamn hands," he says proudly, making me cringe at the thought of the comments I made in the car about what a brilliant kind of imagination the designer must have had. Fuck me, why do I always have to go and open my mouth too soon? Though I'm not gonna lie, I'm kinda impressed. It only makes sense why he's so sore about having this place taken away from him. This was supposed to be his home, the property he raised a family and grew old in, and now his uncle is living out his dream. Fuck, I'd be pissed too.

"WHO'S THERE?" comes a voice hollered from deep inside the house, making my back stiffen. Levi steps in a little closer and I don't doubt he's prepared to save me if all hell were to break loose.

Roman stops at the opening of a massive formal living room and silently waves me in, and with Levi's hand still resting on my lower back, I step through to the impressive room. Naturally, the lights are out and it's nearly impossible to see the finer details of the room, but from what I can make out, it's fucking gorgeous.

Huge windows fill the side wall, each exquisitely dressed with expensive curtains that have been pulled back at the sides. There must be at least ten windows along the wall, spanning what I'm assuming is the whole length of the property. Hell, if all the furniture were moved out of the way, this room could host the best kind of parties.

There is seating for at least a hundred people and it's clear that this room was designed specifically for the man of the house to lead some very important meetings, though the kind of meetings that would be held here are certainly not the kind of meetings I want anything to do with.

"YOU CHOSE THE WRONG FUCKING HOUSE TO BREAK INTO. DO YOU KNOW WHO I AM?" the voice says, sending a chill down my spine.

Roman chuckles to himself. "Shit," he says, glancing at Levi. "Can you hear that? Hasn't even seen us and he's already shit-scared."

Levi laughs and leads me toward a stunning couch. I take a seat and watch as Roman picks the darkest corner to sit in while Levi steps around the back of my couch, always hovering close. "What do we do?" I murmur, glancing across at Roman who sits with his gun resting on his thigh.

"We wait. He'll come to us. No need to go hunting."

"And then what? We just kill him?"

"Something like that." His eyes sparkle with excitement and it throws me off. I always seem to forget just how much they love this fucked-up little lifestyle. This is their domain, their heaven. Why would they ever want anything different?

Levi's hand falls to my shoulder and I glance up at him as he holds his finger to his mouth in the universal sign for silence. "Shhhhh," he whispers. "Listen."

My brows furrow as Levi's hand falls away from my shoulder. I concentrate on the heavy silence until the frantic sound of someone dashing from room to room upstairs catches my attention.

A sick smile twists over my face and I can't understand why it thrills me so much. The guy thinks he's being discreet, moving around the mansion as though he has the upper hand, but his heavy footsteps are like a map leading us directly to him. Just as Roman said, we don't need to worry about finding him, he'll come to us.

The heavy silence lingers in the room, and as the seconds tick by, my nerves get stronger. It takes nearly five long minutes for Antonio to move downstairs and another few before he even ventures to this side of the mansion, but when he does, both Roman and Levi shuffle around, making sure they will have the advantage.

A moment passes before Roman glances at Levi and nods toward the opening of the formal living room. My gaze snaps toward it and I suck in a breath seeing the tip of a gun pushing into the room, shortly followed by their cousin's face.

Antonio peers into the room for a long second, taking in his cousins before glancing at me through narrowed eyes. He assesses the room, probably wondering where Marcus is, but it's not like the brothers are about to spill secrets, especially ones that let this asshole know that Marcus is alone, weak, and vulnerable.

Coming to terms with his late-night visitors, Antonio hesitantly steps into the room, his gun prepared and ready in his hands. "Cousins," he beams, his fake bullshit shining through loud and clear. "What an unexpected visit."

CHAPTER ELEVEN

Roman slowly stands and Antonio flinches, turning his full attention toward him, though somehow managing to keep an eye on Levi. "Was it really?" Roman questions. "Unexpected?"

Antonio swallows hard. "Of course," he says, his eyes flicking between the two brothers. "Your father gave you a mission this week, one I suppose you are still working through considering I have not yet heard any news."

"Holy shit, you sound like a pompous asshat," I scoff, laughing at this idiot before realizing I spoke the words out loud. My eyes go wide and as he shoots a hard glare toward me, I sink down on the couch, covering my mouth with my hand to keep myself from speaking out of line again. After all, despite having Roman and Levi as protection, Antonio is still mafia and could probably shoot a bullet between my eyes with ease.

Roman sighs, drawing Antonio's attention back to him. "You'd be right about that," he says. "My brothers and I have been working on the mission my father challenged us with, which is strange, considering it has led us to this very home."

Antonio's brows furrow. "What?" he rushes out, confusion deep in his dark eyes. "That's impossible. I'm not manufacturing anything, and I know for damn sure that my father has nothing to do with it either."

"Oh, we know," Levi says, stepping out from behind the couch and strategically placing himself in front of me. "We're the ones stealing it right out from under our father, rebranding his product, and making one hell of a profit off him. It's a good little game we've got going on, but the only issue is that our father is getting a little ... frustrated, and unfortunately for you, he needs somewhere to place the blame. Heads need to roll, and how the hell would we keep running our business if it were ours? You see our little dilemma here, don't you?"

"No," Antonio says, shaking his head. "He'll see right through it. You'll never get away with it. My father—"

"Your father was a fool to leave you this week, just as you were to not see this coming. We were given a week of freedom. You should have prepared yourself. You should have hired protection."

"I did," he rushes out, "Just like everyone else in the DeAngelis family did. They'll never follow you. They fear you too much."

"Precisely," Roman says. "That's why we must start fresh. Weed out all of those too weak to face us, too weak to lead and prosper in this family."

His eyes widen, only now realizing just how far the brothers will go. "But my father—"

"Oh, you don't need to worry about your father," Roman says, discreetly stepping toward him. "Your father will be joining you soon enough."

"You won't get away with it," he repeats, spitting the words like venom in his mouth.

"That's just it," Levi says. "We already have."

A chill sweeps down my spine as those words rock through my chest. *That's just it, we already have.* It's not the first time I've heard that sentence, but fuck, I hope it's the last. They'd said the exact same thing to me the night they dressed me up in their mother's old gown and treated me to dinner. The memory still sends chills sweeping through me.

Antonio raises his chin, deciding to go out with power. "Your father will have your heads for this. When he discovers you're trying to overthrow him again, you'll be put down like the fucking animals you are."

One word stands out to me and I find myself getting to my feet, stepping into Levi's side, and staring across the wide room at Antonio. "Again?" I question. "What are you talking about?"

Antonio scoffs. "Well, well, the little whore has found her voice again," he mutters darkly. "Tell me, did they bring you along so I can enjoy you before they kill me?"

I step forward, putting my shoulder in front of Levi's, showing him just what kind of dynamic we have here. "I asked you a question."

"Why don't you ask your little boyfriends?"

"You and I both know they don't willingly hand out information. But here we are, with the threat of death hanging over you, and you seem to be struggling to keep your mouth shut. So, I will ask you one more time, what are you referring to?"

Antonio glances at Roman, probably certain that if he were to divulge information, he'd get his head blown off, but hell, it seems it's going to end that way no matter what he says here tonight. "Go ahead," Roman tells him. "Share with Shayne why we've chosen you to take the fall. Let her know what a spineless snake you are."

Antonio swallows hard before glancing back at Levi. "Come on, man. It's ancient history."

"Ancient history?" Levi laughs. "Ancient history for who? For you? Maybe, but for us, it's as fresh as though it happened yesterday. You're here living in Roman's home, sleeping in his bed, eating his food, while we are locked up like prisoners, and that weight is on your shoulders."

"No," Antonio breathes. "That was your father's decision. If you need someone to blame, take it out on him."

"We trusted you, Toni," Levi says, his tone lethal and chilling. "We grew up as brothers. We would have given you everything if only you'd kept your mouth shut, but you couldn't. You wanted it all to yourself. You wanted the keys to the kingdom, but they weren't yours to take."

My brows furrow, barely following along with the story. "What happened?"

Roman grins and walks toward his cousin, stepping behind him and making the guy freeze as his head does that weird tilting thing that tells me he's slipping into his serial killer alter-ego. "Antonio here was like a brother to us," he explains, glancing up at me with those manic eyes, making sure I'm hanging on his every word. "As Levi said, we grew up together, trained together, learned to survive together, but there was something different about him. Wasn't there, Toni?" he questions, stabbing his gun hard into his back, making Antonio flinch as his life flashes before his eyes. "Toni was greedy. He wanted to rule the kingdom just like we did, and for a while, we loved that about him. He could have ruled by our sides, and we would have been unstoppable."

"Please, Roman," Antonio stutters, his eyes flashing back to Levi, pleading for all he's worth. "I can make it right. I swear, I'll get you out of there. You'll be free men."

Roman laughs and turns his attention back to me, his eyes darker than I've ever seen them. "Ten years ago, we set out to overthrow our fathers. I was barely nineteen, but I saw something in my brothers nobody else saw. We would have thrived with the world at our feet. We were going to take it all, but that wasn't enough for Toni. He realized, just like the rest of us, that if we were out of the picture, he would have eventually inherited it all. So he put a target on our backs. He went to our father, only left himself out of it, and here we are, ten years later, locked up as our father's toy soldiers."

Tears sting my eyes as I look back at Roman and I find myself moving closer to Levi. Despite my feelings for them right now, it's impossible not to see how Antonio's betrayal tore them to pieces, and fuck, I might be losing myself here, but I want them to get what they're owed. I want them to rule the DeAngelis family. I want them to thrive and overthrow their father, and damn it, I want them to make Antonio suffer. If it weren't for him, their father would never have locked them up. Roman would be Giovanni's second in command and living in this beautiful home he built while Marcus and Levi stood proud, free in the world living the life they've always dreamed for themselves.

Antonio robbed them blind, and for that, I'm going to enjoy watching him suffer.

Raising my chin, I walk toward Antonio and stand before him, not missing the way Roman holds onto him just a little bit tighter, making sure he doesn't try anything. "Look at you," I mutter, my gaze shifting up and down his body in disgust. His lack of muscle, poorly defined cheekbones, and the eyes that are so similar to the ones I know, only so much duller. Honestly, I've never been so disappointed. "You're pathetic. You're like a copy and paste version of your cousins, only something went wrong."

Levi chuckles behind me and I take that as my cue to continue. "I don't know you, nor do I want to, because from what I just heard, you're nothing but a spineless, backstabbing piece of shit who doesn't deserve to rule over a fucking sandwich let alone a goddamn kingdom. But who are you kidding? You don't have what it takes. Sure, you might have had the drive to get you there, but what would you have done once you reached the top? You would have been overthrown in seconds."

I laugh to myself, grinning up at the loser, seeing perfectly how his reign would have played out, especially with men like Roman, Marcus, and Levi to watch out for. "Do you really think someone who shit his pants at the first sign of a break-in has what it takes to remain in power when there are men like Roman, Marcus, and Levi gunning for your position? Your throat would have been slit in mere seconds, but you don't need to worry about that now. Roman is going to kill you tonight, and fuck, you better not spill a drop of blood on his expensive floors."

Quickly glancing up into Roman's obsidian eyes, I see the sheer thrill pulsing out of them, and damn it, why does it make me so happy? I look back at Antonio, smirking at the way his knees shake and his skin grows clammy with nervousness. "I can tell by the glistening in Roman's eyes, he's really going to enjoy this. I'm just sorry that Marcus doesn't get to be here to watch the show. But don't you worry, I'll film it just for him. It will be like his very own, private snuff film. I bet he'll love it. It'll be like all his Christmases come at once."

Levi laughs, and as I turn around and take in the overwhelming pride stretched over his face, something warms in my dead, cold heart. Though once this moment is over and we're back in the Escalade, I know things are bound to go back to the way they were. "Come on," I tell him, nodding toward Antonio before holding out my hand. "Give me your phone so I can capture this for Marcus."

Levi strides toward me, not skipping a beat as he hands me his phone. "A snuff film would be great, but you know Marcus, he likes to be in on the action. You're best to call him on FaceTime."

I grin up at him, hating how much I love the way his eyes sparkle with joy. "I like the way you think."

"Ha," he scoffs. "You say that now."

I shake my head as I pull up Marcus' contact details. "Don't ruin a good thing."

Levi laughs and strides past me, putting himself right in front of his cousin as I hit call and hold up the phone. "This is going to be fun. Just like old times, only now, you're the fucker who'll be on the ground screaming for mercy."

Antonio spits something venomous in Italian and I ignore him to smile sweetly up into the screen. It rings three times before Marcus answers the call, his handsomely rugged face appearing before me. He gets one look at me and his brows furrow. "Shayne?" he questions. "What the fuck is going on? Why do you have Levi's phone?"

"SURPRISE!" I call, reangling the camera to get his brothers and Antonio in the background. "Don't be mad, but I kind of got distracted when going downstairs for pain meds and ended up on a field trip. But Roman kinda explained what went down with this fucker, and seeing that you can't be here in person, I didn't want you to miss out on all the fun."

Marcus raises his brow, astonishment settling into his feature. "Damn, babe. Not gonna lie. This is almost as sweet as being woken up to your tight little cunt dropping down over my cock. Woah! Is that Antonio? Hey man. How's it been? Long time no talk," he says, smirking through the camera before continuing. "Look man, I really wish I could have been there to see you off, but it is what it is. I hope you rot in hell, you backstabbing little fuck. Oh, and by the way, I railed your mom when we were sixteen. She was a bit sloppy, but fuck man, she knew what she was doing."

"Get fucked," Antonio roars just moments before a loud shot rings out.

A piercing scream tears out of me just as Levi's hand curls around my arm and throws me down to the ground. The phone goes sliding under one of the many coffee tables and I peer over it to watch as Antonio slips out of Roman's grasp and spits a few more angry words in Italian. His gun aims toward me and I shriek just as it goes off again, narrowly skimming past my face and piercing the window behind me.

I slam down to the ground, dropping lower. "Holy fuck," I gasp. Levi warned me this could get messy and that Antonio would see me as a target, but damn, I hadn't actually thought it would happen. Though the fact that Antonio has been able to get two shots off only goes to show he truly does have some level of skill, but he couldn't possibly be a match for Roman and Levi. At least I hope not.

My face squishes against the expensive tile and I'm just about to compliment Roman on his pristine taste in home decor when I hear Marcus' familiar tone. "SHAYNE," he hollers through the phone. "What the fuck is happening? I don't see shit."

"Oh, fuck. Sorry," I rush out, reaching under the table and scooping up the phone. The mix of adrenaline and painkillers pulsing through my veins making it so much easier to push through the pain.

I flip the phone around, giving Marcus the best view as Roman slams his gun into Antonio's back again, letting off three quick shots, none of them kill shots but definitely enough to cause a slow and painful death, giving them just enough time to play with him first.

Antonio drops to the ground and I cringe, watching the way his blood spills out onto the floor. "Damn," I mutter. "I told him not to spill any blood. Do you know what kind of scrubbing it'll take to get that stain out of the grout?"

"You're shitting me, babe. The blood splatter is the best part," Marcus says. "Could you get a little closer? I need to see the life fading out of his eyes."

"Oh, yeah. Of course," I beam, more than happy to give a helping hand where needed.

I crawl across the floor and end up laid out on the tiles, my face only inches from Antonio's as I hold up the camera for Marcus to see. "Hey dude," I say, looking into Antonio's dulling eyes. "Rough night, huh? Bet you wish you were anywhere but here."

Antonio spits at me and I cringe, pulling back in disgust. "Don't fucking spit at my girl, man," Marcus roars through the phone. "Who knows what kind of germs a little bitch like you has been carrying around."

Before he can respond, Levi grips Antonio's arm and flips his body so he's staring up at the high ceiling, pointedly not meeting either of the brothers' sharp gazes. "I don't need to remind you what happens to men who go talking shit," Levi says, reminding me of the night we were in the industrial area with Draven Miller. He lost his tongue that night … and a few other things, and something tells me that Antonio is about to join that exclusive little club.

Levi crouches down and shoves his hand right into Antonio's mouth, cringing as the fucker bites him so hard that he draws blood, but a little biting never stopped Levi. I should know, I've bitten him more times than I can count.

Roman leans down and grips Antonio's lower jaw and tears it down, snapping the bones in one easy crack, leaving Levi free to pull out his tongue. Then without a second of warning, Levi pushes a short dagger right through the center of it like a piercing, anchoring it out of his mouth. "You watching, Marc?"

"Yeah, man," Marcus says over the sound of Antonio's grunts and muffled cries, the excitement in his tone flowing freely through the big living room. "Make it splatter. NO, WAIT. Do you think you could shoot it off?"

Roman scoffs, stepping back to check all the angles. "There's no way in hell. He'll get his big-ass nose first and if he goes from over here, he'll end up going straight through his head, then it's game over."

I gape up at them. "What the fuck is wrong with you?" Roman and Levi stop what they're doing to look at me before I roll my eyes and scoot out of the way. "I know you guys were raised a little … differently, but surely you have a little common sense? If you can't go from the top or the bottom, take it from the side. There ain't no nose or brain in the way then."

Both Roman and Levi turn their gazes down to Antonio before stepping to the side and studying this brand new angle. "Well, damn," Roman says in appreciation before glancing back at Levi. "She's got a good point. This might just work, even with a bad shot like yours."

"Get fucked, man. My aim is fucking perfect."

Marcus scoffs and turns his attention back to me. "What did I tell you? You're gonna be a perfect mafia wife."

"You gotta quit talking shit," I tell him, glancing back up at Levi to find him standing over me with a gun pointed down at Antonio's face. "Oh, fuck. WAIT! Let me move out of the way first. You guys have already scarred me enough as it is. I don't need an accidental bullet wound to go with my collection of scars."

Levi's hand falters as I shuffle myself out of the way, and as his eyes skim toward mine, I see the darkness sweeping over him again. "Now why did you have to go and say something like that? Now my head is all messed up. I can't concentrate."

"Fuck that," Roman says, shoving him out of the way while pulling his gun out quicker than Marcus could whip his dick out. "I'll do it."

"No fucking way," Levi snaps back, taking his shot before Roman beats him to it and making me jump as the loud *BANG* echoes through the room.

"Holy fuck," I gasp, blood splattering around the room like a fan, hitting everything and everyone in its path. Nausea swirls deep in my gut as my lips twist into a disgusted sneer. "That is so fucking gross."

"HA!" Marcus laughs. "That was brilliant. Where's the tongue? Did he get it?"

I glance back at Antonio whose face has turned a ghostly shade of white, and I quickly realize he only has a few precious moments of life left before the book closes on what I'm positive was a pathetic existence. But there are more important things to worry about because there ain't no tongue in that bloodied mouth of his and it's certainly not laying limp at my feet. "Ummmm ... he got the tongue alright, but I couldn't tell you where it went."

"Then find it. You need to bring it to me."

"What?" I gasp. "I'm not wrapping that thing up and bringing it home. It'll probably give me an STD."

"You gotta do it, babe. That tongue cost me ten years of my life. I need it on my shelf like a fucking trophy."

"Technically," Levi butts in, "it should be on my shelf. I shot it off."

"Only because I gave you the idea. Take an eyeball, or better yet, one of his actual balls. The tongue is mine."

Roman crouches down, his sickening stare lingering on Antonio's body. "I want his spine," he mutters, the darkness in his tone sending chills sweeping over my skin and leaving a trail of goosebumps.

"Ooooookay," I say slowly, turning away from the almost dead body as I start my search for the tongue. "This just got a little too weird for me. I'm out."

And just like that, I end the call, knowing the good part is over, and as I find the scrambled mess of bloody tongue laying haphazardly halfway across the room, I hear Levi's irritated tone as he mutters to himself. "Fuck, he's dead. I wanted to feel his heart beating in my hand just once before I crushed it."

CHAPTER TWELVE

The jar of shredded tongue dangles from my fingers as I try not to gag, but let's be real, with the way Roman was driving back to the castle, the thing was bouncing around in the jar as though it had a life of its own … well, I guess it once did. Either way, it's fucking disgusting, and after what Roman and Levi put me through, I could barely believe when they refused to hold it for me.

Those damn assholes.

I almost hate myself for enjoying tonight, but I'm putting it down to the strong painkillers pulsing through my system. I'm sure had my mind been clear, I would have seen the horror that was going on around me, instead of encouraging it. Hell, seeing the sparkle in the boys' eyes almost got me off. Seeing them in their zone, dominating and laying their traps to overtake the DeAngelis family is nothing short of the hottest thing I've ever seen. It's a real shame that they're a bunch of psychotic heathens, otherwise, I'd allow myself to truly fall for such strong-willed, powerful men. You know, not considering the fact they tortured me. It kinda kills the vibe.

The Escalade door closes behind me, and as I'm walking back into the castle trying to ignore the jar in my hand, my pained stomach reminds me it's been far too long since I pumped it full of painkillers. I should have eaten and rested my wounds before sneaking out of bed and screwing Marcus blind. But what can I say? Tonight was exhilarating. For just a moment, it made me forget how much I hate them. It was the closest thing to happiness I had felt in a long time … until we got back into the car, and their stony silence brought me right back to my tortured thoughts and memories.

Leaving the boys behind me, each with their own disgusting trophy to represent their greatest victory, I stride through the massive castle, determined to get this shit up to Marcus and out of my possession. Passing the impressive living room, I find Marcus sitting up on the couch, a somber expression etched into his handsome face. Doubling back before passing the entrance, I prop my shoulder against the wall and look in at Marcus, studying his side profile as he stares out the window into the pitch-black night.

"Howdily doodily," I say, groaning to myself the moment the words come out, realizing a guy like Marcus, with the upbringing he had, probably wouldn't get that reference.

A soft, breathy chuckle falls from his lips as the corner of his mouth pulls up just a fraction. "Fat Tony was always my favorite."

I scoff and stride into the living room, placing the tongue jar down on the coffee table before him. "Wow, I shouldn't be surprised," I tell him as I drop down beside him, boldly taking his hand in mine before gently grazing my thumb over the angry red scar I left on his warm skin. "I kinda had you pegged as a Sideshow Bob kinda guy."

"Oh, I am," he says, his lips lifting just a little bit more. "Sideshow Bob always spoke to me in ways that Tony never could, but then, Tony had a kind of power that Bob could only ever dream about. It's a numbers game, babe. To be powerful, you need to align yourself with power, otherwise, you'll end up with your fucking tongue in a jar."

My gaze falls back to the jar and a shudder runs down my spine before I quickly change the topic, needing my mind to be anywhere but there. "What are you doing down here?" I question. "You know your brothers are going to give you a hard time."

"Fuck them," he says. "I've been trapped in that bed for days. I needed to get out. Besides, it's not as much fun locked in that room when you're not there hiding beneath my blankets."

My cheeks flush the brightest shade of red, recalling the way I'd shimmied down under the blankets and took him into my mouth after the second … or maybe the third time I'd fucked him during the night. But what can I say? I simply haven't been able to get enough of him. Hell, if something clearly wasn't getting him down right now, I'd probably already be on my knees, my mouth full and my eyes watery as I choked on his thick cock.

"Now, now," I tease. "Don't be crass in front of the tongue."

Marcus rolls his eyes and pulls my hand into his lap before letting out a deep sigh. "Tell me what you remember about the hooded bitch who shot me."

My brows furrow as I look up at him, taken aback by his question. He's been studiously avoiding the topic of the hooded bitch, so it was the last thing I expected to hear come out of his mouth. "Oh, umm … I can't really tell you much. Her head was down and the hood covered most of her face, but she had blonde hair and it was kind of long and matted, like it hadn't been washed in a while."

"Height?"

"Short," I state. "Maybe an inch shorter than me, but I could be wrong. It's not like we stood back to back with a tape measure and drew little lines over our heads against the drywall."

"Shayne," Marcus grunts, clearly not in the mood to deal with my bullshit rambling.

"Sorry," I murmur, but I'm just not sure any of this is really very helpful. "It was the middle of the night and it was dark. You can't rely on my memory, especially after what happened following that. I've been purposefully trying to forget it all."

Marcus shakes his head. "Don't. The raw fear and emotion from those experiences are what fuel you to do better. It's the greatest kind of catalyst you could know, constantly making you stronger. It'll empower you to always strive for more, and never fall back into the same kind of circumstances that will tear you down."

I gape at him, completely baffled by the strange little way he looks at the world. "If that's your 'learn from your mistakes' speech, it needs work."

Marcus rolls his eyes and gets back on with it, his eyes falling back to the jar. "What did she say? Tell me specifically."

I try to think back to the moment the hooded McBitch snuck into my room. "She was trying to tell me that I need to run from you all. That she didn't want you guys to hurt me the way you'd hurt her."

"Hurt her? What the fuck is that supposed to mean?"

"How the hell am I supposed to know?" I fire back at him. "It's not like the bitch was offering to take me out for a sit-down chat over scones and jam." Marcus gives me a blank stare and I let out a sigh, continuing with the small bits and pieces that I can remember. "She wanted me to run and I refused because we'd only just gone through the whole 'I'm safer here with you guys' bullshit, and she didn't take kindly to that, but it was clearly her main goal. She said it a few times, each time getting more pissed off that I hadn't fallen to my knees and thanked her for such a great idea, which is when she told me that if I didn't comply with what she was asking, she'd force me to run."

"Which is when she shot me, knowing that my brothers would assume the worst," Marcus finishes for me.

"Exactly," I say. "Though there was one moment, I can't exactly remember what led to her saying it, but she referred to you all as hers, like you'd all meant something to her at one point, maybe still do."

Marcus' lips press into a tight line and I stare at him, my heart quickly speeding up. "You know who it is, don't you?"

He glances my way, regret heavy in his eyes. "Blonde hair, you said?" I nod and he closes his eyes for a brief moment, almost as though he can't believe what he's about to say. "Shit, I … it can't be. I saw her die right in front of my eyes, but everything is pointing toward it being Flick."

I suck in a gasp, my brows furrowing as I watch the confusion marring his face. "Felicity?" I ask, my question coming out as more of a baffled grunt. I look down and point out the tattoo of Felicity covering Marcus' ribs. "This Felicity? As in Roman's dead almost-fiancé Felicity."

"The one and only," he confirms.

I shake my head, a fierce jealousy cutting through me at the thought that the woman who once held all of their hearts could still be out there. But more than that, she's close by and more than prepared to try and steal them away from me. Hell, she's prepared and ready to shoot them down if it means breaking us apart. "No," I say. "That doesn't make sense. She's dead. You all saw her die. Felicity is gone and you shouldn't allow yourself to hold out hope for a dead woman. You're only going to hurt yourself. It has to be someone else, another woman who was hard done by you guys, someone who's still hoping to get you back."

"There is no one else," he tells me. "All roads lead to her."

I fall back onto the couch, the fierce jealousy cutting through me like a knife, but as Marcus glances down at me, that jealousy turns into embarrassment. "Look at you," he laughs. "I didn't realize my little Stockholm warrior was the jealous type. What's the matter? Worried that she's gonna come storming back in here and take me away from you?"

I narrow my hard glare at him, not impressed with his bullshit in the least. "More like worried that she's going to come storming back in here and try her luck again, only this time she'll aim between the eyes," I mutter. "But for the record, I don't get jealous, I get even. The bitch shot you. No matter who she is, I want to strangle her, even if it means taking her away from Roman for the second time."

"Good," Marcus says slowly, watching me a second longer than necessary, getting a good read on my emotions. "You have nothing to worry about. Whether it was Flick or not, the bitch will end up in a shallow grave for what she did. You don't get to live and tell that story, especially when a DeAngelis brother is involved."

"Don't I know it," I grumble.

Marcus laughs and I shoot my glare straight back at him. "You better not be laughing at my misery," I snap.

His hand tightens in mine as he brings it up and presses his lips to my knuckles. "I'm not," he says, the smirk still playing on his warm lips. "It's just what you said about not getting jealous. You're a shitty liar, but it's adorable."

I tear my hand free and huff, staring back down at the stupid tongue jar. "I'm not adorable, and I'm not a liar," I mutter, more than aware that I'm lying right now. "I'm a teller of mystery, never giving away what's truly on my mind."

"Yeah," he scoffs. "You're a liar, but only when it counts."

I let out a sigh and kick my feet up onto the coffee table, certain that I should probably be taking some painkillers right about now if I plan to get any sleep at all tonight. "Is that why you've been down here?" I question. "You've been thinking about what happened?"

Marcus nods. "I couldn't get back to sleep after your phone call, and without anyone here shoving painkillers down my throat, my mind wasn't so foggy. I've been able to start piecing things together and realized that there was something familiar about her, but I couldn't put my finger on what. It just doesn't make any sense though. It's fucking with my head."

"If it really was her, don't you think you would know? I mean … the tone of her voice, the way she smelled. You've been hurting over her death for months, longing to feel her presence. I just think if it actually was her, something would have clicked inside of you and you would have just known."

"Perhaps," he says. "But I wasn't in love with her. I didn't hold onto those things about her. If she called me up on the telephone right now, I wouldn't recognize her voice, not the way that Roman would. Things like that didn't matter to me."

"Maybe you should be talking to him about this," I suggest, that same flash of jealousy pressing up against my chest like a dead weight as the memory of Roman's lips on mine comes slamming back into my head. "I'm sure he'd be able to answer some of the questions that I can't. He was the closest to her. He'd know her mannerisms, her voice, the way she moved."

"No," he says, his harsh tone slipping back in. "I can't talk to him about this, not yet. I can't give him hope that she's still alive if she's not. It killed him once. I can't do it again."

"But—"

"No," he says more firmly, gripping onto my chin and looking me dead in the eye, reminding me of the guy I first met when I got here.

"The answer is no. You're not to utter a single word about it unless it's to me in private. Do you understand me?"

I swallow hard and nod. "Yeah, okay," I say, pulling my chin out of his grip. "I get it. I won't say anything. You've got my word, but if you grab me like that again, Marcus DeAngelis, I'm going to perform a reenactment of Levi shooting off Antonio's tongue, but it'll be your dick instead. Got it?"

He narrows his gaze, slowly raising his chin, and in the blink of an eye, that harshness fades away almost as though it never existed. "Damn, girl. You're getting way too comfortable in this castle. I thought you liked it when I grabbed you."

"I do," I tell him. "But only when my back is pressed up against the wall and your cock is only inches away from slamming into me. Apart from that, I'm not your ragdoll. I get enough of that shit from Levi and Roman. I don't need it from you as well."

"Okay," he says. "From now on, I'm only rough when you're begging me for it, but be warned, if you slip up on your word, I'll slip up on mine."

I hold out my pinky. "You've got yourself a deal."

Marcus just stares, having no idea what the fuck I'm doing. So I reach out and curl my pinky finger around his, not bothering to explain the terms of a pinky promise, because honestly, he probably doesn't give a shit.

"So," he says, pulling his pinky free and reaching toward the coffee table with a pained grunt before grabbing a packet of painkillers and a bottle of water. "The blood splatter. Tell me all about it. I didn't get to hear the blood raining down around the room. Tell me it was good. I'm so fucking pissed that those assholes left me behind. I've been dreaming of the day that I got to end that backstabber's life. Antonio and I were closest in age, so apart from my brothers, he was my best friend, the only one outside my immediate family who understood the real me. I didn't have to hide with him, so that betrayal stung the hardest. But fuck, you made me the happiest motherfucker who ever lived by giving me a front-row seat to the performance of a lifetime."

I stare up at him, my brows dipped low as he shakes some pills into his hand and divides them up; a pile for him and a pile for me. He passes them over and I pop them straight into my mouth as he hands me the bottle of water. They slide down the hatch with ease and I hand the bottle straight back so he can do the same. "I know I talk a lot of shit, but have I ever told you just how fucked up you guys truly are? I mean, fuck. Your father skipped a few important steps while raising you. Like … you know it's not normal to dream about murdering people and getting off over the sound of their blood splattering against the tiles? Don't get me wrong, it's certainly entertaining, but I'm almost positive that you're the only fuckers in the world having arguments over which body part you get to keep as trophies."

"Hmmm," he murmurs, leaning back on the couch as his arm drops around my shoulder. "How strange. All these years I've been thinking it was completely normal. I'll be sure to bring up my father's parenting failures during our next business meeting."

"Solid plan," I tell him, unable to keep the smirk from stretching over my face. "Just be sure to keep my name out of your filthy mouth when you do it."

"Consider it done."

And just like that, I stretch my leg out and knock the tongue jar right off the table—out of sight, out of mind—giving me just that tiny bit of peace to close my eyes and rest into Marcus' side, finally giving myself the chance to drift off into a peaceful sleep, only one more question lingers on my mind.

"Marcus?" I question, refusing to glance up at him, too afraid to see what might flash through his eyes. "Earlier tonight in your room when we were talking about what your brothers did to me, you made a comment about how they knew what you felt for me and … what does that mean? What do you feel for me?"

Marcus adjusts himself beneath me and pulls me in a little tighter before dropping his chin and pressing his lips into my hair. He doesn't move for a long moment and the silence quickly fills the air as he thinks of what to say, making sure he doesn't mince his words. "I don't mean for this to hurt you, but I don't fucking know. I'm not in love with you if that's what you're asking, but I know that if you were to have died or gotten away, it would have killed me. I've never been in love before, I don't know how that's supposed to feel, but just know that you mean a shitload more to me than anyone else who's ever walked through that door. You mean something to me, Shayne. Something important and I don't want to let that go."

I nod against his side, his words sending a wave of warmth crashing through my body. "Okay," I tell him, feeling myself slipping into unconsciousness. "But if that were to change, if something happens and you suddenly didn't feel the need to keep me around, would you let me know?"

"That's not going to happen," he says so damn sure of himself. "Now sleep, you've had a long night."

CHAPTER THIRTEEN

ROMAN

Shayne's bite mark lingers on my arm and I stare down at the perfect impression of her teeth, bruised and scarred, a chilling reminder of the fresh hell she went through at my hands six days ago.

I'm the worst fucking thing to have ever happened to her. I knew this world was going to kill her, I just never expected it to have been so soon and by my hand. She was supposed to thrive here, she was supposed to be our fucking queen, and now she can't even look at me.

What the fuck have I done? She screamed until her lungs gave out, she cried and begged us to listen, begged us to stop, but I wouldn't hear it. I couldn't see past my own fury to see that she was telling the truth, to see that she had our backs just as we should have had hers. All I could see was Marcus bleeding out on her bed, Levi's hands in his chest, struggling to keep him alive, and Shayne running with nothing but fear in her eyes.

I didn't even stop to question it. My mind was fucking set. She did this and she was going to pay.

I can still feel the warmth of her blood on my hands as the shard of glass pulled free from her stomach, the pressure of her body squirming beneath me as I held her down for Levi to hurt. These images flow through my mind like rapids, constantly rising and threatening to pull me beneath their frothy surface. The same screams I've delighted in are haunting me, reminding me what I've done.

I've killed countless men in my time. I've watched them choke on their own blood, smelled the fear in the air as their lives were brutally taken, and I fucking loved it. I've always washed the blood off my hands and moved on to the next victim, but I can't do that, not with Shayne. Her blood had stained my hands and no matter how much I scrub it away, the marks will never fade.

She deserves so much better than this world, but I won't ever let her go. Not now, not after tasting those lips on mine. I'm in too deep and the worst part is that she doesn't even know. She hasn't got a fucking clue about the effect she has over me and my brothers, not even Marcus. He'll never admit to her just how deep his affections run. Hell, the fucker wouldn't even know it himself. He's in love with her and he has no fucking idea because he's never been taught what it means to love.

We've been conditioned to believe that to love means to be weak. It's part of the reason my father took Ariana away from me. We were too close, too real, and he couldn't fucking stand it. What a fucking brutal lesson that was.

Trying to put the intrusive thoughts to the back of my head, I focus on Shayne's bite mark. It's still red and raw, even after so many days. But since the moment Marcus woke up and confirmed she was telling the truth, this bite has served as a constant reminder, not letting me forget for even a moment what I've done.

This bite mark serves as a symbol of weakness, a pledge to earn her forgiveness, a vow to be a better man for her. Not that she'll ever take me after what I've done, but I have nothing but time to make it up to her, to be whatever she needs in the world until she finally sees just how fucking good we could be. She's had a taste for it now. I felt the way she melted into my arms, how she consumed my kiss like it was her last moments on earth, and whether she's prepared to admit it or not, she feels something for me, which is exactly why I can't bear to see her bite fading from my arm.

Dipping the tattoo gun back into the small ink pot, I get straight back to work. Relishing the pain of the fine needles digging into my skin as I start my outline, more determined than ever to see this mark on my arm until my dying days.

I will never forget what I've done to her and this will serve as my reminder of her pain, a reminder of what I took from her.

Fuck, just the look in her eyes when she bit me will haunt me for the rest of my life. I could have pulled away, but even while putting her through that horrendous pain, I still wanted to offer her that tiny bit of relief. How fucking sick is that? I wanted her to punish me. I wanted her to take her pain out on me, and I'll fucking do it again.

Minutes pass as I capture every little detail of her bite, making sure to get the redness and bruising just right as the weight and guilt of what I've done presses down over my shoulders. I don't want to miss a fucking thing when it comes to this tattoo. It needs to be the perfect representation of just how fucked up it was.

I get halfway through shading the deep crevices her teeth left behind when something catches my eye and I glance up out my bedroom door to find Shayne peering in. Her shoulder is pressed up against the door frame as she wears a relaxed expression, but the tightness in her eyes tells me she's anything but.

Pulling back off of the tattoo so I don't fuck it up, I keep my hard stare on her, nervousness flickering inside me. I used to be able to read her like a fucking book, but this week, she's been so closed off. She's a fucking mystery to me and showing up in my bedroom is the biggest mystery so far.

She eyes me warily and it's no secret that she's hesitant about being here. She doesn't trust me anymore, and I don't fucking blame her. She used to look at me like I held the secrets of the world, but now there's nothing but darkness and hurt in her stunning blue eyes and it kills me.

"What do you need?" I question, doing what I can to keep the usual harsh tone out of my voice, wanting her to know that no matter what, she's welcome. But to be completely honest, not sounding threatening isn't something that comes naturally to me.

Her gaze drops to my arm and a hint of regret flashes through her eyes, regret that I don't quite understand. "What are you doing?" she asks hesitantly, her brows creasing as she slowly creeps another step into my room.

I adjust the angle of my arm so that she can clearly see her perfect mark left on my skin for all of eternity. "I couldn't bear to let it fade away."

Her eyes widen in horror as she barges deeper into my room, gripping my arm and yanking it up in front of her to get a better view. "Is that my teeth? What the fuck is wrong with you? Why would you do that?" she shrieks, dropping my arm heavily back to the table with a loud thump, rattling the small ink pots. "Are you insane? Wait, of course you are. What a stupid fucking question."

I raise my brow, patiently waiting for her to get it all out, and only when I think she's done do I give her my explanation. "It's a reminder," I tell her. "When I look down at the imprint of your teeth, I see the pain in your eyes as clearly as though it was happening right in front of me. I don't want to forget what I did to you, Shayne. It's not something that I will allow to get swept under the rug in time. This here," I say, pointing down at the half-shaded piece of work, "this is going to ensure that I never fuck up like I did before. It's the motivation I need to be better, to do better."

Shayne clenches her jaw as her gaze drops away, not wanting to meet my eyes. "I still think you're fucked in the head," she mutters, not ready to speak with me on such a deep level, and who the fuck would blame her?

My heavy stare lingers on her face until she has no choice but to look my way. "Why are you here, Shayne?"

She swallows hard and a flicker of nervousness flashes through her haunted gaze. "I, ummm … there's been something on my mind," she explains. "And I don't want some bullshit answer, dancing around it. I need the cold, hard truth."

I sit, patiently waiting as she contemplates whether she actually has the balls to ask me what she needs to know. A moment passes and I arch a brow when the words don't come flying out of her mouth. "What is it?" I question, my usual no-bullshit tone sneaking back in.

She lets out a breath and fixes me with a hard stare, only she looks like a cub trying to roar. "Why did you tell me that Marcus was dead?"

My back stiffens and my muscles tighten as I watch her. I had expected a lot of things to come out of her mouth, but not this, at least not yet. She was bound to come looking for answers eventually, but I was certain that she wasn't ready. Hell, maybe she still isn't but I'm not about to deny her, not after what I've done.

Looking her dead in the eye, I give her the cold, hard truth just as she asked, knowing that it's not what she wants to hear. "I had to know where your loyalties lied," I tell her. "I needed your raw, honest reaction to learning Marcus was dead. I needed to see how it hurt you, or if it hurt you at all."

Her eyes search mine, her head shaking in disbelief. "You're a fucking monster," she murmurs, her voice dropping to a low whisper.

I nod, knowing all too well. "Yes, I am."

"So, what happened?" she questions. "Was my grief not believable enough? Were the tears and heartache not enough to convince you? I was a fucking mess, and yet you still doubted me."

Raising my chin, I let her see the horrors deep inside my eyes. "I did doubt you," I tell her, slowly standing and making my way toward her. She eases back a step before deciding to hold her ground, on some level knowing that I'm not going to hurt her. "I didn't trust you. I questioned your loyalties and I wanted to see you hurt like I was."

Her brows furrow and the fear instantly seeps out of her gaze only to be replaced with confusion. "Like you were? What's that supposed to mean?" she demands, standing a little straighter. "Marcus was fine and you knew it. What do you have to be hurt about? Me? Because I tried to run again? Because I was allowing myself to get close with your brothers, but not you? It makes no fucking sense. You had nothing to be hurt about except for your own goddamn actions."

I clench my jaw as her words hit something hard inside me, something I refuse to believe exists. I step closer, hating how clearly she can see through the hard exterior that I've worked years to perfect. "Why are you really here?" I demand, narrowing my gaze on her baby blue eyes and feeling the anger rising high in my chest, only the anger is aimed at myself for failing to conceal the real man who lies beneath, the man my father has conditioned me to bury.

Shayne stares back up at me, not backing away from the relentless brutal stare coming her way. "I want you to train me."

I scoff. "You're fucking kidding, right? Why would I want to do that?"

"Because I asked you to," she seethes, stepping closer into me and shoving me hard in the chest. "Because despite the shit you've put me through, I still have a will to survive."

"No."

"It's not a negotiation," she tells me. "You put your hands on me and in return, you will teach me how to survive. I don't expect to learn how to take down someone like you who's been training all their life, but at the very least, you will train me how to get away so assholes like you can't hurt me again."

I shake my head. After the bullshit the Miller brothers pulled on her, I had every intention of training her, but not now. She's not ready. I reach out and brush my fingers over her shoulder, watching the way she flinches at my touch and shrugs away. "How the fuck do you expect me to train you when you can't stand the thought of my touch?" I snap my arm around her waist and yank her in hard against my chest, instantly smelling that sweet taste of innocence, an innocence I want nothing more than to destroy. "You can't bear to be close to me, and yet you want me to throw you around on a training mat, sneaking up behind you and putting you into hostage-like situations to get out of? You're too weak. You're not ready."

"I don't care," she seethes, getting her hands up between us and pushing back against my chest, forcing herself free. "I'll deal with it, but what I won't do is walk out of here without getting exactly what I want."

"You don't know what you want."

She narrows her eyes and if looks could kill, I'd already be dead. "Don't act like you know anything about what I want."

"I felt your lips on mine," I tell her, walking back into her again, refusing to allow her any personal space, but hell, she's the one insisting that she can handle it. "I felt your body melt into me. I've committed your moan to memory. I know exactly what you want."

"Good job," she spits. "You were able to read my body's reaction to you, but it's nothing different to what it does around Marcus or Levi. Congratulations, you're nothing special, just one of many. The only difference is that they've had me, tasted me, felt me coming on their rock-hard cocks, while you can only dream about it."

Fucking hell, my little Empress is playing to kill, and damn it, that one stung like a fucking bitch, but nothing has ever made my blood boil more.

"Here's the deal," she continues. "You and I both know that if Marcus could, I'd be asking him, but he's out, at least for now. I won't be asking Levi because that fucker is only going to dump all his bullshit feelings and guilt on me, and I'm not nearly ready to have that forced on me. So, you're all I've got left. You're a broody asshole who's terrified of himself. It's guaranteed we can do this without you begging me to forgive you. You're my best shot, so you're going to train me just like you would anyone else."

"And when I touch you?"

"I'm gonna flinch," she spits back at me. "I'm going to remember what you did to me and I'm going to hate every fucking second of it, but damn it, I hope that every single time I flinch away from you, it makes you feel like shit. If you do this, and you somehow manage to teach me how to evade people like you, then I might even consider letting you off the hook."

My brow arches and I hold her stare. "You don't mean that," I mutter. "You'd forgive me?"

She shakes her head, her eyes narrowing to lethal slits. "There you go doubting my word again," she seethes. "But that's not what I said. I said I would let you off the hook. I didn't say shit about forgiving you, and you'd be a fool to assume I ever could."

I hold her stare for a long moment before finally letting out a defeated sigh. "Fine. We'll start next week once you're better."

"No," she snaps. "I'm done putting this off. Fuck the stitches. I want to be ready. We start tonight." Then without another word, she turns and strides back out the door.

I stare after her in complete disbelief. No one has ever busted in here making demands and gotten away with it, not without losing their life … or at least a few fingers. Yet somehow she manages to trample all over me and I allow it to happen.

Fucking hell.

Dropping my ass back into my chair, I pick up my tattoo gun just as my phone rings on the table beside me, and just like that, my whole fucking mood comes crashing down. My father's name flashes on the small screen. For a moment, I consider just how sweet it would feel to throw my phone across the room and watch as it shattered against the hard stone walls of the castle. But then I have to order a new phone and go through the long, painful process of restoring it from the old one, and honestly, fuck that. There's nothing more tedious than having to remember my fucking password and then trying to figure out the goddamn cloud.

Letting out a sigh, I put the tattoo gun down and pick up my phone, pushing out of my seat as I hit accept and bring the phone to my ear. "Father," I grunt as Levi appears in my doorway and watches me through a narrowed gaze, hating my father's calls just as much as I do.

I put the call on speaker so Levi can hear as I stride toward my bedroom window, staring out at the wide expanse of property that doubles as our prison. "Tell me you're not so fucking stupid to kill your own damn cousin. Your stench is all over it."

I glance back at Levi and take in the smirk resting on his lips. "The fuck are you talking about?" I spit, mentally seething at his tone. "What cousin? We haven't killed anyone ... well, at least not anyone important to you."

"Antonio," my father mutters. "He was murdered at his father's property last night. Are you sure you had nothing to do with it?"

"You mean *my* property?" I question. "But good fucking riddance to the little prick. He had it coming, especially after what he did to us. If only I could have gotten to him first. It's a shame, I've been waiting for the day I got to take his pathetic life."

"*He had it coming?*" he repeats as though I'm speaking another fucking language. "What in the hell is that supposed to mean?"

Levi strides deeper into my room, tucking his drumsticks in the back pocket of his jeans. "Probably fucked the wrong bitch," he explains. "You know he was getting busy with Ronaldo's wife, right? Keeping it in the family. It was only a matter of time. You know how

Ronaldo gets when someone fucks with what's his."

"Ronaldo?" Father demands, the thought of one of our many other cousins having anything to do with this fucking with his head. It's shit like this that will set off one hell of a chain reaction. "Are you sure?"

Levi grins as his venomous gaze sweeps up to mine. "As sure as the fact that I'll end your miserable life one of these days."

Ahhh, fuck. The sorry idiot just had to go and push the boundaries. He's just fucking lucky my father is too busy trying to figure out how to deal with this mess before it can turn into a fucking bloodbath. After all, the moment news reaches Antonio's father, he'll be out for Ronaldo's blood, and once Ronaldo is buried and gone, his father will be coming for Antonio's. It'll be like fucking magic to watch, one after the other, dropping like fucking flies until there's no one left. My brothers and I won't even have to lift a goddamn finger.

My father skims straight over Levi's comment. "Where are you with these new manufacturers? You only have one day left. You better make it count."

I roll my eyes and let out a sigh. "We found one of his dealers. He was a dead end. Wouldn't give us a name so we put him down," I say, thinking back on my old dealer, Julius, who learned the hard way what it means to steal from us. Though, it's a shame because he was a good fucking dealer. Let's just hope that his new replacement can pull the same kind of strings and more, but if he double-crosses me, he'll suffer a much worse fate than his boss before him.

"Fuck," my father mutters. "Twenty-four hours left, boy. Don't mess it up."

The line goes dead and I turn to Levi, a smirk cutting across my face. "You heard the man. We have twenty-four hours of uninterrupted freedom. We better make it count."

His eyes darken just like mine, and for a brief moment, a flicker of guilt sails through my chest at the idea of leaving Marcus behind, but he'll be more than alright with Shayne in his bed to keep him company. Though, she's bound to be pissed when I don't show up for tonight's training session. She thinks she can handle it, but she's not even remotely ready. By walking out now, I'm doing her a favor.

"Let's fucking do it," Levi says, and not a moment later, my tattoo gun is switched out for a real one and I'm out the fucking door, more than ready to remind this town who the fuck owns it.

Chapter Fourteen

The big-ass wolf crushes me as he drops his heavy body over my lap and makes himself at home. His brother . . . or sister, jumps up on the couch beside me and drapes over me like a blanket, the two of them together almost suffocating me. "The fuck do you think you're doing?" I demand, hating that I kinda like it when they show preference to me over their delusional, psychotic masters.

I wriggle a good portion of my body free and stare down at the big fuckers. "You guys just need someone to love you, don't you?" I question, feeling my shitty mood slowly begin to fade away. I was supposed to start training with Roman last night, so it's only natural for me to have wanted to strangle the bastard when I showed up for a session that he had absolutely no intention of turning up to. I fumed about it all night, well, until Marcus gave me something better to do. But damn, that asshole is going to get a brand new one the moment I see him.

They were out all night, and according to Marcus, they had some old friends who had forgotten just how thrilling it was to spend the night with them. Naturally, it was time for a reminder, and I couldn't help the chill that swept down my spine. I'm all too acquainted with their friendly ways and I don't wish it upon anyone. I haven't seen them all morning, so I'm assuming they're still out settling scores, but the moment they're back, Roman is going to get one hell of an ass whooping and it's going to be the best time of my life.

The wolves look up at me like some kind of alien mother trying to take them as my own, and as I relax back into the couch, content with being crushed under their massive size, my hand threads into their thick fur, scratching their heads. "So, like … are we friends yet?" I question, only to get a sharp glare from the one across my lap, silently telling me to shut the fuck up.

I roll my eyes and give him a nudge, only he doesn't move an inch. "Listen up, you big murder puppy, if you're going to use me as a human doggy bed, then the least you can do is not be a little shit about it," I tell him just as a foul, tangy smell tears through the air. "Oh, hell no," I shriek, holding back a gag as the murder puppy raises his head, looks me dead in the eye, and lolls his stupid tongue out, his eyes sparkling with laughter.

The smell wafts around the room, consuming me with its all too powerful stench and I can't hold back the gag. "Alright, motherfuckers. Get off me."

I shove my hands into their sides and push until they finally get the hint to give me space. They take their sweet-ass time climbing down, making a point to show how unhappy they are about the situation. When I finally get to my feet and rush out of the room to take a deep breath of clean air, they come bounding after me. "For fuck's sake, what is wrong with your guts?" I demand as I make my way into the massive dining hall, the two wolves hot on my heels.

I bust through the big double doors and just like always, at this time of the day, there's a massive spread of food across the long oak table. My stomach growls at the wafting smell. It's well past midday and I spent all morning sitting in the living room, waiting for Roman and Levi to get home from their night of fun-filled murder. I was too pissed off with them to worry about eating breakfast, but now I can hardly wait.

The past few days, I've been eating soft foods as that's all my raw throat and stomach have been able to handle, but I'm done with that shit. If I'm going to get back to the old Shayne and learn how to thrive, then I need to start eating right.

After filling up my plate and dropping my ass down into Roman's favorite spot, I dig in, smooshing food down my sore throat and sedating the dragon that lives within. I get halfway through when movement to my right catches my eye and I find the two wolves, sitting patiently, salivating over my lunch.

My brow arches and I glance back at the table. "Are you guys hungry or something?"

The bigger of the two stands, his eyes going wide as excitement seems to pulse through him. "Well, shit, you should have said something." I get up and scan over the selections, wondering what makes up a good meal for a wolf. I mean, I should probably bypass the salads and go for the good juicy steaks. I bet they'll appreciate that shit.

I fill up some plates and place them on the ground, positive that they probably have their own food bowls in here somewhere. One wolf stands, barely giving me the chance to get out of his way before he barges in with those sharp teeth, while the other waits patiently, taking his time.

Glancing around the room, I check for water bowls and grin to myself when I find two plain white doggy bowls under one of the many impressive fireplaces. Grabbing a sharpie from the long hallway table behind me, I stride over to their empty water bowls and pick them up.

Grinning to myself, I write 'DILL' and 'DOE' across the fronts of their bowls, filling them all the way up with water and placing them back down. "There we go," I say, proud of my work, and even more proud that the big wolves finally have names. After all, these wolves are more than just weapons, they're our pets and all pets should be loved and cared for.

The bigger, more energetic one with the jet-black fur and stanky guts will be Dill, and his brother—or maybe sister—the more placid and patient one with a softer face, will now be known as Doe. Together they will be the famous DeAngelis Dill Doe wolves, feared by all who dare step in their way.

I laugh to myself as I go to make my way back to my half-eaten lunch when the familiar sounds of Levi's drums sound through the castle and my eyes go wide. "THOSE MOTHERFUCKERS!"

Dill and Doe barely pay me any notice as I barge out of the dining hall and storm up the stairs, relieved when my stomach doesn't scream at me. It's been a week since that night, and while there's still plenty of pain, my day-to-day routine has been getting a shitload easier.

Following the sound of drums, I barge my way into Levi's bedroom without knocking. I've never actually been in here and I'm sure the room is full of all sorts of secrets that I'll be more than happy to explore another time. As for now, this bastard needs an ass whooping.

Clocking me the second the door flies open, he stops playing and looks my way, and for a moment, I'm taken back by the rare sight of undress. His body is unlike anything I've ever seen. So broad and toned. He's a work of art with those stunning tattoos, and my mouth waters at the sight.

"Where the hell have you been?" I demand. "And more importantly, where the hell is your jackass brother? I've been sitting with those big-ass wolves for hours in the living room waiting for you assholes."

As if not realizing that he's doing it, he begins drumming again softly, making it easier to hold a conversation. "We've been home for hours," he says as the muscles in his arms roll, flex, and bounce with every hit.

"No, you haven't," I shoot back at him. "I would have seen you come in."

His shoulders bounce with a shrug before he winks, his lips pulling up into a devilish smirk. "Came in through the back."

I clench my jaw, closing my eyes and trying not to be affected by his devilish charm. "The back?" I screech. "What the fuck is wrong with you? Who does that?"

His brows furrow as his foot starts on the bass, his knee slowly bouncing as his eyes remain locked on me. "What's the matter, Shayne?" he questions as I see the gentle sway of his cock through his grey sweatpant as his knee bounces.

My gaze drops down his body, quickly becoming mesmerized by the sight and inwardly hating myself for being so damn obvious about my attraction to him. But fuck, I'd forgotten just how crazy I was about this guy on the drums. Maybe it's the way he bangs them with such determination that I feel the vibrations right down in my soul … or maybe it's just that cock.

Without even realizing it, I inch closer toward him. "I, ummm … Roman," I say, getting completely off track and trying to remember why the hell I was so mad with them. You know, apart from the whole torture thing. "He was supposed to train me last night. I need to know how to defend myself."

Levi rolls his tongue over his full lips as his gaze drops down my body, watching the way I react to him. "He didn't mention it," he explains. "Last night was our last shot at freedom. Our free pass from our father was ending. Had to make it count."

My arms cross over my chest and I only just refrain from rolling my eyes. "And did you?" I murmur, my voice barely audible over the sound of Levi's drumming as it gets faster, louder, and more erratic, the bass vibrating right through my chest.

"What do you think?" he murmurs, desire pooling in his eyes.

"Have I ever not made it count?"

Fuck me. Why do I hate him again?

I step in even closer, walking around his set as I brush my fingers along the cool drums, sucking in a gasp as the sticks come down beside my fingers, bouncing them right off the drum with their force. Heat floods me and I know there's no way in hell I'll be able to resist him.

"What are you doing?" he questions warily, seeing the same desire in my eyes. He shakes his head, knowing all too well where this is going, but unlike me, he has the control to hold himself back, though I don't think he wants to. "Don't, Shayne. You don't want this."

"Oh, but I do," I purr, letting my fingers fall to the center of my chest and slowly drawing down between my tits, separating the silk material of my dressing gown. It falls off my shoulder and a soft breeze from the small open window hits my skin.

I tug on the small tie at my waist and allow the silk to fall right from my body, pooling on the ground at my feet before stepping over it and slowly walking around Levi. My finger gently presses to the top of his hand as his drumming slows, distracted by my touch.

It trails up over his strong arm, flowing freely over his warm skin until I reach his shoulder. I move in right behind him and press my body against his back, closing my eyes with the intense pleasure of feeling him like this. Despite my every thought telling me that I should pull away from him, that I should be disgusted with myself, I just can't. He's got me right where he wants me and I won't dare stop, not now, not until I've had more than my fill of him and my knees are shaking beneath me.

My hand moves over his shoulder to his wide chest and I feel his heart beating like a challenge, daring me to make it pulse so much faster, and damn it, I'm here for it. "Shayne," he mutters, the warning clear in his voice.

"I want you to fuck me while you play your drums, Levi," I tell him, leaning into him and feeling my tits press right into his back. "I want you to fuck me so damn hard that I forget why I hate you."

"You can't bear the thought of my touch," he reminds me. "How the fuck do you expect me to give you what you need?"

"Like I said," I say, lowering my hand to his sweatpants and feeling his rock-hard cock through the soft material. I slip my hand inside and curl my fingers around his thick cock. "Give me what I want. Make me forget why I hate your touch. Replace those memories with something that's gonna make me scream for a whole new reason."

My hand moves up and down and we both groan as I pull back from him and move around to his side, my tits level with his full lips. "You once told me not to play games with you. If I want something, I need to ask for it. Well here I am, Levi. I've asked, and I'm not going to ask again. So, what's it going to be? Fuck me while you play or I'll go and fuck Marcus instead. Take your pick."

My fist tightens around his cock before pausing, the silent threat lingering in the air, a threat I know he won't be able to risk. "Fuck," he grunts, leaning back and curling his arm around my waist, and with one easy move, he lifts me over his lap until I'm comfortably straddled over him, my bare pussy pressed right up against his throbbing cock.

"When you run out of here hating me, remember that you asked for this."

"I'd tell you to trust me, but it'd fall on deaf ears."

Levi clenches his jaw as his arm tightens around my waist again, slightly raising me up as he loses his sweatpants, allowing his thick cock to bounce free. He lines himself up and I feel the tip of his cock slowly moving around my entrance, mixing with my wetness and proving just how badly I want this.

Without warning, he drops me back down and his thick cock plunges deep inside me, stretching me wide as a satisfied groan tears from deep within my chest. "Oh, fuck," I mutter, my arms flying around his neck and holding on tight as my legs lock around his waist, securing me in place.

His knee bounces below me as his foot hits the bass drum and I gasp, his cock flinching deep inside of me as my body jumps, the momentum from his knees sliding me up and down his cock with a brutal deliciousness.

Levi doesn't skip a beat, doing it again and again before flipping the drum stick in his hands and getting stuck into his intoxicating rhythm. His body tenses around me, flexing and rolling with each practiced movement as I bounce over his cock.

His low groans send shivers down my spine and make me feel more woman than ever before. I clench my pussy, letting him feel just how tightly I can squeeze him. "Fuck, Shayne," he rumbles as I throw my head back, practically swinging from his strong neck as I arch my back and push my tits up.

His gaze drops to my body, passing over my tits as they bounce wildly before looking down between us at where we connect, watching the way my pussy moves over him, coating his cock in my sweet, glistening juices. And just like that, his intoxicating rhythm kicks up a notch, bringing with it a whole new intensity.

"LEVI," I cry. "YES."

Bass. Snare. High hat. Bass. Bass. Snare. Tom toms. And fuck, he hits that bass all over again.

My pussy clenches, the tension building rapidly within me as he proves a million times over that this is just as I always thought it would be. It's fucking everything, and damn it, I can barely breathe.

Our bodies grow sweaty, and with one quick move, Levi yanks my body back into his, keeping me pressed right up against him. My lips fall to his neck, tasting him, kissing him, and loving the way he groans as my tongue trails over his warm skin. I bite down, not enough to draw blood, but enough to let him know just how hard I need it, and fuck, he knows how to satisfy a woman.

His cock slams deep within me, and without warning or even a thought for my aching clit, I come undone, his relentless cock getting me off in the best possible way and destroying me like never before. I explode around his cock, shattering into a million tiny pieces as I pant and scream his name until I'm sure that every motherfucker in this haunted castle knows what the fuck is going down in here.

"Ah, fuck," Levi grunts, slamming deep inside me once again and shooting his load, filling me with his warm seed. My pussy continues convulsing around him, relentlessly squeezing as I clench my eyes, feeling the pleasure rocking right through my body, singeing my every nerve ending with an electrifying, delicious burn.

His rhythm slows on the drums as his chest rises and falls with rapid movements against mine, and damn, I don't think I've ever come like that, especially without some kind of stimulation to my clit. That's grounds for a fucking award, but I'm not going to lie, she's feeling left out.

A loud clapping comes from the door of Levi's room and my head snaps around, taking in Roman leaned up against the doorframe. "What a show," he applauds, his face an emotionless mask, desperate to keep his true feelings hidden. "You want to learn how to protect yourself, then get your ass downstairs. Now."

Rage burns through me at his audacity and I release my arms from around Levi's neck, more than ready to throw myself off his lap and annihilate his moronic brother. "Where the fuck do—"

Roman walks away before the sentence even comes out of my mouth and I clench my jaw, more determined than ever to raise the freshest kind of hell. That doesn't even sound like enough. How does one summon a demon and get it to do your bidding? I was never good at math, but I'm sure I can figure out a pentagram.

Levi drops his drumsticks on top of his snare and meets my eye, wariness flooded in those deep depths of darkness. "You good?" he questions.

I nod, knowing he's not referring to his brother. "For just a little while, you made me forget," I tell him as I slowly rock my hips back and forth, groaning with the sweet pleasure. Hell, I bet a guy like Levi has never been fucked slowly.

His brows crease and I watch as the pleasure rocks through him like a fucking knife through the chest. He really has never felt something like this.

His hand falls to my waist as his other drops to my ass, slipping down to the most forbidden parts of my body as I keep rocking back and forth, feeling the intense way that his cock sails in and out of me like a sensual massage, rubbing and stretching my walls.

Closing my eyes, my head tips forward and I do nothing but feel as my hand slips down between us and gently rubs my clit. "Oh, God," I moan, my subtle movements making Levi's warm seed seep out of me and spread between us, making the best kind of mess.

My pussy clenches as my clit screams in happiness, and as my hips rock just a little faster, taking Levi at a deeper angle, another orgasm tears through me, slow and agonizingly intense.

My pussy shatters all over again and I don't dare stop, keeping my hips moving as his fingers dig into my skin. Then just as he's about to come, I pull back, planting my feet on the ground and depriving him of his most carnal urges. "You made me forget for a little while," I repeat, his face dropping in realization. "But you and I ... we'll never be the same."

And with that, I step over his strong thighs and walk out of his room with nothing but a mess between my legs and the world's worst case of blue balls behind me.

CHAPTER FIFTEEN

Taking my sweet-ass time, I show up in the training room over forty-five minutes after Roman demanded my attention with a smug grin stretched wide over my lips. The fuck knuckle couldn't possibly think he was going to get away with standing me up last night, then leaving me in a pissed-off rage on the couch all morning waiting for his bitch ass.

No, life is never that simple, and if minor inconveniences are the way to drive him to the brink of insanity, then that's exactly what I'm going to do. Though, it's hard to tell just how far I'll have to go. He's probably already taken a few trips to the brink of insanity, so I wouldn't be surprised if he's developed some kind of immunity. Besides, getting under Roman's skin is one of my all-time favorite pastimes, and he knows that better than anybody. Perhaps it'll be good to get a little bit of normalcy around here.

I barge through the door, making sure it rebounds off the internal wall with a loud bang, but it doesn't startle him as I'd hoped. It doesn't even make him flinch. Fuck, all I get from him is a narrowed glare as he curls his hands into fists at his side. "What fucking time do you call this?" he demands, taking slow, deep breaths, trying to calm his erratic, wild emotions.

"This," I say. "Is called a whole lot of bullshit. You can have the shits at me for showing up just a little late while you have the audacity not to show up at all. Fuck you, Roman. I'm not your punching bag. If you say you're going to do something, then do it. I thought you were a man of your word."

He opens his arms out wide and indicates around him. "I'm here, aren't I?"

My arms cross over my chest and I want to hate myself for putting me in this position, but what choice do I have? I've been thrown around like a fucking ragdoll since coming here and I won't allow it to happen again. I won't be weak, even if it means allowing Roman to get too close for comfort, then that's what I'll do.

"You're an asshole," I seethe, pausing in the doorway to glare right back at him only to be shoved out of the way as Marcus and Levi come striding in behind me to watch the show.

"Can we just …" Roman groans, his frustration getting the better of him as he pauses to let out a breath. "Let's get this over and done with. There are a lot of basics to cover."

A seriousness comes over me and I do what I can to leave my issues at the door and look at him as nothing but my new self-defense instructor. I walk deeper into the room and step up onto a soft-fall training mat, stopping directly in front of Roman. I keep my distance, still hesitant to get too close. Though, I had no issues when it was Levi. Perhaps I'm holding onto a little more resentment for Roman than I am for Levi. After all, I had the beginnings of a relationship with Levi before all this shit went down. On some level, I felt like I knew him so much more, though how well can anyone truly know one of the DeAngelis brothers?

"You're going to have to get closer to me, otherwise this ain't gonna work."

I let out a nervous breath and try to hide my shaky hands, but he notices them a shitload faster than I ever could. "I'm not going to hurt you, Empress," he says, lowering his voice to keep our conversation private from his brothers, trying to hide the fact that deep down inside, he's not the heartless soldier his father has strived to create. "This isn't going to be easy. I need to put my hands on you and I will be throwing you down, holding you down, gripping you just like I did *that night*. You're going to hate it. You're going to scream, and you're going to tell me to back the fuck off, but I'm not going to do that, and it's going to make you hate me more."

I shake my head, my determination winning out over everything else. "I won't," I insist.

"You will," he tells me, his tone not wavering as he takes a quick step toward me.

His arm snaps out and his fingers curl around my throat before yanking my body close to his. Fear rattles me and a loud, ear-shattering scream burns my throat like never before. My hands slap out at his strong vice-like hold as the panic tears through me like a bullet. "LET GO OF ME," I wail, my chest constricting as a sharp lump forms in my throat.

Roman releases me immediately and just stares at me with a knowing gaze, not a hint of that usual smug attitude coming at me as he proves his point in less than a second.

Marcus races in, putting himself between me and Roman as I back up a few steps, the images and memories rushing through my mind like a swarm of murder hornets, destroying everything in their path. I take a shaky breath, trying to calm my racing heart as my hands shake miserably at my sides. "No," Marcus says, eyeing his brother with disdain before slowly turning toward me. "You're not ready. I'll train you instead."

"Don't be fucking stupid," Roman says. "One missed punch to your chest and you'll go down like a sack of shit. I won't allow it. She's training with me. She's just going to have to wait until she can manage to be near me without having a panic attack."

My brows furrow as I step around Marcus. "Fuck no. I told you, we're starting this now. I want to learn."

Roman shakes his head. "It ain't gonna happen. What I just did, grabbing you like that is nothing, and you couldn't bear the feel of my touch. What's going to happen when I grab you by the ankle and start dragging you through the room? Are you going to piss your pants and start screaming like a bitch, thinking you're back in that cave? Face the facts, Shayne. You're not ready."

I step up closer to him, raising my chin in defiance, the fear of history repeating itself greater than the memory of the past. "I can do this," I spit, my voice breaking with unease and nervousness as the determination in my eyes shine so much brighter. "Now, train me."

Roman and Marcus watch me for a long, intense moment before Marcus finally steps away and returns to the side of the room with Levi, both of them watching me all too closely, but they're not what's got my attention.

Roman just stands there, his gaze lingering on my hard stare. He steps toward me again and my knees begin to shake, the need to back up racing through me. It was different in his room last night. I knew he wasn't going to touch me, and damn well knew that he wouldn't hurt me, but right here, I've given him permission to touch me in any way he sees fit and the things he's going to do to me will most likely replicate those horrendous things he's already done.

"Alright," he finally says, his tone low and threatening, making fear trail through my blood like lead. He walks around me, his stare not leaving me for even a second. I sense him coming to a pause directly behind me, and the fear of having him at my back is nearly crippling. "Lesson number one," he says, snapping toward me, his arm curling around my neck as he pulls me into a chokehold, his other hand coming down over my mouth, keeping me from being able to scream. "Never turn your back on your enemy. When I walk around you, you walk with me. Always give yourself the advantage."

Then just like that, he releases me, giving a slight shove to push me away from him, knowing that I need my space. I gasp for air but not because he was blocking me from getting any. I spin around, turning to face him the moment my panic is under control. I look Roman dead in the eye. "Do it again," I tell him, swallowing hard over the lump in my throat. "That's how Lucas Miller grabbed me in the club and how your father's henchman grabbed me before the car exploded. Teach me how to get out of it."

Roman watches me, hesitation flashing in his eyes. "Are you sure?" he questions as Levi slowly begins creeping in toward us.

I nod. "I'm sure."

An agonizing moment passes before he finally agrees and indicates to the space in front of him. "Come here," he says, his voice low as he strains to keep it from coming across threatening, something he clearly doesn't have much skill with.

My knees shake as I slowly put myself back in front of Roman, and this time, he moves into me slowly. He curls his arm around my throat and tightens just enough for me to feel it there as his hand presses over my mouth, leaving me enough space to scream if need be.

I feel his breath against my skin at my ear as his body presses in flush with mine. "Okay," he says. "If someone has you like this, they're more than likely going to attempt to drag you back."

I nod, the haunting memory circling my mind like a ferris wheel at a dodgy town fair. "What do I do?" I ask, my voice timid and nervous, muffled by his hand.

He moves his pinky finger over my mouth. "Grab it," he says. "I'm going to hold you tighter and when I do, you're going to yank my finger back as far as you can while slamming your elbow back into my stomach. You're going to wind your attacker, and in most cases, they'll be forced to release you. When that happens, you run forward and scream for help."

I nod, going over my steps in my head.

Pinky. Elbow. Run.

That's not too hard.

"Are you ready?" he questions.

I nod and he doesn't hesitate, yanking his arm around me tighter. Panic sears through me but I stick to my list of instructions. Gripping onto his pinky, I yank it back, and as his hand comes free from my mouth, I slam my elbow into his stomach, knowing Roman can take the hit, despite being shot through the waist only a week ago.

He releases me and doubles over with a slight cringe. He was prepared, though had I caught him off guard, I'm sure I could have winded him.

With Roman off me, I race forward and stumble right into Levi's arms. He catches me and fixes me to my feet, gripping onto my shoulders and holding my stare until he knows that I'm alright. "You good?" he questions.

"Yeah," I say, letting out a hard breath. "Questions like that are only going to ensure that you're left with blue balls. How did that go by the way? Did you take a cold shower or were you forced to spend the next twenty minutes going ham on your cock because nothing felt quite as good as me?"

Levi shoves me back at Roman. "Go again. She's fine."

Roman scoffs and catches me, gripping my arm and putting me

back into position. "Alright, this time, there's no warning. One second you're dancing with your friends at the club, the next second, you're being dragged away, okay? I want you to react on instinct, and this time, pinky and elbow at the same time."

Roman backs up a few steps, taking his place behind me so that I can't see him coming. He waits a few moments, letting it drag out to make it more spontaneous, then all too quickly, he's there, snapping his arm around my throat like a fucking psychopath. He immediately drags me backward, just like he would if he were on the hunt.

Forgetting all about the pinky, I slam my elbow back into his stomach, much harder than I had before, and as he eases up on my throat, my fist flies straight down, cracking him right between the legs.

Roman drops to his knees, releasing me in mere seconds before falling forward and catching himself on his palms. "Holy fuck," he grunts, blowing out his cheeks before slowly letting out a slow breath. "That wasn't part of the plan."

I cringe, feeling a little sorry for the guy, but then, he also held me down and tortured me so there's that. "Sorry, I panicked," I tell him. "But at least I got free, right? That's cool."

Roman shakes his head. "Not. Part. Of. The. Fucking. Plan."

"You have no one to blame but yourself," I tell him, pride swirling deep inside my stomach at being able to evade one of the famous DeAngelis brothers. "It felt too real. You didn't tell me you were going to start dragging me away. I wasn't prepared."

"What can I say?" he grunts, "Dragging unsuspecting women around by their throats is one of my favorite things to do. I got a little carried away."

I shrug my shoulders. "Innocent mistake," I tell him, eager to keep going. "Get up. Let's go again."

Roman holds his hand up and waves me off. "Levi. You're up, man. I just need a minute … maybe two."

I turn to look back at Levi and he scrunches up his face. "You're not going to nut punch me as well, are you?"

"Who knows? It's all part of the thrill, don't you think?"

Levi sighs and steps in closer. "Fine," he says, his tattoos peeking out from the neckline of his shirt, daring me to bite them. "But we'll try something different. We've got a lot to cover."

The next hour flies by with the boys teaching me everything they know about evasion techniques, but to be completely honest, they're a bit rusty as they're not usually the ones who need to do the evading. Roman and Levi show me what they want me to do, sometimes demonstrating on me and other times using each other. Only when they use each other, there's a subtle brutality that goes with it that tells me their normal training sessions are anything but gentle. Every now and then, Marcus throws his two cents across the room, and because he's not standing here in front of me, the boys swiftly ignore it for their own advice, which only serves to infuriate the devilish god across the room.

As time ticks by, it gets easier to focus, easier to accept the feel of their touch on my body and their general closeness. Only that all goes to hell when Roman comes at me with a surprise attack, grabbing my body and throwing me down to the soft-fall training mats. My back slams flat against the ground and he comes down on top of me, his weight pinning me to the ground.

A terrified scream comes tearing out of me before I even know what happened, and after a short moment, I will myself to breathe. "Not going to hurt you," he reminds me, his dark eyes unapologetically piercing into mine, demanding me to focus. "Get yourself free."

Swallowing hard, determination crashes through me like a wave and I give it my all, fighting him off me as he holds me down, his skill way too advanced for my limited knowledge. Had we been out at a club and he'd been an attacker with less than respectable intentions, I would have been fifty shades of fucked.

He doesn't ease up and I hear Levi close by, instructing me on what to do as Marcus roars from across the room giving me conflicting demands. Frustration quickly weighs me down and my moves become sloppy, slow, and predictable.

Hopelessness floods me and just when I'm about to tap out and admit defeat, the two massive wolves come bounding through the open door of the training room. They race toward me, their ferocious snarls echoing through the room as they bare their teeth.

My eyes bug out of my head as they run with lightning speed, barely giving me a chance to scream before they're surrounding us. "Fuck," Roman grunts, pulling himself up higher and curling his arms around my face, keeping me buried beneath him and protecting me from their vicious attack, certain that these wild animals have finally cracked.

I hear Levi moving in closer as the wolves' snarls continue. They come in by my head, standing over me and as Roman slowly pulls up off me, his brows marred with confusion, I realize that it's not me the big wolves are snarling at. It's Roman, and fuck, they're not happy about the way he's holding me down.

Roman pulls back off me, raising his hands to show his innocence and as he gets up, the wolves move forward on either side of me, forcing themselves between me and Roman.

"The fuck is going on?" Marcus questions, somehow now right by my side. He grips my arm, and despite his injuries, he's able to tear me right up to my feet in one swift move.

I shake my head, having absolutely no idea. "I … I don't know," I say, watching as they bear down on Roman, ready to tear him to shreds. "I thought they were loyal to you. They don't even like me that much."

Roman scoffs. "They don't," he says. "But they're still wild animals. They're loyal to no one but themselves. Something must have happened in the last twenty-four hours because when I left last night, they had no issue with me."

I shrug my shoulders. "I don't know. I fed them your lunch and filled up their water bowls, but apart from that, I haven't done anything."

Roman sighs, his body relaxing just a little. "Fucking hell," he mutters. "They're going to protect the hand who feeds them, and seeing as though you gave them a gourmet fucking meal, they're all about the Shayne show. Congratulations, you've stolen my wolves out from under me. Now call them off."

My eyes bug out of my head. "What?" I shriek. "How the hell am

I supposed to do that?"

"Your wolves," he says. "Your problem."

I clench my jaw, his irritating attitude completely fucking with my mood. Hell, perhaps I should let them go, teach him a lesson or two, but unlike the boys, I don't have that brutal nature inside me. Though, that doesn't explain why I enjoyed that visit to their uncle's property the other day.

Letting out a sigh, I snap at the wolves. "Oi, assholes," I demand, my tone full of authority. They react immediately, their snarls halting as they glance back at me. "Cut the shit." Without another word, they back off, releasing Roman from their hold before pressing out of here like they haven't got a care in the world.

I gape after them in amazement. Do I really have my own pack?

"What the fuck just happened?" I murmur as the familiar sound of cars barreling down the driveway fill the room, instilling the kind of fear into my chest that only ever comes when Giovanni is about to pull some twisted shit.

"Fuck," Marcus says, frustration washing over him. "The wolves are the least of our problems now. Guess Father has come to collect. Our week of freedom is officially over."

CHAPTER SIXTEEN

The front door swings open and I watch with distaste as four armed guards storm into the foyer, their guns locked and loaded, acting like a bunch of over-privileged SWAT assholes. They circle the foyer, one of them always with their eyes on Giovanni's three sons, who do their best to look bored of their performance.

"Don't fucking move," one of the guards says, moving directly in front of the three boys and holding his gun out at them as the others continue searching for threats. I scoff and lean back against the wall, crossing my arms over my chest. How ridiculous do these guys have to be to leave just one guard to watch over the three brothers? By the time he could get one shot off, the other two brothers would be bearing down on him, making him regret every decision he ever made.

It's a joke, and Giovanni was a fool to approve this shit, unless he enjoys watching the way his sons so effortlessly take out his guards.

The three other guards return a moment later. "It's clear," they say into their tiny little radios resting on their shoulders, making me laugh. They really did go all out for this special occasion. Though, I guess their last encounter with Roman out in the driveway didn't exactly go as planned. They need every advantage they could possibly get.

Not a moment later, Giovanni comes barging through the front door with another six guards and I roll my eyes as he steps into the foyer and instantly looks at his sons in disgust. "Sons," he says, raising his chin as the guards fan out around him. "I assume seven days was a satisfactory time to complete your task. We'll retire to the dining hall. I have some questions regarding your cousin, Antonio, and the other … things you've been up to during your week. Following that, you will show me to this motherfucker who's been undercutting me and I will take it from there."

Roman straightens, stepping forward to take point on this, and knowing all too well that he doesn't have anybody to hand over, he plays along. "Of course. Let's not waste any time."

Roman turns on his heel and begins stalking toward the massive dining hall as the guards follow suit, not allowing him out of their sight for even a moment, but when Marcus and Levi don't move a muscle, I find myself grinning. They're too fucking sneaky, separating themselves and forcing the guards to break apart. It's a clever move, one that they should have seen coming.

A guard comes face to face with Levi, a forced sense of authority poorly masking his fear. There's a familiar glint of mischief in Levi's eyes, like the excited look of a child on Christmas morning. "Move," the guard spits, jamming his gun right into Levi's stomach and staring him down. That look would have me dropping to my knees, but not Levi.

Levi grins, tilting his head to the side in that way I used to find scary as hell, only now it does nothing but turn me on. "Say please," he taunts, knowing the guy doesn't have the guts to pull the trigger.

The guard clenches his jaw and just as he's about to cause a much bigger scene, Giovanni pushes him out of the way. Without missing a step, he curls his fingers into the front of Levi's shirt and pulls him in until his face is mere inches away from his son's. "I'm not here to fuck around," he growls, his tone so low that I feel the vibrations right through my chest. He shoves Levi hard in the direction that Roman had just disappeared. "Get your ass moving."

Levi laughs and after a pause, takes pity on his old man and starts walking. "Always a pleasure, Father," Levi calls over his shoulder. "Always a fucking pleasure."

Marcus laughs and glances down at me before lifting his chin, silently indicating for me to follow Levi. I don't skip a beat, trailing after him as Marcus falls in behind me, not allowing my back to be unprotected at any time. Marcus walks with his head held high despite the pain he must be feeling inside, but he won't dare let on that he's been injured, especially with so many other men in the castle.

Giovanni follows us with his men, and as we walk into the massive dining hall, I find Roman already sitting back in his favorite spot, his gaze locked in a venomous stare on his father.

The guards fan out around the room and glancing back at Marcus, he gives me a pointed stare—a cold reminder that when in the presence of Giovanni DeAngelis, I would be smart to be seen and not heard.

I nod and walk around the massive table, putting myself against the wall behind where Roman sits, the furthest position away from Giovanni with almost one of the quickest escape routes through the adjoining kitchen door.

I keep a sharp eye on Giovanni, just as his sons do, not one of us trusting him in the slightest. He strides forward and takes a seat at the massive table as though he has every right to be there. Fuck, he even acts like his sons are the ones intruding on him. His arrogance knows no bounds, and it only serves to piss me off more.

"Antonio," Giovanni says, his gaze sweeping across the room, locking on each of his sons. "What do you know of his murder?"

I suck in a breath, my heart leaping right out of my throat as I do everything I can to not let on that I know anything about it. Fuck, if Giovanni thought for even a second that I knew anything, I'd be tortured for information, and damn it, I would break like a fucking twig. I can't go through something like that again. Nerves flicker through me, but taking in the boys' carefree expressions, I do what I can to relax and act cool.

Roman raises his chin, his gaze narrowing on his father's. "I've already explained it to you," he says, "Toni had been fucking around with Monique for three years. Ronaldo was bound to find out at some point, but good fucking riddance. It's about time someone got their claws into that little snitch. I'm just pissed that Ronaldo beat me to it. I would have cherished every moment alone with that asshole."

Marcus scoffs from across the room, slicing his sharp gaze to his older brother. "Not if I got to him first."

Giovanni slams his hands down on the table. "This is not a fucking joke," he roars, his voice traveling right through the whole fucking castle.

"Sounds like a fucking joke to me," Levi mutters, throwing caution to the wind.

Giovanni stands, his chair flying back in his show of rage. "Do you have any idea of the consequences that will come of this? If Ronaldo killed your cousin, war is guaranteed. Your uncle will not stop until Ronaldo's head is in his hands."

The two wolves come barging through the doors of the dining hall. They pause by the entrance, their sharp stares traveling around the room, and judging by the way their fur stands at the back of their necks, they can more than read the tension.

Dill and Doe's stare comes back to me, and without question, they make their way through the room, the guards flinching with every padded step. They drop their furry asses on either side of me and I swallow hard, hating how Giovanni watches them and takes note of whatever this new protective relationship is that they have over me.

Doe's head comes right up to my chest as she sits beside me and nudges me with her side, a silent message that she's got my back. I shift beside her, concealing my hand as it knots into her thick black fur, needing her comfort more than I could have known.

"Damn, Father," Roman says, his head tilting again, taking the attention off me and the wolves while getting back to the riveting conversation. "It almost sounds like you wish we were the ones to have taken his life."

Giovanni lets out a frustrated huff and falls back into his seat, his heavy gold bracelet clanging against the table. "I almost do," he spits. "Your uncle would come for you, but he's too weak. He'd never survive it and it would end there. But once my brother takes Ronaldo's life, there's no stopping the chain of events that will follow. This will be the start of the end. The DeAngelis family will dwindle until there's no one left."

What. A. Fucking. Shame. It's almost as though they planned it that way. How strange.

Power flourishes deep inside my chest and I have to force myself not to grin like a fucking psychotic witch at the mere thought of the DeAngelis family tearing themselves apart from the inside out.

Levi sits back in his chair, sipping on a whiskey. "Just say the word, Father. We'd more than happily intervene. You know we've got the power to stop it right in its tracks. All it would cost you is our indefinite freedom."

Fear flashes in Giovanni's eyes before he calls on every ounce of control within himself and covers it up like every murder he's ever committed. "No," he growls, his tone low and threatening, knowing exactly what his sons' freedom really means for him. "That's out of the question."

Roman laughs. "Let me get this straight. You'd prefer to risk a civil war and lose three quarters of your family, destroying your kingdom than free your only sons? Are you *that* scared of us, Father?"

"Hear me and hear me well," Giovanni spits through his teeth. "I do not fear you. You're a bunch of lost little boys who don't know where to draw the line. No, I don't fear you, I despise you."

Tension rises in the room and the wolves both stiffen at my sides. My hand knots tighter into Doe's fur as I do everything I can to shrink back and melt into the wall behind me. A showdown with the most senior member of the DeAngelis family is not somewhere I want to be. Hell, these wolves better be prepared to get my ass out of here Jacob and Renesmee style, otherwise, I'm fucked.

I watch the boys closely, keeping my stare locked on each of them, terrified of this becoming a bloodbath, but they each just sit still, looking far too relaxed, but that means nothing around here. These brothers have the uncanny ability to go from zero to a hundred in the blink of an eye.

The silence thickens and I watch the moment that Marcus decides he's had enough. His eyes sharpen as the corner of his mouth pulls into the smallest smile that anyone else in this room wouldn't be able to see. I hold my breath, the unknown weighing down on my shoulders as he clutches his knife, and with a practiced, awe-inspiring skill, launches it across the room.

I gape at the blade, my eyes widening in horror as it sails cleanly through the air before cutting right in front of Giovanni's face, slicing the very top layer of thin skin that rests on top of his nose. The knife doesn't stop, hurtling through the air until it finally comes to a plunging halt in the wall, the elegant handle protruding just mere inches from one of the guards' faces.

Silence fills the room and it's so damn loud I could hear a pin drop against the exquisite tiles. Levi watches his father with a keen eye as blood pools at the surface of his skin, dripping from the tip of his nose as Roman clenches his jaw, pissed at Marcus for pulling such a stupid stunt.

My heart thunders wildly in my chest as the guards prepare themselves, but Giovanni just holds up a hand, a silent message to wait as his stiff gaze rests on Marcus. I swallow hard. I've already been through the fear of thinking he was dead, and though I could probably hear his heart beating in this heavy silence, something deep inside my gut tells me he's already a dead man.

Giovanni stands and takes a napkin before making a show of wiping the drop of blood from the tip of his nose. He drops the stained napkin to the ground and I watch in horror as he slowly walks toward Marcus, putting himself directly behind him. Marcus fixes his stare on Roman, and I have no doubt that if Giovanni tries anything, one quick nod from Roman would see Marcus ending his father's life.

Giovanni's hand twists around the front of Marcus' throat and squeezes tight as his other hand trails down the front of his chest, only stopping when his hand is directly above the healing stitches. Then without warning, his hand constricts, squeezing the flesh below. "That was a bold move," Giovanni seethes as Marcus keeps his stare on Roman, not even flinching despite the world of pain he must be enduring.

My heart aches, breaking into a million tiny pieces as Dill growls on my right, his teeth bearing in anger. Giovanni glances at the wolf before smirking and finally releasing his hold on his son, leaving the front of his shirt stained with blood, but all that matters is how the hell he knew. The boys sure as fuck wouldn't have said a word to their father about the shooting, and I know I haven't … so who?

Giovanni laughs as he remains way too close to Marcus for my liking. "Now, onto business. Where the fuck is this manufacturer?"

"I have a better question," Levi states, standing to the same height as his father and leaning forward, resting his knuckles against the big oak table. He keeps his venomous stare on his father. "Tell me again where my mother is?"

Giovanni watches him for a long moment, his brows furrowing. "She's buried in the DeAngelis family tomb on my property, just where she's always been. Why would you ask me that?"

"Really?" he questions. "We haven't been down there for a while. Perhaps at your next business dinner we'll pay her a visit. I do wonder what we might find."

I hold my breath, my gaze snapping right back to Giovanni who just stares, understanding dawning in his lifeless eyes. "Where's my manufacturer?" he demands, refusing to comment on the woman locked in a freezer at the top of this very castle, the woman who was supposed to be his everything, his wife, and the mother of his children. I can only imagine how she died. I bet it wasn't a great life, filled with misery at his abusive hands. She would have been property to him, just as I'm supposed to be to his sons.

Roman stands along with Levi. "You see, that's just the thing,"

Roman says, a smirk playing on his lips. "We don't have your manufacturer."

Giovanni looks taken back. "What did you just say to me?"

"You heard me. We don't have him. Don't know who he is. Don't know where to find him. Don't even really care to be perfectly honest with you."

Giovanni grips onto a knife that lays like a welcome weapon on the table and jams it deep into the polished oak. "I gave you a week to find that bastard and you're telling me you failed? What the hell have you been doing all this time?"

Roman shrugs his shoulders. "Been busy," he says. "I've had other scores to settle. Kinda ran out of time to care about your problems."

Giovanni yanks the knife out of the table and throws it at Roman. My heart stutters in my chest as his hand shoots up with impossible speed, catching the blade between his pointer and middle finger mere inches from his eyes.

A gasp tears from my throat as Giovanni roars while his sons simply stare at him like a child having a tantrum. I guess that's exactly what's going down as they prove for the millionth time that he has lost all control over them. Only he'll continue with his extravagant displays at his business dinners because once the rest of the family knows their most dangerous and lethal weapons have minds of their own, they'll all run for the fucking hills.

He makes his way back to his seat but remains standing, leaning on the table much in the same way that Levi does. "What do you know?" he spits, the rage in his eyes like nothing I've ever seen before. "You said you found a dealer."

"That's right," Roman says with a slight nod. "A dealer whose loyalties to his boss far outweighed his fears of you. He didn't speak, didn't even crack."

Giovanni shakes his head, confusion marring his eyes. "That's not possible, even the most feared men break at the idea of the DeAngelis name." He begins pacing the floor as Dill grows bored by my side and trots off toward his water bowl.

Marcus catches his movement and glances down at the wolf, his eyes narrowing in suspicion before glancing back at me. "What the fuck did you do to their water bowls?"

My eyes bug out of my head. What the fuck does he think he's doing bringing this up and drawing attention to me like this?

"It's …" I start, swallowing hard as Giovanni's gaze swings toward me, irritation deep in his eyes at speaking in his presence. "I, umm …" Fuck. I let out a shaky breath and muster up the courage to find my voice. "Enough was enough. The wolves needed names, so that's what I did."

Marcus narrows his gaze on me. "Dill and Doe?"

I nod. "Yes, Dill and Doe. The infamous Dill Doe wolves."

Roman gapes at me, his eyes going wide. "You stole my fucking wolves out from under me and then had the fucking audacity to name them after a fucking silicone cock?"

I shrug my shoulders and glance back at the wolves who look so damn happy to have the attention on them, hell Dill is even raising his head up and showing off his incredible pedigree and shiny coat.

"I ain't sorry," I grin, holding back a laugh. "You should have named them when you had the chance. What's done is done. Besides, it's written in sharpie and they like it. They've accepted their names and now there's no going back."

"ENOUGH ABOUT THE FUCKING NAMES," Giovanni roars. "WHY IS THIS LITTLE WHORE STILL ADDRESSING YOU LIKE SHE HAS RIGHTS IN YOUR HOME?"

Marcus stands, making three for three and sending a wave of nervousness through the guards as he turns his ferocious glare on his father. "Because she does, and one day, she's going to fucking rule over the world you created. Watch your back, Daddy Dearest. Shayne isn't the little bitch you thought her to be. She's a fucking goddess."

Well, fuck.

Giovanni looks back at me and what I see buried deep in his eyes is enough to send anyone to their grave. He pushes off the table and slowly walks around it, stalking me like a fucking predator as his sons are left to do nothing but watch. He puts himself right in front of me and I don't miss the way that Roman shifts, discreetly stepping closer to his father.

"You're nothing," Giovanni spits at me, slowly moving even closer until I can smell his revolting breath hitting my skin. "I will end you one of these glorious days. Mark my words, girl. I will destroy you."

A chill sails down my spine and as he leans in even closer and I close my eyes, mentally preparing myself for the worst, Levi's flat tone rumbles through the room. "It's a rival family," he says, making his father flinch and spin around to take in his son, holding his stare and demanding an explanation. "The manufacturer. It's the only thing that makes sense. It has to be another family moving in. Why else would the dealer be too fucking scared to break? He wasn't from around here, he didn't know."

Giovanni moves away from me, his eyes going far away, deep in thought as I let out a breath. Roman captures my gaze for a moment, silently checking on me and I nod, despite not really being sure.

"Another family?" Giovanni states, the seed planted perfectly in his mind. "Who?"

Roman shakes his head. "Moretti family," Roman suggests. "They've been known to dip their fingers into our business in the past. What's to stop them from trying it again?"

"No," Giovanni says. "Gia Moretti is a fucking bitch, but she's not stupid. She wouldn't dare."

Giovanni goes quiet, thinking about what he just said, and as the seconds tick by, his jaw clenches tighter. "FUCK," he roars, his hands curling into fists at his side. He glances back at his guards and just like that, he storms out of the dining hall, his men following behind him like a bad smell and finally putting this shit show to rest.

"So," Marcus says, his gaze traveling to me before dropping to the wolves. "You really had to name them that?"

I shrug my shoulders. "It was either that or Ball and Sack. The options were hard but I think I made the right decision in the end."

CHAPTER SEVENTEEN

Roman reaches across the table, gripping the bottle of whiskey and bringing it straight to his lips as he drops back into his seat. "Fuck, I hate that bastard," he says as we hear the familiar sounds of the front door slamming behind his father's henchmen. He takes a long pull of whiskey before lowering the bottle, only to throw it across the room and listen as it smashes against the drywall.

Levi grumbles, dropping back into his seat. "Well, there goes the fucking whiskey," he says, left with no choice but to reach for the bottle of bourbon.

I let out a sigh and walk across the room, grabbing a few napkins as I go. I scooch my ass back onto the table in front of Marcus and dangle my legs on either side of him. His strong hands grip my thighs, thinking he's about to get lucky, only to groan as I reach for his bloodied shirt and pull it over his head.

"Shit," I mutter, seeing the mess his father left behind. I immediately get to work, pressing the napkin against his wound, trying to control the bleeding. "I think these are going to have to be restitched."

Marcus glances down and lifts my hand off his chest to see the mess below. "Damn it," he mutters to himself, confirming my suspicions and prompting Levi to get up and walk across the room. He pushes through to the kitchen, returning a moment later with a small first aid kit in his hand.

Levi moves in beside me and grabs Marcus's chair before spinning him around to face him. "Here," he says, handing him the bottle of bourbon. "You're gonna need this."

Marcus takes the bottle and lifts it to his lips. "How the fuck did he know?" he questions, his eyes narrowed to slits as he gets lost in thought.

"I was wondering the same thing," I tell him as Levi uses the table beside my ass to set up a surgical space. "It doesn't make any sense. I doubt any of you guys happened to mention it in passing, and I sure as fuck haven't spoken to him. So, how would he know? Does he have cameras? Has he been watching us?"

Roman shakes his head. "No, if that fucker had cameras in here, he would have killed us a long time ago."

"Then what?" I question, glancing over my shoulder at Roman as Levi gets to work, bypassing the whole numbing thing.

Roman's lips press into a hard line and for a moment, his eyes go jet-black. "The hooded bitch," he says. "Who else?"

My gaze shuffles back to Marcus and his dark eyes tighten, knowing exactly what's on my mind, but before he gets a chance to stop me, the words come spilling out of my mouth. "Marcus thinks it was Felicity but he's too much of a bitch to tell you."

Levi's hand pauses over Marcus' chest and Roman just stares, looking like a fucking avenging angel. Marcus sighs, realizing just how big the can of beans is that I just spilled all over the floor.

Roman stands, his eyes glued to mine as venom begins pulsing through his veins. "What the fuck did you just say?"

I turn on the table, angling myself between the three brothers. "Stop acting like I said it just to fuck with you. You heard what I said."

"Felicity is dead," he says, the anger bubbling in his tone. "I watched her die before my fucking eyes. I held her as she took her last breath and now you want to come to me with this shit, trying to tell me that the woman carrying my baby is the whore who shot my fucking brother?"

I shrug my shoulders and press my lips into a tight line. "What if she didn't die?"

"She was dead, Shayne. I've killed more people than you could even imagine. I know the fucking difference between dead and alive. I've replayed that moment over and over again. She's fucking dead."

I swallow hard, glancing back at Marcus who's gone awfully quiet. "The woman who shot Marcus had dirty blonde hair. I could see it peeking out from under the hood, so her hair was long. She was shorter than me, slim and I could tell by her voice that she's been through some shit. She referred to you all as 'mine' like she had a personal relationship with each of you. She told me to run because she didn't want what happened to her to happen to me. It just … you have to see it like I do. Who else could it be? Is there some other girl you've hidden away, someone else who you've not told me about?"

Levi shakes his head. "There was no one else. At least, no one else who we were all close with. There have been plenty of girls."

"All of which are buried out in the woods," Roman mutters, his mind clearly swarming with grief.

"What if it is, though? What if she's been out there this whole time?"

Roman stands, leaning onto the table and shooting a hard glare at me. "You're not fucking listening," he says. "How could it be Felicity? I watched her die in my arms. Five fucking months ago. She bled out on the ground beneath me. My knees were soaked in her blood and I felt the very moment she went limp in my arms. She stopped breathing. Her heart stopped beating. SHE. FUCKING. DIED. It's not her."

I swallow hard and glance back at Marcus. He could have been wrong. It could have been some other girl who thought she'd been done wrong by the DeAngelis brothers, who thought she had some ridiculous claim over them, but my gut is telling me to trust my instincts, to believe the impossible.

Realizing that now is not the time to push the topic, I let out a sigh and look back at Levi, watching as he skillfully dips the small needle into Marcus' chest and effortlessly makes the issue go away. "Who's Gia Moretti?" I ask, my gaze shifting back to Roman, making sure that he's doing alright after that bomb drop. "I thought the plan was to pin it all on Antonio."

"It is," he tells me, not taking his eyes off what he's doing as Marcus drains the bottle of bourbon. "All roads will eventually lead back to Antonio, but why can't we have a little fun before we get there?"

A grin cuts across my face and I shake my head, the amusement all too real. "So, who is she then? The boss' wife? She sounds hot."

Roman scoffs. "Gia is the fucking boss. She's the head of the Moretti family, not someone who you want to meet in a dark alley. She makes us look like child's play."

My eyes bug out of my head and I glance back at Marcus, waiting for him to tell me that Roman is fucking with me. But he raises his brow and nods, and damn, the sparkle in his eye tells me he's not just impressed by this woman, but he's got a little crush.

"Well, shit. Isn't she going to be pissed that you put the blame on her for this shit?"

Roman shrugs his shoulders. "Probably," he says, something dark flashing in his eyes as he pulls out another bottle of whiskey from under the table, instantly making Levi's brows draw down in irritation. "There are two things people like us hate. Not being acknowledged for our … *achievements* and being blamed for someone else's."

"So, doesn't this mean that she'll come for you then?"

Marcus scoffs. "Nah, not Gia. She's got her heart set on my father so she'll go after him before coming for us, but she likes to bide her time. He'll be dead before she gets her chance, and we'll already be rising up. I wouldn't be surprised if she changes her tune. She's a smart woman. She knows what's good for her. She'll keep out of our way and we'll honor her by keeping out of hers."

Letting that sink in and wanting to give Levi space to work on Marcus, I scoot off the edge of the table and make my way around to Roman before dropping down into the seat beside him.

He narrows his gaze at me as I reach forward and grab an apple out of the fruit basket. I take a big bite and glance back at him to find his stare still heavy on me. "What are you doing?" he questions, liking his space more than anything.

Swallowing my bite, I glance back at Levi and Marcus to find them already lost in a private conversation, probably trying to work out a screwing schedule between themselves that will keep all parties involved as satisfied as ever.

Turning back to Roman, I let out a sigh and allow myself to be vulnerable for just a moment. "I, uhhh … I didn't mean to get under your skin or bring up bad memories when I said that thing about Felicity being the one to … you know. I just wanted you to know where my head was at," I explain. "Marcus mentioned it to me when we got back from visiting Antonio, and it's just circled my head a few times since then. I just think if she were still alive, all arrows would point toward her."

Roman shakes his head. "You don't think that I spend every fucking waking hour of my life wishing she were still alive? Fuck, Shayne. You've got no fucking clue, do you? Get the idea out of your head. She was good and honest. The last thing she would have ever done was hurt Marcus. You don't know what you're talking about."

I nod and slowly slide my hand across the table until my pinky finger is pressed up against his, knowing that after what he did to me, I shouldn't feel guilt for bringing up something so painful, but I do. It's there and it's killing me that he's hurting. "Like I said, it wasn't my intention to bring it up to hurt you. I just needed to talk out the theory because I knew Marcus wasn't going to."

Roman pulls away from me as though my touch physically hurts him and everything inside of me breaks. For the past week, it's been the opposite way around; me flinching every time he gets close to me, and while the circumstances are very different, I kinda get it.

"I was planning on marrying her," he tells me, keeping his voice low. "Did Marcus tell you that? I had the ring and everything. All that was left to do was to propose and she would have been all mine. But I waited. I wanted to make it special for her. I wanted to wait until I could get her out of this fucking castle, so I foolishly went to my father, thinking for just one night, he would give us a pass to be free so she wouldn't have to sneak out of here like some kind of prisoner. I wanted it to be a night she couldn't forget."

I shake my head, already seeing the pain in his eyes at telling this story, and considering his brothers would have already known, I'm sure this is the first time that he's ever forced himself to say it out loud. "I got my freedom and had the ring in my pocket. I thought for once in my life, something was going right. She had my baby growing in her womb and I was about to give her everything she wanted."

Roman lets out a heavy sigh, the story taking a greater toll on him than I expected. "That night, just before we were due to leave, my father showed up and brought us right into this very room." He pauses, his gaze dropping to the table to where his hands ball into tight fists. "She was so fucking scared. She hated him, just like you do, but she didn't have the guts to stand up to him. She took his abuse as though she deserved it."

"What happened?" I murmur, my words getting caught over the lump in my throat as tears fill my eyes, his raw pain more than I can handle.

"He didn't approve of her as a wife, didn't think she was strong enough to be worthy of the DeAngelis name ... and the baby," he says, his voice breaking. "I never wanted a kid, never thought a baby would be in my future. My brothers and I made a pact as kids. The DeAngelis name was going to end with us, but this baby had other plans. He surprised the living shit out of me and opened my eyes. I went from never wanting a baby to living and breathing only for that unborn child. I was going to tear down my father just so that kid could have the childhood I was never given. I couldn't let what happened to me and my brothers be his future.

"My father showing up that night was the worst fucking thing that could ever happen to us. He didn't know about Felicity's pregnancy and the plan was that he never would," he says, his dark eyes briefly flashing back to mine before falling to his clenched fists again. "We were going to hide that baby until the day my father's heart stopped beating, but when he showed up and saw that tiny round bump, he couldn't take it."

Roman pauses, the memories too great, which is when I notice Levi and Marcus have fallen silent. I glance back at them and see them lost in their own heads, quietly listening to Roman's recap of the past as the haunting memories tear through them like poison in their veins.

A tear falls down my face and I suck in a gasp as I feel Roman's fingers against my cheek. "Don't cry, Shayne. Enough tears have already been spilled."

I swallow hard and pull back, wiping my hands over my face and drying my eyes. "He killed her right there in front of you, didn't he?"

Roman nods. "He gave me a choice. I could either save her life and my child's or I could save my own, and you better fucking believe that I handed myself over quicker than you could have imagined. Nothing was going to take my child's life and I knew my brothers would have followed through. They would have raised my son just as I would have. So my father ordered us into shock collars, then stepped in behind me and drew the sharpest dagger he had."

Roman stops, his fingers gently brushing over the angry, red scar that runs from the top of his brow, over his eyelid, and down to the top of his cheekbone. "I was ready to die, but my father didn't appreciate just how quickly I was willing to throw my life away for theirs. I was his soldier," he says, mimicking his father's tone. "He put too much time and effort into me, and all I'd done was prove to him just how weak I'd become. To love, is to be weak. He wouldn't waste my skill and his dedication on something like that, something so trivial. So, as a punishment, I got this scar, and she got a bullet right through the chest."

A loud gasp tears out of me and I gape at him in horror, my eyes wide as my chest aches, constricting as the pain tears through me.

"No," I breathe, the tears spilling down my face. Without thinking, I throw myself at Roman, my arms going wide before coming down around him. My ass falls into his lap as my face nuzzles into the crook of his neck. "I'm so sorry," I murmur, my tears staining his shirt. "I had no idea it was that bad. I never should have brought it up."

A soft, "I warned you," comes from across the room, and if I wasn't so busy holding Roman like he was my only salvation, I would flip Marcus off.

Roman stiffens beneath me and after a short pause, he relaxes and his arms curl around my body, holding me tight to his chest. "It's fine," Roman mutters. "You need to know because whether you like it or not, you could be faced with the same situation. You need to know what being here really means. Being close to us means you're right in the line of fire. Our father would do anything to control us, to hold something over our heads and force our loyalty, and when it comes down to it, because it will, he will go for you. It's a fact. There are no ifs about it. You need to be prepared."

I pull back and meet his eyes, having already come to terms with every last thing he just said. "I know," I tell him. "This isn't a game for me. Fuck, the scars on my body should be able to tell you that. I want your father's head for the terror he's rained down over the families of my town, over all the innocent lives he's hurt, over you and your brothers … over me. I don't want to be weak. I don't want to be seen as a joke. I want the whole DeAngelis family to fear the sound of my name, just as they fear yours. I want to be powerful like Gia Moretti, and you're going to make it happen."

Roman watches me and I don't doubt that Levi and Marcus are watching closely too. "You're sure about this?" he asks. "There's a big difference between being a tag-along and being a top fucking player. You will never sleep easy again in your life. Do you understand that?"

I nod, remembering the rush I felt as Antonio's life was taken away, the relief when the boys stepped out of the shadows to deal with Draven Miller, and the fierce joy and exhilaration when they dominate a room. I don't just want that, I crave it. I need it. This world is going to corrupt me in the worst ways, but I'm already too deep and there's no turning back now. "I know what I'm getting myself into," I tell him before glancing back at Marcus and Levi. "I want this. I want to be right there with you guys. I'm done cowering. I want to rise."

"Alright," Roman says, tightening his arm around my waist and pulling us both up to our feet. "Then get back to the training room. We have work to do."

CHAPTER EIGHTEEN

Darkness swarms through the Escalade as we fly down the city streets in the dead of night. "Where the hell are we going?" I question, gripping onto the holy shit bar as Roman hurtles over a speed bump like he's some kind of Formula 1 driver.

Marcus glances across at me, his hand pressed against his chest as though he's trying to keep his heart from falling right through the hole. He was too stubborn to admit he wasn't ready to come out tonight. He just had to be here with his brothers, though I see the frustration and pain hidden beneath his eyes. The asshole should be back in his stupid castle with his feet up, madly rubbing one out while he has the place to himself. But business is business and there's no fucking with that.

Idiot.

"You remember that night we went to the club to meet with our dealer?" Marcus questions.

Darkness floods my soul. "How could I forget? That was the night you guys let Lucas get to me."

Roman's hard stare snaps up to the rearview mirror, sending a venomous glare piercing right through to my soul. *"Let?"* he spits. "You think we *let* that happen?"

Letting out a heavy groan, I narrow my eyes back at him, making sure he can see my irritation clear as day, despite the darkness surrounding the Escalade. "You're a bigger idiot than I thought if you think for even one second that I think you allowed it to happen. I was there, remember? I know exactly how it went down. It's called a joke, Roman. Lighten up."

If looks could kill ... goddamn.

A smirk stretches over my lips. Nothing in this world makes me feel more alive than stabbing the knife straight through Roman's strong back and twisting it until he whines like a little baby. Just knowing how deep I am under his skin is my elixir to life. It's like an obsession I can't get enough of. But Roman is so much more than a human pin-cushion, and he proved that to me after his father's visit. No wonder he's so hard, so closed off and broken. I would be too if I'd suffered the way he had.

It begs the question; how the hell hasn't he struck out against his father yet? The brothers are notoriously impulsive. They're reckless and head-strong, yet the patience they have when it comes to their father's downfall is astronomical.

He holds my stare for longer than I can handle, forcing my eyes back to Marcus. Roman would prefer to drive right off the damn road than to be the first to tap out. "What were you saying?" I question, Roman having left my mind in a complete fog from his relentless, addictive stare.

"I was saying," Marcus continues, irritation thick in his tone from being disrupted in the first place. "Tonight, we're checking in with the last guy's replacement, see if he's got what it takes to work under us."

"And if he doesn't?"

Marcus raises a brow, his eyes glistening with a dark excitement. "Well, I'm sure you remember what happened to the last guy."

I swallow hard, hating the rush that rocks through my body. The last guy had cut the brothers short, stole a couple grand right from under them, and as a general rule, Roman, Marcus, and Levi are the only assholes around here allowed to get away with something so devious. He was shot before getting a chance to grovel for forgiveness. His acquaintance stepped up into the lead role with an added incentive that he would be rewarded if he could replace the money the other guy stole.

Nerves rest deep in my gut. It's only been a few weeks since then and the guy had no idea what his old boss was selling, only knew a handful of his customers, so luck isn't on his side. He's going to have to really work to move all the product and impress the brothers. I bet the guy has been shitting his pants ever since his meeting with us. I know I would be, but there's no denying it. He did this to himself. He raised his hand and volunteered to make a deal with the three DeAngelis devils.

"You don't think you've set the bar too high for this guy?" I ask. "How do you know he's going to come through with the goods? He told you that he didn't even know what his friend was selling and now he's got to somehow go out there and sell a whole bunch of that shit. I don't know …" I muse. "I think this guy is going to let you down."

Levi shakes his head. "He won't."

"How can you be so sure?"

Levi turns back to meet my stare just as Roman shoots toward the other end of the city and sends us in the direction of the roughest part of town. "Look where we're heading, Shayne," he says. "Anyone who lives out here has seen a thing or two in their lives. They have connections, all of them, and they know how to get what they need when they need it. This guy was putting on a show for us the other week. There's no way he didn't know exactly what his friend was dealing. He barely flinched when the guy got shot and was the first to raise his hand. This is his moment. He wanted this, so I have no doubt that he'll come through."

"Besides," Roman adds, his tone low and secretive as he meets my gaze in the rearview mirror again. "How could he possibly let us down when there's a pretty girl running the show?"

My brows furrow and I watch him for a moment, his true devilish nature shining through stronger and stronger by the second. "What's that supposed to mean?" I question hesitantly, my nerves flourishing deep in my gut until they completely take over.

"What do you think it means?" he says, his eyes glistening with darkness. "It's not even been twelve hours since you told us that you wanted to thrive in this world, that you wanted to be powerful. So, here's your chance to take the shot, Empress. It's not enough to learn how to shoot a gun or slit someone's throat, you need to prove to me that you have what it takes to run this fucking show."

I glance back at Marcus. Surely he's about to butt in and tell Roman that I'm not ready yet, that his suggestion is as fucked up as they come, but the motherfucker doesn't say a damn word. "You're kidding, right?" I demand, my voice hitching higher and becoming hysterical. "I can't do that. I don't even know what I'm supposed to say, or do ... or, fuck. This is way over my head here. You can't be serious. Are you insane?"

"So, what you're telling me," Roman continues, "is that you can't handle the pressure?"

That motherfucker.

My jaw clenches, the idea of Roman thinking I can't handle it instantly boiling my blood, and damn it, it leaves me absolutely no choice but to storm in there and somehow pull this off.

Fuck, does this make me some kind of gangster or ... what do they even call a dealer's boss? Is there a name for that apart from criminal? A drug lord perhaps? No, that doesn't seem to fit. An organized crime boss? A Kingpin? A narcotrafficker?

Shit, they all sound stupid.

Leaning forward in my seat, I curl my arm around the front of Roman's chest and pull it tight under his chin as he goes on driving like I haven't even moved a muscle. "Don't worry about me," I murmur, my voice low and deadly. "I can handle the pressure."

"You sure about that?" he questions, the pressure on his throat laughable as he pulls up outside a small, run-down property. "This is your one shot. What you do in there tonight will determine what kind of reputation you walk out with, a reputation that will follow you to the grave. If you fuck it up, you will be nothing more than a joke."

"The only joke I see around here is you," I tell him.

Levi chokes back a laugh before quickly righting himself, not in the mood to have his big brother's fist saying hello to his jaw. "What's it going to be, Shayne?" he questions, glancing across at me, watching me as I slowly ease up on Roman's throat.

I hold his stare for a moment before nodding, despite my every nerve ending telling me this is a terrible idea. "I've got this."

"Good," Marcus mutters with irritation, reminding me that he's still pissed I spilled the beans to Roman about his Flick theory. "We're here."

Ahhh, fuck.

My hands shake as they fall back into my lap and I glance out at the run-down property. There's an old wire gate across the front of the lawn that's definitely seen better days. Two of the home's windows are boarded up and it's hard to tell in the dead of night, but I'm pretty sure there's a line of bullet holes spanning the complete width of the home.

This isn't anywhere I should be, but I just had to go and stupidly declare that this was the life I wanted, and for once, I can't blame the brothers for the fresh hell that I'm about to endure.

My finger curls around the door handle and just as I'm about to pull the lever and push it open, I quickly realize that none of the guys are making a move to get out with me. I turn and gape at them, my eyes wide with horror. "You're not seriously going to send me in there by myself?" I question, my determination to do this only going so far. Without the threat of the brothers standing at my back, I'm just some stupid girl wandering into a madhouse and demanding all their cash. I'll never walk out of there alive.

"We weren't," Levi says, his brows arched in amusement. "We just figured you might want a few weapons first but, if you think you can do this all on your own, go right ahead. We'll be here waiting."

I narrow my glare at him, hating how blasé they're being about this, as though this isn't the biggest, most fucked-up thing I'll ever do. Maybe they forget that most kids aren't raised in the mafia, playing with guns and learning the best ways to slaughter their enemies. Don't get me wrong, I had a phase where I'd sleep with a knife under my pillow but that's about as far as it got.

I don't bother responding to his comment. What's the point? They all know what I think about that. Instead, I simply wait as Levi turns back around to the glove compartment and pulls out a small gun. He hands it to me and as he places the cool metal into my hand, I feel as though I suddenly have the weight of the world resting in the palm of my hand.

A sense of false power rocks through me, rattling me right to my core, but I do what I can to mask the unease. "Do you know what you're doing with that?" Marcus questions, looking at me as though he's worried I'm about to accidentally shoot him. Though, it's not him who should be worried.

I glance across at him, lowering the gun so I'm not pointing it at anyone. "I managed to shoot my father, did I not?" I remind him, the memory sitting uneasily in my mind.

Marcus grins. "You did," he says before gently shrugging his shoulders and musing to himself. "Not the shot I would have taken, but effective enough."

"What ever happened to him?" I muse, getting way off track to what I should be focused on.

"Never you mind about that," Marcus tells me, his eyes glistening with a fucked-up kind of darkness that tells me to back away from the topic like it could strike me at any given time.

My lips press into a hard line and I find myself glancing back up at Roman. "How is this supposed to go down?" I question, my voice lowering with a mix of nerves and embarrassment, feeling more than just out of my league and hating to have to admit that. "Do I just storm in there and start demanding what you're owed?"

"That's one way," he agrees, thoughtfully. "Messy, but dangerous. If you go in there, guns blazing, he's going to panic and get defensive, and when a motherfucker like that gets defensive, it's shoot first, ask questions later. You'll eventually get what you need, but it could be easier and done without causing bodily harm or putting yourself in a worse situation."

I arch a brow, wishing he would just tell me what I need to know. "Don't talk to me about worse situations," I mutter, my irritation starting to get the better of me.

"Cool, calm, and collected is how you want to approach this

one," he finally says, ignoring my jibe. "Take it easy. Go in there with confidence and don't allow him to rattle you. You're the boss and he's a fucking bitch hired to do a job. Take what's yours and don't allow him to see how fucking terrified you are."

My gaze drops away. "I'm not terrified."

He scoffs, his lips twisting into an amused grin. "Right."

Letting out a heavy breath, I pull myself together. "Alright. Let's do this. I want to get it over and done with so we can get out of here."

The boys don't hesitate and move into action. Roman cuts the engine as Levi and Marcus bail out their doors without a care in the world, making me desperately yearn for their confidence and carefree nature. Maybe it's the years of brutal slaughters and evasion that have resulted in these cold, hard, untouchable men, but whatever it is, right now, I wish I had a little bit of that magic.

By the time my fingers are curling around the door handle and I'm pushing it open, Roman is there, catching the door from the outside and watching me as I step out of the Escalade. He doesn't say a word and I'm grateful for that. I'm in the zone and I fear that one more 'you've got this' speech is going to send me running straight back into the safety of the Escalade and prove to them I'm nothing more than a fraud playing dress up.

The darkness surrounds the quiet street, sending a wave of silence over the area and something tells me that the people who live out here know when to stand up to defend a neighbor and when the hell to lock their doors and hide away. After seeing the black Escalade rolling down their quiet street, now would be one of those times.

Marcus unlatches the front gate and holds it open for me, allowing me to walk through first to take the lead. I give him a tight smile as I pass and the look in his eyes tells me he has all faith that I can do this.

A soft light shines from between the gaps in the boarded window and I hear the faint sound of hard metal thumping through shitty speakers as the singer screams about … fuck, I don't know what his lyrics are. His scream is like a cat wailing in the dead of night, impossible to decipher. But what it does tell me is that the guy we're meeting tonight is going to be prepared and ready the moment we walk in.

I stand front and center with the three devils from hell at my back, and as I step up to the old, ratty door and raise my fist to knock, Levi clears his throat. My fist freezes mid-air and I quickly look back at him to find him subtly shaking his head.

Right, of course. No knocking. Knocking isn't cool.

Instead, my hand falls to the doorknob, cringing as nerves rock through me. Then before I give myself a chance to bitch out, I give it a hard twist.

Nothing fucking happens.

"It's locked," I seethe, looking back at Levi in a panic.

"Then bust it down."

"I thought this was supposed to be cool, calm, and collected."

The corner of his lips pull up into a twisted smirk. "To an extent."

Letting out a frustrated breath, I back up a step and prepare to bust through this fucker, hoping I haven't already alerted the guy inside to our little visit. Though, if he hasn't noticed the Escalade sitting out front by now, then that's on him.

Taking a deep breath, I will myself to be able to bust down this door. It's not exactly something I've had any practice in, but I guess we all have to start somewhere. Leaning back, I muster up all my strength and just as I bring my foot up, Roman's hand falls to my shoulder. "Move out of the fucking way," he mutters, knowing my capabilities far better than I do.

Without another word, he moves past me and before I can even pretend to be annoyed with him, his foot comes up and slams through the old wooden door. He busts it into a million pieces and the hinges break clean off the frame and it's almost as though he's done this a thousand times before.

My brow raises, more than impressed. I wonder if the guys will set up a few doors in the castle that I can practice on.

Not wanting to waste this moment of surprise, I forge on through the small house, gagging as I'm hit with a foul smell. "What the fuck is that?" I spit.

Marcus grins, reminding me of that twisted psychopath I first met. "That, pretty girl, is the smell of your future." I gape at him, having absolutely no idea what he's talking about until he sighs and lets me in on the secret. "It's a decaying body. Someone got more than fucked up in here."

Gross.

"Move it," Roman mutters, his hand pressing into my back to push me ahead. "You want to find him before he finds you."

Fuck. Good point.

I get my ass moving, following the sound of the shitty, screaming heavy metal until I barge through to a small living room and get smacked in the face with a thick fog. I cough past the smoke, waving my hand in front of my face as I find a guy sitting on a couch, staring straight ahead, high as a fucking kite without a clue that we're even here, but he's not what's got my attention.

The guy I'd seen in the club stands over a bag of cash, furiously shoving it deep into an old duffle bag with nothing but horror written across his face. The boys' pills are spread out over the table in little piles of ten and I watch as the dealer grabs fistfuls of the pills and jams them in with the cash.

Barely a moment passes when the dealer's head snaps up and he takes us in. Relief crosses his features and his hands pause deep in the duffle bag. "Fuck," he breathes, sagging against the table in relief as my gaze sweeps over the rest of the room, searching for the decaying body, but I come up empty. "I thought you were the cops doing a raid."

I raise my brow and stride toward him as the boys hang back by the high dude on the couch. The dealer watches me, curiosity stretched across his face and I don't miss the way his gaze continuously flicks between me and the three imposing men by his living room door.

My gaze sweeps over the table and I trail my finger through the mess of scattered pills and cash that he didn't get a chance to bury in the bag. "Why would you think that?"

Seeing that the boys are leaving this little game up to me, he focuses all his attention on me. "Who else would have the balls to bust in here in the middle of the night? I wasn't expecting you guys to collect for another few days."

"Plans change," I mutter, having absolutely no idea what the original plan was in the first place. My gaze sweeps up from the table to meet his eye, and I do what I can to mimic the boys' cocky confidence and brutal stares. "It looks to me like you were attempting to run."

His eyes bug out of his head, fear rattling him at my suggestion, and damn, the power that rocks through me at being able to invoke that kind of reaction is like nothing I've ever felt. "No," he rushes out, his gaze snapping back to the three brothers. "I swear, I thought it was a police raid. I wanted to get all your shit out of here so they wouldn't take it. I haven't forgotten what you did to Julius when he couldn't deliver and that won't be me."

I walk around the table, getting uncomfortably close to the man and I don't miss the way Marcus flinches behind me, barely held back by Roman's hand. "Say that I believe you," I tell the dealer. "It looks as though you've got a lot of product still to move."

He nods. "True," he says, panic flourishing in his eyes. "But I have your money. All of it."

My brows furrow and I spare a glance at the boys, seeing the same confusion mimicked in their dark gazes. "How is that possible?" I question. I'm no math whiz and certainly wasn't any good in business studies during school, but I know the basics and this simply doesn't add up.

"Hear me out," the guy blurts, darting across the room and making me flinch toward the gun jammed in the back of my pants. He slams his hand over the light switch, rushing back to the old duffle bag and turning it upside down. As the contents spill out, half of it falls to the ground, and I feel the boys moving in for a closer look. Something tells me this isn't how their deals usually happen, but the boys say nothing as they wait for me to take the lead.

"Go on," I tell him as he desperately tries to separate the cash from the pills.

"I, uhh … I didn't mean to present this to you in quite a mess. I was planning on heading out tomorrow to get a briefcase like Julius had," he explains. "Like I said, I wasn't expecting you for a few days. I thought I'd be better prepared."

"Money is money," I tell him. "It doesn't matter how it is presented, as long as it's all there."

He swallows hard and drops his gaze back to the table. "So, uhh … I'm sure you know that I'm not the only dealer in town," he says, referring to the men that Giovanni would most likely have in place, selling exactly the same product, just with different branding. "I may have stolen his customers out from under him with a few little white lies and charged double, claiming it's a more potent pill, designed to get faster and longer results."

I raise a brow, unsure if that's cool with the guys, but I'm not going to lie, I'm impressed. "You consider yourself a businessman, huh?"

The guy swallows hard and nods. "Yeah, I mean … if that's okay. I didn't mean to step on any toes or change anything you guys had already implemented, but I got the feeling that I could do things how I liked as long as I got your money at the end of the day."

Glancing up at Roman, I catch his slight nod and I turn back to the dealer. "That's fine, as long as you're aware that undercutting Giovanni's dealers is not a smart move. However, you're responsible for your own business plan, so if and when they find out what you've been doing, that's on you. You will not get our protection, not unless it is earned and rewarded."

The guy nods and I can't help but get a goody-two-shoes vibe from him, wondering how the hell he got mixed up in this world in the first place. He seems so hard on the outside with his metal music, sharp jaw, and venomous stare. But he's got a smart business mind, and if the boys were hiring, this guy should be at the top of their list.

He nods. "That's fine. I understand."

"Right," I say, dropping my gaze back to the table. "Show me where you're at."

The dealer yanks the chair out and drops down into it before getting started bundling up the cash. Most of it has already been divided into groups so he's quick to count out the initial fifty grand that he owed the boys. "That's what you asked for," he says, sliding the pile toward me before sliding a much smaller one my way. "And that's the extra 2k that Julius owed," he adds, his gaze shifting toward Roman. "You mentioned that if I made up for that, there'd be a bonus."

Roman narrows his gaze, seeing so much more cash left on the table, and considering how many more pills he has to sell, I'd say the guy has earned it. Roman nods and just like that, the guy sighs in relief and turns his attention back to me. "There's an extra thirty grand, plus potential for another fifteen. I tend to sell a shitload more on a Friday and Saturday night, so I have enough to get me until then, but I'll need more product … you know, assuming you want me to keep selling for you."

I nod. "You've done well," I tell him, scooping up the first 52k and dumping it back into the duffle bag before scanning over the remaining cash and dividing it up. I push ten grand toward him. "Consider this your bonus for a job well done," I say before sliding him another five. "And this is your incentive to return the same figures at your next check-in."

The guy gapes up at me and considering the shithole he lives in, I can safely assume that fifteen grand is more money than he's ever been given. "You're fucking kidding me," he breathes, his eyes wide in disbelief.

"You do well for us, and we will reward you, but screw us over like your friend did, and you'll find yourself in a shallow grave. Is that clear?"

He nods furiously and I fear that his whole damn head will rock right off his shoulders. "Yes, ma'am," he rushes out. "I won't let you down."

Ma'am? Fucking hell.

"See to it," I say, grabbing the duffle bag and leaving him the remainder of the pills to move. "Expect to see a fresh batch of pills before the weekend," I tell him, not doubting for a second that the boys will most likely double up on his stockpile and run him until he's dry.

Without another word, I turn and walk out of the guy's home with my three beasts following my every step. My heart races, wildly thundering in my chest until we break out through the splintered front door. "What the ever-loving fuck was that?" I breathe, inhaling a deep breath of fresh air.

"Not bad," Levi tells me, taking the heavy duffle bag from my arm. "You presented yourself perfectly, though, I saw the nerves shining through like a fucking beacon, but I don't think he saw it. There's potential in you yet."

"Gee, thanks," I mutter, pushing my way out through the small gate.

"Don't get cocky," Roman tells me. "It doesn't always go down as easily as that. Next time, you might just be forced to put a bullet through someone's head."

I let out a shaky breath, still unable to believe that I just collected seventy-odd thousand dollars of drug money during a home invasion and walked out like I was invincible. "That was oddly intoxicating," I tell them, gripping the door handle and yanking it open as I turn back to the three brooding assholes behind me. "But you owe me a fucking drink."

CHAPTER NINETEEN

Stars dance across the night sky as Roman drives us back toward the city and away from the disaster zone that their new favorite dealer calls home. "Where are we going now?" I ask, giddy as the high from being such a bad ass still blossoms through my chest.

Roman scoffs. "Home. We've done what we needed to do."

My face twists with disappointment. "Seriously? We're going home?" I question. "That's lame. We should go out and celebrate. Tonight was awesome. No one died, I didn't see that decaying body, and I fucking rocked it. Besides, I recall telling you that you all owe me a drink and I expect payment sooner rather than later. No," I rush out, remembering that I don't take no for an answer, not anymore. "Now. I want payment now."

"Tough shit," Roman laughs, though his laugh doesn't seem so amused or genuine. "You can have a drink back at the castle. We've already broken our father's rules by being out tonight. There's only so much we can risk in one night without being caught."

"He's right," Levi says. "In just the drive over here, do you have any idea how many calls would have been made to the cops? We're wanted fugitives all over the country, on every fucking 'most wanted' list there is, a lot of them with shoot to kill orders. We can't stay out longer than necessary. Besides, have you ever been detained by the FBI? It ain't fun. It's not really something I plan on doing for a second time."

I let out a heavy groan, more than frustrated by their 'old man get home to bed by 7 pm' behavior. "Geez, for the most dangerous men on the planet, you sure know how to kill a woman's vibe. Aren't guys like you supposed to know a thing or two about having a good night? Because … and I don't mean this in a bad way, but you sound like a bunch of boring fucking assholes who are too scared of their daddy to break curfew."

Roman slams on the breaks as Marcus mutters a string of curses beside me, his jaw clenched and eyes hard. The Escalade comes to a screeching halt in the center of the city street, and had it been twelve hours from now, the city would have been packed with bodies.

Roman twists around in his seat, leaning through the center, and before my eyes even get a chance to bug out of my head, he's there, curling his thick fingers into the front of my shirt and yanking me into him. "The fuck did you just say?" he demands as I try to channel that cool, calm, and collected vibe from back in dodge-alley.

"You heard me," I tell him, proudly, not letting him hear the wavering in my tone. "You're too scared of Daddy to break the rules. Live a little, why don't you?"

"Utter those words to me again and I swear to fucking God, Shayne, I will break the jaw they come from."

"Then prove it," I challenge. "Take me out. Give yourself freedom and stop living by his rules. Do you hear sirens coming after us? Do you see the FBI creeping in around the corner? No. We're free. Tonight is ours to get fucked up and enjoy ourselves. When was the last time you got to do that?"

Roman's eyes narrow to slits as I hold his stare, willing myself not to break, and when we hear the familiar sound of Marcus lighting up a joint, his fingers loosen just enough for me to wriggle free. "The fuck are you doing?" Roman questions, looking at his younger brother.

Marcus takes a long, heavy drag and I watch as he blows out a perfect ring of smoke. "You heard the girl. She set down a challenge and I'm not one to pass up a good time. We're taking her to get fucked up DeAngelis style, and if she dies of alcohol poisoning, then that's on her. Let's give her what she asked for," he says before pausing to take another long drag. "I just need a minute to let this sink in. If I'm going out tonight, then I want to enjoy it … actually," he adds, glancing through the front to meet Levi's amused stare, "got any of those pills? I'm gonna need something a little harder."

"Get fucked," Levi says, grinning back at his brother at the idea of going out and getting fucked up like a bunch of rowdy teenagers. "You're not taking anything harder with the pain meds I already have you on. There's a fine line between getting fucked-up and fucked-over.

You ain't dying tonight, bro."

Roman scoffs. "No one is fucking dying because no one is fucking going."

"It's cool man," Marcus laughs, leaning forward to clap him on the shoulder. "Just drop us off and you can take your bitch ass home."

Rage burns in his eyes as he reaches back, grips Marcus by the arm, and pulls him forward just enough to clock the fucker right in the jaw. Marcus laughs louder as I fly back against the chair, determined to get out of the way if this somehow turns into an all-out brawl in the back of the car, but apparently, one punch is all Roman needs as he rights himself in the driver's seat. "You're asking for trouble."

Marcus rubs a hand over his jaw as Levi watches the show like it's prime time television. Hell, all he needs is a bowl of triple butter popcorn and he'll be right for the night. "Nah man," Marcus says. "We're asking for the freedom we've been deprived of for the last ten years. Make it happen, brother. Join the rebellion."

I shrug my shoulders, failing to hide my mischievous grin. "We could take a vote," I tease, knowing exactly how that would go. Roman glares at me through the mirror and I let out a sigh before scooching forward to the edge of my seat and leaning over the side of his. He watches me cautiously as the last time I did this, I shoved my arm around his throat and epically failed at choking him.

My arms drop over each of his shoulders, one hand dangling down his big frame as the other rests against his chest, feeling the rapid beat of his heart beneath. "Come on, big guy," I purr as my hand slowly roams over his wide chest. "When are you going to take back what's rightfully yours? Come out with us. We can even go to your favorite dive bar, or we can go find one of those assholes that you need to settle a score with; whatever helps you relax and have a good time. I won't even try to run from you guys. I just want to go out and have a good time. Then come tomorrow, everything can go back to how it was. I won't even whine when you come at me with your usual Roman bullshit."

His hand falls to mine over his chest and he holds it still as his thumb moves back and forth across my skin, but considering the way he still glares at me through the mirror, I doubt he even knows that he's doing it.

Silence fills the Escalade and the tension rises, everyone impatiently waiting for Roman's final decision. Though it's not like we wouldn't just go without him like Marcus suggested, but having him there would make it feel right.

Roman sighs and his hard gaze finally falls away from mine before focusing out the windshield at the empty city street. "Fine," he finally says, giving in. "But we're doing this my way."

His foot slams down on the gas and the momentum has me flying back in my seat, only Roman grips onto my hand, not letting me go for even a second. He speeds through the city and after only a few turns, Marcus and Levi seem to relax as though they know exactly where Roman is leading us.

The Escalade comes to a stop at a liquor store and as Levi goes to get out, I start listing off all the different kinds of things I need to get tonight going. Only after the fourth item, Levi looks back at me with a blank expression. "You don't expect me to remember all that, do you?"

I let out a sigh and pull my hand free from Roman's tight grip. I shove myself out through the door and tumble out onto the asphalt. "What the fuck do you think you're doing?" Levi hisses, looking around and double-checking that no one is about to come running out at us.

I look up at him, the confusion clear across my face. "What?" I demand. "Stop looking at me like that."

He shakes his head and grips my arms, pulling me in close beside him so that I don't somehow get away despite telling Roman that I wouldn't. "Someone might see you," he hisses, keeping his voice low. "You may have forgotten that you're supposed to be a kidnapped prisoner, but the rest of the world hasn't."

"Correction," I grin up at him, striding toward the liquor store. "The rest of the world thinks I was mauled to death by a bear. Besides, I was a nobody in that old life. Trust me, everyone has already forgotten who the hell I was."

Levi pulls me in closer and slips his hand into the back pocket of my jeans, getting a good handful of ass in the process. "Impossible, Shayne. No one could ever forget you."

Ten minutes later, I come striding out of the liquor store with a cheesy as fuck grin on my face as Levi walks beside me, a massive box of selections in his arms. Apparently, just choosing one is a lot harder than it sounds. Hell, Marcus and Levi are proof of that. I don't ever want to choose between them, but if they want to take me on at the same time, I won't have any issues with that either.

We get back in the car and within the next two minutes, Roman is bringing the Escalade to a stop once again. "Where the hell are we?" I question, glancing out at the empty city streets to see nothing but high-rise buildings around us. "I don't see any clubs or bars."

"We're not going to a club or bar," Roman says as Marcus grips the neck of the whiskey bottle and gets an early start on our little party. "You want to live on the edge, Empress, then that's what we're going to do."

Roman's gaze shifts up and my stomach drops as I follow his stare right to the very top of the highest building I've ever seen. "That's, ahhh … not exactly what I had in mind."

"It's the rooftop or nothing," he says. "I'm not risking putting either of my brothers in prison because of your need to get fucked up. So, which is it? We can go home, or we can go up."

"Up," I tell him, my lips twisting into an excited smirk as my fingers curl around the door handle. "Always up."

The boys follow my lead and within moments, we're bypassing the building's security and stepping into the dark elevator. "How the hell did you do that?" I ask, wishing we were able to turn on a few lights, but apparently that would draw too much attention. "The alarms should have gone off."

Levi grins as the elevator door closes behind us. "It'd be pretty fucked up if we couldn't get into our own goddamn building."

My eyes bug out of my head, but I doubt they'd be able to see it in this darkness. "You own this?" I sputter, thinking of how much a building like this would cost.

No one responds as the elevator sails up through the levels and my stomach does that weird twisty motion sickness thing that happens every time I get into one of these. The silence begins to kill me but, considering just how high this building is, I have a feeling that we're barely even halfway up.

The ride to the top takes at least a full minute before the door opens and the warm breeze forces its way inside. "Holy shit," I breathe, looking out into the night to see the wide expanse of city lights surrounding us. I step out of the elevator with the boys right at my side, gaping in awe. "I've never seen anything like it."

High-rise buildings surround us, but nothing is as tall as the one we're standing on. This has to be the biggest building in the city.

The breeze is relentless, but what else was I supposed to expect from a rooftop like this? I should just be grateful it's flowing against me, brushing my hair off my face instead of hitting me in the other direction and pushing me right off the fucking roof.

We make our way to the edge and I peer over the side, my heart racing in my chest. "This is literally the definition of insanity," I muse as Levi drops the big box of drinks and starts rifling around for what he wants.

I watch him with a keen eye, loving the soft glow of the city lights that brushes against his skin. It's simply stunning. All three of them are, and while I'll happily let both Marcus and Levi know exactly how I feel about their handsome, rugged appearances, I won't dare peep a word to Roman. Though … I think it's safe to say that he knows exactly what kind of effect he has over me.

I can't help but spread my arms out wide and close my eyes as the wind sails through my hair. "God. This is the freaking life," I breathe, channeling my inner Kate Winslet on the Titanic. "Doesn't this make you feel so damn free?"

The boys don't respond, but I know they're feeling it. Why else would they bring me up here?

We pass the bottles of hard liquor around and I show off my skills as I mix all my favorite drinks and fully relax for the first time in what feels like years. With the lack of food in my stomach, it doesn't take long for the buzz to sweep through my system and have me feeling like a fucking goddess on top of the world.

After taking another sip, I creep right up to the edge as I feel power pulsing through my veins. I've been on fire tonight and nothing can take that away. The breeze is my best fucking friend, and just as I feel as though I could fly, a body presses in behind me as a black blindfold comes down over my eyes.

A soft gasp pulls from deep within me and my hand flies back to his thigh, gripping tightly, terrified that one little wobble would have me truly flying over the edge. I've survived all odds over the past few months, but there are some things a girl simply can't come back from. My brains splattered all over the sidewalk is definitely one of them.

"What are you doing?" I breathe as hands slowly begin moving over my body.

"Shhhhhhh," he whispers, his low tone making it impossible to tell which brother is pressed against me. His hands tighten on my waist as his skilled lips fall to my neck, forcing a breathy moan from between my lips. My hand falls on top of his as it skirts across my body, slipping under the fabric of my tank and skimming over my skin.

Hoooooly shit. Am I about to get fucked up here?

Another hard body moves into my side, hovering over me with every intention of destroying me. My heart begins to race as excitement pulses through my veins. His hand falls to my thigh, slowly trailing up my leg until his thick fingers are dipping into the front of my pants and flooding everything below the border with the most brutal kind of need.

Now this is what I'm talking about. A girl can get down with their brand of crazy.

A soft gasp pulls from deep in my chest and I reach out to him, pressing my fingers to his tight abs. Neither of them say a damn word and it's impossible to tell which is which, but I'm so here for it.

His hand pushes deeper into the front of my pants just as the hands at my waist grip the flimsy fabric of my tank and tear it clean off my body, letting the warm night breeze slam against my bare skin. He doesn't waste a second releasing the fabric and letting it fly in the wind before his hands are sailing over my body, cupping my tits as his thumbs roll over my nipples, feeling as they pebble beneath his touch.

"Oh, fuck," I moan softly, tilting my head toward the skilled man at my side, needing to feel more of his brother's kisses on my neck.

The hands dip lower into my pants, skimming over my clit and making me jump. His thumb works tight circles over it as he continues to my entrance, slowly pushing two thick fingers deep inside me. A needy moan sails between my lips, telling them just how ready I am for a night of kinky rooftop fuckery.

A tight grip curls around my chin and rips my head in the opposite direction, and before I even know what's happening, lips crush down over my mouth. I sink into his kiss, loving the feel of his tongue slipping inside my mouth and taking ownership of my every desire.

Hands continue moving over my body, teasing my tits, working my clit, brushing past my ticklish waist, but as the kiss consumes me, I realize that there's more than just four hands.

Pressing my body back, I try to focus on what I feel around me. A hard chest at my back, tight abs to my left and … pressing my hand out to my right, a set of thick, strong thighs that could destroy a woman with one easy go.

What in the sweet baby Jesus is going on here? I must be imagining this. All three of them?

Holy fuck.

Marcus, Levi … and Roman's hands on my body giving me undeniable pleasure. Fuck, knowing my luck, Roman is probably sulking on the other side of the rooftop and I have the night security guard all kinds of chuffed that he gets to have a little fun while on duty.

No, they're too possessive to share with anyone else. It's definitely Roman. I just wish I knew which was which. All I need is for the breeze to change direction and I'll be able to smell their unique scents.

Nerves shoot through me but the blindfold helps. There are no expectations here. This is them making me feel, and damn it, I never knew I needed this so bad.

My ass grinds back and I feel just how hard he is at my back. Not wanting the others to miss out, my hands drop to the left and right, skimming over their impeccable bodies until I find the tops of their pants. I slip my hands inside and my eyes flutter closed beneath my blindfold as my fingers curl around two massive velvety cocks.

The hands at my back drop to the waistband of my pants and yank them down, forcing the fingers out of my pussy for only a moment as the material sails down my legs. They're pulled from my feet and I kick them away as I hear the familiar sound of a belt buckle being undone behind me.

My legs are kicked apart, spreading them wide, and without missing a beat, those same thick fingers are pushing back inside me as I feel the breeze rushing against my pussy.

A breathy moan tears out of me as I feel that hard cock at my back again. He steps in closer and grinds against me, and just like that, I know that I won't be leaving this damn rooftop without that cock slamming deep inside my ass. No. Matter. What.

The hands are addictive, too much as they roam over my skin and make me feel more alive than ever.

The two on either side of me drop their pants and give me more freedom to work their delicious, big cocks. My fists pump up and down as my thumbs roam over their tips and circle over that small bead of moisture at the top. A thrill shoots through me and I can't resist releasing them and lifting my thumbs to my mouth, tasting each of them at the same time.

A groan pulls from the back of my throat as the guys seem to move even closer, their determination and desire knowing no bounds. Taking them again, I give a show worthy of their attention as those thick fingers continue slamming deep inside my pussy.

Needing more, I press my ass back, and whoever it is that stands at my back, reads my every need like a fucking road map, the directions set out in stone. He reaches around me, his fingers pressing at my mouth, silently demanding that I open wide. I do exactly as he wants and his fingers slip between my lips. My tongue rolls over them, coating them until he decides that it's enough and pulls them free.

A soft gasp pulls from deep within me as his soaking fingers instantly drop to my ass, spreading around my hole until he pushes them inside me. I push back, taking them deeper and I can feel his smile against my neck.

He works my ass, preparing me for what's to come as my pussy is thoroughly fucked by his brother's skilled fingers.

My soft breaths quickly turn into needy pants as they rock my world like never before. Like fuck, I'm standing at the highest point of the city, bare fucking naked on the edge of a high-rise rooftop with the three DeAngelis brothers worshipping my body as though they couldn't live without it. This is easily the best moment of my life. I've never felt so alive, so fucking powerful.

The brother to my right drops to his knees, forcing me to release his velvety cock. He moves himself beneath me, somehow getting between my legs without any of us falling off the goddamn roof and I bite down on my lip as he reaches up and takes my hips.

The fingers pull free from my cunt and a soft cry builds within my chest until the brothers begin lowering me down. My knees spread wide and with skilled precision, I drop down right over his cock, filling me to the brim as I feel his firm balls hitting my ass.

"Holy fuck," I groan, my fist tightening on his brother's cock and making him flinch, reminding me just how much power I hold in this situation.

My hips start rocking, taking him even deeper with each movement, my hand falling onto his shoulder to steady myself. I sense the brother behind me, dropping to his knees as his hand comes to my hips, slowing my movements. He shuffles in closer until I feel his cock at my ass and I lean forward, giving him all the access that he needs.

I suck in a breath, trying to relax. This isn't something I've done many times, and the few times I have, it was a disaster. But I know the boys will take care of me and make me wish we'd been doing it all along. He starts pushing into me and I tighten my hold on the cock bouncing near my face as I take him deep.

I let out a breath, getting used to the way he stretches me, and as my nipple is sucked into someone's mouth, I focus all my attention on that, helping my body to relax into their welcome intrusion. They wait for me, letting me decide when I'm ready to keep going, and after a short moment, I start moving again, testing the waters as I rock my hips forward and back, feeling the way they each move inside me at the same time.

"Oh, my God," I mutter, clenching my jaw as the overwhelming pleasure rocks through me. My nails dig into whoever's shoulder I'm gripping as I slowly get used to it and start working my body to its fullest potential. I can't say that I've ever taken two guys at once, but fuck, it's good. I've never been so full, so stretched and desired. It's like nothing I've ever felt.

Their bodies move with mine as my fists continue moving up and down, and as I get all too comfortable, I turn my head toward the cock bouncing by my face and pull him in closer. My tongue slips out, wetting my lips and finding his tip right there.

My tongue pokes out again, immediately tasting him and I can't resist closing my mouth over him. My head bobs up and down, taking him right to the back of my throat as I sense all of their eyes on me. My tongue roams up and down, circling and teasing his tip as my hand remains at his base, squeezing him tight.

His hand works into my hair, bunching and knotting into it until he's able to take control of my rhythm, but he doesn't dare. He lets me take the lead as my body is rocked around from the two cocks buried deep below the border.

Fingers tighten on my skin, and I know that tomorrow I'll wake with a perfect road map of fading bruises to tell me exactly where they've been.

My pussy clenches as fingers fall to my clit, massaging tight circles and bringing my body right to the edge. One cock rubs against my walls and I groan against the cock working its way to the back of my throat.

My ass is stretched to capacity, and at any moment, I'll be a fucking convulsing mess on the ground.

Feeling that familiar burn deep inside my stomach, I rock my hips faster, taking one deeper as the other pulls back like a well-oiled machine, always giving me exactly what I need. I pant around the cock in my mouth as my nipples are pinched and teased, my ass cheeks grabbed and squeezed while my clit is rubbed furiously, setting my body on fire.

I take it all, desperate to be their one and only little whore.

FUCK. It's everything and more.

I get faster and faster, my desperation taking control and consuming my every thought. The boys groan and grunt but I'm too far gone to even try to work out who the sounds are coming from until finally, my world implodes, and my orgasm tears through me like a fucking explosion.

My pussy shatters and I cry out, the sound muffled around the thick cock in my mouth. My ass clenches and convulses as my body is destroyed in the best damn way, but I don't dare stop, riding it out and soaking up every damn ounce of pleasure.

My eyes roll in my head as fingers bite into my skin, the guys so close to their breaking point, and fuck, I want it. I want them to fill me with their seed. I want to feel them pouring themselves inside me and claiming me in the most primal way possible.

I want to be theirs. All of theirs, and damn it, I won't accept anything less. I should be running for the fucking hills, especially after what Roman and Levi did to me, but I can't. My feet are permanently rooted in their lives. I'm not going anywhere. I will see this through right to the end. The good, the bad, and the ugly.

My earth-shattering high continues, spasming, convulsing, and shaking as the cock buried in my ass thrusts forward, taking me so much deeper. I cry out, gripping tighter onto the shoulder in front of me to keep us all from toppling over the edge of the fucking roof as the hand in my hair tightens and I taste him coming in my mouth, shooting his warm seed right down my throat.

I swallow everything he's got as his brother slams up into my pussy, grabbing my waist with a fierce primal groan. He gives me everything he's got and pours himself into me, claiming me as his own.

I groan, loving every damn second of it as I keep moving, rocking my hips back and forth while pushing back against his brother in my ass. He picks up his pace and with one more brutal thrust, he comes hard, shooting his load deep inside me.

My body slows and as the thick, velvety cock is pulled from between my lips, my body sags forward with exhaustion. I slam against a hard chest and he holds me up as his brother slowly pulls out of my ass, being careful and treating me with every kind of respect.

I catch my breath as I bury my face into the body beneath me, trying to find the energy to get up, but I've never been so exhausted. I know I came up here with the intention of getting fucked up, but this isn't quite what I had in mind. It was incredible though, and a much better plan than I had come up with.

A moment passes before hands are at my waist, pulling me off their brother and helping me to my feet. The blindfold remains on as a big shirt is pulled over my head and falls all the way to my knees, keeping me covered. I let out a sigh, smelling Marcus all over me. When the blindfold slips from my face, I find him standing before me, as Roman and Levi already sit on the edge of the roof, drinks in hand and legs dangling over the city. Letting out a sigh, I know that I will never be able to work out who was where during that whole experience.

"You good?" Marcus asks, his gaze roaming over my body as Roman studiously ignores me, more than content pretending he had nothing to do with that.

I grin up at him, knowing no matter what, Roman simply just can't resist me, just like his brothers. They've destroyed and claimed something inside me, just as I intend to do to them. "I've never been better."

And with that, I drop down beside Levi, take his drink right out of his hands, and throw it back as I feel their warm cum slowly seeping out of me.

CHAPTER TWENTY

Nerves rattle my body as Marcus leads me through their creepy little underground playground. Out of all the things I thought I was going to do today, this wasn't it. Before he came and demanded that I take a walk with him, my day was supposed to consist of nothing but nursing my wicked hangover. Apparently, at twenty-two, I'm supposed to just shrug that shit off.

Asshole.

Perhaps my night of reckless drinking wasn't my brightest idea, but I'm not going to lie, that rooftop certainly had its perks. Perks that I'll be demanding to see again. I mean, once a girl has experienced all three of the DeAngelis brothers at once, there's no going back. Normal one-on-one missionary sex is officially ruined for me, but if I'm being honest, it was ruined the first time Marcus put his hands on me down in that fucked-up little cell.

Sensing my nerves, Marcus places his hand on my lower back and leads me through the underground playground. It's creepy as hell, and after shooting my father in the knee only a week and a half ago, I'd hoped I'd never have to come down here again. It's cold and filled with the most horrendous kind of fluorescent lights that showcase every drop of dried blood on the ground. Hell, even the echo of our feet on the cold concrete is enough to send chills sweeping through my body.

We pass multiple empty cells, but when we start passing cells that are covered in blood splatter and dangling bodies, my stomach sinks. The deeper we get, the fuller it becomes with bloodied and bruised men calling out at me; some demanding freedom, some looking for water, while others call out abuse and sexist slurs. "What's going on down here?" I murmur, keeping my voice so low that Marcus would have to strain to hear it. "All these people weren't down here last week."

His lips pull into a hard line and he nods. "I know," he mutters. "It seems my father has been using our playground a little more than we'd realized. At least it explains why all of his men had been down here that night. He must be up to something. I bet those assholes weren't expecting to see Roman out there like that."

I nod, remembering it all too clearly. "He practically tore them to shreds," I tell him. "I don't get how he's still alive. That many guards against just one man. It's not possible."

"When you've got the kind of training that we have," he says, his gaze shifting over the cells with a sick desire, "anything is possible."

"Cut it out," I tell him, drawing his focus back to me and not all the things he'd like to do to his father's prisoners. "We're here to teach me how to shoot, not so you can start dreaming about all the wicked things you'd like to do."

Marcus grins, his gaze darkening with excitement. "I know," he tells me. "But wouldn't it be better to learn to shoot with a real target? After all, shooting a stationary target is very different from the courage you need to actually shoot a human being."

I narrow my gaze at him. "How old were you when you first shot someone?"

His face scrunches in thought as we continue walking past the rowdy prisoners. "Umm, maybe seven or eight," he muses, watching my face as it morphs into horror. He laughs and drops his arm over my shoulder as though this is the most casual conversation we'd ever had, though I guess in his line of work, it kind of is. "It's not what you think. I had been practicing shooting with Levi. Roman already knew what he was doing with a gun so he didn't have to put in all those hours like we did, and it just … kinda happened. I didn't mean to shoot him in the ass. It was an accident."

"Wait," I say, slowing my pace to focus on his eyes. "Who'd you shoot in the ass?"

He cringes and glances down at me, looking as though he's breaking some kind of pact just by discussing this with me. "Roman," he finally admits as an amused grin pulls at his lips. "He still has the scar, but I was sworn to the grave to never speak of it again."

I can't help but laugh and immediately feel guilty about it as I remember the prisoners around me. "What happened?"

"So, Levi and I had just finished up and we were cleaning our guns and putting them away, but Roman had just finished his own training and he was being a fucking asshole. He was always like that. I kinda hated the guy. He expected so much out of us. He wanted us to always be better, to do better. Our capabilities were never good enough for him, but now as an adult looking back, I see it for what it was," he says, pausing for a beat as he gets way off track. "Roman wanted us to be the best because anything less wouldn't be good enough for our father, and when you're not good enough, you're as good as dead. He saw what we were too young and naive to understand. I guess the asshole was protecting us even back then."

"Ah, the noble gentleman as always," I laugh, still thinking about the bullet hole in Roman's ass.

"Anyway," he continues, "we were putting all our shit back and Roman came in to tell us that the shots we'd taken weren't good enough, and he was right, they were shit. But back then, I couldn't control myself, still can't sometimes. It sent me into a rage and I just lost control and pulled the fucking trigger."

I let out a sharp gasp as he takes his little stroll down memory lane, laughing to himself about the fond times he had growing up. "The bullet lodged straight into his ass and the fucker screamed like a little bitch. My father had my fucking balls for it, but it was worth it to see that prick sitting on one of those blow-up donuts for the next few months."

I gape up at him as we finally pass by the last prisoner and move into the state-of-the-art shooting area the boys have built down here. "So, he just let you get away with it?" I ask as my gaze sweeps over the array of guns and targets, most of them done up with a picture of their father's face stapled to them.

Marcus laughs and pulls up the side of his shirt to show me a faded scar hidden within the beautiful lines of his tattoo. "Nah, the asshole took my kidney for that one a few years later then sold it on the black market for his first car, but I can't blame him, that car was nice. One of a fucking kind."

"Holy shit," I breathe, my eyes wide. "I don't know whether to be happy or sad that I never had a sibling."

"Happy?" he questions. "Why the hell would you be happy about not having a sibling? That was a good, brotherly-bonding story. I got away with shooting him in the ass and he got to take a kidney. It's a win-win situation. Didn't you hear the part about the car? One. Of. A. Kind."

I shake my head, unable to comprehend just how far gone he truly is. "You know, every time I start to convince myself that you're just like the rest of us, you go and prove to me just how wrong I really am."

His brows furrow as he takes a gun, looking it over before glancing back at me. "What's that supposed to mean? How else are brothers supposed to show affection and bond?"

"Ever heard of football or video games?" I laugh, nervously taking the gun he hands me and looking down at it like it could strike me at any time. "I mean, I don't have a brother, but I'm pretty sure that's how it's supposed to go."

Marcus scoffs and comes to stand right behind me, adjusting my posture and turning me to face the target at the end of the lane. "I'd rather burn in hell with all the assholes I've sent down there," he tells me. "Now focus. You know the basics, but in our line of work, you can't afford to miss. Speed and precision are crucial."

Over the next few hours, Marcus takes me over everything I need to know, and while I'm far from perfect and still have many hours to log down here, I can confidently use a gun. Though, whether I'd actually be able to aim it at another human being is a whole other hurdle I will have to fight through.

Three hours turn into four and when my arms are aching so bad that I can no longer pull the trigger, he finally eases up on me. It leaves me wondering what a training session with their father would have been like. Marcus is going easy on me now, but to get to the elite level they're on, their training would have been brutal, consistent, and terrifying; something no kid should ever have to endure.

We start packing everything away, and after the long walk back out of here, we finally break into the warm afternoon sun. Marcus can't help but glance around like a soldier, making sure we're not about to get shot from afar, but all we see are the Dill Doe twins racing out in the distance, weaving in and out of the big trees at the start of the thick woods.

We make our way back toward the grand entrance of the castle and I find myself lost in thought. "Can I ask you something?" I mutter, feeling as though I'm about to cross some invisible line that I was never aware of in the first place.

Curiosity sparks in his dark eyes as he watches me, and after a short pause, he nods. "What's up?"

"I never really sleep well after drinking, so I woke up pretty early this morning and was just wandering around when I saw Levi. He was coming down those stairs that lead up to Snow White's room and he seemed … off, like it's tearing him apart having your mom here. He went back to his room after that, but he didn't sleep, just played the drums all morning, like he was trying to forget her."

Marcus lets out a heavy sigh and he stops me at the bottom of the stairs, not wanting to have this conversation anywhere closer to the castle. "Levi was young when she died, only four or five. He doesn't remember her, not in the way that Roman and I do," he explains. "I think he has one memory of her reading him a bedtime story a few nights before she was killed and he's held onto that tighter than he's held onto anything. Having her here now .. at least being aware of her being here, he feels like he's let her down. We all feel like that, but it's hitting him the hardest."

"Shit," I murmur, feeling as though there's got to be something I can do to help him.

Marcus places his hand on my lower back and starts leading me up the stairs. "Roman and I," he continues, "we have countless memories to fall back on, but all Levi has is that one bedtime story and her decaying body upstairs. I don't blame him for trying to hold onto that."

I nod, hating how much their pain hurts me too. "Why would your father do that to her?"

He shakes his head. "The fucking question of the century," he mutters, not doubting for one second that he would get the information out of him if it's the last thing he does. "We always believed that she'd been put to rest in the family tomb on my father's property. Hell, every fucking year we'd break out of this hellhole and risk a trip to the tomb just to see her, but after all these years, she's been left up in a lonely castle to rot. We could have helped her, buried her somewhere nice."

"You will," I tell him, "and after that, you're going to make your father pay."

"Damn fucking straight," he says, reaching for the front door and groaning when it doesn't open. "Fuck. I thought I left this propped open."

My eyes widen, gaping up at the big castle. "How the hell are we supposed to get back in?"

Marcus steps back and scans over the massive building. "Never thought I'd be needing to break back in," he mutters as his gaze travels to the far corner of the property and scans over the huge, overgrown maze that they chased me through only a few short weeks ago. "How do you feel about taking a little stroll through the maze again?"

"Fucking hell," I mutter, the idea making me want to break out into hives. "What are my other choices?"

"Going up through the cellars."

"Shit," I sigh. "Maze it is."

We start making our way toward the massive hedges of the maze and I stare up at it, remembering just how daunting being on the other side of this thing was. Though it's late afternoon, and with the sun shining, surely it won't be half as scary in there.

"I've been meaning to ask you something," I say, realizing that a second probing question to do with his mother probably isn't a smart move, but hell, I'm already on a roll.

Marcus glances at me and raises his brow as he tries to figure out the best way to get us on the opposite side of this hedge wall. "Yes?" he says slowly.

"You know that first night when you guys dressed me up in that black gown?"

He narrows his gaze on me, not liking where my line of questioning is going. "What of it?"

"Was that really one of your mother's old gowns?" I muse, nervously glancing up at him. "Because I know you guys are a bit fucked in the head, but getting off on a random chick wearing your mom's old clothes is just weird."

A howling laugh comes tearing out of him as he attempts to scale the side of the hedge. "Holy fuck, babe. How long have you been wanting to ask me that?"

I shrug my shoulders. "A while."

He shakes his head as the branches snap under his weight and he drops back down to the ground beside me. "It wasn't my mother's dress," he laughs, shaking off the shallow cut that starts at his elbow and trails all the way down to his wrist. "I don't know who's fucking dress that was, but it looked fucking good on you."

"Oh," I breathe, the relief pulsing through my veins. "So you guys don't get off on …"

"No fucking way," he laughs. "We get off on your fear. Levi just likes to fuck with chicks like that. Tell them something so off-putting that it makes their skin crawl. With everything going on, I'd forgotten he'd told you that."

Something eases within my chest and realizing that their mommy issues aren't as fucked up as I thought, I step into Marcus and offer him my foot. "You're going to have to throw me over," I tell him, both of us quickly realizing that this is the only way.

"Alright," he says. "But for the record, if you faceplant on the other side, it ain't my fault."

Taking hold of his shoulder as he makes a brace under my foot, I meet his eyes and nod. "Deal," I tell him. "Now make me fly."

After fifteen long minutes of Marcus attempting to catapult my body up and over the high maze walls, we finally break in through the back door with only a few minor scrapes and bruises. We come in laughing and within moments, we hear Roman's amused tone hollered through the massive castle. "Oi, Marc. Where the fuck have you been? Come and check this out."

We follow the sound of his voice and the closer we get, the easier it is to make out the familiar sound of a news broadcaster giving the world its latest breaking story.

Turning into the big living room, we find Roman and Levi hovering around their massive TV, too worked up to be able to relax back into one of their many luxury couches. As we walk in, Roman glances back and I don't miss the way his eyes scan over my body and linger on my face.

"What's up?" Marcus questions, walking deeper into the living room and glancing up at the TV, figuring out that whatever is going down has something to do with this news story.

"Check this out," Levi says, grabbing a remote and hitting rewind, watching closely to make sure he doesn't go too far back.

I creep in between Marcus and Roman, my brows furrowed as Levi gets it to the right place and hits play.

"Breaking news," the stunning news anchor says, her platinum hair instantly making me jealous that I've never had the funds to do that on my own, let alone maintain it afterward. "The DeAngelis family war continues."

An odd thrill shoots through me and my back straightens as I hang on her every word, watching as an image of a man I've never met appears on the screen. "Ronaldo DeAngelis was found dead in his family home late last night. This comes only a few days after his cousin, Antonio DeAngelis was murdered on his family property outside of town. Both of these men have links to the DeAngelis mafia family and are both nephews of Giovanni DeAngelis. The police have launched their investigation into these vicious murders, but it is unknown whether these killings are linked."

The news story continues with the finer details of these murders as I gape at the screen, unable to believe how it's all playing out. "Holy shit," I breathe as Levi lowers the volume, not interested in the details we already know. "It happened just as you guys predicted."

"Sure fucking did," Levi says with pride. "Just you watch. My father will be in a rage when he calls Roman within the hour to make sure it wasn't us, but he already knows the truth. It was Antonio's father, Victor, retaliating for his son's death."

"So what now?" I ask as Marcus steps closer to the TV, grabbing the remote and turning the volume back up as he watches the rest of the story.

"Now, we sit back and watch the show unfold," Roman says, walking across the room and filling a small glass with perfectly round ice cubes and his expensive whiskey. "Our father is the eldest of five sons. Giovanni, Victor, Joseph, Phillip, and Louis. Victor is our father's second in command; he has five of his own sons. Well, now that we've killed Antonio, he's down to four. Joseph has kept his nose clean as far as we know. He doesn't want anything to do with the family business. Phillip is just as dirty as Victor, though he'll keep his distance from this particular war because he has two young daughters. Louis is the youngest of our uncles, and Ronaldo was his only son."

My ass crashes down onto the couch as I try to go over everything he just said, trying to wrap my head around the DeAngelis family tree but I think I'm going to need someone to draw it up. "That's … a lot of people you need to get out of the way."

Roman shakes his head. "Not exactly. A few of them will be regrettable deaths, but it's meticulously planned out that those who will survive at the end of this will be easily swayed to the dark side. We will not have to worry about their loyalties as we already own them."

I stare blankly across the room, tuning out the news story playing in the background. "So, who's next?"

Levi drops down beside me, his arm falling over the back of the couch. "My guess? One of Victor's remaining sons. They are hot-headed, and after learning that Ronaldo killed their older brother, his death won't be enough for them. They'll be out for blood and go for Ronaldo's wife or his father … most likely his father considering Antonio's relationship with Monique. But they are too inexperienced to go up against a man like Louis. He will slaughter them and once he's done that, he will go after Victor."

"But the ball is in Louis' court, right? After Victor killed Ronaldo. It should be his turn to retaliate, not Victor's sons."

"Technically, yes," Roman says. "But in the real world, you strike when you can. War is not a forgiving game, nor is it fair. Louis is a patient man who would prefer peace within the family, but once Victor's sons come for him and he gets a taste of blood, he won't be stopped. Not until Phillip steps in."

"No shit," I breathe, reaching across and grabbing Roman's expensive whiskey right out of his hands. I throw it back before he gets a chance to rescue it, needing the hit more than I need my next breath. "This is … literally insane."

"One by one his soldiers will fall," Roman says slowly, his eyes darkening with his sinister plan. "My father loses his inner circle, and every death brings us one step closer to freedom and power."

"Just wait until the wives get involved," Marcus murmurs, excitement brewing in his devilish eyes. "Ariana won't know what hit her." And not a moment later, he drops down on the big two-seater couch across the room and looks back at Levi with an amused smirk. "You know, Shayne thought you were serious when you told her that black gown was Mom's? She thought we've been locked in this big castle, getting off on chicks dressed as our dead mother."

"Well, fuck," Levi laughs. "We're screwed in the head, but even we know where to draw the line."

CHAPTER TWENTY ONE

Wrapping a warm towel tightly around my body, I perch on the edge of the bathtub, coils of steam still filling the air. I've never been lucky enough to have a bathroom with under-floor heating and a heated towel rack, but now that I've experienced the good stuff, there's no going back.

The sweet smell of warm vanilla sugar reminds me of home as I pull my favorite lotion from the bag of toiletries the boys lifted from my apartment and squeeze some into my hands. My feet have been used and abused in the worst possible way since being here, but this week, they've been given a chance to really heal. The deep cuts from running through the woods and scraping across the asphalt haven't done them any favors, and while they have a long way to go before I can classify them as fully healed, they're looking and feeling a shitload better than what they were.

A pained groan pulls from deep in my chest as I rub the lotion into my sore feet before slowly moving up my calves and doing everything I can to minimize the look of each of my scars. Some will fade easily, but others will be there until the end of time.

I get halfway through putting lotion on my lower body before the mirror finally becomes clear and I focus on the scars that are harder to hide. Pain tears at my chest with each welt that I focus on, remembering the exact moment I received it.

The fading ridges where Lucas Miller carved his marks are woven haphazardly through the shallow gashes that Levi and Roman left on my skin. The oldest scars mean nothing to me, just silver lines left by an angry man, fueled by power and control. But my stomach spasms in waves of dread and grief as I take in the puckered, red gashes that tell a very different story. That betrayal is something I may never heal from; both mentally or physically.

I've spent the better part of my morning training with the boys downstairs, and just like the other day, Levi and Roman yelled orders at me while Marcus stood by, wishing he could be the one to drop me to my ass. Though, he'd also be the one to kiss it better afterward.

With no other plans for the rest of the night, I pull the clip free from my hair and let my long brunette locks fall down my back in soft waves. The towel falls to the ground as I stride from my private bathroom, feeling a million times better than I have in weeks.

The soft silk dressing gown catches my eye and I walk toward it, not wanting the hassle of getting completely dressed at this time in the evening.

I push my arms through the opening of the silk gown and let the soft material brush against my skin. I'll never get used to this. In the space of only a few weeks, I've gone from haunted prisoner to queen of the castle, and I freaking love it. But what the boys did to me on top of that high-rise building with the breeze on my naked body is my favorite part of this whole experience. It was so damn good that I haven't been able to get it off my mind since, and as I loosely tie my dressing gown and allow the beautiful silk to fall off my perfectly lotioned shoulder, I know exactly what our night will be filled with.

My tongue rolls over my bottom lip, and after taking a lingering look in my bedroom mirror and pinching my cheek for a natural glow, I realize this is as good as it's going to get.

My hand skims along the polished banister as I make my way down the stairs. Levi's drums rumble through the castle and I follow their hypnotic sound, remembering exactly what he could do to a woman on those drums.

Walking through the lower level of the castle, I find the boys hiding out in the massive room they'd used for the party they'd hosted, the very night I'd ended up on Draven Miller's radar. Levi sits across the room at his drum set, his eyes already on mine as he plays, instantly making my body heat.

Roman sits on the same couch he'd been on with Ariana before she decided to take advantage of the scared kidnapped girl while Marcus hovers at the bar, fixing himself a drink as he takes a long drag from a joint.

I feel Marcus' hot stare on me as I stride through the room, but I know how easy it would be to get him on his knees. Levi would take me anyway I want him, but the challenge here is Roman.

We haven't spoken about what happened up on that roof. It's been avoided harder than I've tried to avoid my father. But if I can just get close enough to him to have him touch me like I know he wants to, then I know his brothers won't be far behind and I'll get exactly what I want.

I lock my hungry gaze onto Roman and as I stride toward him, he lifts his chin, sensing me coming. He looks my way and as his stare connects with mine, that usual fire burns brightly between us. He doesn't miss the hunger in my eyes, and as my hands fall to the silk tie at my waist and slowly pull it loose, I see that same hunger reflected in his.

Roman's eyes become hooded and I don't miss the way that Levi skips a beat on his drum, too consumed as he watches me. I see Marcus out of the corner of my eye as he steps from behind the bar. He's slowly trailing behind me, almost as though he's stalking me like one of his many victims, and for the second time tonight, I feel like a damn goddess. Only a goddess would be able to capture and hold the attention of these three men.

Roman places his glass on the small coffee table and relaxes back into the couch. I step in front of him, letting my silk gown pull open an inch, showing off the sliver of skin down the center of my body.

His hungry eyes sail over me, taking me in like his next meal as I silently step in even closer. I see the question on his lips, wanting to ask me what the fuck I think I'm doing being so bold with him, but after his kiss in the foyer and his boldness with me on that rooftop, the ball is in my court to do whatever the fuck I want.

Levi keeps on his drums and the intense beat syncs with my racing heart, sending blood rushing through my system and spreading adrenaline throughout, making me braver than I ought to be. Shrugging my shoulders, I allow the silk dressing gown to sail down my skin and pool at my feet before moving forward and pressing my knee into the soft cushion beside Roman's strong thigh.

He doesn't make a move to touch me and I pause for a moment, my confidence already taking a hit but the adrenaline is too strong, pushing me on. My hand falls to his shoulder, and as I adjust my weight, I bring my other knee up and straddle his lap. My hand slowly moves up from his shoulder and around the back of his neck.

My nails trail up into his hair until I can grab a fistful of his dark locks, tearing his head back and forcing his eyes to mine. I hold his stare and he watches me right back, each of us captivated, breathing heavily as the need slams through our bodies. Then without warning, I crush my lips to his.

I kiss him deeply, taking exactly what I need from him, just as he did to me in the foyer. He instantly reacts to my kiss, moving his lips with mine as his hand finally comes to my waist, circling around me and pulling me in tighter until my bare pussy is pressed right up against his cock, straining through his gray sweatpants.

His lips pull into a grin as I kiss him deeply, our tongues fighting for control until I'm forced to pull away to catch my breath. His fingers dig into my skin, holding me tighter than ever and it's exactly how I thought it would be with him. So powerful and forceful, the dominance always in his corner. Roman isn't the type to give up control and now isn't going to be any different.

His other hand knots into my hair and just as I did to him, he pulls my head right back until my spine is arched and my tits are pressing into him. His lips come down on my neck, sucking hard until he bruises my skin and leaves his mark. In the past, I've bitched at men for doing this, but damn it, the way his tongue rolls over my sensitive skin kills me in the best way.

"Oh fuck," I groan, my eyes closing with the overwhelming pleasure rocking through me.

He releases his hold in my hair and my body relaxes over him. I turn my face to his, desperately needing to feel his lips on mine again, and just before my lips press down over his, I feel his thick fingers slipping between my spread legs and pushing up inside me.

I gasp into his mouth just as his lips crush down over mine, swallowing my cries as his fingers start working inside me, massaging my walls and curling just right so that my eyes roll back in my head. My hips grind down against him, needing more and wishing I could just reach down between us, free his huge cock, and ride him all night long, but judging by the way Marcus creeps in a little closer and the drumming across the room slows, this could very well be another earth-shattering group project.

Roman's fingers work me in the same way that he views life—

brutal, dominant, raw, and controlling. But there's also a hint of selflessness, giving me exactly what I need while not caring about his own desires.

But not for long.

I push back on my knees, making more room between us before reaching down and feeling his hard cock through his sweatpants. My fingers curl into the front of his waistband and just as I'm about to feel that velvety skin beneath my fingers, he pulls my hand free, stopping me. "No," he says, not skipping a beat as his fingers continue working deep inside me.

I pull back and meet his eyes, confusion furrowing my brows. Maybe he's still unsure about how our little dynamic is supposed to work. He's hesitated with me since the very start, so I shouldn't have expected anything different. Leaning back into him, I drop my lips to his strong neck, brushing them over his skin as they move up toward the sensitive space below his ear. "Come on, Roman," I murmur, grinding down against his hand as he makes me feel alive. "Let go. I want you to be with me."

His whole body tenses as his fingers freeze deep within me. "Roman?" I question, pulling back to meet his heated stare, only there's nothing heated about it. His dark eyes are ice cold and full of fury. "Roman?" I question again. "What's wrong?"

He rips his fingers out of me so fiercely that I gasp, but before that gasp has even sailed past my lips, his arm is around my waist, pulling tight. He flips me around, keeping my knees on either side of his thighs as he holds my body flush against his strong chest.

Roman holds my body down, his hand cupped against my tit, squeezing and pinching as his other hand sails down my body with determination. I don't get a second of warning before his fingers are back at my cunt, pushing deep inside me with rough, determined thrusts as his brothers watch on with furrowed brows. "Is this what you want?" he spits in my ear. "You want to be my little whore? Want me to join your little fucked-up harem with my brothers? Fuck us all until you can't fucking walk?"

I swallow hard as he's rough with my body and find myself nodding. "Yes," I breathe, knowing that I want him more than anything, to have all three of them to myself, but unsure why this feels so wrong. This isn't how I imagined it, this isn't what I was asking for.

He fucks me with his fingers, slamming deep inside me over and over again as his grip on my tit tightens, flicking his thumb over the pebbled, sensitive peak. I try to relax into his touch, knowing that if I were to just relax and embrace his dark side, I would probably like it, but it's like my words flipped a switch inside him and he's taking out his anger on my pussy.

I try to pull away from him, wanting to adjust the angle that he pushes into me but his hold is too strong and I'm trapped under him. "Stop," I find myself saying, my voice broken and barely a whisper that I force myself to say it again. "ROMAN. STOP."

He tears his fingers free immediately and releases his hold around my body. "You're too fucking desperate for it," he murmurs in my ear, his voice like acid on my skin. "You don't want this. You have no fucking idea what you're begging for."

I barely catch my breath before he pushes me off his lap, and though he doesn't mean to, I slip straight off the edge of the couch and go tumbling to the ground. Then without sparing a single glance at me, he reaches for his drink and walks away.

Tears sting my eyes as I wonder what the fuck just happened. One second he was into it. He was giving me exactly what I wanted, smiling against me and urging me on. The next second, he was punishing me for wanting something real with him. I want to hate him.

Feeling Marcus' eyes from the opposite couch, I raise my head and meet his haunted stare. I expect him to tell me to shrug it off, that it doesn't mean anything, but he simply stands and looks at me as though he couldn't be more disappointed. He turns and walks in the opposite direction, leaving me feeling humiliated on the ground and reminding me that these are not the normal kind of guys I'm used to dealing with. They're psychopaths. Heathens. Stone-cold killers. And I am nothing but a joke.

The tears fill my eyes and fall down my face, dropping from my jaw onto my chest. My fingers knot into the silk gown on the floor and I pull it up to cover myself, wondering how I could let that happen. I dropped my guard. I allowed myself to feel something for a bunch of men who don't know what it means to even care.

My head falls into my hands and just as sobs begin to build deep in my chest, two hands curl under my arms and pull me up onto the couch. I crash down into Levi's arms and he pulls me in tight next to him, allowing me to cry into his shoulder.

A moment passes and as his hand begins to rub up and down my arm, I hear the soft rumble of his deep tone filling the room. "It's not you," he tells me. "This is all on him. You're there asking him to open up to you, and while he wants that, he doesn't know how to give it to you. It angers him. He's always been so good at everything, been the best, the favorite, and he sees how easily Marcus and I have been able to let you in, and it's breaking him."

I shake my head, my brows furrowed with confusion. "I'm not asking him to fall in love with me. I'm asking him to let me in, to know him like I'm getting to know you."

"I know," Levi murmurs. "There's one thing you need to understand about Roman before attempting to get close to him. He doesn't take orders and he needs to always be in control. Felicity had to learn all of this the hard way, but he won't allow some woman to come in and start fucking with his emotions, and that's exactly what you're doing. He doesn't trust himself when he can't see what's clearly ahead. Then add the guilt that's weighing down on him for even having any sort of feelings for you so soon after Felicity's death."

I let out a breath, cringing as I realize what I've done. "Fuck, I didn't even think about her."

"Roman sees the world in black and white, and right now, you're fucking with his head and forcing him to see all the gray in-between," he explains, holding me tight. "It'll take some adjusting but give him time, he'll come around. Though, he's going to need some space after that one."

"If he wasn't ready, why did he join in on the rooftop the other day?"

Levi lets out a sigh and I raise my chin to watch the expression on his face. "Don't take this the wrong way, but the rooftop was about fun. It was about making you feel something, not us, and certainly not about feeling any connection. He just wanted to see you come, just like the rest of us. It was fun, nothing more. Now, one-on-one, and the way you look at him with expectations, that's different."

I swallow hard and nod as I adjust the silk gown over me to cover all the important bits. "And Marcus?" I question, trying to deal with one thing at a time as I put that information away for later. "Why was he so mad at me?"

"He's not," Levi says. "He's mad at himself for thinking that he was going to get you all to himself."

"What?" I question, my brows dipping low again. "That doesn't make sense. He knew I was interested in all of you from the beginning."

"You saw how possessive he was when I started showing an interest in you, and now he has that with Roman. He'll never admit it, but after what happened with his shooting and when Roman and I … you know, I think he had hoped that you'd pull away from us and he'd have you all to himself."

"And what about you?" I question, keeping my voice low so he doesn't hear how it shakes with nerves. "How do you feel about me wanting to be with all of you?"

His lips press into a hard line as he glances far away across the room, wanting to dig deep inside of himself and give me an honest answer. "I'm cool with it," he tells me. "All three of us are naturally possessive guys. We don't like to share, but for some reason, it works. I don't want to fuck with a good thing. So as long as you're down with this fucked-up little thing we've got going on, then I'm down too. I'm not about to ask you to choose."

"Will Marcus?"

Levi shakes his head. "No, I don't believe he will," he tells me before adjusting himself beneath me and pulling me up. "Come on, let me get you something to eat and you can spend the night with me."

"Okay," I say, letting him pull me along as I try to slip my arms back into the dressing gown. I let out a shaky breath and wipe my eyes, and the moment I step out of the weird little party room, I promise myself that I will never shed another tear for Roman DeAngelis, and I sure as fuck won't be sharing my body with him unless he's groveling on his knees, begging for forgiveness. But like he once said, if he's begging for forgiveness, then his knees better bleed.

CHAPTER TWENTY TWO

"**A**re you fucking kidding me?" I demand as Marcus hands me the skimpiest outfit I've ever seen along with a thick, metal collar to sit around my neck.

"They're not my rules, babe. I just enforce them," he says, the annoyance still in his eyes from last night's bullshit. "We need to go to this party, and if you want to come, then you need to be seen as property."

"What?" I mutter, scrunching my face in distaste while throwing the skanky lingerie and thigh-high boots onto my bed. "That's ridiculous. What kind of fucked-up party is this? I'm not wearing that."

"Then you're not coming," he shoots back at me, clenching his jaw before walking straight out, leaving me with Roman and Levi both staring like they want to be anywhere but here.

Roman sighs and inches forward, and while I don't see an apology in his eyes, there's definitely regret, but unfortunately for him, that won't be enough to be rewarded with my obedience. "Look, Marcus is right. If you want to walk into this party without being kidnapped or fucking raped, then you need to wear that. The kind of people—"

I step into him, raising my chin and letting him see the fury in my eyes. "Get out."

He pulls back, his brows furrowed. "What?"

"Get. Out," I say, my words as clear as day. "Do I need to say it again? Perhaps a bit slower? I don't need an asshole like you coming in here and telling me what I can and cannot wear, and I sure as fuck don't need you telling me that my only options for the night are to either be kidnapped, raped, or objectified by men just as sick as you. So, get the fuck out."

Roman's eyes flash with the worst kind of rage and his hand strikes out, gripping my throat as he walks into me, pushing me up against the wall of my bedroom. "The fuck did you just say to me?" he spits, leaning in closer so he hovers right over me.

"Oops," I tease, having been in this position too many times to know he'd never see it through. "Seems you forgot your manners again."

His fingers bite into my skin and I just grin up at him, still perfectly able to breathe through my nose as my hand shoots out and grabs a fistful of dick. I squeeze hard and watch with delight as he falters, trying hard not to let his panic shine through. His other hand circles my wrist, squeezing it tight to the point of pain, but I don't dare back down. He tossed me around like a fucking ragdoll last night, humiliated me, and abused my body like it didn't matter, and though he stopped when I told him to, he won't be getting away with it, not this time.

I hold his hard stare and let him see the humiliation deep in my eyes, the pain he caused me from his bullshit actions. "No real man would treat their woman like that," I spit, hitting him right where it hurts, and while there has been no conversation about him viewing me as his, we can all see it. "So until you learn how to play nicely and grow a set of real balls, then you'll be releasing my throat, getting the fuck out of my room, and figuring out how the hell you're going to make it up to me." I squeeze tighter on his dick, knowing he feels the pain. "Now. Roman."

He holds my stare for a moment longer, the two of us locked in a battle of domination and after what feels like a lifetime, he finally relents, releasing his tight grip on my throat and backing up a step. He continues staring as I release my hold on his junk and that regret that shone in his eyes earlier is now like a beacon completely taking over.

He doesn't say a word, just stares like he wishes he knew what to say, but what could he possibly say that would make any of it okay? I understand wanting to lash out because you feel backed into a corner, or because someone is wanting something from you that you're not ready to give. But using my body to prove a point, to help release your anger, and to make me feel ashamed and embarrassed ain't it. The fucker can go and fall down a chasm for all I care.

No, that's a lie. I do care and I'd be even more pissed if he died and took the easy way out rather than finding the courage to actually apologize for his bullshit.

Without another word, he finally turns and stalks out of my bedroom much like he did last night. Only this time, he doesn't hold his head quite so high.

The moment he disappears around the corner, I take a deep breath and try to focus on the matter at hand. My gaze shifts up to Levi who watches me like a fucking queen taking her throne. "The skimpy lingerie and collar?" I ask, pointing toward the mere scraps of material laying across my bed. "Is it really that necessary?"

Levi presses his lips into a tight line and nods. "Yeah," he mutters, not that happy about it either. "We need to go to this party. Someone is going to be there who we need to see, and apart from tonight, no one has seen this guy in three years. Tonight is our only shot. It's going to be a fucking shitshow though. It won't be safe. The kind of men there … they're just like us. So I get it if you'd prefer to stay here."

"And risk being alone for your father to come get me? No thank you. I'll take my luck with the rest of the psychopaths, but you haven't explained why I need to wear that."

Levi glances away and he almost looks embarrassed. "The collar and lingerie … they represent ownership, that you're our property, meaning no one else is permitted to touch you without our permission. If you were to walk in there without a collar or leash, you'd be free for the taking, and don't be naive about it—*you will be taken*. If you're coming with us tonight, then you will be wearing that collar. It's non-negotiable. Is that clear enough for you?"

Fuck.

My gaze shifts back to the collar and a heavy dread sinks into my stomach, especially considering how easily controlled I was the last time I wore one of these. During that ridiculous party, all it took was Marcus stepping in behind me and chaining me to the bar and I was trapped until they decided to release me. This collar though, it's something else. It's basically a metal bar that's been bent to fit a woman's neck with a place to screw in a thick bolt at the front. There's nothing sexual about it. It's simply a tool to keep your little slave woman in line.

I swallow hard and nod. "Fine, but if even one person puts their hands on me without *my* permission, I won't be the docile slave girl they're expecting. They will die at my hands. There won't be any second chances like with Draven."

Levi nods, already knowing this but his cringe has my nerves sitting on edge. "Spit it out," I tell him, striding toward the bed and dropping my stupid silk gown that makes me feel anything but sexy now.

Grabbing the ridiculous skimpy lingerie, I start pulling it on as I glance up at Levi, waiting for his response. He lets out a breath, and like ripping off a Band-Aid, he lets the words fly free knowing exactly what I'll think of them. "During this party, it is expected that when speaking to myself or my brothers, you will refer to us as 'master.' If not, it will raise suspicion among the other ... guests."

I shake my head, my jaw dropped open in horror. "If you think for one second that I will ever refer to any of you three as 'master' you're going to be sorely disappointed."

"Then you must not speak directly to us unless we are alone," he explains. "These men ... when I say they're just like me and my brothers, I don't mean this version of us that you have gotten to know.

I'm referring to the version of us you see plastered all over the news. This is not a place you want to be caught slipping up."

I nod and pull on the rest of the lingerie and feel sick to my stomach as Levi steps in behind me and helps to fasten the cheap bondage straps around me to make my skimpy slave look really pop. He doesn't put the collar around my throat and explains that he'll wait until we're pulling up at the location.

My ass crashes down onto my bed and I pull the thigh-high boots up my legs and instantly hate them. I've tried running in boots like this in the past and it's not easy.

Levi gives me twenty minutes to do my hair and makeup and soon enough, I'm making my way downstairs in my ridiculous little outfit with an oversized hoodie covering my body. "You ready?" Marcus demands, his gaze sweeping up and down, and despite how annoyed he is with me throwing myself at Roman last night, he can't deny that he likes what he sees.

"Would I be down here if I weren't ready?" I throw back at him, striding straight past his stupid ass and making my way through to the dining hall. The boys follow my lead as I walk through the main kitchen and down into the small room they spent five years digging a tunnel out of. They shove the old bookcase out of the way without wasting a second, and I make my way into the long, winding tunnel.

It takes us ten minutes to walk right through it, and all too soon, I'm in the back of the Escalade with my nerves on high alert. Roman takes the driver's position as usual with Marcus in the front passenger seat and Levi sliding in beside me.

Roman hits the gas and we go sailing out of the small garage they'd built and out into the thick woods. He keeps his eyes glued to the road the whole time, not once daring to look at the rearview mirror and see the fiery rage staring back at him.

The drive seems to go on forever and I find myself cursing their father for locking them up so far away from civilization. Don't get me wrong, I'm glad that they live so far away from the city. It's probably what's kept most of us safe all these years, but right now, it's an inconvenience to me.

Three long, silent hours pass before the Escalade is pulling to a stop deep inside the windy streets of an old, gothic-looking cemetery. Chills sweep over my body, already hating where we are. "There are no other cars," I comment, looking up and down the streets. I mean, if this were a party, there would be lots of guests … right?

"They're out there," Roman says, his voice low as he watches out the front windshield. "You just can't see them, just as they can't see us."

I close my eyes for a brief second, trying to remind myself that I'm not the scared little girl who first came into this world. I've faced down the impossible. Tonight is nothing more than a weird dress-up party with a bunch of shady dudes. I can do this. I just have to remain in character and then we'll be back inside this Escalade before I know it.

The sound of the thick bolt releasing from the heavy collar has my eyes springing open and I shoot my hard stare across the back seat to Levi who looks guiltier than I've ever seen him. "It's time, Shayne. You need to put it on."

I let out a heavy sigh and nod, allowing him to inch closer to me and lock the collar around my neck. The heavy metal immediately weighs down on my shoulders and the feeling has me wanting to curl into a ball and cry, but there's no way in hell that I'm about to do that here. "Let's just get this over and done with," I tell them once Levi finishes fixing the bolt into place.

We climb out and the boys seem to create a protective shield around me as I strip off the hoodie and toss it back through the open car door before finally walking deeper into the creepiest graveyard I've ever been in.

Massive tombs surround us, and the deeper we get, the more luxurious they become with angel statues and marble stones. I follow Roman's lead and find myself shaking as he comes to a stop right in front of an ancient-looking tomb with big black iron gates with skulls incorporated into its thick metal bars.

My blood turns cold as I watch Roman pull an old key from his pocket. "What the fuck is this?" I breathe as he pushes the key into the lock and turns it. The old locking mechanism jars and makes a loud banging noise that has my whole body flinching with fear.

Roman pockets the key and pushes against the iron gates just enough for us to slip in, and as we do, Marcus steps in beside me and places his hand on my lower back. I meet his stare and see a flicker of nervousness in his eyes which instantly puts me on edge. He's the craziest of the bunch and for him to be nervous … that speaks volumes.

"Come on," Roman mutters, his voice low as he leads the way. "I want to get this done as quickly as possible. I smell a fucking rat."

We follow Roman as he walks through the tomb and my knees shake. I've never been inside a tomb in my life. It's cold and creepy and definitely not a place I want to be. He moves through it with purpose and stops at a marble wall before sliding it right out of the way to reveal an old metal spiral staircase.

"What's down there?" I question, trying to peer ahead only to see nothing but darkness.

Roman glances back at me with a wicked grin, showing me the true psychopath that lives within him. "Why don't you come down and see?"

Asshole.

He doesn't bother to wait for a response as he traipses down the stairs like he's not about to walk straight into a shitshow.

Marcus follows him down into the deepest pits of hell, and not wanting to be last, I fall in behind him. My hand grips the railing, certain that I'm going to fall to my death on these old rusty stairs. I hear Levi on the steps behind me. "Remember, not a fucking word," he murmurs, keeping his tone low, "and if you must speak—*master.*"

I don't respond, but he knows that I hear him.

We walk down another twenty or so steps and the deeper into hell we get, the louder the music and voices become. My knees barely hold me up on the stairs and it's like descending into darkness until we hit the final few steps and a red, foggy glow settles into the air.

We really are descending into hell.

I swallow hard, and as we turn the corner into the party, fear rocks right through me as my jaw hangs open. I couldn't have been more wrong. This isn't hell, it's something far, far worse.

CHAPTER TWENTY THREE

Satanic chanting sounds around me as I gape at the woman lying back on an old marble coffin, her arms and legs chained to the sides as men hover around her, watching on as a man who could only be described as the devil slices into her skin. She screams and wails in agony and my eyes instantly fill with burning hot tears.

"Don't," Roman mutters, reading my mind without even looking my way. "She consented to this. Racing in there all hot-headed is only going to ensure that you go next."

Fuck.

I pull myself back and do what I can to hide behind the brothers as they make their way through the crowded party. When Levi told me these men were just as bad as they were, I thought he had to be exaggerating because no one could be that evil, but seeing the type of men in this room, I was wrong to doubt him.

There are women dressed just like me—scars and all. Some wear their collars with pride while others look as though they're about to break, and those are the ones who make me want to throw down. Most of the men in the room sit on red suede couches looking like a bunch of creeps with their whiskey on the rocks as their sharp, venomous gazes travel over the women in the room, those who already belong to someone else.

Women are being grabbed left, right, and center. Women behind the bar. Women walking around like show ponies. Women being used as human cum pockets. It makes me sick. The whole fucking room is dressed with women, hung like fucking decorations. They stand around the room, chained to fucking pedestals so the sick bastards who ogle them can get off. I've been down here for less than a minute and already seen at least four men forcing themselves onto collarless women.

Hot, burning rage tears through me and I make a point to scan over every single face in the room, committing them all to memory. I don't doubt that every fucker in here is on some kind of most wanted list and if I ever get the chance, I'll be hand-delivering them right to their prison cells, maybe missing a few important body parts.

The deeper into the room we get, the harder it becomes to stomach and I drop my gaze to the ground, unable to take it in for a second longer. The room smells of blood, booze, and sex, and the agonizing screams drown out the heavy music. I can't be here. It's one thing thinking I'm strong enough to have some sort of power in the boys' fucked-up mafia world, but this right here is far beyond anything I could have imagined.

Guests begin recognizing the brothers and stopping them to say hi, and as they take me in, they laugh and congratulate the boys on getting themselves a new girl who knows how to keep her mouth shut, leaving me wondering who the hell they brought here before me and what the fuck went down.

A few minutes pass and after more and more men come in to get an up-close-and-personal view of the country's most feared villains to shake their hand and ask about their dirtiest little secrets, Marcus begins leading me away, keeping me out of the spotlight.

Not having the protection of his two other brothers at my back worries me, but I follow him anyway, more than ready to hide out in the corner of the room. We pass by some questionable things and I do what I can to keep my gaze locked on the ground to appear like the flawless little slave girl who the brothers have trained perfectly.

He leads me right up to a set of stairs, and as he takes the first step, my gaze lifts and widens with horror. "No," I hiss, pulling back on my wrists as he tries to lead me up the small set of stairs beside one of the many pedestals overlooking the party.

Marcus tugs on my wrist, keeping me moving and skillfully disguising my resistance as an awkward fumble. Having no choice, and damn sure that I don't want to draw any extra attention to myself, I reluctantly walk up the few steps until I stand on top of the small platform with a hard column at my back.

Marcus puts himself right in front of me, so close that my bondage-style bra presses up against his shirt. "I don't want to be up here," I hiss as he reaches around me and takes hold of the small cuffs at either side of the column.

"I know," he murmurs, keeping his voice low. "But it's our only fucking choice. I can't babysit you down there, so it's either be up here where we can watch you from afar, or down in the crowd where you'll be taken, just so some dumb fucker gets to say that they took what was ours."

"But—"

"Stop," he spits through a clenched jaw. "You're going to make a fucking scene and put a bigger target on your back. Just stand here and look pretty. That's all you need to do. Don't look at the people around you. Don't focus on the dirty fucking pricks getting off at the thought of having your body. Don't watch the fucking sacrifice across the room, and for fuck's sake, don't try to be a goddamn hero because it will only get you killed. Do you understand me?"

I hold his stare and fight the urge to scream before finally nodding, realizing just how right he is. I'm cuffed to the fucking pole at my back, and while it makes me an easy target, if anyone tried something, there'd be no hiding. The boys would see and they'd be able to do something about it. But if I were down in that crowd, it would be all too easy for someone to pull me away.

Marcus finally drops his gaze, releasing me from his strained stare. He crouches down and takes my ankle. It's not until the cool cuffs are closing around my skin that I realize just how much trouble I'm in. "Marcus," I plead, my voice so low and terrified. "Please. Don't. I know you're still angry about what happened last night, but please don't cuff my ankles. Don't leave me completely defenseless."

He glances up at me and I see the fear in his eyes—the fear of losing me, of anything happening to me here, of walking away when I need him most, but if he is caught going easy on me, he'll be labeled as weak and the masses will turn on him. His gaze drops away almost as soon as it connects with mine and he takes my other ankle before quickly wrestling it into the cuff, leaving my legs spread apart and on view for everyone to see.

And just like that, Marcus turns his back and walks away, leaving me out on display and free for the taking.

He strides back across the room and I keep my stare on him as he steps in front of the bar and pulls out a joint, lighting it but refraining from taking a drag. I find Roman next, he's the closest, and while he appears cool, calm, and collected, he's anything but. His muscles are bunched and tight, ready to spring into action at a moment's notice.

Levi stands across the room, talking to some guy who looks like the kind of guy you'd smile at in a board room only to find yourself locked in his closet with your guts spilling out a few hours later.

They said they were here to meet with someone who's flown under the radar for the past few years, but as I look around, it's impossible to tell who that might be. Every asshole in here is as shady as the next.

My gaze shifts back and forth across the room, constantly watching the stairs by the pedestal while keeping an eye on the boys and making sure none of us are about to get in trouble. I'm on my third sweep of the room when a man and his collared girl steps up to the pedestal.

My body goes rigid as he looks up at me with interest, his gaze roaming over my body as though he'll be abusing it later. The woman wears skimpy lingerie similar to the ones I wear as the man drags her along behind him, a thick chain wrapped around his hand that connects to the heavy metal collar at her throat, a collar that's a shitload tighter than mine.

He yanks her up the stairs and she fumbles after him, her eyes wide and terrified and it's clear that she doesn't share the same kind of relationship with this man that I share with the brothers.

Bruises cover her body, so dark that I see them through the black lace of her bra. Her thighs are the worst, clear marks from his fingers where he's held them apart and abused her for hours on end.

My stomach turns and as she glances up and meets my horrified stare, shame crosses over her face. This poor woman. I can't even begin to imagine the hell she's been through. The brothers have been awful to me, especially in the beginning, but they never once touched me without my consent, and the one time I needed it to stop, he did without question. But this man … fuck, I want to feel the blood splattering against me as I slit his throat.

The podium is small, not meant for so many people so he's forced to walk right by me as he moves around to the other half of my column. He's tall, just like the brothers and despite still being a few feet away, he somehow manages to hover over me. I take a shaky breath as he saunters toward me and as his arm grazes past my body, a chill sweeps through me, making me feel sick to my stomach. He doesn't take his eyes off me as he slowly strides past, pulling the girl behind him.

Darkness flashes in his eyes and there's something so wicked and sinister, it makes my skin crawl. His tongue rolls over his bottom lip, silently telling me that I'll be next. Finally, he moves past me and I'm able to take a deep, shaky breath.

He yanks the girl hard and she fumbles in front of me. Natural instinct has me pulling against my binds, trying to catch her fall, but it's no use, I can't help her like this. She slams down onto her knees and her gaze snaps up to the man who looms over her, terrified of what he will do.

Anger pulses in his eyes, furious that she's made such a scene in front of all of these men. He pulls hard on her chain, forcing her up by the throat, but he doesn't stop, pulling her higher and higher until her toes are barely touching the ground. A soft gasp tears from my throat as I watch his sickening display in disgust, putting on a performance for the men around him, trying to prove just how much of a man he really is. Fucking bastard.

The woman pulls at her collar, desperate for a deep gasp of air and I shake my head, the horror quickly getting to me. Just one move with that collar and he'd snap her neck. I have to help her, but there's nothing I can do apart from watching as every second unfolds right in front of me.

My stare snaps across the room, desperate to find the brothers but not one of them are where I thought they were. Panic consumes me as my eyes go wide, scanning the room again and again. How could they leave me like this, vulnerable and afraid? Why would they do that?

The woman is finally lowered to her feet and the man laughs, looking at her as though she's the most pathetic piece of shit he's ever come across. He pulls her around the other half of the column and cuffs her just as I am, putting her on display for the men who stand behind me and showing off her bruises like a goddamn trophy.

She whimpers behind me and my body shudders at the sound of a sharp slap that cuts across her skin. She gasps and frets, desperately trying to hold it in until he finally moves away from her, walking back around the podium with his dark eyes coming back to mine. I look away, not wanting to look at him for a second longer than necessary, only he stops right in front of me and grips my chin, yanking it up and forcing my stare onto his.

I try to pull out of his grip but without my hands and with the column at my back, there's nowhere for me to go. "Who's your master?" he questions, his gaze glistening with excitement. "My bitch is a little worn out. We'll see if we can make a little trade. I need someone with a little more … fire."

I pull against his grip and shamelessly fail. "I'm not for sale," I spit.

He laughs, finally releasing my chin. "We'll see about that."

His sickening stare lingers on me a moment longer before he finally walks away and steps down into the crowd, giving me a chance to breathe again. I close my eyes, trying to calm my racing heart. Only when I feel that small sparkle of courage lighting up within me, I stretch my fingers back, desperately trying to reach the girl who shares my column.

My fingertips brush over her broken nail and I feel as she retracts, absolutely terrified. "It's okay," I tell her, turning into the column so she can hear me better. "I'm not going to hurt you. My name is Shayne."

A moment passes before I feel her fingers reaching out for mine and I grip onto them as best I can. "I'm Jasmine," she tells me, her tone so weak yet somehow so strong.

I squeeze her fingers and she grips onto mine just a little bit tighter.

"He's been hurting you, hasn't he?"

I'm met with silence as she immediately understands the depth of my question. She knows I don't mean getting roughed up by this psychopath. "Yes," she finally says, her voice breaking, confirming my suspicions. "All the time. I just … I want it all to end. I just wish he'd put me out of my misery and kill me but he likes to see me broken … bleeding."

Tears fill my eyes and I will them away, desperately wanting to be strong for her. "I'm going to get you out of here."

Jasmine scoffs at my comments. "That's nice of you," she tells me. "But nothing can get me out of this. Look at us. We're cuffed to a fucking pole with goddamn collars. The best thing you could do for me is to convince one of these pricks to put a bullet through my head."

I shake my head. "You need to be strong, Jasmine. I promise, I will do everything that I can. My … *masters,*" I spit, "we have a different kind of relationship. They'll help me."

Jasmine lets out a heavy sigh and it's clear that she thinks I'm full of shit. A moment passes before it becomes clear that she's not going to respond, but that's not good enough. I'm not going to allow her to give up. Hell, tonight is probably the only chance she's ever going to get. "Tell me about yourself," I prompt her, squeezing her fingers. "Do you have a family?"

A heavy sob comes from the opposite side of the column and it breaks my heart. "I have a newborn at home," she tells me. "He's only six weeks old and I … I'd do anything to be able to hold his little hand and feel the way his fingers would curl around mine. He's … he's perfect and I … I'm a fucking mess."

"You're not a mess, Jasmine. I promise, I'm going to help you get home to your little boy."

"I don't even know if he's still alive," she tells me. "The night … the night he took me. My husband was at work. He takes the night shift and my little man was in his bassinet. He was nearly due for a feed when that bastard busted in through my front door. I've never felt fear like that in my life. I ran into his room to get him but he caught me first … and my baby … he was just left there all night. He would have been so scared, wondering where his mommy was, but I wasn't coming. Anything could have happened to him."

"Babies are resilient," I tell her, hoping that's true. "He would have been okay, just a little bit hungry. He would have cried for a while and eventually settled himself back to sleep. His daddy would have come home and given him what he needed. They're both okay, just waiting for—"

BANG! BANG! BANG!

Gunshots sound through the fucked-up underground tomb and my eyes widen in fear as all hell breaks loose. Women drop to the ground as their masters pull guns from every fucking crevice on their bodies, grabbing hold of them and using their bodies as human shields.

Men start running while others have more balls than what they're worth, turning this place into a fucking war zone.

Jasmine screams at my back, gripping tighter onto my hand and thrashing against her bonds as bullets sail past her face, lodging into the thick column between us.

Men in black tactical gear come storming into the underground hell with massive bulletproof shields protecting their bodies. "FBI. GET DOWN," I hear hollered through the tomb as the bastards filling this room fire back at them like their goddamn lives depend on it, which I guess they do. Every last dickhead in this place would have an arrest warrant out for them.

Loud, piercing screams rock through the tomb, and my heart races as I thrash against my binds, knowing damn well just how easy it'd be to get struck by a stray bullet. "It's a raid," Jasmine yells back at me, gripping my hand like her only lifeline.

"We have to get out of here," I yell back, my body thrashing and pulling against the cuffs.

"I don't know if you've realized this," she yells back. "BUT WE'RE CHAINED TO A GODDAMN POLE. THERE IS NO GETTING OUT OF HERE."

"They'll come," I spit through my teeth, knowing deep in my gut that the boys won't abandon me like this, even if it is the FBI and they're on every damn most wanted list imaginable. *They will come.*

I see flashes of men racing through the tomb, men who could be the brothers … or maybe they're not. More FBI agents swarm the tomb, unforgiving as they trample over fallen bodies in their desperation to get to those who have been highest on their lists for years, constantly escaping them—men just like the DeAngelis brothers.

Women shriek and scream, barging past the shields in their need to be free of their captors while those very captors shoot at their backs, ensuring their eternal silence. And then just as a bullet lodges into the pillar beside my shoulder, the tomb falls into darkness and sends my world into an overwhelming panic.

CHAPTER TWENTY FOUR

The cuffs tear at my skin as I thrash wildly, my heart racing while the sound of deafening bullets spray around the room.

Terrified screams fill my ears and I don't know if they're mine, Jasmine's, or the women scattered through the tomb being abused by the vile men in the room, taking advantage of the fucked-up situation.

Glass shatters making me flinch, and just when I think I can't take it a second longer, a shadow leaps up onto the podium and hands press against my body. I thrash against it until I hear his calming voice. "Shayne," Roman rushes out, his hands flailing over my arms and legs, making sure everything is intact. "Are you hurt? Shayne?"

I shake my head violently. "No, I … I don't think so," I rush out as his hands grip me tighter, trying to calm me and get me to focus. "Get me the fuck out of here."

He immediately drops to his knees and grips my ankles, madly searching for the release on the cuff in the darkness. He holds onto me, his big body acting as a protective shield as he quickly works to free me from the podium.

"Marcus and Levi?" I question, glancing over his head and trying to find the two possible loves of my life in this horrendous darkness.

"They're fine," he says, freeing my ankle and quickly moving on to the next. "They know how to handle themselves, but if they're worried about you, they're going to do something stupid."

Fuck.

My other ankle comes free and he flies back up, his massive body hovering over mine as he works quickly on my wrists. "I won't have time to remove the collar," he yells over the sound of bullets raining down around us. "Just get the fuck out of here. I can cover you but you need to fucking run. Fast."

I swallow hard and nod as my first wrist is freed. "I'm not going anywhere without Jasmine."

His gaze snaps up to mine, his brows furrowed as his fingers continue working the release for the second wrist cuff. "Who the fuck is Jasmine?"

"The girl behind me," I rush out. "He hurts her. I'm not leaving her."

Roman shakes his head, his eyes burning with a fiery rage. "We don't have fucking time for your bullshit games, Shayne. We need to go. Now," he says just as I'm freed from the column. He takes my hand and starts to pull me away. "The cops will find her and get her to safety.

You need to get out of here."

"NO," I roar, pulling back on his sharp hold, ripping my hand free, and racing back around the small podium until my body hovers in front of Jasmine's. She meets my fearful eyes as she thrashes against her binds. "I'm not leaving without you."

"Get me out of here," she begs, flinching as another bullet plunges into the column above our heads. "FUCK."

I immediately get to work, my fingers fumbling with the cuffs as Roman barges back into me, the searing rage in his eyes knowing no bounds. His strong arm scoops around my waist and he hauls me back, tearing me away from the woman I so desperately promised to save. "NO," I scream, clawing at Roman's back as a painful sob tears from my chest. He pulls me away from her and the fear in her eye kills me. "I promised. I promised her. She has no fucking hope like this. She'll be dead before the cops can get to her. Roman, please."

Regret shines heavily in his dark eyes, but he has one thought and one thought only—get us the fuck out of here. "She's not our fucking problem. Let her master risk his life instead."

"HE RAPES HER. ALL THE FUCKING TIME. HE'S NOT COMING FOR HER."

"Please, don't leave me," she wails, pulling harder on her binds, her face a mess of smudged mascara. "Please. Help. Help me. I just want to go home to my baby. He needs me."

I tear at his back, my nails digging deep crevices into his skin. "PUT ME DOWN."

"FUCK," Roman roars, his frustration getting the better of him.

He spins around and drops me to my feet before shoving me hard. My body falls toward the girl and I dive for her ankles as Roman takes her wrists.

She panics at having Roman so close to her, and I don't doubt that she's able to recognize him from all the haunting stories we've seen splashed across the news, but her will to survive shines through and she's not blinded by the fact that right now, Roman is the one person standing between life and death.

She's freed within moments and Roman grips my hand, shoving his palm against my back and pushing me toward the edge of the podium. He jumps down, bypassing the stairs and tugging me with him, catching me before I get the chance to fall. He reaches up and does the same with Jasmine, not being quite as careful with her, but all that matters is that she's free.

We barge through the bodies as Roman does his best to barricade us from the shots. His gun is out and proud, shooting off perfect shots despite the chaos surrounding us. We get halfway through the crowd before three FBI agents bear down on us, their biggest prize ever in their sights.

"FUCK," Roman roars, his eyes darting left and right for some kind of way out but they come too fast, determined to capture the most feared fugitive in the world. "GET DOWN," Roman yells back at us just as a spray of bullets come hurtling toward our faces, the agents more than willing to sacrifice me and Jasmine if it means getting to Roman.

He shoves me down hard and I drop to my knees, pulling Jasmine down behind me.

Roman groans, clutching his arm and my eyes go wide. "You've been shot," I gasp as Jasmine's fingers are crushed beneath a heavy boot.

Roman clenches his jaw and glances down at his arm. "It's fine," he hisses as the FBI agents close in on us. "Flesh wound."

"But—"

"No, you don't have time for this bullshit," he says, digging his hand deep into his pocket before pressing the key to the Escalade into my hand. "Get the fuck out of here. Run as fast as you fucking can. We will come for you."

I gape at him, my heart racing in the worst kind of way. "What?"

"NOW. GO."

Fuck.

Pain tears at me as I watch Roman get to his feet and face down the FBI agents like a fucking warrior, and with one last lingering glance, knowing this could be the last time I ever see him, I take Jasmine's hand and fuck right off out of there.

We race and weave through bullets and bodies as the agents step out of our way, seeing that we're nothing but victims fleeing for safety. I'm sure they'll come looking for us later, but for now, they have much bigger problems.

We break out through the crowd, leaving the wild gunshots behind us as we hit the spiral staircase. My hand grips onto the banister as I bolt up the stairs while Jasmine clutches onto me, her energy quickly dwindling but she pushes through, determined to get out of here. She has a family at home, a baby who needs her, and all I want to do is find the brothers and bring them with me. My priorities are as fucked up as they come and after the shit I've involved myself in over the past few months, those agents should be arresting me right along with the rest of the bastards in this room.

A stampede of blood-soaked women follow behind us, and though my heart breaks for what they've been through, I have to zone out their frenzied wailing to help myself. We're not in the clear yet. Not even close.

Guilt soars through my gut at the thought of leaving Roman to face those agents. Surely he's not going to kill them. They're innocent men just doing their job. But the thought of Roman being carted away in cuffs is more than I can handle. If it's him or the agents, I can't say that I'd make the honorable decision.

Where the fuck were Marcus and Levi? Surely they'd have his back. They'd make sure he got out of there.

I have to believe that they're all going to be alright.

We break out through the top of the spiral staircase and race toward the big iron gates locking the tomb. My hands curl around the metal bars and violently shake them. Roman didn't lock it after we walked through it, but I'm damn sure that we weren't the last ones to come through here.

A hand curls around my arm and tosses me aside, sending me flying into the concrete wall. Glancing back over my shoulder, I see one of the creeps from down in the tomb pulling his gun to shoot through the lock. His foot comes up and kicks out the gates, and with self-preservation on his mind, he races out into the night.

Jasmine and I don't hesitate, racing out after him with wild, erratic movements. I grip her hand, tugging her toward the Escalade hidden deep in the shadows, both of us stumbling over our ridiculous heels.

The gunshots deep in the tomb echo through the night, fading with each step we take, and as I glance back over my shoulder, I see men in uniform closing in on the bastard with the gun. The man turns and aims his weapon at the agents, but he's taken by surprise when one man springs from the shadows and tackles him to the ground. The agent slams him onto his chest and pries the gun from his hand, waiting for backup to cuff the piece of shit.

I see agents looking toward us with interest and suspicion but with so many arrests to make down in the tomb, they reluctantly let us go.

We reach the Escalade in minutes, though it feels as though we've been running for hours. I hit the unlock button on the key fob and we dive into the car. Panting heavily with wide, terrified gazes, I lock the doors and hit the button to bring this bad boy to life.

The engine rumbles beneath me as I quickly adjust my seat to reach the pedal, then the second I can, I hit the gas and get us the fuck out of here, knowing the boys will come. They have to.

The momentum has Jasmine falling back into her seat, but she quickly adjusts herself and clips her seatbelt into place. I go tearing out of the old cemetery, having absolutely no idea where we are. All that matters is getting away from the shit show behind us.

We break out onto the main road and I allow myself a moment to breathe before glancing across at Jasmine who silently cries beside me.

"Are you good?" I question, my gaze sweeping over her bruised body. "Did you get hit?"

She shakes her head and quickly scans over her body, the adrenaline pulsing through her veins making it impossible to feel a damn thing. "I … I think I'm good," she rushes out, her eyes still wide and panicked as she continually turns to glance out the back window, making sure we don't have a tail. "What the fuck was that?" she breathes. "I … I …"

"I know," I murmur, my chest still viciously rising and falling with gasping breaths. "That was all kinds of fucked up, but we're alive and that's what matters."

She nods, focusing on taking slow, deep breaths as she stares out the front windshield. "It's over," she breathes, the relief washing over her like a wave. "It's really over."

"Well," I say, not wanting to be the bearer of bad news. "First off, I have no idea where we are or how to even get out of here. Second, we don't know if your kidnapper was killed, arrested, or if he got away. We just … we don't know, but we need to get somewhere safe until we can figure it out."

"Right," she says, letting the reality of my words begin to sink in as she sits forward in the Escalade and starts pressing buttons on the GPS. "My place. I need to get home, let them know that I'm okay."

I cringe. "I … I don't think that's such a good idea. You said that's where he took you from, so if he goes looking for you, that'll be where he starts. We can … I, shit," I sigh. "Before I was taken, I had an apartment in the city, but I was being evicted and I don't know if it's even still my apartment anymore, but it's the best I can think of. Mrs.

Brown down the hallway, she'll let you use her phone. We can call your husband and figure something out until my guys come for me."

"Come for you?" she questions, her horrified gaze slowly sweeping to meet mine. "What do you mean? Who ... who was that guy back there? The one who freed me?"

"Roman DeAngelis," I tell her, watching as her eyes widen with the worst kind of fear. "That's who took me. A few months ago, the three DeAngelis brothers broke into my apartment and claimed me. They'll come and then we'll both be safe."

She gapes at me as though I'm speaking another language. "How the hell would we ever be safe with the DeAngelis brothers? They're ... they're murderers."

I shake my head. "I mean, they are, but they won't hurt you, not if I ask them not to. They'll protect you and help you get back to your family. My relationship with the brothers ... it's changed since being kidnapped. They care for me."

"What kind of messed-up Stockholm bullshit is this?" she demands, her hands flying to the door handle and trying to pull it open. "Stop. Stop the car. I want out."

"STOP," I yell at her, reaching across and grabbing her arm to keep her from attempting to turn herself into a road pancake. "Stop being stupid. Think about it, if Roman didn't give a shit, he would have left you there. He helped me save you. You need to trust me. They will help, and if anything, they can make sure that he never comes for you again. Your family will be safe. He'll never hurt you again."

Jasmine watches me for a long drawn-out moment and I'm forced to turn my attention back to the road before she finally sighs, presses the button on the GPS to lead us into the city, and rests back in her seat. "Okay," she says with a shaky voice, deciding to trust me with her life despite only just meeting me. "What now?"

"Now," I tell her. "We figure out how the hell we're going to get these collars off our necks."

It takes two hours and a nearly empty tank of gas to get back into the city and as I pull the Escalade into my old parking space, tears fill my eyes. I hate this apartment, but it was the only real home I ever had. I never thought that I'd get the chance to come back here.

It's after three in the morning, and considering that we're both wearing bondage-style lingerie, thigh-high boots, and thick, metal collars, I couldn't be happier to be pulling into a dark underground garage covered in shadows.

We climb out of the car and as I'm walking around to meet Jasmine on the other side, my gaze sweeps past the back window and freezes. My body goes rigid as I gape into the trunk space to see a body staring up at me with dead eyes. "What the fuck?" I screech.

Jasmine comes running around and peers into the back, her eyes going wide with horror before she promptly throws up all over her thigh-high boots. "Come on," I tell her, curling my hands under her arms and trying to yank her up once she seems to have recovered.

"That … that body … was in there this whole time."

"Apparently," I mutter as she gets on shaky feet beside me. I curl my arm through hers and pull her along, hoping to God that between now and whenever the boys decide to come get me that no one decides to go peeking. "I guess now I know where the boys disappeared to during that stupid party."

Jasmine scoffs at my casual use of the word 'party' and she'd be right to. What we just went through was anything but a party. It was hell in human form.

We make it up to my apartment and after trying the handle a few times and finding it locked, devastation washes through me, but I refuse to turn back now. I take a step back, and just like Roman had done at the new dealer's place and his uncle's property that was supposed to be his, I slam my foot into the door and kick the bastard down.

My attempt is nowhere near as impressive as Roman's, but it weakens the door just enough that Jasmine and I can shove our bodies into it and push it the rest of the way open.

We go falling into my apartment and my head quickly snaps up, glancing around to make sure we're not busting in on a terrified family, but everything looks the same. My old shitty couch, my crooked canvas print on the wall, even my empty fridge.

An hour later, we're both showered, clothed, and fed after I found a twenty dollar bill stashed between the couch cushions. Our collars still rest heavily around our throats, and while mine isn't comfortable, I know Jasmine's must be causing her all kinds of hell. At some point, we're going to have to figure out a plan. How to get in contact with her family, how to get these collars off, and how to get me back where I belong. This place doesn't feel like home anymore.

We sit together on my old couch, both of us lost in our thoughts, and while I've come to learn that things like tonight are common in the brother's dark world, I can't even begin to imagine what's going through Jasmine's head.

Hours pass as we each stare at the blank wall where my good TV used to be before my father stole it, neither of us able to clear the horrendous thoughts to allow us to sleep. "You can take my bed if you want to," I tell her, knowing damn well that I'll be sitting in this same spot until I know the brothers are alive and coming for me.

"No, it's fine," she says, looking completely exhausted. "It's your bed, you should—"

BANG.

My door barges open, the handle slamming straight through the drywall before it rebounds and catches on a heavy boot.

Jasmine screams as my eyes widen with fear, snapping up to the face that's haunted me my whole fucking life.

My father.

He stands imposingly in my doorway, his filthy stare locked on mine as I slowly shake my head, unable to believe how he's here right now. The boys let him out into the woods with the wolves. He should be dead.

My heart races as I take him in. He's got a crutch under his arm, holding himself up after I shot out his knee cap. Thick, red gouges cover his arms and legs and I don't doubt that they belong to the wolves, but how did he get free? Those wolves are natural hunters. It shouldn't be possible … not unless they were recalled or instructed only to play with their food.

FUCK.

My feet hit the ground and I start backing up as he steps over the threshold into my small apartment. Jasmine whimpers on the couch, her eyes flicking back and forth as she tries to work out what the hell is going on, fear of being taken again clear across her bruised face.

My father walks with a limp, dragging his leg behind him as he slams the door shut, the sound echoing through the whole apartment complex. His lips pull into a sickening smirk, and as he draws an old, rusty knife from the waistband of his pants and stalks me through my apartment, I know without a doubt that he's after revenge.

Only one of us is going to make it out of this alive, and after the bullshit I've been through tonight, this motherfucker better fucking bring it because this bitch is not in the mood.

"Jasmine," I say, refusing to take my eyes off my father while knowing that my two training sessions are nowhere near enough to teach me how to come out of this alive, but with my father's injuries, luck might just be on my side. Either way, it's a risk I'm willing to take. "Stand behind me. I'm going to teach you what it truly means to survive."

CHAPTER TWENTY FIVE

MARCUS

"**W**ell, that didn't quite pan out how I expected," I mutter as I rub my raw wrists, the anger slowly boiling beneath the surface. Those motherfuckers must get off on cuffing us because they sure as fuck made it count. I've got to be honest, it's not the first time I've been in handcuffs, but it's sure as fuck the first time I didn't get hard over it.

"I told you I smelled a fucking rat," Roman spits, wiping his forearm across his face to mop up the blood staining his skin.

Levi hashes in the pin code to release the back door of the prisoner transport vehicle and the automatic lock unhinges. It was all too easy getting the transport officers to give us what we needed, and I can't lie,

I might have enjoyed it too. They should have been smart enough not to transport us together. Everyone knows that the three of us work best when we've got each other's backs.

It's been a shit of a night for too many fucking reasons, but for the most part, I think we actually had nothing to do with it. We weren't supposed to be there tonight. We weren't on any guest lists and sure as fuck didn't warn anyone of our surprise visit. The FBI raid was meant for someone else—someone who just happens to already be dead in the back of our Escalade. They got lucky that there happened to be so many other big names for them to arrest, but when there are big names, you better bring big guns.

The FBI were severely understaffed for such a big operation. They were out of their league, but they couldn't have known there were going to be so many players there tonight. Hell, we didn't even fucking know, and if I were given another hour to play, I would have evened a few more scores while I was at it.

I can't deny that tonight we had timing on our side. Had we skipped out and waited for our target's next appearance, we would have missed our shot at ending his miserable life. He was too powerful in this world, too determined. We had to put him down. When we overthrow our father and rise in power, he would have come for our throats to take our throne, and unfortunately for him, we're not going to be fair rulers.

It's just a shame that all of these fucked-up events lead to us losing sight of Shayne. She was so fucking scared, her eyes wide and haunted, but there was a determination there, a fire and will to survive that I respect. I have a good idea where she is, and the second we can, we'll be taking her sweet ass home, but if she's not there and she's taken this opportunity to run, I will personally rain down hell over her.

I jump down from the back of the transport vehicle, stretching my neck to either side, feeling that sweet crack at the top of my spine. Roman strides around to the driver's side and shoots out the locks. He reaches in and hauls the driver's body out before moving out of the way as it drops to the asphalt with a heavy thump.

He climbs up into the bloodied driver's seat, his fucking ego too big to allow anyone else the privilege, and I follow suit as Levi climbs into the back holding cell of the truck. The doors slam and Roman takes off just as I open the small window between the front seats and the back, finding Levi grinning at me as he makes himself comfortable.

"We've gotta make this fast," Roman says. "This truck probably has a tracking signal on it. We need to ditch it as soon as we can."

"Too fucking right," Levi says. "I'm too pretty for prison."

I scoff. "Not as pretty as me."

"You're both ugly motherfuckers," Roman mutters, switching hands on the steering wheel and cringing as the bullet wound across his arm starts to give him hell. "Either of you still have your phones? I want to check the GPS location of the Escalade before we start driving hours in the wrong fucking direction."

"Nope," Levi says as I shake my head. "Those bastards stripped me bare. Took everything I had on me. I was only seconds away from having a cavity search. That fucker wasn't even gonna use lube."

Roman glances through the small window at Levi, his brow

arching. "You would have liked that," he teases. "Did you have anything incriminating stored on your phones?"

"Nothing more than what you would," he says. "We're as good as fucked. You know they'll be able to pinpoint the location of the castle."

"Come on," I murmur, my eyes locked in the distance, prepared and ready for any threat. "They've always known where we've been. They just don't have the proof they need to make it stick. It's all hearsay and rumors. We're too fucking careful."

"Don't believe that for a fucking second," Roman says. "They have everything they need to take us right to the slaughterhouse, especially after what we just did to their transport driver, but they're too deep in Father's pocket. Either way, someone tipped them off about tonight's party."

"It could have been anyone," I tell him, nodding up ahead to an old gas station. "There were hundreds of people there tonight, most of them with kidnapped girls who would have done anything to be freed. Tonight wasn't an attack on us, we were just stupid enough to walk straight into a trap."

"I told you I smelled a fucking rat," he says, repeating the same words that he's said at least a million times since our capture.

"Whether there was a rat or not, we needed to go to that party," Levi says, reminding us of the reason we ventured out to that bullshit in the first place. "We did what we had to do and now I just want to go get Shayne back. We promised her that she was safe with us, and now look what's happened."

Roman scoffs. "If you're going to start crying, close the fucking window so I don't have to hear it."

"You're one to fucking talk," he shoots back at Roman. "What was that bullshit with her last night anyway? She was practically throwing herself at you and you made her feel like a piece of shit."

Roman clenches his jaw and stares out the front windshield as he pulls off into the gas station, but all I can seem to do is replay last night over and over again in my head, and the memory of it all instantly puts me in a sour mood. I was doing my best to try and forget that I'm not enough for her.

"What are you moping about?" Levi says. "You're just as bad as he is. Shayne is too fucking good for both of you. She was hurting last night after Roman's little stunt and all you could do was walk away because you're too fucking proud to admit that you're falling in love with her."

"The fuck did you just say?" I demand, whipping around to glare at my brother through the wire mesh window, desperately wishing that I could punch my fists straight through it and strangle the bastard.

"You heard me," he throws back. "You're in love with her and it's turning you into a little bitch, and instead of manning up and accepting it, you're pushing her away and making her feel like shit over it. What's the matter, big brother? Too afraid to admit that you're only human?"

Fury ripples through me and I grip the window cover and slam it shut, blocking out his big fucking mouth. He doesn't know what he's talking about. He clearly got knocked around too much as a kid. Roman and I sure did enjoy using him as a punching bag as a kid, perhaps we hit him a little too hard.

I stare out the window as Roman drives around the gas station, finding the best place to park to keep the truck hidden from the road and all I can do is huff. Levi might be onto something, but there's no way I'm about to admit it to him. He's right. I feel things shifting between Shayne and me. She's not just the girl we took; she's something real, something I don't want to lose. But in this world, to love is to be weak. Roman knows that all too well. Every girl he's ever gotten close to was destroyed under my father's thumb, and if I allow myself to really fall for her, I don't doubt that she will end up as nothing but a pawn for my father to use against me.

Roman brings the transport truck to a stop behind the gas station and we're quick to pile out. "Maybe we should just leave him in there," I suggest as Roman unlocks the back door.

"Nah," he says. "Then we'll have to come back and bail his ass out later and I'm too fucking tired to make another trip. We could just knock him out and stuff him in the trunk."

"Sounds like a—"

"Get fucked," we hear from inside the truck. "If either of you assholes try anything, I'll open an artery while you sleep."

Roman rolls his eyes and opens the back door. It doesn't take long to ditch the transport truck for an old Jeep that's barely holding it together and before I know it, we're flying down the highway toward the city.

We drive a few hours and Roman navigates toward Shayne's old apartment as though he knows the directions by heart, but after stalking this place for three months before taking her, I guess it's fair to say that we do. I know every fucking building surrounding hers, every fucker who lives within her complex, and where the best places are to eat in the neighborhood. Those few months leading up to her kidnapping were fun, but nothing was better than once we actually got her.

Roman pulls into the underground garage and I can't lie, it's a relief to not have to park far away and walk our asses over here just to see her like before. We find the Escalade almost immediately, but it's not hard. The car sticks out like a fucking unicorn taking a shit in the middle of a country club wedding in this neighborhood.

He pulls up beside it and the moment my feet hit the asphalt, I glance across the back window and double-check that our friend is still exactly where he's supposed to be, but it's not like Shayne was going to do anything with it apart from stare at it while her knees gave out. Though she's getting better at accepting our fucked-up lifestyle. Hell, I think it even excites her, which does nothing but get me rock hard.

Wanting to get back to the castle, we take off up the dodgy stairs and break out onto her floor only to find her apartment door broken and propped open. We take off faster, storming toward her apartment, each of us in a boiling rage, unable to handle the fear and terror of the unknown.

If someone fucking hurt her, I will burn the whole fucking world down just to make it right.

I break out in front of my brothers and slam my fist against the door, letting it swing open with a devastating blow only to be met with a piercing scream.

We barrel into the small apartment, the fond memories of the night we took Shayne pulsing through my thoughts. A girl sits in the corner of the kitchen, her arms wrapped around her legs as her whole body shakes, the collar around her neck telling me that Shayne picked up a stray. "Who the fuck are you?" I demand, rushing deeper into the apartment with my brothers hot on my heels.

"She's not important," Roman says, rushing toward her and grabbing her shoulders, squeezing them hard as I notice the trail of blood leading through the living room, down the hall, and pooling at the bathroom door. "Where's Shayne?"

"B … bathtub."

I take off, my stomach dropping like a lead weight as the haunting memories of Lucas Miller rushes through my head like a sickening carousel stuck on repeat. Shayne and bathtubs have a love-hate relationship, one that makes me want to tear the spine out of every fucker who's ever looked at her wrong in her life, and if tonight is a repeat of that one horrendous night, I'll be fucking livid.

I storm down the hallway, determined to get to her. If that's her fucking blood staining the floor, I'll have no fucking choice but to put this motherfucker to rest. Nobody hurts my girl.

It takes three wide strides to reach the bathroom with my brothers barreling behind me. My hand grips onto the door frame as I propel myself into the tiny bathroom and come to a screeching halt.

Shayne stands before me, her arms crossed over her chest as she stares at me with crippling fury. "Where the fuck have you been?" she screeches as her father lies in a pool of blood in her cramped bathtub, his eyes glossy and lost. "I was expecting you hours ago."

I gape at her, needing a second to catch up as my brothers spill into the bathroom, taking up every available space as they look down at the almost dead body, rotting in the bath. "What the fuck is going on in here?"

"You assholes were supposed to deal with him," she seethes, hot, angry tears in her eyes. "How is he still alive? The wolves were supposed to kill him."

Roman shakes his head. "This ain't on us. Blame the mutts," he tells her. "Those wolves are temperamental assholes at the best of times, and you know that. It's not our fault that he was no fun to play with."

Shayne lets out a huff and I step toward her, reaching out and gripping her arms. "What happened?" I murmur, meeting her wide, haunted eyes. "And why is there a stray in your kitchen?"

She shakes her head. "I couldn't just leave her there," she tells me. "She has a family at home, a newborn baby and a husband, and that asshole took her right out of her home and has been abusing her ever since. He rapes her all the time. Just take a look at her. Her body is like a fucking map of the abuse she's endured from him. If I just left her … what if he came back for her?"

"Babe," I say slowly, shaking my head. "She's not our problem. We can't take her. She belongs to someone else. We can't risk bringing that kind of heat down over us, not now."

Shayne pulls out of my grip and in the same moment, slams her hands against my chest, pushing me back a step and narrowly avoiding the stitches below my pec. I can't lie, I wish she'd hit it and make me bleed. There's something so satisfying about her hurting me, just like the steak knife through my hand. That was my turning point when I realized that I was going to keep her.

"YOU LISTEN TO ME, MARCUS DEANGELIS. I SAID WE'RE TAKING HER, AND THAT'S WHAT WE'RE GOING TO DO," she roars, anger turning her creamy skin a warm shade of red. "If you don't like it, you can fuck right off and shove a goddamn baseball bat up your ass while you're at it because that's what life is like for her. Have you ever had someone force themselves on you? Do you know what it's like to be terrified every moment of your life? To have a man take advantage of your body in the most brutal way? No, you don't, so you're going to shut the fuck up, help me get rid of my father for good, and then you're going to be a fucking gentleman and help her down to the car so we can get the fuck out of here. I promised her she was safe with us and that she would never have to fear him again and I swear, Marcus, if you make me a fucking liar, I'm going to tear your testicles out through your throat."

I stare at her unblinking as my brothers fall quiet around me. "Okay," I finally say as Roman lets out a frustrated sigh behind me. "We'll take the girl, but she stays one night and one night only. After that, she's on her own."

Shayne nods and takes a breath, my words seeming to ease something inside of her soul as she relaxes back against the bathroom wall, the cool tiles pressing up against her heated skin. "Okay," she breathes before shooting her glare toward the gasping man in the tub. "Now what am I supposed to do about that?"

Levi steps a little closer, judging the mess in front of him. "Why's he in the bathtub?" he questions, his lips pressing into a hard line.

Shayne shakes her head and it's clear that this was a spur-of-the-moment decision. "I … I don't know. He was bleeding everywhere and staining the carpets. I'll never get my deposit back, well … I was so late on my rent anyway. It's not like I was going to get it back in the first place, but my landlord would have made me pay for damages."

Levi scoffs. "You don't need to worry about that."

"Huh? Why the hell not?" Shayne demands, her gaze snapping to Levi's as her brow furrows with confusion.

I find myself smirking as Roman looks back at her. "Let's just say that we had an unfortunate run-in with your landlord a few hours before we took you and we couldn't risk him running his mouth so we may have squeezed his chunky ass through a meat grinder. That bastard sure clogged up that machine though."

Shayne gapes at us and my brows start to furrow, wondering what could possibly be wrong with that. We did her a favor. The guy was an ass and jacking off on her bed with a pair of dirty underwear. If we didn't take her, he eventually would have. "You killed him?" she gasps. "What the hell is wrong with you?"

"Look at the bright side," I tell her. "You're not evicted anymore and all your stuff is still here."

"Gee, great," she beams, her sarcasm coming through thick and loud. "How lucky."

I roll my eyes as Roman pulls a gun, wanting to get this shit over and done with. He holds it up, aiming it right at her father, and just as he's about to pull the trigger, Shayne inches off the wall. "Wait," she rushes out. "I want to do it."

Roman glances back at her, his brow arching as he watches her through wary eyes. "Are you sure?"

She glares back at him. "I shot him once before, didn't I?"

Roman rolls his eyes and steps out of her way, having learned which battles to choose when it comes to this little spitfire. He passes Shayne his gun, and she steps up in front of her whimpering father.

Shayne raises the barrel with absolute venom in her eyes, stirring something deep within me and as she takes aim, I shake my head and let out a heavy sigh. "Four hours down in the playground and you didn't learn a thing?" I question, stepping in behind her and adjusting her body weight. I raise her chin, pull her shoulders back and fix her hold on the gun. I step back and look over her stance. "If you're going to do this, make sure you do it right."

She glances back at me, her brows furrowed as her gaze shifts up and down her body. "Like this?"

Maxwell Mariano musters up his last ounce of energy and shakes his head, seeing a difference in her from the last time they were in this position only two weeks ago. "Shayne, I'm your papa," he says, trying to pull on the heartstrings that he was responsible for fracturing. "You don't want to do this."

"Hey," I say, holding up my hand to shush him. "Don't be rude. She needs to concentrate. She's going to be pissed with herself if she misses. Don't distract her."

Shayne focuses again, clenching her jaw, and as her father's voice sounds through the small bathroom again, her body flinches and her whole posture changes, undoing everything we just went over.

"Come on, man," I groan as Shayne drops her shoulder. "I'm trying to teach her something here. You're fucking with her technique and that's just uncalled for."

Levi steps in beside me, lifting his finger to his lips. "Hush now," he tells her father.

Shayne takes a deep breath and raises her chin, she adjusts her posture and gets into a comfortable position. A smug as fuck grin tears across her face and damn it, I've never been so attracted to this woman in my life. My dick grows hard in my pants, straining against the metal zipper as I roll my tongue over my bottom lip, the excitement building deep within me and sending a wave of adrenaline coursing through my veins.

"Just so you know," she tells him. "While you're rotting in the fiery pits of hell, I'm going to fucking shine. Every chance I get. I'm going to shit all over your dirty name until the whole fucking world knows just how much of a piece of shit you truly were. And for the record, I'm going to have everything you ever wanted in life without having to lift a goddamn finger. I'll be living it up in a fucking castle with more money than you have ever seen, high on the knowledge that I will always be better than you." She moves in closer to her father, leaning over and pressing the gun right between his eyes as hers seem to shimmer with the most dazzling happiness. "You're nothing to me, just a dirty stain on my past that I've already forgotten. Fuck you, Father. Your reign of terror over me is finally over. I'm free."

BANG!

CHAPTER TWENTY SIX

After hours of rotting in the back of the Escalade, the decaying body only goes to fuck with my day some more. "What the fuck?" I demand, interrupting Jasmine's description of her kidnapper as the door opens and the smell all but smacks me in the face. Marcus smirks, barely having taken his eyes off me since I decided to take control of my life and put a bullet through my father's brain. "Don't just stand there. Do something about it. I'm not driving all the way back to your stupid haunted castle with this big bastard stinking it up. I mean, what even is that? Did shit leak out of his asshole now that it's not clenched? It smells wet."

Marcus just smiles, watching me like he's in awe, hanging off my every word, and after a long, narrowed stare, he finally opens the trunk before reaching in and gripping the body. He hauls it out and dumps it straight into the old beat-up Jeep parked beside us—a Jeep that wasn't there when I parked the Escalade in the early hours of the morning.

With the back cleared out and free, Levi dumps the three duffle bags of my clothes into the vacated space and my face twists in disgust, wondering just how much of that dead body is left behind and now marinating my things.

Roman starts the engine and puts every window down, cranking the air conditioning to relieve the Escalade of the smell, and the way Roman gets down to business suggests this isn't the first time a dead body has been rotting in the back.

A minute passes and with the early morning sun beginning to creep into the sky, we get a move on. It won't be long before people start making their way to work or getting up for an early gym session, and we do not want to be here when they do.

I take the center in the back, assuming that Jasmine isn't comfortable enough to sit directly next to one of the boys, considering the way she flinches every time they come near, but I can't blame her, especially after the bullshit she's been through over the past few weeks. Roman takes the driver's seat as usual, but when Marcus goes to take the back beside me, I shake my head. "No fucking way," I tell him, pointing toward the front. "You have decaying body juice all over you and I just showered. You're sitting up front."

Levi smirks and shoves him out of the way before climbing in beside me and hooking his heavy arm over my shoulder, making Jasmine jump as his fingers unintentionally brush over her fragile shoulder. Not wanting to make this harder than it needs to be, he keeps his hands to himself and we get the fuck out of here.

Keeping only a few of the windows down to mask the boys from the rest of the world, we pull out of the darkened underground garage into the lonely city streets. Roman takes off at full speed, his dark, obsidian eyes narrowing in the rearview mirror as he takes in Jasmine beside me. "Right," he says, getting back to business. "Who is this guy? Start from the top."

Jasmine swallows hard and gives the same explanation she'd given me while we were cuffed to the column, only taking all the emotion out of it. "He broke into my house a few weeks ago. I'm not sure how many days have passed. I lost track of days after the first week. It was the middle of the night and my baby was asleep in his room. I tried to get to him first but I was banged around and taken. All I really remember after that is the sound of my baby crying. The noise had woken him up."

"Do you know what the guy's name was?" Roman questions, casually skimming over all the other details that guys like Roman and his brothers are already too familiar with. Bad guy breaks in, roughs up the girl, takes her as his own. Hell, it's similar to my story.

Jasmine shakes her head, her eyes filling with unshed tears. "I don't know. He made me refer to him as master, but one night he had a visitor and I could only hear a muffled conversation, but I think the person referred to him as James."

Marcus lets out a frustrated huff. "That could be anyone," he says. "What else? Any distinctive features? Hair? Height? Tattoos?"

She swallows hard and shrugs her shoulders. "No tattoos. He's just like everyone else. Looks like a normal guy. Dark hair, dark eyes, average height. There's nothing special about him, nothing that makes him stand out."

"She's right," I say. "I saw him when he put her up on that podium. He looks like some kind of try-hard CEO in a fancy suit. He gave me the creeps. He stopped and asked me who my master was and when I said I wasn't for sale, he acted like that wasn't going to be a problem for him. I'd recognize him if I saw him again."

Levi's hands ball into fists, not liking the idea of someone attempting to take what's his as Roman mutters from the front seat. "Look, you can stay with us for the night. Make some calls and figure yourself out, but no more than that. I don't know this guy. He could be anyone and I'm not putting my neck out for you or risking my brothers' lives," he says. "If he comes looking for you, sure, we'll happily put him down, but we're not going on a witch hunt for you."

She nods as a wave of sadness comes over her. "I understand," she says in a small voice, having hoped that the brothers would move heaven and hell to save her and be her unexpected heroes, but if that's what she was wanting, she's going to be sorely disappointed. These boys only do things that immediately benefit themselves … and I guess me too.

"You're going to be okay," I tell her in a small voice, trying to keep our conversation somewhat private. "Call your husband when we get back and organize a place to meet. We'll drop you off and after that, you guys should take the fuck off. Change your names and build a new life in a different country, somewhere he won't find you. You're going to be fine. Get yourself a gun and learn how to breathe again."

Jasmine swallows hard and gives me a forced smile that doesn't reach her eyes, though I see the gratefulness buried deep below her grief. She's glad to be out of there and happy to be able to see her family again, but the haunting memories are going to kill her. She's going to need one hell of a therapist after this.

We get an hour into our trip when Roman veers off the pavement, pulling up a cloud of smoke as he turns onto a dirt road, following a sign that reads 'JOE'S AUTO SHOP.'

"What are we doing?" I question, sitting up straighter to peer out the window.

"You want those things off your necks, don't you?"

My hand falls to the heavy collar and relief pulses through me as I turn my gaze to Roman. Warmth rushes through me. He could have easily waited until we got back to the castle and had one of his brothers free us, but this just goes to show that sometimes, he's not the cold-hearted asshole he always strives to be. A beaming smile spreads across my face. "Fuck yeah."

Roman pulls up at the front roller door of the shop and we all peer around for a quick moment. "Nobody's home," Marcus mutters, noticing what we all do—there are no cars, no lights, and judging by the thick chain and lock hanging from the front door, nobody has been home for a while.

We pile out of the car and Levi fucks around in the back of the Escalade as we make our way to the door. Jasmine sticks right by my side, still not trusting the boys, but knowing that right now, they're her only hope. Levi meets us a moment later with a massive pair of bolt cutters and I stare at him in wonder. "You just keep those in the back of the car?"

His brows furrow as he glances back at me. "You don't?"

Fucking hell.

Turning my attention back to the door, I watch as Levi steps in and cuts through the thick chain like it was nothing but a piece of wet paper. His muscles roll and I'm completely mesmerized until I remember that these assholes are the ones responsible for putting me into this stupid collar in the first place.

We waste no time, rushing inside and hitting the lights. Marcus walks through the place like he's in his element, knowing exactly what he's looking for as he reaches back and takes my hand. He leads me through the dirty shop and my face scrunches, smelling something that isn't sitting well with my stomach.

Jasmine sticks with me as Marcus leads me to a bench, pushes me down, and takes off toward a workbench. He scurries through some things, looking high and low until a grin stretches wide over his face.

He pulls down some kind of circle-shaped saw contraption and I gape at it in horror. "What the fuck is that?" I screech, the thought of what he plans to do with it sinking in and weighing down on my shoulders.

"It's a grinder," he says, walking back toward me while searching the shop for an outlet. "It'll slice through that collar like butter."

Ahhhhhhh, shit. I should have known. When it comes to the DeAngelis brothers, nothing is ever easy.

"Here," Levi says, yanking off his shirt and stepping into me. "It'll be hot and sparks are going to come at you like fireworks," he explains as he threads the shirt through the small space between my neck and the collar and spreads out the rest of it to protect as much of my skin as possible.

"No," I say, flying up off the bench and trying to yank the shirt out from under the collar. "Absolutely not. This is insane. What kind of fucked-up idea is this? You're not putting that thing anywhere near me. What happened to the key?" I demand as my fingers go to the small, bolted lock at the front of the collar.

Levi's face pulls into a guilty cringe. "When we were processed by the FBI, they took everything I had on me. The key is gone. This is our best shot."

"FUCK."

I pace around the dirty shop taking long deep breaths as my hands ball in and out of fists at my side, desperately trying to give myself a pep talk. It's nothing. Just a big-ass sharp blade spinning at a million miles per hour right by my neck. Not a stupid idea in the least. It makes all kinds of sense.

Shit. I'm fucking screwed. And here I thought I was going to die during some brutal attack, and all along I was going to be taken down by a spinning blade.

I allowed this to happen. What the fuck is wrong with me?

My terrified stare locks onto Marcus. "You better make it fast and I swear, if you tear through my skin, I'm going to come back from the dead and haunt your ass like never before."

"It's cool, babe. Believe it or not, this ain't my first rodeo."

My eyes bug out of my head and I gape at him, wondering when in the fresh hell he would have had to do this before, but instead of asking the question of the hour, I turn toward Roman and Levi. "You two are going to have to hold me down."

Levi nods as Roman cringes. "I don't think that's such a good idea," he says, his gaze sweeping to the healing tattoo on his arm, the tattoo that has done nothing but remind me of what happened the night Marcus was shot every time I see it.

"I'll be fine," I tell him, my jaw clenched, not wanting to get into the finer details with Jasmine here. "Just do it."

Roman holds my stare for a long moment before finally nodding, and a part of me wonders who this is supposed to be harder for—me or him?

Marcus plugs in the grinder and it fires to life, the horrific sound of the blade spinning scaring the shit out of me as I make my way back to the bench. Levi helps me lay down before spreading the shirt over my face and body. He grips my hand and I squeeze tight as I feel Marcus move in beside me, his strong thigh pressed up against my arm.

Ahh, fuck, fuck, fuck.

Clenching my eyes, I swallow over the massive lump in my throat as I feel Levi and Roman press down over me like a vice. With my full attention locked on the grinder, I don't even notice Roman's strong hands holding me down.

Marcus brings the grinder over the collar and the sound of the blade cutting into the thick metal has me wildly thrashing and fretting beneath the boys' strong hold. The collar heats up just as Levi explained, and I feel the sparks hitting the part of my skin that the shirt doesn't cover.

The smell of burning metal hits me and I clench my eyes, willing it to be over. Levi's thumb moves slowly across my skin and I focus everything I have on that.

Seconds tick by before Marcus cuts the power on the grinder and pulls back. "It's done," Marcus mutters as Roman grips my arms and helps me sit up. The metal is hot and they wrap their hands in old rags to pull the collar from around my neck until I'm finally free and able to leave the last of the night in my past.

I take a shaky breath but before I can completely recover, Marcus is looking at Jasmine. "You're up," he tells her.

Her eyes bug out of her head but seeing that I'm just fine, she reluctantly takes my place on the bench. Levi threads his shirt through the narrow space at her neck just as he had for me, and I cringe as Roman moves in to hold her down.

Jasmine whimpers and I can't help but feel for her knowing what a powerful man holding her down must be doing to her right now.

Marcus makes quick work of her collar and before I know it, we're making our way out of the shop, letting the heavy door fall shut behind us. I step up to the side of the Escalade as Marcus and Levi walk around the opposite way to get in, but I find myself reaching out to Roman, gripping onto his elbow as he reaches for the door handle.

"What is it?" he questions, pausing as he glances back at me, the soft breeze of the early morning brushing against our bodies.

My lips press into a hard line and allowing myself just a moment of vulnerability, I step into him, and press up onto my toes. My lips briefly brush against his cheek before I lower myself until I'm flat on my feet. "Thank you," I murmur. "You didn't have to stop and risk us getting caught. I appreciate it."

He watches me for a long moment, his eyes narrowing to tight slits. "I thought you had the shits with me?"

"Oh, I do," I grin. "I'm just too exhausted to put the effort into being a bitch about it, but don't you worry your pretty little head. Come tomorrow, I'll be more than happy to make up for it."

I don't say another word as I pull the door open and scooch across the backseat of the Escalade, getting comfortable between Jasmine and Levi.

Roman takes off just as he had earlier and after ten minutes back on the road, the exhaustion proves too much for Jasmine to handle. Her head droops forward as her eyes give in and she falls into a deep, fretful sleep. I press against her face, gently tilting her head to the side to rest against the window so she doesn't hurt her neck, and after a short moment, a light snore sounds through the car.

Marcus leans forward, his hand outstretched as he presses a few buttons, letting the soft music fill the cramped space, drowning out the boys' murmured conversation so she can sleep in peace.

Levi's fingers immediately begin tapping on his thigh as his knee bounces, perfectly in tune with the music and I find myself watching him. He's so damn skilled. I could have only ever dreamed of having that kind of talent as a kid, though I was more about the guitar, not that I ever had the money to get one for myself—nor would I want to.

My father would have pawned it for cash or cheap alcohol.

Levi catches me staring and looks down at me, taking in the pain within my eyes. Without a question, he reaches for me and pulls me up onto his lap so that I'm straddling him. "You're fucking stunning," he tells me, brushing the hair back off my face and skimming his fingers down my neck, taking in the heavy bruises and blisters the collar left on my skin. "We never should have taken you there."

I agree wholeheartedly, and just when I'm about to tell him exactly what I thought of that stupid party, something else comes flying from between my lips. "I murdered my father."

Levi nods. "You did," he tells me, his eyes glistening with something dark. "Don't let the guilt eat at you. I saw how you stood proud, how you enjoyed every fucking second of it. Let that feeling consume you, corrupt you. Don't you dare shed a fucking tear for that bastard. Come and join us on the dark side, Shayne. You'll thrive there and you'll be our fucking queen, ruling over the three of us. We will kneel at your fucking feet if you asked."

"You really think so?" I question as his hands fall to my hips, pulling me in closer.

He takes the front of my black tank and tears at the fabric until I'm left bare before him, my tits mere inches from his full lips. "I fucking know so." And just like that, his hand curls into the back of my hair and pulls me in, crushing my lips to his.

He kisses me deeply, and as his tongue sweeps into my mouth, I realize that I have absolutely no idea when I stopped hating him. At some point, the fear of being around him faded away, and I unknowingly forgave him for what he did after Marcus was shot. All that pain somehow faded and left me with nothing but admiration for this terrifying man.

"I don't want to be your queen, Levi," I murmur against his lips as he grinds up against me, his hard cock rubbing against my needy cunt. "I want to be your equal."

"You can never be my equal," he tells me, his brothers silently listening from the front seats. "Not when I already hold your life above mine."

And without another word, he reaches down and strips me of my sweatpants. His thick cock is pulled free, and after curling his strong arm around my waist and adjusting my position, I sink down on top of him. He fills me to the brim, stretching me wide as his veiny cock moves against my walls. His lips come down over my pebbled nipple and as he teases me with his skilled tongue, I fuck him with everything that I've got while his brothers watch the show with jealous, heated stares.

CHAPTER TWENTY SEVEN

The Escalade pulls to a jerking halt and my eyes snap open, finding an army of black SUVs surrounding the front of the castle. My heart leaps out of my fucking chest, thundering wildly as a loud gasp tears from between my lips.

"Fucking hell," Marcus spits, taking in the dramatic show of force as both mine and Jasmine's gaze sweep over the cars. My mind instantly takes me to the FBI, assuming they've come to collect their escaped prisoners, but seeing the old bastard standing front and center, my mood takes a deep dive.

"What the hell does he want?" I demand, my arm flinging into the back to grab a new tank out of my duffle bag to replace the one that was torn to shreds by the satisfied beast sitting beside me. The boys' father stripped me bare once before, and I won't be allowing him to look at me like that ever again—no matter what the cost.

Roman growls deep in his chest and slowly begins creeping the Escalade in closer, knowing damn well there's no escape here. We have no choice but to face the firing squad about tonight's little excursion. The boys have been caught red-handed, and I don't doubt that will come with consequences, consequences that will most likely extend to me. "Any bets that one of those little FBI bitches on my father's payroll put in a call the moment they clocked us in that fucking tomb? Look at that smug fucker," he continues, gently shaking his head. "He's here to remind us who's fucking boss."

Marcus scoffs. "Not even that army could convince me that he holds any cards here. He might look smug, but the fear in his eyes shines brighter than those fucking diamonds around his neck."

A smirk plays on my lips as I notice Jasmine's shaking hands beside me. "You're going to have to stay in the car for this one," I tell her as I fix my tank back into place. "Trust me, you don't want anything to do with this guy. On better thought, you should probably duck down and hide. It's best that Giovanni doesn't even know you're here."

"Gi—Giovanni?" she sputters wide-eyed and terrified, her fear mirroring mine the first time I saw the douche. "As in Giovanni DeAngelis, mafia boss?"

"The one and only," Levi mutters beside me, the irritation clear in his voice, knowing all too well what a random visit from his father could mean. "Welcome to the shit show."

Roman brings the Escalade to a stop right in the center of the black SUVs and lets out a heavy sigh before turning to face me. "Remember—"

"I know," I murmur, rolling my eyes as I cut him off, more than used to the routine by now. "Seen and not heard. I got it the last hundred times."

"Could have fooled me," he mutters before glancing toward his brothers. "Don't fuck this up. I'm not in the mood to spend the day cleaning up your messes. I just want him out of here so we can figure out what the hell to do with this chick."

He turns his attention to Jasmine. "Keep your head down," he tells her, the venom in his eyes ensuring her compliance. "Don't make a fucking noise. Don't scream. Don't run. Don't even fucking peek out the goddamn window. Is that clear? If you hear shots, you close your eyes and hope to fucking God that you don't get hit. This ain't none of your business, but if you try and make it yours, I will see to it that you don't live to tell a damn soul."

Her eyes go wide as she nods her head, more terrified of Roman than she's been this whole time.

I let out a heavy sigh. "Are you kidding me? Do you have any idea how much effort I've put in trying to get her to trust you enough to stop shaking? And then you have to go ahead with that bullshit? Fuck's sake, Roman. Thanks a lot."

Roman narrows his dark stare. "I'm not playing your fucking games, Shayne. I couldn't give a shit if she trusts me or not. That's her problem, not mine, but if she foolishly decides that she can trust me, knowing what she already knows of me, then that's her mistake. Now, get the fuck out of the car so we can get this over and done with."

I roll my eyes, but he doesn't give me a chance as he pushes his door wide. As if on cue, the army of douchebags raise their guns and Marcus lets out a frustrated sigh. "Just fucking great. Tasers."

Levi shrugs beside me and opens his door as well. "Beats the shock collars."

"Clearly you've never gotten a taser to the nuts," Marcus murmurs, pushing his door wide.

The three brothers get out of the car as one and I quickly follow after Levi, making sure to close the door behind me to keep Jasmine hidden as she slides down to the floor space. The feel of having the taser guns trained on me makes my stomach turn with unease, but considering the other option is a gun loaded with bullets, I can learn to live with it. Truth be told, those tasers are more than likely aimed at the boys, not me. I'm not seen as a threat to these guys, and for good reason too. My ability to gouge out flesh with my nails has nothing on the gruesome shit the boys can do with their bare hands.

The four of us walk around the Escalade, moving toward Giovanni who stands fifteen feet away.

Twelve feet.

Ten feet.

Nine. Eight. Seven.

Without warning or even a chance to scream, every single fucking trigger is pulled and the sharp metal prongs of the tasers dig into my skin. In an instant, I drop to the ground, my body spasming in pain as I scream out, the agony too much to bear.

Hot tears sting my eyes but the pain only lasts a few seconds before it fades away, leaving me numb and gasping for breath. Marcus hovers beside me, on his knees with his tight fists pressed against the driveway and it only takes me a moment to realize I wasn't the only one taken down by the brutal shock—all four of us were. As I raise my head off the ground, I find Giovanni standing right in front of us. "It was so nice of you to join us."

What a fucking asshole.

Anger pulses through my body. Where the fuck does he get off pulling fucked-up stunts like that?

Roman is the first to recover, getting to his feet as he grabs hold of the metal prongs and pulls them off his skin, though I'm not surprised. A guy like Roman probably spends his day tasering himself just to build up some kind of resistance to the shock, training himself for moments just like this. The fucker probably gets off on it.

Marcus' hand skims over my bare waist as he gets to his feet, but that's all I get from him. He's willing me to stand on my own, determined not to show how much he cares for me in front of his father.

The boys don't say a word to their father, just silently stare as I get up on shaky feet, wishing I had stayed hidden in the back of the Escalade with Jasmine.

"Start talking," Giovanni spits, looking over his sons like they're the scum of the earth. "Where the hell have you been? You are on strict orders to remain in the castle, so imagine my surprise when I get a call telling me my fucking moronic sons were arrested by the FBI."

A smirk pulls at the corner of Roman's mouth, more than pleased with himself for calling it. "Business," he says, not offering any more than that.

"Business?" Giovanni roars. "The only fucking business you have is mine. What the fuck were you doing at that party? Who were you meeting?"

Marcus grins and I know he's about to shit all over the limitations Roman just put on him. I can all but hear Roman's defeated sigh. "Why?" Marcus questions, his eyes sparkling with that usual *I'm up to no good* gleam. "There were some big names at that party. Which one of them has you shaking in your boots?"

Marcus gets hit with another fucking taser and I almost cry out as he drops to his knees beside me, but instead, I just stand tall, trying not to let my emotions show as he curses in pain at my feet.

Giovanni grins, Marcus' show of pain doing nothing but getting him off. "When will you learn, son?" he mutters, crouching down to meet Marcus' heated stare. "You will never beat me. Surrender. Tell me what I want to know."

Marcus tears the prongs off his skin as a clammy sweat begins taking over. "You're a fucking bitch," he tells him, pronouncing each word like gospel.

Giovanni's hand cracks out, breaking across Marcus' skin with a loud slap.

"Enough," I growl, pushing myself between Marcus and Giovanni and being careful not to touch him despite my hand flinching at my side. I feel Marcus stand behind me, his big body hovering way over mine. "You call your sons moronic, yet you have them locked up in this ridiculous castle and they still manage to defy you. How many times are you going to hurt them before learning that it only makes them stronger and fuels their desire to destroy you?"

Giovanni glares at me and just as I expected, his hand comes hurtling toward my face. I flinch back just in time as Roman's hand snaps out, catching his father's wrist, just like he had that night many weeks ago. Without a moment of pause, Roman shoves his father's hand back into his chest with such force that he stumbles back a few steps, each of his henchmen flinching with the hit.

"You are out of line, girl," Giovanni spits, barely looking at me as his foul stare slices toward Roman's, who I have no doubt is silently brooding at my idiocy to step in his father's line of sight while on a witch hunt.

Roman steps toward his father and I grin at the way his eyes tighten, fear pulsing through his veins. "Tell me, Father," Roman muses, enjoying this way more than he will ever admit. "How did those agents know about that party?"

"You think I had my sons arrested?" Giovanni scoffs as something catches my eyes up past the grand entrance of the castle.

Roman silently steps around his father, making his body stiff at having his son at his back while his others remain in view, knowing all too well just how perfectly they work as a group. "You tell me," he murmurs darkly as a figure appears at the top of the stairs, a figure that instantly grinds on my nerves. "You have the connections to pull it off and the motivation. How easy your life would be if your three sons were locked away behind bars. You wouldn't have a care in the world, but that's where you're wrong. If you think for even a second that we wouldn't have a pull, even from behind bars, you're going to be sorry. Watch your back, Father."

Giovanni scoffs, discreetly stepping to the side to see all three of his sons at once as his bitch of a wife sails down the grand entrance as though she owns the place. "Don't insult me," Giovanni spits. "If I wanted to get rid of you, I would put a bullet through your miserable brain. Don't assume that I take part in playing ridiculous games like you do."

Roman laughs and walks back toward his brothers as Ariana steps in beside her husband, handing him a drink like the perfect little wife, only her gaze is locked on me.

My lips pull up into a sneer as her stare trails over my body, taking in every last scar. It takes me a moment to remember that the last time we saw each other, the boys wrapped me perfectly in a gown that covered the extent of my injuries, but here in this cropped white tank, my body is on show for the world to see, every one of my scars telling a loud and horrendous story.

I expect her to be taken aback, or at the very least look a little shocked by the scars, but instead, a smugness creeps into her expression and the bitch almost looks happy about the hell I've endured.

A wicked smile crosses my lips, knowing exactly what kind of cards I hold in my hands. "See something you like?" I question, letting her and everyone else around us hear the double meaning in my tone.

Ariana blanches for a moment, knowing just how dangerous this could be for her, but after forcing me to spread my legs when I was vulnerable and terrified, then demanding I repay her kindness during

Giovanni's business dinner, I kinda hope this gets her in a bit of hot water. Karma's a bitch and is best served with a face like mine.

She quickly recovers, doing her best to put on a show for her husband, though something tells me she puts on a good show for him every damn night. Her knees would be just as bruised as mine, only mine are bruised for a very different reason. "I'm just glad to see those boys finally put you in your place for that smart mouth of yours."

I roll my tongue over my bottom lip. "I'd bet you'd love to see just what this smart mouth can really do," I tell her, loving the tightness in her eyes and wondering if by any chance she might have been the hooded girl that shot Marcus, though my gut still screams Felicity. "Why so smug, Ariana? Is there something you're hiding? Something you want to confess?"

Giovanni turns his attention on his new wife, his eyes narrowed to slits, having every reason not to trust her, and considering he blackmailed her until she stood at his side, he shouldn't trust her. This bitch is as vile as they come. "What does she speak of?" Giovanni demands, spitting his words like poison in his mouth.

Ariana shakes her head. "I haven't got a clue," she says. "I met the girl once during your dinner party and tried to be nice and look where that got me. She's just another jealous bitch trying to cause problems. They all do, you know that better than anyone."

Giovanni scoffs as though everything she just said makes perfect sense before he turns his attention back on me, his lips pulling up in disgust. "Then what are you waiting for?" he questions his wife. "Go and deal with it."

"Gladly," she says, her shoulders pulling back in excitement. She strides toward me, her expensive red-bottom heels clicking against the asphalt as her gaze sweeps over my body. She shakes her head as though what she sees is so pathetic, it's not even worth her time. "You better watch your tongue," she murmurs, keeping our conversation private. "I am not somebody you want to mess with."

"Really?" I laugh. "That's cute. Though, I wonder if you've realized yet that holding my tongue isn't exactly one of my strong points."

Her face falls, seeing just how serious I am about destroying her for what she did to me. "I swear, you little bitch," she murmurs, her voice hitching a little higher, creeping into dangerous territory of spilling her own damn secrets. "If you say a goddamn word, I will cut your bloody tongue out. Don't think I won't. I will destroy you."

"You see, that's just the thing," I tell her, remembering that night during the business dinner when my rejection pushed her over the edge and all I got was a bitch slap before she stormed away, making me realize with complete certainty that she couldn't be the hooded girl. "I don't think you will. You don't have what it takes, and deep down, you know it. You're just flailing around like the rest of us, hoping you don't get a bullet through the head. The only difference between us is that you've had years of practice, pretending like it bounces right off your shoulders. Though, just between you and me, I think you cry all night and binge eat ice cream and peanut butter because you don't know how to control the fear. You're an actress, Ariana, and that's all you'll ever be."

She stares at me, swallowing hard and having no clue how to

respond to that, so instead, she looks back over her shoulder and sneers at her husband. "I'm bored," she says like a whiny brat. "Wrap this up. I want to get out of this dump."

The corners of Giovanni's lips pull into a smug grin as he watches his bitch of a wife strut past me, bumping my shoulder harder than any woman has the right to. All is silent apart from the clicking sound of her heels on the driveway as she strides away, trying to hold her head up high. Not a sound is made until she opens the door of Giovanni's car, slides into the back, and slams it shut.

Giovanni glances back at his sons. "Last chance. Who were you meeting with?"

Levi's head tilts and a sick excitement pulses through me. "How did my mother die?"

Giovanni stares back at him, his brows furrowed, confused by Levi's sudden change of topic, though I'm not. Too many questions have been raised about their mysterious mother, the woman up in the tallest tower of this castle, frozen in her glass coffin. It's been plaguing Levi's mind, though he hasn't said anything, I can sense it. It was only natural for him to seek out answers eventually.

"I ... why is that necessary?" Giovanni asks. "I am not here to spend hours talking to you about your mother. You are no longer a child."

"I am not searching for stories, Father. I am searching for answers," he says, stepping forward and stalking his father, making adrenaline pulse through my veins. Levi doesn't stop until he's standing right in front of him, his impressive height towering over Giovanni. "I'm not going to ask you again," he says as some of the guards switch out their tasers for guns. "How did my mother die?"

Giovanni narrows his eyes, the hard tick of his jaw is a clear indication that he's losing control. "I wrapped my hands around her fragile throat and I squeezed until she stopped breathing," Giovanni spits, stepping impossibly closer into his son until their noses are almost touching. "Your mother was a useless swine and did nothing but baby you. She was destroying my legacy, filling your minds with ridiculous stories and unconditional love. She was weak, and every moment you spent around her made you just as pathetic. You should be thanking me," he spits. "Without me, you three would have been average, just as useless as she was. You never would have had what it takes to stand in my place, but now look at you. I created you in my image."

Levi's hand snakes out like a rabid python, cutting around his father's neck with impossible strength, squeezing just like Giovanni had done to their mother. Levi raises his hand into the air until Giovanni's feet are dangling above the ground, having the complete power to snap his neck like a damn twig.

I wait anxiously, my knees shaking, silently daring Levi to put an end to all this bullshit and take him out, but before he gets a chance, the harsh metal prongs of another taser pierces his skin. Levi falls to the ground, his knees crushing against the asphalt as his jaw clenches in agony. He hastily releases his father, and Giovanni shakily catches himself, grabbing the bottom of his suit jacket and straightening it up.

Before Levi's body has even stopped convulsing on the ground, Giovanni gets the fuck out of here like the scared little bitch that he is.

CHAPTER TWENTY EIGHT

The black SUVs careen down the long driveway, taking off like fucking rockets as they hurtle toward the front gates, more determined than ever to get the fuck out of here. "What the fuck did I say about starting shit?" Roman demands, pissed off with each of his brothers, but I'm not going to lie, I can't find it in me to be upset, that was the most entertainment I've had in my life. That shit is worthy of an award. A Grammy? Emmy? A Tony? Which is the one for big stage performances? Because damnnnn, put that shit on a stage in front of thousands of people and they would have received a standing ovation. Fuck the mafia, put these bitches in tutus.

Marcus scoffs as we all turn to face the Escalade that looks all too lonely in the massive driveway by itself. "Like you're one to talk," he mutters as we move toward the big black car. "What was with all your, *tell me, Father, how did those agents know about that party* bullshit? I couldn't let you have all the fun, now could I?"

Roman doesn't respond, knowing damn well that Marcus is right. Though there's no denying that Marcus and Levi were a little more demanding in their approach. At least they were able to get a few answers out of their father, even if they weren't the ones they were hoping for.

It's only been a few minutes since Levi was knocked down by that taser again, and he hasn't spoken a damn word after hearing exactly how their father murdered their mother. Though, they had to have expected it. Surely they couldn't have been so blind to believe she died some other way, but then, they were only vulnerable kids. Who knows what their father would have told them about her sudden death.

Marcus reaches out and grips the door handle of the Escalade and tears it open. "Come on," he says, his voice low and demanding, leaving no room for argument. "Out."

Jasmine's head snaps up, her eyes wide as her gaze snaps to Marcus. She peers up, peeking her head over the window edge and peering out into the massive drive to see that the threat is now gone. She lets out a shaky breath as she scrambles out of the Escalade quicker than she ran for the exit in the tomb.

Leading her up the grand entrance, we find the front door left wide open and relief surges through me knowing that I won't have to scale a fucking maze bush just to get back inside. My body is too tired for that crap. I just want to find a bed and crash in it, and honestly, it doesn't even matter whose bed it is at this point.

I get Jasmine inside and before I even get a chance to show her around or tell her where the bathroom or dining hall is, Roman is there with a phone, handing it over. "Go and call your husband," he tells her. "Do not give him your location or tell him who you are with. We will take you to him. Understood?"

She swallows hard and nods, her eyes still wide as she scurries out of the foyer and toward the massive staircase. She drops down on the third step, hugging the banister as though it's her only lifeline. We all watch her for a moment as she enters the phone number, and after a long pause, she sobs at the sound of her husband's voice.

I can't help but glance at Roman again. He's really trying to make things up to me, though I can't be certain what for. It could be for the whole slicing and dicing incident after Marcus was shot, or for rejecting me in the den and making me feel like a pathetic, desperate whore. Either way, I appreciate it.

With Jasmine sorted out, I cross through the foyer and step into the massive living room, my heart breaking as I find the two wolves passed out on the floor, just like I found them after Giovanni's last visit. "For fuck's sake," I mutter, my jaw clenching as I bend down in front of them, holding my hands out in front of their mouths to feel their warm breath brushing against my skin.

Certain that they're still alive, I drop onto the big couch and get comfortable, scooching down and propping my head against the armrest as the boys trail in after me. Each one of them mimics my expression as they see the wolves on the ground, and just as I had, Levi takes it a step further to double-check they're still breathing, knowing his father's sick antics all too well.

Roman sits directly across from me and I can't help but grab the half-empty water bottle from the coffee table and launch it at his head. "The fuck was that for?" he demands, his eyes pulsing with an uncontrollable rage, his emotions already too messed with to be able to function like a normal human being.

"Your taste in women fucking sucks," I tell him. "Ariana? Really? She's a fucking bitch. God, I hate her. What the hell were you thinking?"

Roman clenches his jaw and glances away, trying to calm himself as Marcus and Levi smirk, the agreement clear on their faces, though they don't dare speak it out loud.

Roman shoots his sharp glare back toward me. "You don't know what the fuck you're talking about," he tells me. "She's had a hard fucking life and has been screwed over with every turn she took. Go easy on her. It's because of her relationship with me that she's trapped under my father's hold. She has every fucking right to be wary of you."

I scoff, shaking my head as I listen to his explanation. "Right, so you're telling me that after ten or so years, she's never been able to get away from him? Never been able to run or disappear despite the unlimited cash and resources she has access to?" I question, looking him dead in the eye. "How many times has she taken off on a jet to vacation in Italy or France? How many times has she easily slipped out of your father's home and spent the night here or out at some dodgy club without question? I'm sorry Roman, but I don't know if you're blind or just stupid. That woman has power over your father and she loves it. She's not suffering in that big-ass mansion, she's his perfect, doting wife. She gets everything she wants, and while it may not have started that way, it definitely is now. You're just too racked with guilt to see it. She's using your emotions against you."

Roman stands, his jaw clenched. "Stop," he growls, his stare boring into mine.

I sit up on the couch, not breaking his hold. "What's the matter, big guy? Don't like it when someone throws some cold, hard facts at you?" I stand and walk around the coffee table, putting myself right in front of him as I feel his brothers' eyes locked on the show, waiting for Roman to lose control. "I grew up around bitches like her in the worst kind of area. I know a snake when I see one, and that woman is the biggest one of all. She's got you wound around her little finger and you can't even see it. I bet if she called you up right now with some sob story, you'd drop everything and run to her side."

Roman just stares, refusing to answer me, so I raise a questioning brow and turn to his brothers, more than ready to wait all day to get the information I need. Realizing I'm not backing down, Levi lets out a heavy sigh. "She's right, man. Ariana calls, you go running."

Roman glares at his brother for a long moment before letting out a sigh and dropping back onto the couch, his gaze locked on the coffee table, knowing damn well I'm right.

Letting out a breath, I sit my ass down on the edge of the coffee table, keeping my gaze on Roman. "I'm sorry," I tell him. "I'm not saying this to be a bitch or anything, I just don't like to see how easily she's getting away with playing you. If anything, I should be trying to become her new best friend to figure out how the hell she does it."

Marcus scoffs. "No need," he mutters darkly. "You're already doing a fucking great job at it."

My lips pull into a smirk. "What's the matter, Marcus? Am I a little too deep under your skin?"

He glances away, staring out the window as though I didn't say a damn thing and I turn my attention back to Roman.

"Why?" Roman finally says. "What's the fucking point in trying to play me? She gains nothing by having me at her side."

I shake my head. "That's where you're wrong. You're the biggest player in this game and once you've overthrown your father and stand at the head of the family, you're going to have more power than Giovanni ever could. She can sense that just as clearly as I can and having you at her disposal makes her more powerful than you could ever know. With a click of your fingers, she would get anything she ever wanted. You're her free ride to the top."

Roman's hands ball into fists on his thigh as the realization and anger begins pulsing through him and I find myself standing and moving toward him. I climb onto his lap, straddling him while keeping a small distance between our bodies, not wanting him to get the wrong idea and push me off him like he did the other night. "Hey," I say, demanding his full attention. "Don't get pissed about it, get even. Cut the bitch off and let her fumble through this fucked-up world like the rest of us. You've already done her enough favors."

He shakes his head. "It's not as easy as you think it is," he mutters. "What my father holds over her ... my brothers and I owe her our lives. The reason we're able to breathe right now is because she gave everything up to save us."

My brows furrow as I glance back at Marcus and Levi to see sober expressions on their hard faces. Marcus nods as Roman's fingers uncurl from his tight fists and rest against my thighs. "It was just like with Flick," Marcus says. "Only she was about eighteen and barely out of high school."

"What happened?"

"Same old shit that happens every time I get close to a girl," Roman says, fixing his hard stare on me, a silent reminder as to why he refuses to ease up and accept the fact that there's something growing between us. "We were pretty fucking close in high school. First love and all that shit," he mutters, rolling his eyes as though the admission physically hurts him. "My father hated it and right after locking us up in this fucking castle, he swooped on her."

"What did he do?"

Roman sighs. "Put a bullet through her mother's head and then promised to do the same to her baby brother. Her assignment was clear, stand at his side and eventually become his wife. If she failed at any point, or refused him, he would take our lives too and she'd be left with nothing."

I narrow my gaze and slowly shake my head, doubting their father. "Was he not bluffing? He's threatened death a million times and you're all still breathing."

Levi sighs and grabs the collar of his shirt, moving it across to show off a faint scar just under his collarbone. "He wasn't fucking bluffing," he says bluntly. "Her baby brother died the day I got this. He was only fourteen and it left her with no one. He was her only remaining family. My father wiped out everything she had until she had no choice but to lean on him, and after all these years, she's stuck by his side to ensure that he doesn't take our lives too."

I swallow hard and turn my gaze back to Roman, finally understanding why he moves heaven and hell for her, but there's still no denying that I'm right. She's a snake, and while life might have been hell for her ten years ago, she's more than adapted to this new lifestyle filled with luxury and power.

I adjust myself so that I sit sideways on his lap and relax into him, my brows drawn, deep in thought. Something still doesn't sit right with me and I refuse to accept that the boys will simply continue catering to her every need and desire because of a decision she made ten years ago.

"What?" Roman murmurs, his hand low on my back. "You're thinking so fucking loud that it's giving me a headache."

Levi and Marcus raise their stares to watch me as I struggle with my thoughts, trying to make sense of them. "I don't know," I mutter, keeping my gaze locked on the wolves sleeping peacefully on the ground. "I just … I don't trust her. She's a snake."

"She's not the hooded bitch," Marcus says, reading into it. "I'd have known if it was her. That girl was too short and too blonde to have been Ariana."

"I know," I agree. "It's not her style. She'd prefer to bitch about me to Roman than go to all the effort to storm in here with a getaway car and try to convince me to run, but something else just isn't sitting right with me. I don't trust her."

"You don't have to," Roman tells me. "I barely trust her myself, but I respect her and owe her my life. She may be playing the game now, but ten years ago, she sacrificed her life so my brothers and I could live. So while I don't expect you to get along with her, I do expect you to make a fucking effort. Once we overthrow our father, she will be ruling right along with us."

My jaw clenches as fierce jealousy and anger pulses through me. Despite the fact that I want the boys all to myself and don't like to share, the very idea of her having a part of what they promised me angers me like never before. I don't expect to have any power in this world once the boys are head of the DeAngelis family, but I expect to have the kind of respect that comes along with being theirs, and to have to share that role with a bitch like Ariana is like a slap in the face.

I pull off of Roman's lap as the fury takes over. "Absolutely not," I spit, stepping over Dill as I make my way back to my original couch and flop down. "Think about what you're asking of me before you go saying stupid shit like that."

Marcus laughs, the amusement tearing across his face. "Well, fuck. I thought I was the one with jealousy issues."

"I'm not fucking jealous," I spit, lying right through my teeth. "I just don't want anything to do with the bitch who spread my legs while I was too fucking scared to say no. And for the record, I'm holding each of you assholes accountable for that shit as well, so bite my fucking perky ass. It's her or me."

Marcus laughs hard. "Aww fuck, you're feisty when you're jealous, huh?"

Crossing my arms over my chest and bringing my legs up on the couch, I focus my hard stare across the room, doing my best to ignore him before I get the stupid idea to throw myself at him and strangle the life out of him. After all, I'm a cold-blooded killer now.

The wolves begin to stir on the floor beneath me and as I drop my attention to them, Jasmine awkwardly appears in the entryway of the huge living room with Roman's replacement phone in her hands. She glances at him just briefly before dropping her gaze, not having the strength to hold onto it. "Ummm, your phone was buzzing with a new text," she mutters, still hovering in the doorway despite clearly wanting to hand the phone back.

She waits right where she is as Roman looks back at her, raising his brow impatiently, though she still doesn't make a move until he lets out a sigh and holds out his hand, wordlessly welcoming her into the living room to hand over the goods.

Jasmine scurries in and quickly hands the phone over. "Did you work out a plan with your husband?" Marcus questions before she gets a chance to bolt.

Jasmine nods. "I did," she says, her eyes slightly bugging out as she takes in the snoring wolves on the ground. She swallows hard and tries to turn her attention back to Marcus. "He's packing our things right now and I'll meet him tomorrow with our son and take off."

"Just because you take off," Marcus says, "doesn't mean that bastard isn't looking for you. Be smart about it. You have a baby to protect and assholes like that will use that against you."

"Ahh, fuck," Roman growls, the fury wafting off him in waves. All eyes turn toward Roman and the small distraction gives Jasmine the chance to bolt out of here like her ass is on fire. She races back out to the big staircase and falls back down on the third step, hugging the side and watching her surroundings as though something could jump out at her at any moment.

Roman stands and paces across the big living room, his lips pressed into a hard line as his gaze continuously shoots toward mine only to drop away again. His hand pulses at his side as his other looks like it could crush his phone with one easy blow.

"The fuck is going on?" Levi questions, getting frustrated with Roman's endless pacing.

He stops just in front of the coffee table as Doe stretches up and walks toward him, sensing his frustration and demanding a scratch. Roman tosses the phone to Levi and does everything he can to avoid my hard stare. "She was fucking right," he mutters between a clenched jaw, struggling to contain his rage as the words coming out of his mouth sound like the hardest words he's ever had to say. "Ariana is a fucking snake."

My back stiffens as Roman's stare finally comes back to mine, a glimmer of guilt glistening in his dark eyes, though the concern keeps me from shitting all over this sweet turn of events. "What did she do?" I demand as a chill sweeps through my bones and my stomach tightens, not liking the look on his face.

Roman swivels his gaze back toward Levi, watching as he takes in whatever is on the screen and I find myself standing, desperate to know what the hell is going on. Levi's jaw clenches, and as his stare snaps up to mine, Marcus steals the phone right out of his hand.

"What is it?" I demand, sick of not having an answer.

Indecision, concern, and unease filter through Levi's gaze as he looks back at Roman, the two of them having some kind of silent conversation. I can't help but feel that whatever is on the phone, not only has something to do with me but is about to change the game.

Marcus' eyes widen as he looks down, and when he doesn't tell me what I need to know, I race in and snatch the phone right out of his hands. I back up a few steps, giving myself a moment to take it in before the boys can take it off me, but they hold back, letting me see it for myself.

My stare locks onto the small screen to see a video sent by a private number, and as I open the video, nerves rush through me. The video is dark and looks like some kind of security footage from an old dive bar. There's a timestamp at the top dated a few weeks ago, but that's not what's got my attention.

Ariana sits at the bar, a drink in hand as she faces a man I never thought I'd ever see again. Lucas Miller. They're deep in discussion, and it's clear by their reactions to one another that there's certainly no friendship between them. This right here is business, and the only kind of business that Lucas Miller has anything to do with is me and bathtubs.

I swallow hard, tears springing to my eyes as the memories of that night come crashing back. "When was this?" I ask, despite the date being clear across the top. My head is too fucked up to go back and try to work out exactly how many days ago Lucas attacked me.

Roman lets out a heavy breath and I can all but see his heart breaking as his trust in Ariana crumbles right before us. "That timestamp is from the night before Lucas attacked you," he says, his head hanging forward, refusing to meet my eye. "This is on me. I told her where we were going to be, thinking she might be up for a night out. She bailed, said she already had plans. I never fucking thought those plans were stabbing me in the back."

My hand fists around the phone, squeezing it tight as the need to rain hell over Ariana crashes through me. She did this. She told Lucas where we were going to be. She set me up and that's why she was so fucking smug seeing my scars this morning. She put them on my body just as much as Lucas did and that bitch will pay.

Rage pulses through me as I stride across the room, putting myself right in front of Roman and grip his chin just as he does to me. "Believe me now?" I spit, having every fucking ball in my court and holding back on the childish, *I told you so.* "That bitch will go down, right along with your father, and if you think for even a second that I'm bluffing, you're going to be sorely mistaken."

Chapter Twenty Nine

Barely a moment has passed since learning of Ariana's betrayal when I find all three of the brothers storming down their massive staircase dressed in black, telling me that shit is about to go down. "What are you doing?" I rush out, following them as they storm into the garage, throwing the door wide and barely working out who will pass over the threshold first, their determination to make heads roll shining brighter than I've ever seen.

"The only reason we haven't moved on our father yet was because of Ariana," Roman mutters as they all stride toward a locked door within the garage. "She's shown her cards, and from here on out, our protection no longer extends to her. We move on our father tonight."

My eyes bug out of my head as I watch the guys break through the locked door to a room full of weapons. It's a fucking armory in here. Machine guns, pistols, daggers, throwing stars, things that I don't even know the names of. They're lined against the wall just like I'd expect at the freaking CIA or SWAT headquarters. No, more than that. The military. The goddamn SEALS. This shit is insane.

I gape at it all as I look around, absolutely amazed yet terrified at the same time. There are grenades and boxes of dynamite, things that I would have been thrilled to never see in my entire life. "This," I breathe, losing my words. "How?"

Levi glances back at me for a brief moment, too distracted to give me his full attention. "We've been preparing for this for ten fucking years. What you see here is only a portion of the weapons we have on standby."

"Shoes," Roman cuts in, his gaze sweeping down my body. "Go and get proper shoes. Black hoodie and whatever the fuck kind of pants you're comfortable in. We're not fucking around tonight. If you're coming, you need to be prepared."

I swallow hard, my eyes bugging out of my head as I realize just how out of my league I'm going to be on this, but this is their shining moment, their victory, the one moment they've waited the past ten years for. There is no way in hell that I'm about to miss it.

Without another word, I race out of the garage and dart up the stairs, passing a wide-eyed Jasmine on the stairs. She gapes at me, her brows furrowed, clearly able to see that something is about to go down but having absolutely no idea what. Knowing damn well that those boys will leave without me, I make quick work of stripping out of my sweats and following their lead where the uniform is concerned.

I pull my hair out of the way and add a pop of red lipstick. The boys may make their black uniform look so damn good, but I need the crimson lips to remind myself that I'm not the weak, pathetic girl they kidnapped a few months ago. I'm a warrior, and I will stand at their side.

Nerves rock through my body but I push them down. What could possibly go wrong? We're only four people standing against Giovanni's whole damn army.

Fuck.

I must be out of my mind.

Hurrying back down the steps, I pass Jasmine again, her brows still furrowed as her eyes fill with concern. "What's going on?" she rushes out, racing after me into the garage, only to pull herself up short, seeing the brothers loading the back of a fucking military-grade truck with all sorts of weapons.

Roman pauses and looks back at her, his face scrunching as he tries to figure out what the hell to do with her. Indecision crosses his handsome features before taking a step toward her and digging the Escalade keys out of his pocket. He tosses them at her and she fumbles to catch them. "Time to go," he tells her. "Take the Escalade and meet your husband. Ditch it in a remote area, pour gasoline over it, and light it up like a fucking bonfire. I don't want a scrap of evidence left on that thing. Got it?"

She swallows hard, her gaze flicking back to mine before finally nodding. "Got it."

Jasmine hovers in the corner of the garage, watching as the boys load up the truck and I stand back, knowing that I'm only going to be in the way. "Get in," Marcus tells me, carrying some kind of machine gun that looks like it weighs a million pounds. He strides past me, the determination hard across his face as he makes his way to the garage door that hasn't been opened in years. Then without warning, he lets loose on the machine gun and sprays bullets over the complicated locks that Giovanni installed.

Jasmine screams and drops to the ground, her hands curling protectively over her head as I race for the back seat of the truck. Roman climbs into the front, grinning as he watches Marcus in his zone while Levi gets in the front passenger side, shaking his head at Marcus' performance.

The lock breaks free of the garage door and Marcus turns back, slinging the machine gun over his shoulder and striding back toward the truck. The grin on his face is like nothing I've ever seen before.

He climbs in the back beside me, laying the gun over his lap like some kind of pet before leaning back out his door. A loud whistle tears from between his lips and Dill and Doe come bounding into the truck, jumping up onto the back seat before bounding right through to the back. They drop down with impeccable car manners and before Marcus even has the door shut, Roman is hitting the gas and speeding right through the front garage roller door.

It tears off its hinges, flying out onto the driveway and crushing beneath the massive tires of the truck. I grip onto the door handle as my body is tossed around, and as Roman speeds past the Escalade that still sits in the center of the huge driveway, I glance back just as Jasmine comes tearing out of the garage after us and rushes toward the Escalade, more than determined to get herself out of here. I don't blame her, my first few hours in that creepy castle were a nightmare. I would have done anything for my freedom.

Knowing the chances of ever seeing her again are slim to none, I turn back and get comfortable in my seat, hoping to whoever lives above that she can get herself back to her husband and be freed of this world for good.

The drive is long and silent as I stare at the back of Roman's seat, my knee bouncing with nerves. Doe launches herself over the backrest and drops her big body onto the space between me and Marcus as her heavy head falls into my lap. I wonder if she senses my nerves. My hand falls to her head, subconsciously scratching behind her ears, and before I know it, Roman is pulling up in front of his father's home.

The truck comes to a stop right in the center of the massive circle drive and we each stare up at the mansion the boys once called home, the place they grew up in, and the home where they received the most horrendous abuse. "Something is up," Levi says, their plan to get the drop on their father backfiring. "They should have caught us at the front gate and been out by now."

Roman stares ahead, his skilled gaze sweeping across the front of the property before he finally shakes his head and hits the gas again. "They're not home yet," he says, taking off around the side of the property to hide the truck. "Plan B. We take them from the inside."

Without warning, Roman's foot flattens to the ground and the truck takes off like a rocket toward the house. A piercing scream tears from the back of my throat and my head burrows into the wolf's fur as the truck sails straight through the massive floor-to-ceiling windows of the dining room that I'd only been in a few weeks ago.

"The fuck are you doing?" I screech as Roman drives the truck right through the house until he's dead center of the massive foyer. No one responds as they pile out of the car, almost as though they can read Roman's mind perfectly.

"What the hell is going on?" I demand, fumbling around like a fucking idiot, watching as they unload weapons and storm around the foyer, setting up the perfect ambush. The wolves jump out and race toward the front foyer windows, watching and waiting for a threat, already on guard despite not receiving a single order.

"Uhhhhh hello?" I say, waving my hands around and demanding attention. "Mind clueing me in on the plan here? What am I supposed to be doing apart from not getting killed?"

Roman jumps down from the high balcony of the second level that overlooks the foyer and glances back at his brothers, his brows furrowed with indecision. He shrugs his shoulders. "I guess … she could just … hide," he suggests, knowing my limits all too well.

Marcus watches me for a moment, narrowing his eyes, deep in thought. "Nah," he says, shaking his head. "She'll end up doing something to get caught. Give her a knife. She has good instincts when it comes to stabbing people."

My eyes bug out of my head. "A knife? No way. I don't plan on getting close enough to any of your father's guards to have to use a knife. Give me a gun."

Roman scoffs. "I'll pass on that one," he mutters. "I've copped enough bullets over the past few weeks without having to worry about an accidental one from you. Besides, you won't be going after the guards. They're too experienced. You'll be overpowered in seconds. You're going after Ariana."

I suck in a breath. "You want me to kill Ariana?"

Levi shrugs. "I figured you'd just fuck her up like Lucas did to you, but if you want to kill her, then that's your decision. Watch those nails though," he offers. "Those sharp as fuck nails are a fucking bitch."

"Good to know," I murmur, trying to act as though I'm not completely horrified about all of this. "How is this supposed to go down anyway?"

Dill and Doe both stand with raised hackles, their low growls rumbling with menace. "I guess you're about to find out," Roman says, moving around the back of the truck and grabbing a few things. He takes hold of me and pulls me in until my body is covered by the open truck door. He straps a knife to both of my thighs, pressing one into my hand, and for good luck, he shoves a gun into the back of my jeans. "Don't fucking shoot me," he warns as I distantly notice that the knife in my hand is the same one that Marcus had gifted me the night he chained me to the fucking ceiling and fucked me until I couldn't breathe. "There are only so many bullets I'm willing to take for you before it's gonna start pissing me off."

I swallow hard and nod. The guy definitely has a point.

We hear the sound of Giovanni's convoy making its way down the massive driveway and the nerves bubble through my system. Roman jumps back into the truck and drives it right out of the foyer to hide it out of the way, and as the boys position themselves behind the exquisite pillars surrounding the wide room, it looks just as Giovanni had left it.

Not a noise fills the foyer as Roman returns and points out the best space for me to stand before taking the pillar across the room, putting equal distance between him and his brothers. The wolves flock to my sides, ready to protect me if needed.

Leaning back just a step, I get the perfect view of the mansion's grand entrance and find Giovanni's guards making their way toward the door. There are only half as many guards as what they had this morning when they blindsided us with those damn tasers, and a part of me is grateful for fewer casualties. "What do you see?" Levi questions, his tone lowered, not wanting to give us away.

"Maybe fifteen or so guards," I tell them. "They're halfway up the stairs. They have those fucking tasers on their hips, and guns on the other. I can't see any other weapons, though I'm sure they're there. They look relaxed, as if they don't suspect anything."

"My father?" Roman asks.

"Only getting out of his car now," I say, pulling in closer to the wall so that the guards don't see my face hovering by the side window. "Ariana is just getting out now too. She looks pissed, as though they've just had a fight or something."

"Shit," Levi mutters, irritated as he switches out his gun for a knife.

"What's wrong?"

"The guards will be here long before my father. They'll warn him and give him time to flee," he explains. "If this is going to work, we need him here. We're going to have to take out all of them by the time he makes it up the stairs, and we have to do it without alerting him to our presence."

Well, shit.

"How the hell are we supposed to do that?" I hiss.

"Not by getting to use my fucking grenade, that's for sure," Levi mutters to himself, clearly disappointed that this bloodbath isn't going to be quite as destructive, loud, and dramatic as he'd hoped.

Marcus steps out from behind the pillar and meets my eyes with a dark, twisted smirk across his lips, looking like the psychotic heathen I know him to be. He raises his hand and the sharp blade of his knife catches in the light before he draws it across the base of his throat. His eyes widen, feigning terror before he puts on a crowd-pleasing performance of pretending to die.

I gave him a hard stare. "Was that necessary?" I hiss again.

He shrugs his shoulders. "You asked, babe," he says before slicing his gaze toward the door, hearing the guards at the electronic keypad. He winks back at me and holds up his finger to his mouth, reminding me to keep quiet.

My hands shake and I find myself fretting behind the pillar, but my chance for panicking is gone. The door pushes open and the guards pile in, their murmured conversation instantly filling the massive foyer.

They walk through the space without a care in the world and I hear soft laughs as they discuss what fucking heroes they are for tasering the boys and getting them to their knees. All I can do is shake my head. Their laughs will only ensure their deaths are just a little more painful.

Fuck, the boys are going to enjoy this.

A moment passes, and just when the front door falls closed behind the final guard, the games begin.

Roman moves first, silently slipping out from behind his pillar and stalking behind them. He grabs the closest guard, his hand immediately wrapping around his mouth and snapping his neck before he even gets a chance to scream. He silently lowers the body to the ground and moves on to his next victim. Marcus steps out, grabs hold of a guard, and pulls him behind the pillar. I see scuffling and blood splatter, but again, the other guards don't notice a damn thing.

Levi is too far across the room to risk stepping out just yet, but not Marcus, he moves out to join Roman in the fun. I can't help but notice the blood splattered across his face as the rest of it blends into his soaked shirt.

Roman and Marcus move through the foyer like ninjas, silently taking out guards like they were being paid to do it and the moment Levi can, he joins in. He takes out a guard with a sharp knife straight across the neck and the soft gurgle from his throat alerts the other guards just as the blood splatter hits the wall with a loud splash.

A gag is caught in my throat as the remaining six guards spin around and take in the chaos at their backs. The three brothers look at them like the angels of death, moving like lightning toward them and not giving them a chance to call in back up before they're on them. They go for their guns but the boys are too quick, leaping in and taking out two in a matter of seconds.

Their bodies whimper and fret on the ground as blood pours

from their arteries and flows across the room. Marcus grabs one of the guards' tasers and shoots him with it, getting a sick enjoyment out of the hell they put us through this morning, and as he drops to his knees and groans in pain, Marcus finishes him off with a knife right through the chest.

A guard gets away and starts bolting for the front door, leaping over fallen bodies. My eyes bug out of my head. He can't get away. Another second and he could warn Giovanni. That car ride was far too long to risk having to come back and do it all over again.

Knowing I'm way out of my league, I dart out from behind the pillar and race after him, but before I can even get close, a knife whips past my face and plunges deep into the back of his neck, piercing right through his throat as the sound of his gurgled choking fills the foyer. The guard drops to his knees and his eyes widen, realizing this is the end of the line for him.

His hands pull at his throat, his airway completely cut off, and not a moment later, he drops heavily to the pool of blood beneath him.

I stand in the middle of the foyer, gaping at the scene, and as I look back at the boys, I find them down to the last three ... no, make it two.

The blood covering the expensive marble floor is like a fucking pool, splashing up around the boys' heavy boots. All I can do is stare at it in disgust. I've never seen anything like it. So many bodies ... so much death all at once. I'm just glad that I never got around to breakfast this morning.

I back up toward the window to stay out of the way and can't help but glance out, seeing Giovanni and Ariana on the opposite side of the big door. I suck in a breath. "Time's up," I warn the boys, remembering exactly why we're here.

The door handle twists and the boys get the job done.

Roman goes for the throat of one guy as Levi takes the guts of the other. The door springs open, and just as Giovanni steps through, the sound of the two final guards sloshing into the pool of blood sounds through the quiet foyer.

CHAPTER THIRTY

Ariana's wailing scream tears through the foyer as she barrels through the door after Giovanni. Both their eyes are wide, taking in the massacre around them as Giovanni's three sons stand in a mess of blood, looking like a bunch of kids who've just had the best day of their life at the playground.

It's as though I'm watching in slow motion as Ariana's chest rises and falls with erratic, wild movements. Her gaze sweeps over the three boys before trailing down to the fifteen bodies scattered on the ground, trying to figure out how the hell this happened so fast. There were only a few seconds between the guards entering the mansion and them trailing up the stairs behind them. In theory, what just happened here shouldn't even be possible, yet here we are.

Giovanni walks through the foyer, kicking bodies out of his way as he makes a show of taking in the destruction, though it doesn' go unnoticed that each of his steps takes him further away from his sons. "Quite impressive," Giovanni says as Ariana foolishly remains by the door, assuming that in this room, she is the safest of all. "Was this supposed to be retaliation for this morning?"

I laugh and Giovanni turns on me, his wild stare piercing through me like one of the boys' knives before quickly flickering toward the wild animals that stand by my side. "This here isn't retaliation. This is the end of your reign," I tell him, striding across the room as though I have every right to take point on this as the wolves move forward, letting their intentions be known while also keeping their eyes on Roman's subtle commands. I step in beside Roman and hold out my hand as I take in the anger deep in Giovanni's stare before making a point of turning my attention on Ariana. "And it all starts with her."

Ariana takes a hesitant step back, having expected a lot of things to come out of my mouth, but definitely not that. "Her?" Giovanni spits as I hear the faint *drip, drip, drip* of blood falling from the hem of the boys' shirts. "What the hell are you talking about?"

Roman places his phone in the palm of my hand, not saying a word as he lets me have my moment. I walk toward Giovanni while still keeping my distance and bring up the video from the bar as a soft growl tears through the room. I hold up the phone and let the video play, and while it would mean absolutely nothing to Giovanni, it's the difference between life or death for the woman cowering by the door.

Ariana's back stiffens as her eyes widen with horror, sucking in a loud gasp. Her gaze quickly falls to mine, knowing exactly what this means and exactly what I want. She swallows hard and turns her stare to Roman's, shaking her head. "It's not what it looks like," she murmurs, backing up another step, knowing that even though I'm taking point, Roman is the one she needs to be wary of. "Roman, no. You've got it all wrong. I had nothing to do with it."

"Nothing to do with what?" Giovanni spits.

Roman doesn't respond as I laugh. "Really, now?" I muse, glazing over Giovanni's question as I stride past him to get closer to his wife, knowing just how much being left in the dark must be pissing him off. "Because it looks a lot like you're sitting in a dive bar in the middle of the night, meeting with the guy who kidnaped and tortured me the very next day. Now, I'm not one to believe in coincidences, but you gotta admit, something seems a little … shady with this one. Don't you think?"

She shakes her head, her gaze flicking toward Giovanni's. "I … I didn't," she says, her ability to lie appalling. I mean, damn. At least put a little enthusiasm in it. "I swear, I had nothing to do with it."

Giovanni steps in beside me and tears the phone out of my hand before looking over the video for himself. In an instant, his big hand crushes the phone until the screen cracks. He throws it hard against the wall and steps toward his wife. His hand cracks hard against her face and something tells me it has nothing to do with her meeting with Lucas Miller but more so the fact that she stepped out of his home in the first place.

He leans into her and she shakes. "I will deal with you later," he seethes before turning back to his sons, knowing the show is only just getting started, only the moment he turns his back, Ariana grabs the door handle and goes to make a break for it.

"NOOO," I scream, not nearly close to being done with her. I bolt after her but the second I go, a knife sails through the air with absolute precision and plunges deep into her hand, pinning it right in the center of the big door—a skill that only Marcus DeAngelis could possibly pull off.

A loud, agonizing scream tears out of Ariana as she stumbles forward, her weight pressing against the door and slamming it closed with a loud bang. She grips the hilt of the knife with her other hand, giving it a hard pull to free herself, but the blade is lodged so deep in the door that she doesn't have a hope of getting it out.

Realizing just how fucked she is, she turns around with heavy tears in her eyes and looks to Roman. "Why?" she cries, her mascara smearing all over her face. "Why are you doing this? I've done nothing but protect you all these years. Doesn't that mean anything to you?"

Roman steps over the body at his feet and I don't miss the way that Giovanni discreetly adjusts himself, something I'm sure the boys are all too aware of. "I've told you a million times, Ari. War is not fair. If you stab a knife in my back," Roman says, his eyes trained heavily on hers, "is it not expected that I stab one straight through yours? Only I would have the decency to do it face to face."

Roman stops walking and stares at the woman who has crushed him, the woman who he thought he could trust with his life, but she's nothing but a power-hungry bitch. "There's only one thing that I don't understand," he says as Giovanni watches on with a cautious stare. "Why did you do it? Shayne means nothing to you. She's a nobody. She holds no power. No threat. Just the kidnapped daughter of a dead man. Why hurt her?"

Jealousy sits in her eyes and she clenches her jaw, staring back at the man who she once loved. "Because you were going to fall in love with her," she finally says, the admission coming out like nails on a chalkboard. "I could already see it, after just that first time. You were going to fall in love with her, just like Marcus and Levi would have. You were all mesmerized by her, just like you were with Felicity. I wasn't going to let that happen again. I only just got you back."

"Got me back?" Roman spits as Giovanni straightens, anger wafting off him like a bad smell. "Let us get one thing straight. I might have thought you were hot in high school, maybe let you suck my dick every now and then, but you have never had me, not even close."

Ariana shakes her head. "That's a lie," she spits through her teeth. "I know you, Roman. I know you better than anyone in this room. You don't mean that. You loved me. You always have, that's why you keep coming back."

"I keep coming back?" he questions. I know it must be hard for him because, even though he's denying it, I know that once upon a time, he truly did care for her and maybe has all these years as well, but that is more than over now. "Or do you keep showing up? There's a difference, Ari. A big fucking difference."

"No," she says, the hard sobs getting stuck in her throat. "I did it to protect you. She was going to destroy you. You would have followed her blindly. It was supposed to be me by your side. We were going to do this together. We were going to be more powerful than anyone, with people kneeling at *my* feet."

Roman laughs and looks across at me. "Why don't you show her what Lucas Miller did to you that night," he suggests.

A grin stretches across my face and I feel a warm fuzziness settling into the pit of my stomach, knowing that Roman doesn't mean for me to *show* her my scars. After all, she's already seen those.

My hand falls to my thigh and I yank on the knife that sits in the tight holster, having absolutely no idea what happened to the one Roman placed right in the palm of my hand. I stride up to her, a wicked excitement brimming in my chest. Ariana's eyes are wide and she looks at me in fear. I bet Lucas told her exactly what he had planned, but never in her wildest dreams did she expect the tables to turn on her like this.

My gaze sweeps over her body, taking in the miles of flawless flesh that I can't wait to decorate, just as Lucas decorated mine. Her eyes spit venom, a silent message for me to watch my back, that if I were to go through with this, my life wouldn't be worth living. But I disagree. If I don't settle this score, I would never be able to live with myself.

"Where to start?" I muse, taking the tip of the blade and gently sailing it across her skin. The blade trails over her arm and leads down to the hand that's pinned to the door. "You know what he did to my arm?" I question. "I still remember it so perfectly. The way his blade dug into my skin. How it stung. How I wanted to die." Then without warning, I press down on the blade, letting it pierce her flesh just as Lucas had done to me.

Her screams consume me, giving me life and making my blood pump faster. I yank the blade out and immediately stab it deep into her thigh until I feel her bone beneath the tip of the blade, right where he got me, reliving the memories all over again. "This," I seethe. "This is what you did to me. What you put me through."

"ENOUGH," Giovanni roars as his hand curls around my arm and throws me down on the floor at his feet, the gun at my back falling out of my waistband and sailing across the marble tiles. The wolves instantly bare their teeth as they creep forward, pissed off with what they see.

Giovanni turns to face his sons, his gaze glossing over the protective wolves and noticing how his sons have all crept in closer. "You mean to tell me that you're putting on this ridiculous show just for her?" he spits, kicking his leg out and hitting me in the ribs. "She's nothing, and yet you stand there and allow her to mutilate my wife?"

Marcus laughs. "Yet at any point, you could have stepped in and stopped her yourself. You could have saved your wife all of this humiliation and pain. Hell, you could have even freed her from that knife pinning her to the door, but you haven't. What kind of husband does that make you? No," he continues. "Don't answer that. The fact that your wife was out in dive bars meeting men like Lucas Miller in the middle of the night answers that. Right along with the fact that your first wife lay dead in a glass coffin, rotting away at the top of your sons' prison."

"Watch your tone with me, boy."

Levi laughs. "Careful, Father. You don't want to piss him off. You know how Marcus gets once he's got the taste for blood. It's nearly impossible to stop him and it looks like you're his next victim."

Roman shakes his head, holding out a hand that has the wolves backing down. "No," he says, a slow grin stretching over his face as he meets his father's stare. "He's mine." Giovanni's face falls as his three sons begin to stalk him. "The guards and Ariana, that was merely for our entertainment, but you, Father. You're what we've come all this way for."

"You locked us up for ten years," Marcus says, his tone lowering to a venomous whisper. "You took our freedom. You chained us to a fucking castle when we should have thrived. We should have ended you the night Antonio whispered in your ear. We were wrong to have let it go on for so long, but Ariana needed our protection."

"That's over now," Roman says. "And now there's not a damn thing standing in our way. Your reign is over. The DeAngelis family is ours."

Giovanni stands tall, staring his sons down as though he's hoping this is all some kind of bad dream. "They will never follow you," he spits. "You're nothing but a joke, all three of you. My brothers will stand against you and destroy you before you even see it coming."

"Your brothers will destroy each other for us," Levi says as Giovanni backs up closer to his wife, her whimpers barely audible against the overwhelming tension in the room. "They've already started."

Giovanni's brow furrows as understanding dawns. "This family war," he spits as though his sons are the most despicable creatures on earth. "It was all your doing."

"Every single move was perfectly planned and crafted for years," Roman says, his dark eyes swarming with victory, this very moment is the one he's been waiting so damn long for. "There is no win for you, Father. Your throne is ours."

Giovanni's hand whips back to Ariana and grips the hilt of the knife, yanking it out as she screams in agony, and as the boys go to make their move, Giovanni drops down like lightning, the bloodied knife at my throat and his strong arm curled around my chest.

He yanks me up off the ground as his sons come to a stop, their eyes showing what they refuse to say out loud. "What's it worth to you?" Giovanni spits as the knife digs deeper into my throat, a soft trickle of blood trailing down my chest. "Would you sacrifice her life just to prove a point? To prove you're stronger than me? You're not. You're all weak. Look at you, halting at the idea of losing this common whore. I should do you a favor and take her life myself."

Roman's jaw clenches as he meets my eyes, his hands balling into fists at his side. No one says a word, hearts racing erratically all around the room as Ariana takes her shot to tear open the door and fuck off out of here. Though she's not important. The boys will find her eventually, but right now, Giovanni has their full attention.

With the door open at his back, he takes a step back, dragging me through the door only to have the three boys stepping with him. He starts backing down the stairs and his sons match his every move.

"Where will you go, Father?" Levi questions, seeing that he's aiming for one of the many cars at the bottom of the stairs. "Will your brothers take you in once you explain that your sons have finally outplayed you? You will be the laughingstock."

I stumble back as he takes another step and Giovanni holds onto me tighter, crushing my chest beneath his steel grip. "You can take my home and scar my wife, but you will not take my throne," he spits, his breath on my face as we hear the sound of Ariana taking off in one of the many black SUVs. "I will come for you, and when I do, your whole castle will crumble."

Giovanni reaches the bottom step as his sons just stare, knowing damn well that it will never get to the point where he will rise up again. Men don't usually rise once they're six feet under. The boys stop their descent and as Giovanni reaches for the door handle, Roman's hand slides back for his gun.

He meets my eye, waiting for my move, but even with a knife at my throat, I'm not quite done. I have one more card to use, and I won't stop until its power has singed him like his abuse has singed his sons. "When you make their castle crumble," I spit, my nails digging into his arm at my chest and trusting that Roman could get a bullet through his head before his knife could dig into my skin. "Make sure you go extra hard for that wife of yours, after all, your sons have been passing her around like a piece of used meat for years. No wonder she found it so hard to get over Roman. You must be so proud. They fuck like champions, but that bitch of yours, she really knows how to make a girl feel special. I wonder, how did it feel when she shoved her tongue down your throat right after it was buried in my cunt? I bet you could taste this little *common whore* in your mouth all night long."

Giovanni roars, and as I feel his muscles flinching behind his blade, Roman's hand whips out as mine flies back, stabbing the sharp blade of my knife into his thigh. Giovanni roars, the anger pulsing through him like never before just as he catches sight of the gun.

Roman pulls the trigger and I'm pushed hard to the ground as Giovanni flies back, dodging the bullet in a way that only a skilled man with years of experience could do. Then before my scraped knees even have the chance to bleed, Giovanni is diving into the open car door and taking off down his long drive.

Fury pulses through my veins, watching him get away. I can only imagine what the boys must be feeling. They had him right there in their grasp. They were going to get everything they wanted, everything they've been waiting for, but I was standing right in the way. If I had only moved out of the way, if I had scrambled after he pushed me, they would have succeeded.

"You okay?" Marcus questions, striding down the final few steps as he takes my hand and helps me to my feet.

"Fine," I mutter, staring out past the driveway and watching as Ariana hits the main road and takes off like a bullet with her husband hurtling after her. "I'm sorry," I tell them. "I should have—"

"No," Levi says, staring after his father as well. "We'll get our chance. He's a proud man. He won't be able to resist coming for us after what we just did. He'll want to prove he still has what it takes to hold us down, and though we may have the keys to the kingdom now, as long as he's still breathing, he still owns it. This war is only just getting started, Shayne. What you experienced tonight wasn't even the tip of the iceberg."

CHAPTER THIRTY ONE

Blood trails between my tits as I walk back in through the front door of the boys' childhood home. My knees hurt from being thrown down on the stairs and my ribs are definitely bruised from Giovanni's kick, but the sting on my neck is what's killing me. It's really not that bad compared to the fresh hell I've been through in the past, but either way, it's a bitch. It's like getting a papercut and it makes me want to scream.

My gaze sweeps over the fallen bodies that take up the foyer and my stomach clenches. I've seen men gutted and murdered in the most brutal ways since getting caught up in this world, but those men deserved it. This here … I don't know. What if these men weren't the bad guys and their only mistake was being hired by a bastard like Giovanni DeAngelis? What if they had a family at home, a newborn baby, or a doting wife?

I try to put it to the back of my mind. What's done is done. It's not like I can go back, line them up, and interrogate them with quick-fire questions about their life before handing them over to boys to end their life. I have to find a way to be okay with this because, even if I hadn't been here, this would have eventually ended the same way.

Closing the door behind me, I ignore the rush of guilty pleasure that pulses through me at seeing Ariana's blood stained on the back of the massive door. I wish I could have played with her a little longer, let her feel the kind of hell she put me through, let her suffer just like I did, but she won't be gone for long. She'll get what's coming for her. It's only a matter of time.

Making my way to the stairs, I take the long way around, not wanting to walk through the pools of blood or step over the dead bodies like they don't matter. I grip onto the railing and make my way up the massive staircase, not really knowing where we go from here. I'm almost certain that the boys intend to stay here from now on, seeing as though they brought the wolves along with them, but one can never be too sure when it comes to the DeAngelis brothers. Though if they are staying, I'm almost positive that they'll be doing a raid on the castle to get every single weapon out of there. Sooner or later, they're going to need them.

The mansion is incredible, modern and sleek with a slight gothic feel to it, though that could be the dead bodies downstairs. The ceilings are high and the rooms are massive. I've never been in a property quite like this, you know, except for the other time I was here, but I only saw the coatroom and the dining hall so it doesn't really count.

I wander around, searching for a bathroom to clean up in when I push through the door to what must have been Ariana's room. My mouth hangs open. It's fit for a fucking queen in here with its own private living room, a massive walk-in closet bigger than my whole apartment, plus a private bathroom that has my mouth watering. I thought my bathroom back at the castle was impressive, but that's got nothing on this.

I find myself hovering in the massive room, picturing her life here. She would have had everything she ever wanted, only she had it with the wrong DeAngelis.

Walking into the massive closet, my fingers skim over the designer gowns and past the massive fur coats that I could never afford in my whole lifetime. I find myself glancing down at my cheap jeans and black hoodie. How pathetic.

Seeing the blood soaking through my clothes, I pull them off and dump them on the floor, not giving a shit about staining the pristine carpet as I make my way through the luxurious closet, searching for something to wear that wouldn't get me mugged on the street.

Walking through the closet in nothing but a sheer black bra and thong, I find myself admiring the impressive wall of color before me. The shoe racks are sorted by color and there must be at least a thousand different options. Boots. Stilettos. Wedges. Runners. Anything a woman could dream about having on her feet, Ariana had it right here at her fingertips.

Unable to help myself, I pick up a black pair of stiletto pumps with gorgeous red bottoms and slip my foot straight in. It fits like a fucking glove, and judging by the smooth, pristine red bottoms, these gorgeous heels have never even been worn.

What a fucking waste. I'll have to keep them and show them a good time.

Taking my new heels for a walk, I find a secluded section deeper in the closet with nothing but a button on the wall, and hell, I'm only human. I press that damn button with everything that I've got and gape as the wall fades away to show off the massive collection of jewelry. Diamonds stare back at me, the whole wall sparkling like Marcus' eyes when he gets to play in blood. Bangles, bracelets, necklaces, rings. It's like Tiffany's threw up in here and forgot to clean up after itself.

"Spank me, Daddy," I murmur to myself. "I've been a bad, bad girl."

I scoop up a diamond bangle and slip it over my hand before finding another and then another. Necklaces dangle between my breasts, some right down to my belly button while others barely pass my collarbone. I shower myself with diamonds, filling my fingers and ears with the most exquisite pieces. I must be wearing millions of dollars and I fucking love it, though I'm all too aware that this is nothing more than dress up. A girl like me could never even dream about this kind of luxury.

Finding a sheer, *I just killed my husband* robe, I slip it over my arms and let the soft material hang from my shoulder, feeling like a fucking rockstar. Damn it, if the boys ever take this room away from me, it's not their father they'll have to worry about. I'm in a dream right here and up until this moment, I didn't even realize this was something

I ever wanted. I guess sometimes we don't know what we like until it's shoved right in our faces—the three murderers downstairs are the perfect example of that.

Stepping toward the mirror, I take myself in, and just as a shiver trails down my back, Marcus steps in behind me, his arm curling around my body as he watches me through the mirror. His dark eyes are filled with the most intense desire, and I can't help but wonder if this is what he likes, but as his fingers move to the blood slowly trailing down my chest, I realize that I couldn't have been more wrong.

It's not the diamonds and heels that get him off, it's the blood.

His fingers trail through my blood before raising them up. He gently presses them against my lips before smearing them across my face like smudged lipstick. His hand curls into my hair without warning, tearing my head back and turning my face until his eyes are directly on mine.

Those delicious lips crush mine and he kisses me deeply as his hand slips inside the sheer gown and trails down to my panties. His fingers slip inside and I grip his arm, pushing him further as the desperation slams through me.

"Shayne, babe, where are ya?" I hear Levi calling from the main door of the bedroom. I pull my lips free from Marcus' and he drops straight to my neck, making me groan just as Levi appears in the entrance of the massive closet. He pauses, taking in the scene before him, and sees the red-hot desire and need in my eyes.

His tongue rolls over his lips as hunger pulses in his eyes and damn it, unlike his brother, he's all about the diamonds and heels. "Fucking hell," he breathes as I feel Marcus' thick cock grinding up against my ass.

I meet Levi's heated stare and grin back at him. "Fuck me, Levi. Make me scream."

Not one to disappoint, he strides into the big closet, removing his stained black hoodie as he goes. He wears no shirt below and my gaze sweeps over his defined abs. My mouth waters just looking at him. He steps in front of me and I trail my fingers over his body as Marcus removes his hoodie behind me.

Levi takes my thigh and raises it up high until the bottom of my stiletto heel is propped against a shelf just by his waist, spreading me wide as the sheer robe falls open, showing off my toned stomach and thigh.

He moves in close as Marcus presses against my back, his bare cock right there. He takes the robe and slides it down my arms, letting it fall in a messy heap at our feet as Levi captures my lips in his, his hands roaming over my skin and sending shivers all over my body.

Reaching behind, I take Marcus in my hand, feeling just how hard and ready he is as his lips come back to my neck, his tongue trailing up my skin to that sensitive spot below my ear, making me flinch with satisfaction. My hand tightens on his cock and his responding groan is all I need to feel that familiar flooding between my legs.

I have to have them, and I have to have them now.

Levi's cock grinds against my pussy through his jeans and when his hand scoops around my body and unhooks my bra, I couldn't be happier. He cups my tits, squeezing them firmly, knowing I want to be man-handled and treated like a bad girl in a rich man's world. He pinches my nipple hard and I gasp before he soothingly rubs his fingers over it, feeling how it hardens beneath his touch.

My hand moves up and down Marcus' cock, and as my thumb roams over his strong tip, I feel that bead of moisture. Releasing him, I bring my hand to my mouth, and with his eyes locked on mine, I graze my thumb over the tip of my tongue to taste him.

His eyes pulse with hunger and he grips the back of my neck before slamming his lips down on mine in another bruising kiss. I gasp into his mouth, melting into him and meeting his intense desire with my own. My hand falls back to his cock and I work him harder.

Levi's pants come undone and his heavy cock springs free, falling into his big hand, but before I can take it in my own, he drops to his knees. Marcus' lips fall back to my neck and as I gasp for air, my gaze falls to Levi as he strokes his cock and inhales, breathing in the scent of my arousal. He smirks with a cockiness that has my pussy clenching for a good pounding, and as he meets my eyes, I know that he's about to give me exactly what I've been asking for.

He leans in, tearing my panties from my body and closing his warm lips over my clit. My body spasms as I gasp and grip his shoulder for support, still squeezing Marcus' cock. Levi grips the bottom of my heel on the shelf and slides it along, spreading my legs wider and giving him all the room he needs to fuck me up.

His tongue works me just as I knew it would, flicking over my clit as he sucks. I groan low, my knees already weak, and when his fingers push up into my cunt, I know that I'm not going to survive this. His fingers stretch me and curl just right, hitting that spot that has my nails digging into his strong shoulder.

Marcus reaches down between my legs, feeling where his brother's fingers push up into me and with a smirk against my neck, he pushes his fingers in too. My eyes widen as I suck in a deep breath, Levi moving his fingers up and down as Marcus splits his and slowly massages on either side. "Holy fuck," I gasp as Marcus' other hand slips around my body and squeezes my tit, his thumb circling my pebbled nipple.

My pussy quivers, never feeling anything like it but when Levi's tongue flicks over my clit one more time, I explode.

My orgasm tears through me much sooner than I'd expected and I clench down, my pussy spasming as I squeeze both their fingers. "Fuck, that's right," Marcus murmurs by my ear, his breath on my neck sending goosebumps over my skin as his brother refuses to let up on my clit, making my knees shake as I clench my eyes, the high like nothing I've ever felt.

Their fingers keep working me and each little movement has my pussy clenching tighter as it continues convulsing, making me groan and throw my head back. "Ride it out, baby," Marcus tells me as I grip my other tit, squeezing it tight.

My eyes clench as I finally come down from my high. Levi pulls back, releasing my clit as both he and Marcus pull their fingers free from my pussy. Marcus brings his hand up and grins. "Open wide."

His fingers dive into my mouth and his grin widens. "Suck."

My fucking pleasure.

My mouth closes around his fingers and I suck them hard, roaming my tongue over them as I taste my arousal. His eyes flutter and it damn near makes me come all over again. "I'm gonna fuck that tight little cunt," he promises me. "You better be fucking ready."

His fingers pull free as Levi stands in front of me, slowly working his hand up and down his thick, veiny cock. He meets Marcus' eyes over my head and nods. "You can take that sweet cunt," he tells him, glancing back at me and seeing the raw hunger in my eyes. "I want her mouth."

Well, damn. Who am I to say no?

A grin stretches across my face and he sees the absolute determination in my eyes, but more than that, he sees the challenge. "Then take it."

Without hesitation, Levi pushes my foot off the shelf and grips the back of my neck. He pulls me in close and crushes his lips to mine, and when he inches back, I hold his stare, putting on a show of licking my lips. I reach out and take his cock in my hand, roaming my thumb over his tip as an intense satisfaction tears through his eyes.

I press my ass back against Marcus, letting him know I'm ready for whatever he's going to put down, and not a moment later, I'm braced against the shelf and taking Levi in my mouth. I take him deep, wanting to impress him as Marcus kicks my feet wide, spreading me open to show me the time of my life.

His fingers work my pussy, mixing with my wetness and spreading it up to my ass. He teases me, taking his cock and rubbing his smooth tip over my clit as Levi curls his hand into my hair and takes control, holding me still as he slowly fucks my mouth.

Marcus' cock pushes into me and I gasp as his thumb pushes into my ass at the same time. I push back, and he gives me exactly what I want. He pulls back until I feel the tip of his cock at my entrance and he slams straight back in, making me jump. The boys take it easy, both of them fucking me slow, but so damn hard. One in as the other comes out. It's a hypnotic, intoxicating rhythm.

They start picking up their pace and I slip my hand between my legs, rubbing tight circles over my clit as I take them both deep. Marcus rests his other hand on my back, keeping me down, and I push back against him more. He fucks me hard, his rhythm picking up until my eyes are rolling in the back of my head.

He doesn't let up on my ass and that slight pressure is enough to drive me wild.

"Fuck, little one," Levi murmurs, his hand curling tighter into my hair as my tongue works his tip. He groans low, his breath coming in short, sharp pants. I work him harder, rolling my tongue like a fucking pro, wanting him to feel it all, until he's certain no other woman could ever make him feel this way.

Marcus groans, the breathy sound forced through his clenched jaw, and I can't help but squeeze down around him, increasing the intensity. That familiar burn begins building deep inside me as I work my clit, rubbing furiously as the need for release almost becomes too much.

I want it all and I need it right fucking now.

Levi fucks me hard, his cock hitting the back of my throat and forcing tears to my eyes, but I don't dare let up. Whatever he needs from me, he will get. Period.

It builds and builds, and when Marcus takes his hand from my back and grips my hip, I know he's right there with me. Levi is barely hanging on, already waiting for me. Marcus' fingers tighten on my hip, digging into my flesh, and I come hard, turning into a spasming mess.

"Fuck," he hisses on a low breath as I feel his hot cum pouring into me. He doesn't let up and I sure as fuck don't stop squeezing, taking everything he has on offer just as Levi groans, spurting hot pulses of cum into the back of my throat.

I swallow him down as my knees shake, and as I reach an all time high, Levi pulls back, freeing my mouth just moments before a breathy moan tears from between my lips. "Holy shit," I gasp with Marcus' thumb and cock still buried deep inside me.

I straighten myself up and plaster my back against Marcus' chest and he curls his other arm around my waist, holding me up as he slowly pulls out of me. My knees go weak and I want nothing more than to crumble to the ground and do it all over again. "That," I say, resting my hand over Marcus' on my waist as I meet Levi's satisfied stare. "Every. Fucking. Day. Is that understood?"

Levi steps into me, gripping my chin and tearing it up to meet his heated stare. "Your wish is my fucking command, but if you come showered in diamonds and heels like this, I'll tear my fucking soul right out of my goddamn chest and give it to you."

His words hold more weight than ever as I reach up and rest my hand against the side of his face. My lips barely graze his as Marcus moves closer behind me, his cock hardening once again. "This time,"

I tell them, feeling that desire lighting up inside me. "I'm going to fuck you slow and you won't come until I say so. Is that clear?"

Marcus grins against my neck. "Just say the fucking word, babe, and I'll give you anything you want."

CHAPTER THIRTY TWO

"Stupid fucking wolf," I scream, slamming through the back door of the massive DeAngelis family mansion and taking off at full speed after Dill, the bane of my existence. He bolts toward the thick forest that runs directly behind the property and a frustrated, gurgled scream tears from the back of my throat.

My bright purple, ten inch, silicone suction cup dick hangs from his wolfy mouth, and I want nothing more than to beat his bitch ass with it. I swear to God, the second this wolf decided to make me part of his little pack, he's been going out of his way just to mess with me.

"Get back here you big turd," I scream, knowing damn well that he's racing out to hide my purple, veiny cock with all the other shit he's stolen from me over the past few days. "If you leave teeth marks on that bad boy, I swear, I'm gonna slap you with it."

That goddamn wolf! I'd never touch a strand of fur on his body, but shit, it feels good to threaten abuse right now.

I bet he fucking loves watching me race after him with his little wolfy giggle. He knows damn well I'll never be able to catch him. I can only imagine what the boys would think of this if they knew what kind of fresh hell their little wild pet was giving me. Doe, on the other hand, is a complete angel, and as long as I supply her with the goods, then she keeps coming through with the love. Not Dill though, he's a fucking mutt. It's almost comical that the thing he's currently racing off with is exactly what he was named after. Perhaps he figured it out and that's exactly why he's punishing me. I wouldn't put it past him, Dill and Doe are some of the most intelligent creatures I've ever met.

It's been three days since we stormed the mansion, three days since Giovanni took off, and three days since anybody has heard from him. In the real world, I'd be thrilled not to have heard from that piece of shit, but right now, it scares the life out of me. Not hearing from him means that he's biding his time, putting a plan together, and waiting to strike. Giovanni won't stay down for long. His kingdom is being threatened and he won't go down without a fight, but he should be warned, his kingdom is already ours.

I've done whatever I can to try and put the impending war to the back of my head. I've showered myself in the luxurious riches this mansion holds. The first night was fun, exploring the mansion, learning all its exquisite little secrets, and seeing the rooms the boys grew up in despite them being as plain as a ham sandwich. Day two was about playing dress up and seducing the boys with all the pretty little things I could find in what is now my closet. It was exciting at first, dressing the part of the perfect mafia bitch to stand by their side, but it's getting old fast. I've had my fun, and while I'll take full advantage of the things in that closet as much as I possibly can, it's not me. While those clothes make me feel like the most heavenly creature on earth, it almost makes me feel like a stranger in my own skin. I'll take an old tank and sweats any day over clothes that are uncomfortable and shoes that give me blisters.

My feet pound against the manicured grass as I sprint after Dill and as he breaks out into the thick forest behind the property, he slows just enough to make me think I've got a chance. The forest is thick and overgrown and I can only imagine what scary little nightmares have gone down between these trees. This forest would be a goldmine for the cops, assuming they had the balls to actually go after Giovanni, but what's the point? He'll be dead and buried before they get the chance.

A brief thought flickers through my mind that I probably should have mentioned something to the boys about me taking off after the wolf, but where's the fun in that? Had I stopped to chat, Dill would have been long gone and my chance of getting all my things back would have bounded away with him. Besides, I'll be ten minutes at most. If the boys really want to panic over ten minutes, then that's on them. I stuck by them after they did horrendous things to me, so if they think I'm about to run now, they've got another thing coming.

"DILL?" I call out, the thickening woods creating a canopy over my head and blocking out the natural sunlight. I look around, trying to figure out which way to go. "DILL? Come on. This was fun for like …

three seconds. Give me my dick back."

I groan and as I hear a soft twig breaking, a grin pulls at my lips. "Gotcha, motherfucker."

I turn and bound after him, knowing damn well that he's playing with me. Not even the boys would be able to beat the wolves at this game. I just have to hold out hope that he gets bored of the game and gives up before I do.

A ruffle of leaves to my right has me spinning and peering through the thick bushes, only movement to my left has me spinning back around. My heart begins to race. Now, I wasn't the smartest kid growing up and I more than failed a few classes, but what I do know is that Dill can't possibly be in two places at once.

"Dill?" I murmur, my gaze flicking back and forth between the two sounds, only now just realizing that perhaps running out here wasn't my brightest idea.

A soft growl tears through the thick trees and my gaze snaps to the right, finding Dill creeping toward me, the fur on the back of his neck raised high as he stalks forward, the purple silicone dick dropping from his mouth. He snarls as though he senses something and I find myself backing up toward him, knowing that despite fucking with my day, he wouldn't hurt me.

He creeps in closer, his shoulder rubbing my hip as he slowly passes me. "What is it?" I murmur, my gaze wide as his growls rumble through the forest. My fingers dig into the fur on his back, needing him closer as his sharp gaze sees something that I just can't.

He steps in front of me, nudging me back and I take the hint, creeping back and getting ready to run when a sickening laugh echoes through the forest. "You can run," the chilling voice says. "But you can't hide. Not from me, and certainly not in my fucking woods. I know every fucking rock, twig, and leaf."

I suck in a whimpering gasp as Giovanni steps out from the shadows, his smug grin making me want to hurl. I back up another step. It's one thing being brave with the boys at my back, but out here, I've never been so alone.

My hands shake at my sides as I creep back another step, my heart racing with fear.

Giovanni looks at me as though this isn't even worth his time, but the sparkle in his eyes tells me he has me right where he wants me. "That's just the thing," I say, my voice breaking as I force the words out over the lump in my throat. "This isn't your forest anymore."

Giovanni smirks, the amusement clear in his eyes as though he's watching a cub trying to roar. "You're brave," he says, ignoring my comment and taking another step toward me. "I have to give you that. You have a set of balls that men twice your age could only dream of having, but those balls are going to get you in a lot of trouble."

I shake my head. "You need to leave," I warn him. "Your sons will come looking for me, and they will not be so forgiving again."

The wolf growls and adjusts his position as Giovanni creeps in closer. "My sons are weak," he spits. "And they proved that to me when they sacrificed everything they've always wanted to save you. They will not make it in this world, not when they are too concerned with your well-being. You are going to cost them their lives."

Giovanni takes another step and Dill snaps out, his ferocious snarl warning Giovanni what would happen if he were to take another step.

Giovanni pulls up short, his gaze dropping to the wolf as though he barely notices him there, yet just the sound of his growl has the hairs standing on the back of my neck. How could Giovanni be so calm around him, so collected, and careless?

"You don't know what you're talking about," I say, stepping back, my knees shaking as Dill remains right where he is, putting distance between us and opting to keep closer to Giovanni.

"So naive," he taunts. "You choose to believe the best in them, but when it comes down to it, they will destroy you. Don't be fooled, Miss Mariano. I know my sons. But it won't matter, not now."

My back presses against a tree and I fumble back, my heart racing, not giving a single fuck that I look like a terrified rat, showing all of my cards. I was an idiot to think that just because I was gaining strength and working my way up in the world that I could handle anything they threw at me. I'm so fucking out of my depth, it's not funny. "Wh … what's that supposed to mean?" I question, stuttering over my words.

"Your father, Maxwell Mariano. He is dead, correct?"

My brows furrow and I nod, not knowing where the hell he could be going with this. "Yes. I killed him myself."

"As I thought," he muses, watching me like a tiny little fly landing right in the center of Venus fly trap and waiting for it to slam shut and destroy me. "There is still the question of your father's debt, and as his sole living heir, that debt now falls on your shoulders, and on top of that, you now owe me for putting your hands on my wife."

I shake my head, the determination creeping back into my soul. "No. No fucking way. I had nothing to do with my father's debt. That's all on you. You're the idiot who so willingly gave your cash to a deadbeat piece of shit like him. Don't blame me for your mistakes. And as for your wife," I spit. "She put her hands on me. She forced me to spread my legs so she could put on a little show for your sons. Take that one up with her. I don't owe you a goddamn thing."

Giovanni laughs, his eyes darkening in the same way that his sons' do, warning me that this is only the beginning. "You should have stayed locked up in that castle, playing the role of the innocent little damsel. You were safe there," he warns me as his hand moves and I see the muted sunlight glistening off the sleek metal of his gun. "Your time is up, Shayne."

Fuck.

I don't hang around.

I take off like a fucking bullet, bolting through the thick trees, not sure which direction I'm heading but any way that's further from Giovanni is a bonus. A terrified scream tears out of me as I faintly make out the sound of Roman's name on my lips.

My hip slams into tree trunks as fallen branches scrape past my legs, slicing deep into my skin.

The wolf snarls behind me as I hear the rhythmic sound of his paws slamming against the hard earth. Giovanni grunts and as a growl fills the forest, the gun rings out, the loud *BANG* vibrating through my chest.

Dill lets out an agonised howl that tears right through my chest, my eyes widening with horror hearing Doe's returning howl back at the mansion, the sound filled with heartache as her brother and best friend falls.

Hot tears sting my eyes as heaves of grief overwhelm me, but I keep running, knowing that if I stop for even a second, I'll be next.

My feet slam down on the ground, catapulting me through the thickening forest as my whole fucking world flashes before my eyes. Tears stream down my face. I should have stayed in the fucking mansion where the boys could protect me, where Dill would have been safe.

I stumble over a rock and just as I catch myself to keep going, a strong hand knots into my hair and yanks me back. My ass slams down onto the hard ground and the last thing I see before blacking out is the butt of Giovanni's gun coming down over my face.

Hands grab at my body and my eyes spring open with a panicked gasp to find two men hovering over me, gripping my arms as they pull me from out of the back of a black SUV. I fight against them, trying to pull my arms free as my feet come down on an old gravel road.

They hold me tight, painfully dragging me along as I see Giovanni stepping out from the passenger side of the SUV. He strides toward an old, abandoned house that sits in the center of a huge property out in the middle of nowhere, right where nobody would think to look for me. The windows are boarded up and the door looks as though it's falling off its hinges. It's the perfect place for a man in hiding.

It's well after nightfall, but when Giovanni stalked me through the forest, it was barely even midday. At least eight hours must have passed, and eight hours in the car could put me anywhere. The boys will never find me out here. I'm fucked.

The guards pull me along and I drag my feet, trying to make it as hard as possible, but even if I did manage to get away, where the hell am I going to go? There isn't another property in sight and we're surrounded by nothing but the hot desert.

The small door is pulled back and the men shove me in, letting me fall over the threshold. I barely manage to catch myself before someone is there, a hand jabbing into my lower back as Giovanni strides in behind me, the old wooden door slamming shut and echoing through the empty home.

There's nothing here but an old, torn-up couch with piss stains and a small fold-up table with beer cartons, an empty pizza box, and playing cards. Guns lay scattered around the house and I take note of each one, but something tells me that I won't be in a situation where I can get my hands on one of them.

A muffled, wailing cry tears through the small house and my eyes widen in fear, desperately searching but not even close to finding where the noise came from.

"Put her with the others," Giovanni says, his eyes filled with laughter as he strides past me and grabs a bottle of wine from the kitchen table. He walks back toward the door. "Call me if there are any changes," he throws over his shoulder, sparing me one last haunting stare.

Giovanni disappears and I swallow hard, being left with the two guards as they jam their hands into my back and push me across the room. I stumble forward, barely catching myself against a locked door, and watching in horror as they pull me away and shove a key deep into the lock.

The door pulls open and all I see is darkness. The smell wafting in has me gagging, and as I'm pushed through, my foot steps down onto a rickety spiral staircase, much like the one in the tomb. My body trembles and I shake my head, pulling back, refusing to see what horrors they have down here, but they push me harder, forcing me to keep going.

Pained cries and curses come from deep below and fear rattles through my chest as my feet barely keep up with the guard's hard pushes. We get halfway down and a small string is pulled above and a dim yellow light shines through the darkness, showcasing the horrors that Giovanni keeps hidden below.

The whole basement has been fitted out with old, dirty cells. There are broken and battered women all around me. Some weep while others just stare at their cell walls, wishing something would just come along and put them out of their misery.

"No," I breathe, red-hot tears filling my eyes as I try to fight my way out. "NO."

A hard slap cracks across my face and I whimper under the force as it knocks my head right to the side and I fall down the remaining stairs. Hands capture my arms and I'm yanked back to my feet before being tossed toward the hard cell. My face smashes up against the cold, metal bars as a man steps in behind me, keeping me pinned to the bar as the other guy unlocks the empty cell.

The door slides open, the metallic *BANG* echoing right through my chest, and before I get the chance to pull back and fight him off just as the boys taught me, I'm thrown hard through the opening of the cell. I fall forward, my body crashing against the dirty, damp ground as I hear someone across from me screaming in agony.

Panic tears at me and I spin around, flying to my feet just as the heavy metal bars slam closed, locking me in. I scream out, gripping onto the bars and pulling hard. "LET ME OUT," I wail, shaking the bars as though I could somehow tear free. "PLEASE," I sob. "LET ME OUT."

"It's no use," a bland, exhausted voice comes from the cell beside me. "There's no getting out of this one. You've doomed us all."

My head whips around and I stare at the woman through the dim light, something familiar about her tone. My brows furrow and I move across my cell to get a better look and suck in a breath as I find Ariana, her body beaten and bloodied, the scars I left on her body nothing compared to what her husband has done to her.

I fall back a step, my back slamming up against the opposite wall as guilt weighs down on me. I did this to her.

Dropping to the ground, my knees crumble in the dirt as my face falls into my hands. I'm a fucking monster. What has this world turned me into? It's one thing to want revenge on a woman who set me up for the worst torture of my life, but this isn't what I wanted. She was supposed to have gotten away. She took off in the guard's SUV and I came to terms with the fact that was the end. I was never going to have to see her again, never have to think back on what happened, but here she is, staring me in the face and blaming me for the fresh hell that she's endured at her husband's hands.

The same pained cry from earlier tears through the room and the labored breathing that comes with it has my head whipping around and searching through the thick bars. Seeing only a faint shadow in the darkness, I crawl across the ground, my knees screaming in protest until I finally see her, curled in on herself, whimpering in pain.

"Hey," I call out, gripping onto the bars. "You're going to be okay. Just hang in there, okay. The pain will go away soon."

She lifts her tear-streaked face and those bright blue eyes lock on mine as her dirty blonde hair falls in matted waves around her waist. "Nothing is ever going to be okay," she says as her hands curl around her swollen, pregnant stomach and screams in agony as a contraction tears through her.

Horror rips through me and all I can do is stare. Her voice is so damn familiar, but her face, it's the exact same one tattooed across Marcus' ribs.

"Felicity?" I gasp, getting to my feet as I look back at the poor girl, gripping onto the bars as desperation tears through my chest. My gaze locks on her pregnant belly, the bruises on her face, the blood smeared between her legs. She can't do this. She's too weak.

Felicity meets my horrified stare, her eyes telling me so much more than her words ever will. "I tried to warn you," she breathes as my eyes widen in understanding. "You should have run when you had the chance."

"It was you," I murmur, my heart racing in my chest as she screams again, the contraction sending her into a whimpering mess with sharp, agonized pants. "The woman in my room. You shot Marcus."

She meets my hard stare, not sorry in the least. "I did what I had to do," she spits through a clenched jaw, clawing at the bars to try and find just a little bit of comfort. "Marcus is a fighter. He would have been fine."

"They think you're dead."

Felicity laughs, her haunted stare raising to meet mine. "Aren't we?" she questions, sweat coating her skin. "Look around us, Shayne. We're never getting out of here. Not even the great DeAngelis brothers can save us now."

CHAPTER THIRTY THREE

Felicity's pained cry tears through the dirty basement and every soft whimper and groan kills me. Call me a fucking pushover, but how can I hold my grudge against this woman while she's currently in labor with Roman's child, the one he so desperately wanted, the one he grieves every damn day?

I grip the bars tightly, my knuckles turning white as my knees shake with the worst kind of anxiety. "Come on, girl," I breathe, not sure if I'm speaking to Felicity or giving myself a mental pep-talk. "You've got this."

"HAVE YOU EVER PUSHED A FUCKING WATERMELON OUT YOUR VAGINA?" she roars. "NO! I don't think so. I don't fucking got this. I can't do this. It's too early. He's not ready yet. I'm barely eight months."

Fuck.

My grip on the metal bar tightens and I rattle it, desperately needing to get to her, to somehow help or get her comfortable. What kind of shit show have I been thrown into? My head aches from where Giovanni hit me, but that's the least of my problems now. I don't know shit about giving birth, but I'm almost certain that if the mom is all tense and panicked, it couldn't mean anything good for the sweet baby trying to claw its way from between her legs. "You need to relax," I tell her, trying to be as soothing as possible, but the terror in my tone comes through loud and clear. "Take slow deep breaths like they do in the movies."

"Relax?" she screeches. "Relax? How the fuck do you expect me to relax? I'm giving birth to a fucking baby in a—AHHHHHHHH." Her screams quickly turn into heavy, pained sobs that get caught in her throat. The contraction passes and she raises her tear-streaked face, the devastation and horror deep in her eyes. "What's the point? I'm going to die," she cries. "He's going to kill me the second this baby comes out."

I shake my head, pulling on the bars again. "No," I breathe. "He won't. You're going to get out of here. We all are."

Ariana scoffs from her cell across the room. "What a fucking joke. We're all dying down here and the sooner you figure that out, the better."

"Shut the fuck up, you jealous whore," I spit, sending a venomous glare her way only to see her slumped back in her cell. She's completely given up on life. "For the record, Roman thinks you're trash, nothing but a whore to be passed around between his brothers, and definitely not someone worth keeping around. Think about it, he's crept out of that castle a million times over the past ten years, and not once did he come to save your bitch ass. But you're right, you will be dying down here, but you'll be dying alone."

Turning back to Felicity, I find her an absolute mess. "Don't give up. Do this for your baby," I tell her, willing her to hold it together. "Just think about holding him for the very first time. Seeing his little face, hearing those little cries. You can do this. I know you can."

Felicity swallows hard and adjusts herself again, the movement making her groan in pain. "Fuck," she says, gasping for breath, her panicked stare coming back to mine. "I think it's time."

My eyes widen in horror. "Shit, are you sure?"

She nods, her head bouncing with erratic movements. "What … what do I do?"

I shake my head, having no fucking clue. "I … I don't know," I panic. "Can you feel its head?"

I swallow hard, watching as she adjusts herself again, making space to move around as she reaches down between her legs. "Oh, fuck," she cries, whimpering in fear as her eyes come back to mine. "I can feel him."

"Then I think it's time to push."

Ariana's irritated groan tears through the underground dungeon and I try shaking the bars again, wanting nothing more than to tear them right out of the concrete and throw them at her caveman style. Perhaps one might fly right through that big mouth of hers and shut her up for good.

Seeing the overwhelming fear and panic in Felicity's eyes, I quickly realize there's no way in hell she's about to do this by herself and that baby is going to be the one to suffer the consequences. Besides, if Roman knew I was just standing here watching the train wreck while both Felicity and his baby were in trouble, he'd kill me himself, and this time, he won't be fucking around.

My whole body shakes and the need to get over there fires through me, but I'm fucking trapped and Felicity is looking at me with those big blue eyes, begging to make the pain go away. "HEY," I scream out, having no idea what the fuck I'm doing. "HELP. WE NEED HELP DOWN HERE."

Ariana flies to her feet, her hands clutching at the bars. "The fuck do you think you're doing?" she hisses, her eyes wide with fear, barely able to keep herself up. "Don't bring them down here. Are you insane?"

"Got any better ideas?" I fire back at her.

Ariana scoffs and it makes me want to tear out her throat. "The bitch got herself into this situation, she can get herself out."

"Fucking hell," I mutter under my breath. "I swear to God, if I ever get out of here, I'm going to fuck you up in the worst kind of way and I'll fucking enjoy it."

"Ooooh," she teases. "You spent three seconds with those brothers and all of a sudden you think you're tough. Go ahead, try me. There's no way you're getting out of that cell. We're doomed to rot, and it's all your fucking fault."

I scoff. "You're the unfaithful one here, not me," I remind her as my eyes remain locked on the spiral staircase, willing it to open. "HEY," I scream again. "GET YOUR MOTHERFUCKING SHRIMP DICK DOWN HERE SO I CAN BEAT THE LIVING SHIT OUT OF YOUR DUMBASS, YOU BIG TURD SNIFFING, WAFFLE STANKIN', LAZY FAT CUNT."

Felicity's scream tears through the basement, echoing through the room and making me flinch as Ariana laughs. "You're fucking asking for it, you stupid bitch."

The old wooden door at the top of the stairs opens with a bang and I look back at Ariana with a smirk. "Watch and see how it's done," I tell her. "But just so we're clear, I'm getting out of here and I'm taking her with me, but you, you're going to rot down here until you're nothing but a pile of bones for the rats to chew on."

The guard who'd dragged me out of Giovanni's trunk with a bruising grip is at the top of the stairs. His hard glare is locked on me as he descends, clearly knowing that the string of insults didn't come from anybody else. The old, rusty stairs shake under his weight, and just as he hits the bottom and comes for me, Felicity's murderous screams tear through the basement.

The guard whips around and gets a front-row seat of the alien baby forcing its head through its mother's bits like some kind of horror show. Blood is everywhere and he fumbles back a step, way out of his league, but that small fumble is all I need.

Reaching through the bars, I grip onto the back of his shirt and use his momentum against him, yanking him back toward me with everything that I've got. He falls back and slams his head against the metal bars with a loud BANG and I watch with wide eyes as he drops to the ground with a heavy thud.

"Fuck," I breathe, staring down at him. I hadn't expected that to work, but shit, he won't be out for long.

Not wasting a second, I drop to my knees and reach between the bars, feeling around his clammy body until my fingers curl around the keys. Relief pours through me and I scurry across my cell, my hands shaking as I hastily try to unlock it.

The door slides back with a bang and I cringe, hoping to God that the other asshole upstairs assumes that the sound was his colleague stepping in here to teach me a lesson.

Not skipping a beat, I race across the small basement and jam the key straight into Felicity's lock, but as I'm twisting the key, I hear the voice inside my head telling me that this is my one shot to run. I spare a glance toward the spiral staircase knowing that if I were to stay and help Felicity deliver her baby, I may never get another chance like this again.

Fuck.

Felicity's scream tears through the basement and I let out a shaky breath. If I ran and left her behind, left Roman's baby behind, I would never be able to forgive myself, so instead, I tear her door open.

"LET ME OUT," Ariana calls, standing at her bars and gripping onto them with everything that she's got. "SHAYNE. FUCK. PLEASE. I SWEAR, I'LL DO ANYTHING YOU WANT, JUST LET ME OUT. I'M SORRY. HE'S GOING TO KILL ME DOWN HERE. GIVE ME THE FUCKING KEYS."

Ignoring Ariana's demands, I focus everything I have on Felicity as I fall to my knees between her legs. I meet her eyes as the guard remains out cold behind me. "We only have a minute before he wakes up," I tell her. "It's now or never."

Felicity nods, seeming to get just a little more courage as she pushes herself up against the wall, sitting higher to get comfortable. "Okay," she says through her erratic panting. "I need to push. Don't drop him, okay?"

"Your baby is safe with me," I promise her, knowing that Roman would bust my ass wide open if any harm came to this child while in my care.

Felicity reaches forward, her hands gripping the back of her thigh as she takes a gasping breath and then screams, the sound vibrating right through my chest. She pushes until she's red in the face, takes a quick breath, and pushes again. Tears trail down her face and I feel helpless, desperately wishing for a way to make this easier for her.

The baby inches out and my eyes bug out of my head. "Holy shit," I breathe, staring in awe as I put my hands under his head, not wanting him to drop. "He's coming. Keep going. You're doing it. He's coming!"

Felicity gasps in happiness, a pained smile cracking across her lips as she takes another heaving breath and pushes again, more than ready to tear herself apart if it means getting to hold her sweet baby in her arms. "Fuck, fuck, fuck, fuck," she screams, her fingernails digging into the back of her thighs.

His whole head pops out and I gape at his little face staring up at me as a wave of relief pours over Felicity. "Holy fuck," I laugh, my heart thundering in my chest, wishing that I could see the resemblance between him and his father but at the moment, he's just red and covered in slime. "I see his face. It's all squishy."

"Squishy?" she breathes, adoration in her eyes as her heavy pants sound through the cell.

"Yeah," I tell her, unable to look away from the gorgeous little baby, Roman's newborn son. "Getting the head out; that's the hard part, right?"

She shrugs her shoulders. "I … I don't—AHHHH," she groans as she's hit with another contraction. She pushes again and I take hold of the baby, helping to guide his shoulders out and the moment they're free, the rest of his body comes sailing out like a wet sausage.

My hands fumble on his slimy, wet skin as I adjust him in my arms and make sure that he's breathing just right. I have no idea what I'm doing, but my vast array of movie experience tells me that he's going to start crying any moment now. A smile tears across my face, taking in his beautiful features and noticing that this kid is going to be one hell of a heart breaker. Felicity was right, he really is a boy, one that his father will be more than proud of.

A second passes and then another before his tiny little cry fills the cells and I look up and meet Felicity's tear-filled eyes. "Here," I say, handing him through her legs and putting him into her waiting arms. She takes him greedily, crying happy, relieved tears as she looks down at her son.

I pull my stained shirt off and reach over, offering it as a blanket for her to wrap around her baby and she takes it gratefully, having absolutely nothing else in here but her own body to offer as protection.

Felicity pants as I hear the guard behind me beginning to stir. I turn around, making sure that we still have time and preparing myself to fight him off if that's what it takes but when I glance back at Felicity, her face drains of color. "Something's wrong," she murmurs, her brows furrowing as she holds onto her baby just a little bit tighter.

I look over her, trying to figure out what the hell she's talking about when I feel warmth pooling at my knees. Horror slams through my chest as my gaze shoots down to find blood pouring out of her. I suck in a gasp. "You're bleeding," I rush out, looking around in panic, trying to figure out what the hell I'm supposed to do to help her. "There's too much blood. What do I do?"

My hands hover over her, frozen and shaking as the blood continues to pour and her eyes grow droopy. Do I close her legs, press down on her stomach? Where? How … what am I supposed to do to stop the bleeding? "Flick?" I rush out, my eyes wide and panicked. "What do I do? Felicity. HELP ME. Don't go to sleep. I … I don't know what to do."

Her body relaxes and the baby slips in her arms. "FELICITY," I cry out, grasping onto him as he falls right out of her hold. I cradle him in one arm, barely holding onto him properly as I come up blank, my desperation not helping. My eyes flicker back toward Felicity and hot, burning tears fill my eyes. "NO," I panic, her eyes growing heavy as the blood continues to flow. "Don't go. He needs you. Just hold on a little longer."

Felicity meets my eyes as the harsh reality sinks in. She's not going to make it and no matter what I do, there's not a damn thing that will help her now. "Tell him I'm sorry," Felicity breathes as my tears spill over. "Don't let them hurt my baby."

I shake my head, a sharp lump getting caught in my throat. "I won't," I promise her, knowing that I would lay my life down if it meant keeping this baby out of Giovanni's hands. "I'll find a way to get us out of here. I'll take him home to Roman. He's going to be okay."

Felicity's eyes widen with fear, her hands reaching for her baby again. "No," she panics. "Not Roman. Anywhere but there."

I shake my head, not understanding. "But Roman is his father," I tell her, unable to comprehend what it means to truly keep this baby away from him, and despite her wishes, it's just not something I could do to him. "He thinks he lost this baby. For months, it's been killing him. He would never hurt him. Roman would be the best father a kid could need."

Seeing she is too weak to hold her baby, I take her hand and squeeze it, not wanting her to feel alone in this. "I know," she breathes as a tear rolls down her cheek, her voice barely a whisper. "He would be Roman's whole world, but to be loved by Roman, or any of them, means to live your life in fear. I don't want that for my son. Loving him brought me nothing but pain and suffering. My son," she sobs. "He needs more."

My chest aches as understanding tears through me like never before, her words hitting me a little too close to home. She's right. Every damn word is right. Being loved and adored by the DeAngelis brothers means to live a life full of heartache and fear and while that's terrifying to her, for me, it's never been so exciting.

Tears stream down my face and I know without a doubt that I will not be able to keep this precious child from his father, so I promise her the one thing I can. "Your baby will be safe with me," I tell her. "I swear, he will have a happy life."

Felicity lets out one last breath and the rest of her body slumps against the wall as her hand falls from mine. Overwhelming grief crushes through me and pained sobs tear from deep in my chest as I hold onto her newborn son, crying in my arms.

Unease settles into me. How the hell am I supposed to get us out of here, let alone care for him? All I know is that if I don't get this baby out of here now, he doesn't stand a chance. Sobs tear from deep in my chest as I carefully lay him down on his mother's stomach. He's still attached by the umbilical cord and if I don't figure out something fast, we're both screwed.

Racing out of the cell, I drop down beside the guard and start feeling around his body. He stirs under my touch and the moment my fingers curl around a knife, I throw myself back to my feet and kick him hard in the head, making sure he's well and truly out.

Swallowing hard, I step back into the cell and take a shaky breath, hoping that this doesn't hurt the baby in any way. I pull the hair tie out of my messy hair and tie it tightly around the base of the cord before taking the knife and slicing through it.

The baby cries and I push the knife into the waistband of my pants before scooping him back into my arms. "I'm sorry," I whisper, the tears stinging my eyes as I try to comfort this sweet little soul. Then sparing one last glance at Felicity, I let out a broken sigh and get to my feet, knowing the moment I finally get back to the boys, I'm going to have to explain everything that just went down here, and it is going to crush Roman.

My knees shake under me and I turn to step out of the haunting cell when a voice breaks through the heavy silence. "Where the hell do you think you're going?" Giovanni says, stepping out of the shadows and striding toward me, blocking me in the cell with his big body.

I swallow hard, gripping tighter onto the innocent life in my arms as I start backing up, terrified of letting him get any closer. I pull the knife straight back out, but against someone like him, I don't stand a fucking chance.

Giovanni drops his gaze to his newborn grandson and steps through to the cell, his eyes darkening with whatever sick plan he has. He sweeps his sickening stare toward Felicity's lifeless body, slumped on the ground of his dirty cell. "Shame," he mutters, slowly turning his attention back to me, not even bothering to spare a glance for the weapon in my hand. "And here I was hoping to use her against my son, but I've got you now."

"You've got nothing," I spit and just like that, his hand cracks out like lightning, striking across my face. The momentum of his blow has me falling back against the wall and I scream out as he steps into me, tugging the knife free and closing his hand around my throat, a million times worse than the boys have ever done to me.

I grip onto the baby, holding him tight to my chest, the fear rattling me like never before because now it's not just me I need to protect, but this baby as well.

Giovanni doesn't let up on my throat, just keeps squeezing as his eyes shimmer with a sickening amusement. I feel myself running out of oxygen, my arms growing weaker by the second. It won't be long until I pass out or die and the moment that happens, it's game over.

My hold on the baby loosens and I scramble, fighting to keep hold of him. He quickly starts slipping from my grasp as I gasp for air, only to be met with nothing. Black dots appear in my vision as my lungs scream for oxygen and my hold on the baby fails. He drops out of my arms and I watch through heavy eyes as Giovanni catches him and pulls him into his chest, victory brimming in his eyes.

"It looks like my luck is changing," Giovanni tells me, indicating to the screaming baby cradled against his chest. "Take a good look, Miss Mariano. This right here is the greatest weapon you will ever see. My sons will never see it coming."

And just like that, the last of my oxygen burns out like a useless flame and my world turns to darkness. I'm thrown down on top of Felicity's lifeless body and the last thing I hear is the sound of Giovanni's wicked laugh as he slams the cell's door closed and locks me in, his laugh flowing back up the winding stairs and out the front door, taking the screaming baby, and my last ray of hope along with him.

HEATHENS

THANKS FOR READING

If you enjoyed reading this book as much as I enjoyed writing it, please leave an Amazon review to let me know.

https://www.amazon.com/dp/B09J44TJGP

CONTINUE THE SERIES

SAVAGES - Depraved Sinners (Book 3)
https://www.amazon.com/dp/B09MVXT445

Humpty Dumpty sat on a wall
Savages rising, watch how they fall.
All of the heartache and all of the pain.
Couldn't put me back together again.

There's nothing quite like the smell of a decaying body. Being trapped in a cell with it under the hot, desert sun … now, that's just sick

One minute, I thought I had everything I needed in this dark world, and the next, I was a prisoner to Giovanni's wicked plan. I don't know how, but I will get myself out of here, even if it's the last thing I do.

Giovanni will not win this, and I won't stop until my fingers are curled around his throat and my knife is sinking into his flesh. He's taken everything from me. My freedom, my home … my blood, but he will never have my will to survive.

Roman, Levi, and Marcus are out there somewhere. They're looking for me and won't stop until they have spilled as much blood as it takes to get me back in their strong arms. I have to believe that, because if I don't, I will rot down here. I will lose myself, and I like this new life too much to give up on it now.

This wicked game of life and death just took a turn for the worst and in this war, loyalties will be tested, but just as in war—not everybody will make it out alive.

Eenie, meenie, miny, moe.
Which DeAngelis has got to go?

STALK ME!

For more information on the Depraved Sinners series
join me online with the rest of the stalkers!!
I swear, I don't bite. Not unless you say please!

Website
Facebook Group
Facebook Page
Instagram
TikTok
Threads
Spotify
Pinterest
Bookbub
Goodreads
Newsletter

MORE BY SHERIDAN ANNE

www.amazon.com/Sheridan-Anne/e/B079TLXN6K

DARK ROMANCE STANDALONES

Pretty Monster | Haunted Love | Darkest Sin

Midnight Stage | War Games

DARK CONTEMPORARY ROMANCE SERIES - M/F

Broken Hill High | Haven Falls | Broken Hill Boys |

Aston Creek High | Rejects Paradise | Bradford Bastard

DARK CONTEMPORARY ROMANCE - RH

Boys of Winter | Depraved Sinners | Empire

NEW ADULT SPORTS ROMANCE

Kings of Denver | Denver Royalty | Rebels Advocate

CONTEMPORARY ROMANCE

Play With Fire | Until Autumn | Remember Us This Way

HOLIDAY ROMANCE

The Naughty List | Santa's Dark Secret